Huzama Habayeb is a Palestinian writer who was born and raised in Kuwait, where she started writing and publishing short stories, poetry, and journalistic pieces as a student and later as a journalist. When the Gulf War erupted in 1990, she fled to Jordan and established her reputation as a short-story writer. Her first novel, *Root of Passion*, was published in 2007 to wide critical acclaim and her second novel, *Before the Queen Falls Asleep*, was published in 2011 and received rave reviews, establishing what some critics called 'the new Palestinian novel.'

Velvet is her third novel and was awarded the Naguib Mahfouz Medal for Literature in 2017.

Kay Heikkinen is a translator and academic who holds a PhD from Harvard University and is currently Ibn Rushd Lecturer of Arabic at the University of Chicago. Among other books, she has translated Naguib Mahfouz's *In the Time of Love* and Radwa Ashour's *The Woman from Tantoura*.

T0346461

Velvet

Huzama Habayeb

Translated by
Kay Heikkinen

hoopoe

AN IMPRINT OF AUC PRESS

First published in 2019 by
Hoopoe
113 Sharia Kasr el Aini, Cairo, Egypt
200 Park Ave., Suite 1700 New York, NY 10166
www.hoopoefiction.com

Hoopoe is an imprint of the American University in Cairo Press
www.aucpress.com

Copyright © 2016 by Huzama Habayeb
First published in Arabic in 2016 as *Mukhmal* by The Arab Institute for Research
and Publishing
Protected under the Berne Convention

English translation copyright © 2019 by Kay Heikkinen

All rights reserved. No part of this publication may be reproduced, stored in a re-
trieval system, or transmitted in any form or by any means, electronic, mechanical,
photocopying, recording, or otherwise, without the prior written permission of the
publisher.

Dar el Kutub No. 25356/18
ISBN 978 977 416 930 4

Dar el Kutub Cataloging-in-Publication Data

Habayeb, Huzama
    Velvet / Huzama Habayeb.— Cairo: The American University in Cairo
    Press, 2019.
        p. cm.
        ISBN 978 977 416 930 4
        1. English fiction
        828

1 2 3 4 5   23 22 21 20 19

Designed by Adam el-Sehemy
Printed in the United States of America

Winter's here again
Keep me in your mind
Keep me in your mind
Winter's here again
Fairuz

THE RAIN WAS NOT IN a docile mood. It certainly wasn't flowing, soft, or gentle, nor was it graceful, treading lightly on the earth.

The rain beat down viciously on naked life, its hard drops splitting the rough crust of the earth. Daggers of water pierced the dusty flanks of the ground, thrusting rapidly and in quick succession, as if laden with emotion, or haunted by ancient sorrow, or filled with deeply buried rancor.

The veins of the earth continuously bled black water. The surging water closed the streets, rising to the very edges of the sidewalks. It poured into the lanes, where streams formed, burdened with mud, while the network of sewer pipes disgorged the filth in their bellies onto the roads.

The water poured down like a hail of bullets on terrified windows. Some of the bullets crept in at the edges of the windows, their frames now dislodged, enfeebled by the effects of advancing age. Lightning flashes split the sky, the thunderclaps colliding, scolding men unprotected in the night streets. Men in houses—not fully fortified against the unreasonable effects of nature—protected themselves with television screens devoid of interest, and with cups of consoling tea that had absorbed the brewing vengeance, and that were redolent with winter sage and the stifling breath of small kerosene heaters.

That was the first day of the rain. People allowed themselves to feel betrayed, as the day before, the sun had spread its ripe yellow over half the sky and that general feeling of winter

1

gloom had retreated, even if a deceitful cold sting still penetrated their bodies, through toughened skin. Where was all this angry water coming from? "God's own downpour!" The words rose from some people in an amazement very likely to fall under the heading of blaspheming divine omnipotence. Vendors with display stands spread along the roadsides rushed to gather up their copious wares—combs, hairbrushes, key chains, sunglasses, leather wallets, cases for cell phones—after the earth exploded in springs of water under their displays. Meanwhile, produce sellers scurried to rescue crates of tomatoes, cucumbers, lemons, onions, potatoes, cabbages, apples, chestnuts, sweet potatoes, oranges, tangerines, and pomelos that displayed their maternal firmness on angled display tables along the walls.

On the second day of the rain, the skies were gloomier and the roadways were muddier and blacker. People with pale faces ran about, covering their heads and exposed faces with shawls and keffiyehs against the storming water and buffeting wind. Even so, their steps were heavier at the end of the day, with the weight of the rain descending on their backs in torrents.

On the third day of the rain, which continued with unflagging zeal, the sky awoke in the morning gloomy, dispirited, and very dark. Deep wounds opened in the earth, whose pus overflowed into the asphalt streets, long neglected, whose tar coating had dissolved long before. People walked listlessly, their backs bent, exhausted; the rain slapped their sides and they did not resist or make any real effort to avoid it.

The rain did not stop pouring for seven days. During the day the sunlight was short, so the light diminished, like a hoarse voice fading, to the vanishing point; and at night the darkness thickened, the skies covering the moon and the stars, which went into a long swoon. At times the rain was rushed, as if it wanted to empty everything in the womb of the sky and be done at last with its burden, or perhaps its sin. At other times it slowed, as if its will were feeble, the space between one raindrop and the next becoming wider and longer, as if the sky's mouth had gone dry, before the water once again reclaimed its anger, its lash, and its bluster.

Lakes overflowed on the roofs of houses, and puddles appeared here and there where people walked, while twisting rivers wound through narrow lanes. People got used to leaping in the muddy roads during the days of rain, though they were unable to keep their feet completely out of the puddles that suddenly gaped before them. It was something that in all likelihood made them more impetuous than usual.

The deliberate, monotonous drumming of the water and the heavy downpours were interspersed with pauses, space for the sky to catch its breath and gather new, watery energy. But the bubbling rain was an established fact, as continuous as if it were eternal.

On the eighth day the rain stopped suddenly, just like that, without slowing down or diminishing gradually as a prelude to stopping. All at once the sky went from a jungle of clouds to a desert, and a large sun rose over the world. The rivers of mud in the roadways turned into paths of hard, cracked concrete, as if they hadn't been wet for long days, when languid spaces of morning alternated with long, desolate spaces of evening. But the persistent odor of the water remained in the air and settled into every place, clinging to the bodies of people completely exhausted by the days of water, lurking in the fur of cats stretched lazily on the smooth ledges outside the houses. Inside, the odor dominated the accumulated smells of sweat, urine, kerosene, and the oil used and reused for frying, whose fumes hung in the air of houses crammed with human beings whose flesh, or some of it, had a quarrel with warm bathwater. The odor established itself in the walls, their surfaces cracked and shedding worn paint. It was not a good smell, as it married humidity and leftover decay. It snatched away the air breathed by all beings, and that left the temper of the cosmos roiled and brackish. A trace of something like disintegration clung to the edges of both the water and the air.

The sun was very yellow, and very low over the camp and the people, as close as could be to a summer sun, except that it wasn't burning. This sun was like a discovery, as it was clear under its revealing light how worn down the houses were. It was clear in the rising daylight that fatigue had afflicted people's shoes, their cheap leather holding together only with difficulty, and their old woolen shawls, and their worn coats, some with forgotten mothballs still stuffed in their lined inner pockets.

Nonetheless, despite the obvious feebleness and overall frayed state of life during the violent era of a watery universe, and despite the specter of a wasteland planted by the rain during its dark days, no complaint rose to the heavens, nor was there open grumbling about God's water. People hid the spells of fever that settled in their bodies and bore up under the loosening of their joints and shaking of their limbs, and shut their mouths over the spray of their violent dry coughing.

In general, people's feelings remained hidden. But Hawwa's feelings remained open during the violent, beating rain, yearning for the water, for ever more water. Hawwa loves the sun, but she loves the clouds more. While others crave radiant, sunny, cloudless skies, she prefers them angry, overcast, and frowning, pouring out rain.

Anyway, it's a beautiful morning, she says to herself from behind the window of her house, as she opens it on a horizon no longer wet, on a day when the sun has wakened after a long sleep. Today sun, a vision of summer, and daylight; tomorrow water and companionable winter, freighted with promise. When Hawwa listens a little she can hear jubilant birdsong, and human clamor in the houses of the camp, where life yawns in waking. She hears the clatter of restless souls, and she hears Fairuz singing: "Fly, O kite, fly, O paper and string, I wish I were a little girl again, on the neighbors' roof." The song plays from the radio, Fairuz's voice embellished with pure joy.

Hawwa smiles to herself. She loves Fairuz's paper kite, but she absolutely does not want to be a little girl again.

1

THE RUTTED LANE TAKES HAWWA, and she surrenders to it. She has hardly passed through it when she enters a second rutted lane, still more wrinkled, and then two others, no less corrugated. But Hawwa does not seem careful or cautious as she walks; her feet, in black leather boots with collars of matted brown fur, glide along the path mechanically and lightly, as usual.

Hawwa knows the lanes of Baqa'a Camp well, and they rarely surprise her. She has learned them by heart, with their austere geography, outwardly stable; with their long-standing cracks; with their pockmarks that store dark, sticky wastewater; with their sandy pimples that are no sooner picked off than they form again. She knows their scales, roughening their rugged hands; their hillocks, fresh and muddy or dried; their mounds of cement, dried at the edges of the houses; their random collections of gravel, pebbles, and stones; their puddles of water, accumulated from the wastes of the skies and the houses; and their thin streams that dig narrow furrows. She knows the lanes with the lone plastic slipper, nearly split, overturned on the path, and the sole of a sandal, gnawed at the toes; with the limbs of a half-buried doll, the head showing, implanted with locks of coarse blond hair, one eye gouged out; with the eight hopscotch squares, laid out on a bald patch of earth, their sides not completely straight, drawn with thick blue paint, partly worn away. Hawwa crosses the hopscotch squares, being careful not to step on the lines, in keeping with the rules of the game. In her imagination, which is still active, she casts a stone shaped like a cake of soap, polished on both sides. With a practiced throw she lands it at the heart of one of the squares, without letting it land on any of the faded blue lines or beyond the outside lines.

The biting cold morning air strikes her face, or what shows of it. She covers her frozen nose with a part of the scarf wrapped around her neck, made from amber wool with off-white carnations scattered over it, crocheted with a large hook. She has replaced her cotton head covering with another of a soft wool and polyester blend, colored with intertwining shades of beige, crimson, and cocoa, and wound firmly around her hair and ears. Even so, the air whistles its freezing cold through the threads of the scarf over her ears. She hunches her shoulders over her chest. "Cold enough to cut a nail in two!" She remembers her father's expression from long ago, as she carefully fastens the top button of the black coat hugging her body.

"Abu Lutfi! Abu Lutfi!"

A raucous voice was calling her father after dawn, coupled with a heavy pounding on the iron door of their house, making the walls shiver. They curled up in their beds, hiding their expectant heads under their heavy covers that gave off an odor of humidity, kerosene, and the chill stored in the hidden bodies.

Her father, Mousa, who worked as a builder, hated winter days and hated rainy days. The people in his household also hated winter, and they hated rain, and they hated their father during the rain and the winter, just as they hated him before and after winter. During many winters, as in other seasons, when her mother, Rabia, would cautiously poke one side of his huge back, his senses would rouse all at once, in a whinnying snort. She would pull back fearfully as he turned over on his back, spreading his body over most of the surface of the bed. Once again she would shake him a little, with the palm of her hand bent back; he would raise his long arm, ending in a broad, swollen palm, toward her face, as she pulled back, out of reach. Then he got up, gathering his slack body, the metal bed frame shaking violently, its clatter tearing the dark silence. He sat on the edge of the bed, a mass of lava gurgling in the mouth of a volcano. With the rough soles of his feet, he searched for his slippers and kicked one of them under the bed, by mistake or because of his crankiness. "Fuck you, for the fucking morning!" He took aim at Rabia with his eyes, half closed by the heavy curtains of his eyelids; she lay flat on the floor, trying to squeeze half her body under the bed, stretching her heavy arm as far as possible, to pick up the stray slipper. Then she guided his stony heels into the slippers with her hand. He got up dizzily, with his repelling face, and headed for the bathroom, preceded by continuous coughing, both nasal and rumbling from the effects of the dark phlegm settled in the deep well of his throat. The noise of the spit coming from his moist throat ruptured the air of the bathroom, and from beneath the door came the stench of dark piss, like a cloud, along with the crude sound of a long, thick stream of urine that nearly broke the bottom of the toilet.

Her oldest sister, Afaf, cracked four eggs into the blackened aluminum skillet, and the heat of the olive oil set the glutinous eggs, making four suns gleam in the middle of a foamy white sea. Meanwhile, the water started to tremble in the metal teapot, with its coating of chipped blue enamel; she added two spoons of tea and six of sugar. As soon as the bright yellow of the eggs faded and the foam of their whites subsided, she turned off the gas burner, one of three in the stove, under the pan, as well as turning off the second burner under the teapot. She stirred the water, thickened with tea leaves and sugar, many times, then left it to steep. Wrapping a towel around the hot handle of the frying pan, she rushed off with it, down the fairly high step from the kitchen to the small living room, which Mousa had fashioned by biting off a part of the entrance to the house and a part of one of its two rooms, after his offspring multiplied, so it could serve all purposes, as a bedroom, a dining room, and a room where he could fling himself down in front of the television. Afaf placed the frying pan in the middle of the low, round table, then Hawwa joined her with a tray bearing the teapot, its handle wrapped in a crushed rag taken from the remains of a tattered t-shirt, along with straight-sided glass cups, a plate of Nabulsi cheese, a plate of green olives, a plate with two tomatoes cut into wedges, and a plate each of oil and za'atar, all of which she distributed on the table.

Her middle sister, Sajida, folded the mattresses spread out in the corner of the room where the girls slept, all except the one belonging to Duha, their youngest sister. The small child with her tiny frame lifted her stick-thin legs to the smooth surface of her belly, curling up under the blanket, which was folded over her twice. Her shrinking body and spirit harbored an unshakable peace, at least at that moment; Duha's limbs were not long enough for her to join in the daily toil of life. Hawwa thought that Duha's feminine flesh would probably never blossom like that of her sisters, or at least that she would not resemble her, Hawwa, specifically.

Hawwa, who was younger than Afaf and Sajida, had the largest build among the sisters, and in some ways she was the most a woman. They were convinced that she grew every day; and on the day when she had leaked a stream of dark blood, which traced a wide line on her white thigh and descended to her compact calf and her thin ankle, her mother had been terrified. She had led her to the doctor in the camp's medical facility, and he had confirmed what she feared. "But she's young, really young!" she had said to the doctor. "Oh Lord, what a catastrophe!" she repeated to herself, as she dragged her heavy heart along the street. Hawwa stopped her at a cart selling ice cream. "Yamma, Mommy! Buy me an Eskimo!" Rabia looked at her with compassion for a few seconds. Then the compassion in her eyes was replaced by hot anger and the blood boiled in her limbs; she made a fist of her trembling hand and hit Hawwa's shoulder out of spite, knocking her off balance so that she nearly fell. Before they reached the house, the mother had taken her little girl aside in a lane empty of all but a few flies hovering over a split garbage bag, spilling chunks of rice, a sticky rotten tomato, a wilted cabbage leaf, yellowed cilantro leaves, and onion skins. She leaned over her face and warned her: "Don't you dare let anyone know you've bled! Is that clear?" Hawwa was still crying for the Eskimo she hadn't gotten. Her lips, unstained by the blood-red tint of the popsicle, were puffed up with a mix of tears and snot. The eight-year-old child had known very well why she was crying hotly. But she had not understood why tears were pouring from her mother's eyes, accompanied by suppressed sobbing.

Now, Duha seemed plunged into a deep sleep. The wrinkled end of her thumb, with its nail nearly dissolved from her continuous sucking, rested at the edge of her mouth. The sound of her regular breathing formed an abiding, flowing tune, spreading a passing warmth throughout the room. Hawwa lit the kerosene heater in the kitchen, watching the thin conduits as they were populated by flames. She brought her hands close to the metal body of the heater, trying to store some of the warmth in her body. But what came into her instead was the odor of the sputtering kerosene in its first huskiness, an odor that would remain with her the whole day long. She picked up the stove by its thin metal arm, the burning liquid shaking in its half-full belly, and walked with it to the living room, balancing it with difficulty, not letting it lean to either side. Her brothers Lutfi and Ayid slept on mattresses next to each other in one corner. She put down the heater near the round table, and the flames flared up red. "Lutfi! Lutfi!" She pushed her older brother's shoulder, and the younger Ayid opened his eyes anxiously. She exchanged a conspiratorial look with him, and he went on sleeping, or pretending to, curled up in his place, while she lifted the blanket to cover the shaved half of his head and the recently stitched wound above his forehead. "Lutfi! Get up and have breakfast!"

Her father's coughing rose continuously, as he crossed the small distance from the bathroom to the low tabliya tray table. He took his place on the padded pallet that was his alone, during the long, demanding evenings, and during the days of unemployment or idleness, which he also spent at home—days that were disturbing and exhausting for his household. Her mother sat down near him, but far away enough to give him room to spread his temper unimpeded. She handed him the round pita loaf and he divided it in two, before shouting for Lutfi, through his phlegm: "Lutfi! *Get up!*" Lutfi stood up, while Ayid shrank back under his heavy blanket, hiding his head with its spiky, close-cut hair under it completely.

With a big piece of the bread, folded over, Mousa split off one of the pregnant, sunny eggs in the frying pan, scooping up the entire egg and devouring it. Afaf poured the tea for him in a thick glass cup, then returned it to the teapot and poured it again, the liquid now thicker and darker red. The steam from the brewed tea hung in the air of the room, its aroma blotting out a stale stench. Rabia stretched her hand to the plate of tomatoes and took one quickly, as if pilfering it; she followed it with a small piece of bread dipped in oil and za'atar, chewing slowly. Mousa turned his eyes to where Ayid lay, curled up. He took a long, preparatory sip of tea. He called Hawwa, who was helping Sajida fold Lutfi's heavy mattress, and was stuffing his heavy blanket into the metal cabinet that held the covers and blankets. Her father's voice rose over the creaking of the hinges as she pressed on the bulging cabinet doors with her youthful body, so they would close over the piled-up mattresses.

"Hawwa! Check on Ayid."

Hawwa sent a pleading look to Sajida, who covered half her face with both of Lutfi's pillows and hurried into the other room with them. Hawwa surrendered to the morning obligation, on this morning that was colder than usual. A small piece of plain bread was still hanging from her mother's fingers, as she embraced her with a look of fear mixed with compassion. Hawwa bent over Ayid, who had adopted the position of a corpse thrown randomly in its place. She inserted her hand under his blanket and probed the parts of his body, with a movement that conveyed both thoroughness and deliberation. She withdrew her hand from under the cover and half looked into her father's eyes: "He's dry!"

Mousa got up from the floor like a spring suddenly released. Rabia put out her short arm to turn him back: "Finish your breakfast!"

He shook off her arm and walked to Ayid's mattress. With the edge of his bare foot he pulled back the heavy blanket spread over the cowering body of his son. Ayid bent his legs while clenching his eyes shut. Mousa inserted the broad, cracked sole of his foot between his little boy's legs, feeling the cold dampness below his belly and examining with his toes the spots of urine in the middle of the mattress. His roar pierced the morning in the apprehensive house: "Afaf! The strap!"

Rabia half leaned on a knee, trying to stand up. He forbade her forcefully: "Stay where you are!"

Rabia sat down again, where she was, cross-legged, pressing her fists into her legs, which felt weak and numb. A huge tremor shook Ayid's body. He tried to gather in his scattered limbs, in an attempt to reduce the area of his flesh exposed to the pain, raising his thin arms to his face. Hawwa was preoccupied with covering her brother with his blanket again, and her father pushed her hip with his heavy, stony foot, making her fall on top of him. Rabia pleaded with him to let them go this morning, but the blows of the strap fell thick and fast on Hawwa and Ayid, by turns or together. Hawwa tried to

11

cover Ayid's austere body with her full flesh, its softness apparent under her nightgown, so the blows of the strap flying through the air fell on her hips, her back, and the tops of her arms. Each stripe produced a long moan, as if she were pulling it out of deep pain, cutting across Ayid's screams, which bumped against the ceiling of the room. Her father glared at her: "Shut up! I don't want to hear your voice!"

Rabia was getting up again. Mousa shot her a warning look to deter her, before wrapping part of the strap around four fingers and bringing it down again on their bodies, which clung together. Hawwa put her closed hand over her mouth, pressing hard to stifle her moans, while her body trembled violently. Ayid buried his head between his arms completely, closing his mouth over his suppressed screams, which took the form of a drawn-out groan at each blow that missed Hawwa and landed on his legs or back. Rabia wiped her feverish face, as pain enveloped her body with each sting of the lash shining on the bodies of her two little ones.

When Mousa had finally had enough of them, he came back to the steeping cup of tea that waited for him. Still standing, he gulped down what was left of it. He inspected his empty pack of cigarettes, crushed it, and threw it on the table. His eyes followed Lutfi, who had deliberately remained in the bathroom until after the morning ritual of the lash was over. Now he sat on the edge of the pallet and wiped up what was left of the eggs in the skillet. Mousa's eyes besieged his firstborn until their eyes met. He said, "Give me a cigarette!"

Lutfi soaked a big piece of bread in oil, dipped it in the za'atar, and ate the bite slowly. He followed that with an olive, stripping off its moist flesh in his mouth before throwing the pit on the table. Rabia poured the steeping tea, now a deep red, for him and for herself. He tried to avoid his father's eyes as he reached for the last tomato wedge, saying, "I don't have any!"

Hawwa spread the blanket over Ayid, who continued his suppressed groaning. She curled up beside him, hugging her chest and crying; the tears stung her red cheeks. Her father coughed up the phlegm sticking in his throat, collecting it with noisy snorts and whinnies, then spat it into a little flowerpot sitting on the sill of the room's one window, which was closed. In the past it had held a stunted green plant, which had turned into a dry, woody branch planted in a dark mass of mud amid cigarette butts. As Lutfi chewed his bite slowly, Mousa brought his face close to him and motioned with his eyes, saying, "Search in your socks. You might find a cigarette or two."

Lutfi stretched out his leg and took a pack of his Gold Star cigarettes from the top of his sock, where they were hidden beside his foot, a little above the ankle. Mousa snatched the pack and took five cigarettes, lining them up in his empty pack of Reems. He tossed Lutfi's package back to him, then asked, "And the money?"

Lutfi stifled his wrath as he took back his cigarette pack and counted what was left in it. He looked at his mother, who was opening the neck of her galabiya with her fingers. He lowered his eyes to the floor and took a sip of tea, then another. Then he answered, without lifting his eyes to either of them: "Yesterday I gave Mother five dinars."

Rabia pulled aside the collar of her galabiya, surrendering to Mousa's commanding look. She plunged her hand down to her chest and pulled out the folded bill, which had not yet had its fill of dampness from one of her full breasts. Feeling loss and emptiness in her heart, she gave him the money, and chewed a piece of dry bread from among the crumbs of the meal collected on the table.

It took them some time to absorb the fact that he had left, at last, and that the air of the house was free of his voice and his odor, and that the oppressive feeling that accompanied his presence had dissipated, or at least thinned. Anticipation crouched on their shoulders as they closely watched the final minutes before he disappeared from their day, while he put on his reddish-brown boots with corrugated soles and shanks lined with thick broadcloth, as well as his heavy fatigue jacket and his black leather hat lined with fake fur. The hat had two broad flaps that hung down from the sides to cover his ears, making him look like a hunting dog, with his cautious gait. He opened the door of the house and stood on the stoop, separated from the lane by three steps on one side; he lit a cigarette, holding the smoke in his lungs before breathing it out; he raised the collar of his jacket to cover his chin, and walked away. When the street had swallowed him up, a different life crept into the house, one that was more bearable.

In the kitchen, Sajida pumped the handle of the kerosene stove several times to compress the air, until the fire caught, and its crackle deadened the sound of the morning call to prayer. Hawwa filled the tall, cylindrical aluminum bucket with water from the faucet in the bathroom and carried it to the kitchen, walking like a penguin with wide steps, and making a great effort not to tip the bucket to one side or the other. Her well-muscled arms held the bucket by its two handles; the lashes that marked her back and her arms flashed with pain, increasing or lightening according to the movement of the heavy water in the bucket. She raised the bucket with all the strength she could muster and settled it on the grate of the stove, so the crackling, cawing circle of flame spread out over its bottom. When the water had boiled, she extinguished the stove, wrapped a piece of fabric around each of the bucket handles, and carried it to the bathroom, even more slowly and ponderously this time. She was careful not to tilt it, but a few drops of hot water from a light jolt stung her hands; she swallowed the pain. Ayid sat on the low wooden bath stool, hugging his arms around his trembling body. Hawwa put the bucket on the cold bathroom floor. "I'm cold!" Ayid said, and she took him in her arms. He yelled from the burning of the lashes that gleamed on his arms. Hawwa rubbed his shoulders and his back until some warmth crept back into his delicate flesh, then she stripped off his pajamas, soaked in cold piss.

The steam rising from the bucket formed a warm, smoky cloud. Hawwa took off the galabiya she wore over a white, short-sleeved cotton blouse and navy pants of a cheap, polyester-blend corduroy, which stretched to allow her well-rounded bottom and fleshy thighs to expand at ease. She folded over her pant legs several times, to just below the knee, then filled a metal basin three-quarters full with cold water from the faucet, and added enough hot water from the bucket to make it bearable. She measured the temperature of the water with her elbow, and poured the warm water over Ayid's shoulders. His body recoiled for a moment, until his flesh became accustomed to the refreshing soap and water. Hawwa rubbed his prickly hair with Nabulsi soap, then scrubbed his back, stomach, arms, and stick-like legs with a loofah covered in soapy foam. He moaned at the places where the loofah stirred up the sting of the lashes, but it wasn't long before he surrendered to that feeling of limpness and a certain serenity that comes after great pain.

At eleven years of age, Hawwa was a mature woman, plump, fully fertile, her flesh plainly visible and pliable, slack and yet solid at the same time. She was only three years older than Ayid, and yet she seemed like his mother. Ayid was skinny, with a mousy figure, bowed down. His frame turned inward and his limbs inclined to hunch over in sleep and when he sat, and that made him look constantly frightened. No one knew whether his fear had imprinted itself on his body or whether the fear had arisen from the nature of his body as he grew, and had then bent his spirit. Whichever way it had happened, Ayid was afraid of anything and everything—afraid of rain, coupled with angry thunder and lightning; afraid of the dark night in the street, when he would clutch his mother's hand tightly and walk hurriedly, fleeing from imaginary footsteps that might catch up to him; afraid of the darkness of the night at home, when Rabia would get up on still, black nights and feel her way in the gloom, looking like the ghoul that eats children and sucks their bones in the stories Afaf told him and

Duha; afraid of how his father looked when he came home at the end of the day; afraid of his father's face looking at him; afraid of his father's eyes boring into his eyes; afraid of his father's voice calling him: "Boy!"

Ayid would flinch, but he was careful to answer, "Yes, Yaba!"

On the days when the cold was greater and the piss more abundant, so that his clothes were almost completely soaked, Hawwa carried him to the bathroom. He lay in her arms like a nursing child, his face clinging to her full breast, engulfed in the smell of her morning flesh and aware of a sense of safety in her embrace.

Hawwa was growing every day and every hour. She was ahead of Afaf and Sajida, and beside her, Duha seemed to shrink ever faster. It worried Rabia, especially when Hawwa's breasts began to form, like two pomelos in their early winter yearning. She cut a piece of cloth two yards long and half a yard wide and bound it securely, swaddling her breasts, nearly flattening them. Hawwa told her that she couldn't breathe, so Rabia said she could loosen the band when she slept. During the night, when she lay on her mattress near her sisters, Hawwa abandoned caution and spread out her body, heedless of the darkness and its possibilities, so all of her curves bloomed, even those hidden during the day, and she became a woman.

During the day, Hawwa's body could lug and tote what her sisters and even her mother could not, so her strong, firm frame was put to use for all the hard labor. She carried Ayid's heavy mattress up to the roof, climbing two sets of concrete steps that jutted from the walls in one of the corners of the kitchen. The steps were neither level nor even in size, and over time some of the edges had broken, so they held lurking dangers. One day her foot slipped on one of the upper steps of the first set, as she was carrying a tub of laundry, and she fell backward with the tub, to the bottom step. For a few moments she couldn't get up; her eyes were fixed on the kitchen ceiling.

16

Her mother and her sisters rushed to help her, frightened. But Hawwa pushed up her prone body and stood erect, as if she had never fallen down. She collected the scattered wash and started up to the roof again to hang it out. Then she came down, folded Ayid's mattress and blanket, loaded them onto her back, and took them up to the roof.

Ayid cried on the day Hawwa was married. He was still wetting himself during many winter nights, and during some summer nights as well. He realized that Hawwa's wonderfully sturdy body would not be there in the mornings, to cover most of his body and take most of the stinging lashes for him.

Now Hawwa cuts through the narrow streets of the camp, with which she shares a close acquaintance, in some places an intimate one. The walls of the houses, bearing the signature of misery, poverty, overcrowding, and the inarticulate, injudicious writings of the time, exude the odor of defeated life and exhausted people, who have surrendered to the vicissitudes of their days. As much as possible Hawwa avoids walking in the narrowest lanes, where the odors of exhaustion and coercion stagger together with the smell of frying oil, depleted from repeated use. She likes the wide streets that face the sun, the air, and the sky more comfortably.

With its two parallel rows of wide buttons, descending from the chest to the middle of the hips, Hawwa's coat reaches to the top of her ankles, and flows in a wide skirt from her buttocks. The coat emphasizes her firm figure, her chiseled waist, and the harmonious distribution of muscle and fat in her body, now in its forties, amid flaring fullness in certain places. The edge of her silver dress shows below the coat. When the air strikes her towering form, the skirt of the coat, split in back, swirls around her on either side, and the small, intensely red flowers with a faint touch of silver that are scattered over her dress seem to glow. Hawwa raises her eyes to the ripe sun, intensely yellow, imprinted in the bowl of an intensely blue sky. The copious sunlight that spills everywhere over the camp keeps its heat frozen within. The sun seems like a drawing, still and completely silent, while the icy air rages in the streets, striking bodies violently.

Hawwa buries one of her hands, softened with Vaseline, in the pocket of her coat, and with the other she holds her black leather purse and a thick green plastic bag, bearing the name of a shoe store, which is carefully closed. She hears the sound of strong, successive blows and lifts her head toward the source. She sees Umm Said beating a multicolored carpet hanging from the roof of her house, with a long cane that ends in an oval of woven bamboo.

"God give you a good morning, Umm Qais!"

"Good morning, Umm Said!"

Umm Said's head is wrapped in an orange wool scarf. She complains to Hawwa about the past days of profuse rain, while continuing to beat the damp carpet. The roofs and the floors leaked, and the carpets got wet, and the sewers overflowed, and rot crept onto the people in the house.

"It really killed us, Umm Qais!"

Hawwa lifts her head and smiles in agreement.

Umm Said complains of many other things unrelated to the days of rain, but that resulted from them or are added to them. The bus that Abu Said uses to carry supplies to the school cafeterias broke down, and the washing machine broke at the most crucial time, and her son Said's wife has been sulking with her family for a month. Then she lowers her head, as if she wants to whisper in Hawwa's ear from above. In a voice wrapped in rage and powerlessness, she says that her husband's sister has been staying with them for over a week. She came from West Bank with four of her children. Umm Said stretches out her neck and presses it with her palm, in a meaningful gesture, saying, "A person could suffocate, sister!"

Hawwa consoles her: "God help us all."

Hawwa moves on, giving herself to the hopeful December morning. In some spot deep inside she feels happiness, just as she feels that she loves this wintery morning without needing any reason to love it. With her eyes she sweeps the iron doors of houses, painted with cheap, immoderate, unruly colors, breaking the monotony of the gray surroundings, the walls and the streets: green with the vigor of mulukhiya when the leaves are first picked, edged in cream; mustard yellow with a frame of black; rust red with an apricot-colored lattice for two small windows above the door; sky blue with an arabesque design in pistachio; and amber with edges gilded boorishly, as befits the aesthetic aridity of the place. Hawwa contemplates windows cracked open enough to allow the nectar of the day to creep into rooms still shaking off the slackness of sleep. Her gaze passes over the haphazard maps of Palestine, drawn with red spray paint, like spots of blood plastered on the walls, and the words "Long Live Palestine!" and "Gaza Resists!" next to drawings of hearts of various sizes and colors, with arrows piercing them, some of them crooked. A favorite Fairuz song runs through her head. She hears it clearly: "I belong to my love, and he belongs to me. O little white bird, don't ask me! Let no one scold, let none be shocked—I belong to my love, and he belongs to me." Rapid footsteps follow her from behind; they come very near. She starts, and looks to the side. A man in his sixties passes beside her, his face and eyes lowered, carrying a white translucent bag with bread in it. She silences the song playing in her head. When the man and his footsteps have moved far enough away, she once again plays her piece of Fairuz, and the song blazes anew in her spirit: "My love called me, saying gone is winter's gloom, the dove has returned, the apple trees are in bloom. . . ."

The flow of the song in her head converges with the vibration of her cell phone, announcing the arrival of a message in her mailbox. She slows her steps and puts her hand in the pocket of her coat, picking up the phone carefully. Heat rises to her face. She stops for a bit to contain the light tremor that runs through her body. The tempo of the tremor is always the same, and it's not bothersome. In fact, the tremor can be exciting and enjoyable, and it's sometimes accompanied by a little perspiration. She even intentionally delays opening the message, keeping the tremor and its effects in her body for the longest possible time.

"May your morning be happy." Hawwa reads the message, and wipes the screen of the phone, which is smeared with her fingerprints. She embraces the few words once more, then closes the message box and returns the phone to the warmth of her coat pocket. She wipes her neck, perspiring from the remains of the tremor, under her scarf, and a gust of cold air strikes her. She lifts the collar of her coat, covering her neck, and walks on.

"My love called me, so I went right away. He stole me from sleep, he took my rest away. His way leads to beauty, and I'm going his way. Oh sun of love, spin our story today. . . ."

On the way an idea shines in her mind, not breaking the flow of the song in her spirit; a pristine idea, clear as the sun and the blue sky and this crystal morning: how beautiful life is! How very beautiful, at times.

2

HAWWA CLIMBS INTO THE SMALL bus heading from Baqa'a Camp to Sweileh. She lifts the edges of her coat and her dress off the floor of the bus, marked by filth and the dirt deposited from shoes, and takes a single seat beside the window. She crams the hem of her coat and her dress between her legs, and puts her purse and the bag in her lap. She cracks open the closed window to allow a little fresh air to come in, to suck up some of the enduring stench, resulting from a succession of miserable people, a paucity of soap and water, and sunken leather seats.

The bus is delayed while it fills with flabby bodies, huddled against the cold. Some of the faces are dark from the effects of the darkened sky during the past days of rain, which—added their owners' generally miserable existence—is more than enough reason for gloom of face and spirit. The riders get on the bus with bowed bodies, pressing themselves with difficulty into the narrow seats, all the more narrow as their bodies are enlarged by heavy coats and jackets, lined with padding and packed filling. The bus starts off at last, after a futile dispute between the conductor and a woman in her sixties who is sitting on the outside of a double seat that could accommodate two riders and who has set a large blue bag of waxed burlap beside her in the narrow aisle of the bus. The conductor asks her to put the bag on the seat beside her, but the woman refuses, in order not to pay the price of two riders. The dispute ends at last in favor of the woman, and a thin young man stretches his legs over the huge bag to sit on the inside seat. His fashionable, though not necessarily expensive clothes, his swept-back hair held in place with gel, the penetrating smell of his scent, and the denim backpack that hangs from his shoulder indicate he's a university student. All along the way, the exiting and entering passengers jump over the bag or squeeze their legs to one side as they pass it, unable to avoid bumping into it.

Hawwa prefers the single seats, but often she's forced to sit in one of the double seats. Sometimes she shares it with schoolgirls or university students, who wear the hijab and take extreme care with their makeup and the shiny, eye-catching accessories they add to their outfits, like wide leather belts or rows of silver and gold chains, holding cheap beads, which cover their chests. In their embellished state, framed by the obligatory hijab, they look like rough sketches. Hawwa might share her place with women who are teachers or employees in the middle of their spinsterhood or their married lives; in either case one could see the progressive exhaustion in their faded hijabs, their funereal jilbab overdresses, and their swollen purses, with many outside pockets. But many times, Hawwa resorts to tucking in her body and reducing the space it occupies, as a succession of men sit next to her, greedy for all forms of physical contact and fondling, and sometimes tickling and pinching. Then Hawwa shrinks in on herself, more and more, until—if she cannot make herself any smaller—she's sometimes forced to get off the bus at any stop she's reached, taking another bus or covering the rest of the distance walking.

The bus devours the road at great speed. The clatter of the wheels on the asphalt eats away part of the riders' thoughts and voices. Hawwa grips the metal back of the seat in front of her, to control the shaking of her body and her involuntary swaying, being careful not to bump into the enormous thigh of a passenger who looks as if he works in a garage, and who is standing next to her single seat, supporting himself with a hand on the back of her seat. She happens to notice her watch: it's 10:00 in the morning.

Hawwa was thirteen when she first rode the bus from Baqa'a Camp to Sweileh alone, on her way to Sitt Qamar's house. She had gone twice before in the company of her mother, who introduced her to Sitt Qamar and showed her the way there, and its risks. "Don't talk to anyone, don't look into anyone's face, don't laugh," she cautioned. Hawwa's eyes must remain planted on the floor, she emphasized. She likewise showed her ways to contract her body and confine her ample limbs to the narrowest possible space. But Hawwa did not escape from all forms of groping and rubbing, squashing and squeezing, from conscripts, college students, workers, and even the young conductors: one would brush her rear with his trembling thigh as she boarded the bus, or pretend his arm had unintentionally collided with her breast when she got off. And if the bus shook when it was passing or stopping, or when the driver handled the surprises of the road rashly, then that provided an opportunity for most of the men on the bus to pretend to have lost their balance, and rub against any part of the women's bodies they could reach, while the women struggled and fought to contract their bodies and fold them inward.

Her mother was always reminding her not to allow anyone to pay her fare for her, but often the bus conductor would return her shilling with a wink and she would take it from him, putting it in her pocket without looking at his face. Later she would buy a couple of chocolate wafers with it, or a bottle of Pepsi, which she drank standing at the entrance to one of the shops. It was something she would never admit to Rabia.

At thirteen, Hawwa was a woman of towering stature and many supple bodily features. Her breasts in particular were immense. Sitt Qamar did not suppress her amazement when her eyes fell on them for the first time, especially when Hawwa took off her gray jilbab to stand before her in a pleated, sumac-red skirt that emphasized the breadth of her hips and the luxuriant flesh of her thighs, and in a tight pink stretch blouse that showed her round waist, small compared to her extremely large breasts. Sitt Qamar asked her to take off the blouse. Hawwa hesitated. Sitt Qamar gave her a commanding look, so Hawwa stripped off her blouse and stood before her embarrassed, trying to conceal her uncovered chest and stomach with her arms. Hawwa was alone in the house with Sitt Qamar, who said to her, "Straighten your back!" Then she came up to her and pushed gently on her shoulders, so that Hawwa dropped her arms to her sides, and pulled back her shoulders and back. Hawwa was wearing a bra of limp cotton fabric, which sagged under the weight of her breasts. The cups were small and not deep, and the volcanic breasts were crammed into them, overflowing on either side of the shallow cups, so that under the tight pink blouse they looked as if they were made up of two firmly packed levels of pliable flesh. Sitt Qamar disappeared for a few moments, then returned carrying a black bra and asked Hawwa to put it on. Hawwa hunched over completely as she took off her bra, turning her back to Sitt Qamar, who helped her to fasten the new bra from behind, settling the straps for her. Sitt Qamar showed Hawwa her new shape in a half mirror hung at the entrance to her apartment. The new bra had wide straps made of a thick weave that would not stretch easily, designed to lift unusual weights. The cups of the bra were more like two bowls, their depth a hand span or maybe more, so they contained the breasts completely. The bowls were made of stiffened black lace, so they helped the sturdy straps lift up the breasts. Hawwa contemplated herself in the mirror, amazed by what she saw. The trunk of her russet-colored braid coiled around her shell-white neck, where a hint of faint, pale blue showed under the delicate skin. The black bra framed her white complexion, marked with pink freckles, and her upper half looked as if it were alight. This was the first time Hawwa had seen her body, or any part of it, in this way. It was the first time she had examined the perplexed features of her face, and the first time she believed she could be beautiful.

Rabia had taken Hawwa to Sitt Qamar to learn sewing from her, and to help her with the housework. Sitt Qamar lived in a spacious apartment in a three-story building in an elegant and orderly quarter of Sweileh, where many cars, some with license plates from Gulf states, stood outside houses built of stone and red brick. Some of the cars were so large and luxurious that if they had tried to pass through one of the lanes of the camp, they might have gotten stuck in it, if they even made the attempt. Sitt Qamar's apartment was "roomy and restful," as Rabia later described it to her neighbors. It was made up of three bedrooms, two bathrooms, a living room, and a large parlor, which Sitt Qamar had divided in two. In the larger half she had placed a French salon set of chairs and sofas, in indigo satin fabric woven with gilded beige flowers, and framed with hazel-colored, carved beech wood. The set was surrounded on three sides by small oval tables, made of the same wood, and bearing many statuettes and glass objets d'art, hard for the eye to take in at first glance. In the middle stood a large oval table, its legs endowed with large calves, lushly ornamented. Its surface was draped with a cream-colored chiffon cover with raised, gold-thread embroidery; it covered one side of the wood and left parts of it bare, in an artistic arrangement. The half-bare table was adorned with a single, exquisite vase, its surface opulent with exuberant color and generous gilding. One flower stood in this masterpiece, its wide fabric petals made of golden organza, while its center was embroidered with cream-colored beads that had a rainbow luminescence. From time to time Sitt Qamar would exchange it for a new flower, made of a mixture of organza, chiffon, and silk, of a different design and a different color, according to her mood. Sitt Qamar would answer Hawwa's questioning look by telling her that the old flower had wilted.

Sitt Qamar used the smaller side of the parlor for a long, oval dining table of walnut. It was surrounded by twelve chairs with openwork carved backs and seats raised with stiff foam and upholstered with indigo satin, which went with the satin of the French set. The edges of the chairs were decorated with bronze tacks that Hawwa thought at first were metal buttons. A large, empty bowl of cut glass occupied the center of the table. The dining set harmonized with a buffet of the same wood. Behind its glass doors were carefully arranged rows of white china tea and coffee cups with gilt edges, and transparent, long-stemmed crystal glasses of various shapes and sizes.

In a prominent place in the buffet, covering three of its broad shelves, sat a china set with a vast number of pieces, including a dozen teacups and saucers, a rather tall teapot, a sugar bowl, and a small vessel with a spout, for milk. They were all arranged side by side, along with a dozen large plates, a dozen of medium size, a dozen small dessert plates, three elongated, oval bowls, a dozen small soup bowls, and a large bowl with a cover that had a small opening on one side for the handle of a ladle. Some of the plates had been put on stands to show off the design. Hawwa was fascinated by the details of the painting on the pieces of the set: it was of a beautiful girl, wearing a lilac dress like a bride's, and a young man who looked like a fairy-tale prince, walking hand in hand, their eyes on a lush garden. Hawwa never tired of looking at the parts of the drawing in the middle of a plate, a cup, or the teapot; its details stood out against the shell-white background of the china vessel, the background adding luster to the set. Likewise, she never tired of enlacing her eyes with the look of the lovers, repeated hundreds of times in the buffet without weariness or tedium. She would bring her face close to those of the girl and the prince, and would almost hear them talking together, or maybe they were whispering.

Hawwa asked about them one day. Sitt Qamar closed her eyes and let out a sigh that she deliberately made melodic and dramatic, saying, "Romeo and Juliet." When she noticed that the names meant nothing to Hawwa, she explained that they were two lovers. Hawwa decided that the set must be very valuable, and very dear to the heart of Sitt Qamar, who singled it out for a special ritual of care. Every two or three months she organized a ceremonial cleaning, under her direct supervision: Hawwa would spread a blanket on the floor and place all the pieces of the set on it, taking them down from the shelves gently, one by one. She would wipe them with a damp piece of terrycloth before putting them back in place. If the china clattered because one plate bumped another, or because a teacup strayed from its saucer, or because the cover of the teapot slipped out of place, Sitt Qamar let out an abrupt cry, as if she had been stung, and Hawwa would reassure her quickly that Romeo and Juliet were safe.

Rabia was just as impressed as Hawwa by Sitt Qamar and her home, or possibly more. Sitt Qamar led them to the living room, where she received her clients, which was much less luxurious than the parlor. Sitt Qamar sat on a sofa with three seats, part of a Morris set that was obviously well used compared to the French set, which had retained its newness for years. She invited them to sit down, and they each took a single chair.

With the exception of a cabinet containing a bulky television, as if it had been designed for it, there were not many pieces of furniture in the living room. There was a large, square coffee table with short legs, made of wood, scratched from much use; it could have served as a low tabliya tray table for dining if it had been a little shorter, or so it seemed to Hawwa. Scattered on the table, which occupied a large space at the head of the room, were various issues of *Chabaka* and *Mawed* magazines, bearing the faces of overdressed, overly made-up women, together with dozens of issues of the magazine *Burda*.

A smaller table, different in its wood and design from the large one, was crammed into one corner, next to the sofa with three places. It had a Formica surface, and held a green telephone, two packs of Kent cigarettes, a lighter, a broad glass ashtray containing cigarette butts, and a half-filled cup of coffee. An open bag was tossed on one sofa. A folded piece of red velvet showed from it, with a paper of measurement numbers attached to one edge by a pin.

Sitt Qamar lit a cigarette, looked at Hawwa for a moment, and asked her, "How old are you?"

Hawwa sat stiffly on the edge of her seat, her head bowed.

Rabia answered immediately: "Thirteen going on fourteen."

Surprised, Sitt Qamar nodded. She had imagined she was older than that. Next she asked: "Can you read and write?"

Rabia leapt to answer: "She went up to middle school, year two."

Sitt Qamar was wearing a housedress of white linen, marked with small red carnations. It was sleeveless and short, at least by Rabia's and Hawwa's standards, as it barely covered her knees, and it hung open loosely at the chest. When she sat at ease on the sofa the dress became shorter, and her chest could also breathe more easily from the opening. Sitt Qamar took the ashtray and placed it on the sofa beside her, then took off one of her cork-soled sandals and folded her leg beneath her body.

Again she addressed a question to Hawwa: "Why'd you leave school, Hawwa?"

Rabia intervened, as if defending her decision: "A girl just ends up getting married. . . ." She was silent for a bit, examining Sitt Qamar's legs, and then added: "God guard the girls till then!"

Sitt Qamar tapped her cigarette over the ashtray, and some of the ash flew onto the sofa. She smiled and said, "Do you have a tongue, Hawwa?"

Hawwa raised her eyes a little to Sitt Qamar, exchanged a smile with her, and answered the question with a nod. Sitt Qamar laughed before asking, at last, "Do you know how to make coffee, Hawwa?"

Hawwa lifted her eyes and her head to Sitt Qamar, her mouth opening in a broad smile. Sitt Qamar laughed, long and loudly, and in that moment Hawwa realized that she loved Sitt Qamar, and that Sitt Qamar loved her.

Today the Sweileh market hums with people and cars. It stretches, moves, and gradually becomes animated, in this morning crowned with a yellow sun and a blue sky that seem completely real. Hawwa feels for the cell phone in the pocket of her coat; she rubs its small screen secretly with her fingers; she trusts that her happy morning still has its sun glowing in her message box. She makes her way among the clothing shops, some of which have stuck cardboard signs in their glass windows, with improvised announcements of shattered prices. She fingers the fabric of a cinnamon-colored, broad-cloth jilbab overdress, made in China, on a mannequin at the entrance to one of the shops. The head of the mannequin is covered by a light-yellow scarf that permits a few locks of her brown, wiry wig to shade her broad plastic forehead. Hawwa doubles over the hem of the jilbab and examines its silky lining, a little lighter in color than the reddish cinnamon. She squeezes the fabric in her hand for a second and then releases it. The lone salesman in the shop leaves a half-nude mannequin inside, which he was dressing in a jacket and skirt, and approaches Hawwa, inviting her to come in and see jilbabs of other cuts and colors. Hawwa inspects the back of the jilbab without looking up at the salesman and asks about the price.

"Only twenty. I swear, before the rain we wouldn't have sold it for less than twenty-five."

Hawwa puts her hand in one of the pockets of the garment to measure its depth. She seems disengaged from the jilbab despite her close inspection of it; she does not look at the salesman at all.

From experience, the salesman, in his forties, senses her lack of enthusiasm. He rubs his prickly beard, and pretends to surrender early: "Eighteen, madam—take it at cost. I swear to God, all I'm making on it is two dinars."

Hawwa leaves the jilbab and turns around, moving away.

The salesman calls after her, "Fifteen!"

Hawwa does not turn at his voice, which is engulfed in despair. She feels his eyes boring into her back. She continues on her way, resisting the temptation to stop at adjacent shops displaying similar jilbabs, settling for letting her eyes rove over them discreetly.

She passes a large commercial market with four windows overlooking the street. Piles of discounted merchandise are spread on the sidewalk: bottles of shampoo in large sizes, cleansers, bags of diapers, bundles of paper tissues in nylon packages. Behind them, the store's glass display windows hold giant advertisements for Nabil Frozen Foods, from kibbeh meatballs and cheese samosas to chicken fillets and beef kebab fingers.

Hawwa leaves behind the market and the knot of women that has begun to grow around the cheap discounted goods spread on the sidewalk, and goes into a small store selling kitchenware. The store owner greets her—"Come in, sister!"—and invites her to sit on a worn leather seat in front of his counter. He is atop a step stool in a far corner of the store, arranging water pitchers of frosted glass on one of the shelves. He continues arranging them, placing them according to their shapes and heights, while two women in the opposite corner inspect a set of stainless steel hostess trays. When they ask the owner, who has lost interest in them, about the price, he answers neutrally, without enthusiasm and without looking at them.

"Will you have tea, Umm Qais?" he offers, from atop the three steps of the stool. Hawwa declines, thanking him. The two women leave the store, not much bothered by their lack of any purchase. They gather their jilbabs and heavy shawls, wrapped around their plump bodies like blankets, and walk carefully, so as not to bump into the many vessels resting on the shop floor. Hawwa watches the shop owner fold the step stool and put it aside, then go down some old wooden steps at the back of the store; their groans reach her clearly, one after the other. He returns after a few minutes bearing two cartons, carrying them with great eagerness despite their heavy weight. The shop owner places the closed cartons next to each other on the dusty desk. He wipes their surfaces with a dry towel, then splits the brown tape over the opening of each with a small knife. The cavity of the larger carton is divided into small sections of various sizes by white foam. In the largest lies a teapot, which the shop owner takes out carefully, unfolding the plastic bubble wrap around it. Hawwa cannot suppress the light in her eyes. The shop owner reads her delight and says, "How about that? It's exactly what you asked for!"

Enthralled, Hawwa picks up the porcelain teapot. She rubs its ornate design with her fingers. On the curved surface of the oval teapot sit Romeo and Juliet, close together on a bent tree trunk. They are surrounded by the green foliage of love that Hawwa knows well, against a creamy white background. Juliet's dress is almost a pink fuchsia. The expression of happiness on the faces of the lovers does not differ much from the one that beamed in Sitt Qamar's buffet for so many years. The shop owner passes his fingers over the pieces of the set, counting them: six teacups and saucers, with a sugar bowl and creamer. Hawwa covers the teapot in its bubble wrap and returns it carefully to its place. From the smaller carton, he pulls a porcelain plate covered in the same bubble wrap, with the same design of two sweethearts surrendering to the gentleness of love: a reduced copy of the design is painted in three places on the edge of the plate. He turns the plate over and shows her the writing in English on the back.

"Original Japanese," he assures her; and for greater proof, he brings the plate close to her ear and taps the center with the tip of his finger. "Do you hear the ring?" he asks, as a way of attesting to what he says. Hawwa seems completely convinced, without understanding the meaning of the ring. He tells her that he couldn't manage more than six plates. She holds the plate in her hands as if she were holding a baby she has had after a long wait, her face overflowing with happiness. "It's more than enough!" she tells him. In her mind she's determining the place for the tea set and the plates in the buffet. She will have a buffet in her new house. It won't be enormous, like Sitt Qamar's buffet; it will be small and new, with the scent of newly cut wood, sawn, carved, and painted recently, the aroma of the beginning of life. Hawwa pays the price of the tea set and the plates without arguing, and asks the shop owner to keep them for her until tomorrow morning, when she'll come with a car to pick them up. "I'll keep them safe and sound," the shop owner tells her, as he counts the money and then closes the two cartons with broad tape, making sure it has stuck tightly again and patting it with his hand, reassuring her.

Hawwa hastens her steps, her heart skipping from joy. She grasps the bag tightly in her hand and presses her arm against the purse hanging under it, as if that might calm her heart's fervor. When she reaches the fabric store at last, her panting has subsided. She folds her joyful spirit inside and pulls herself together; she knows that a delight of another kind awaits her. As soon as she enters the store, her eyes are dazzled by the profusion of colors in the dress fabrics, which are lined up vertically, in three sections, stretching from floor to ceiling, on all four sides of the store. Hawwa moves her eyes among the bolts, arranged according to the type of material; when they fall on the velvet section an excitement courses through her, which she has experienced time and again. The feeling still glows, and is renewed. Several bolts of velvet have been spread out, displayed on one side of the cutting table. The plain velvet is mixed with cut velvet, embossed velvet, sculpted velvet, velvet embellished with sheer chiffon or touched lightly with satin, velvet set with beads or embroidered with spangles and sequins. But Hawwa knows her velvet, the one she wants. It must be *velvet*—pure, embodying the spirit of velvet, not allowing any addition to ruin its weave, its touch, its exquisite essence.

When her hand runs over a billow of violet velvet, Hawwa knows that she has found what she's after. The salesman spreads out the folds of the bolt, which holds all the shades of violet, before her on the table. As the fabric rises and subsides between his hands, the aroma rises, the one Hawwa knows and expects. She breathes it in, holding the particles of the sweet scent within her.

Velvet has an aroma unlike any other; that's what Sitt Qamar used to tell her. It's the aroma of warmth, of dormant heat, of depth and expanse; it's the aroma of well-deserved luxury, of pride and restraint; it's the aroma of wishes and desires, of maturity, maturity of love and of age; it's the aroma of clean flesh, of flesh suffused with yearnings and the sweat of lust. But not just any velvet—only plush velvet, velvet in which the most expensive silk blazes; velvet with a closely packed, draping softness that resists pleating; velvet with a hidden flare in the fabric, with a changing, subdued mix of color, with a faint light, a pervasive sheen; velvet with an intimate timidity over the folds of the body, with a touch that emits a rustle, a rustle that does not startle yearning.

Sitt Qamar favored dark shades of velvet, specifically the shades that begin with the sunset at its last breath, and go until the end of the night, because they radiate greater heat. The colors slip from blood red, to purple, to cherry, to lilac, to violet, to aubergine, to indigo, to navy blue, to ink, to deepest blue-green, to smoke, to charcoal, to coal black, at the extreme of black. She favored plain velvet, and she hated multicolored velvet, embossed velvet, striated velvet, embroidered velvet, pebbled velvet, crinkled velvet, crushed velvet, sculpted velvet, cut velvet. Once, a woman brought her a piece of heavy velvet sculpted with broad, raised flowers; Sitt Qamar asked her, with obvious mockery, whether she wanted her to make a dress or upholster a sofa!

Sitt Qamar would bury her nose in a piece of velvet, then rub her neck and face with the recently cut fabric, because its aroma still clung to it. She would fold the piece of fabric twice and lay it on the cutting table, then form it with her hands into the shape of a dress. She would round the imagined neck opening, gather in the waist, and form the lower part into a narrow skirt, reaching the middle of the knees—her knees. Then she would close her eyes while she moved her hands over the temporary sculpture of the dress, as if she were embracing it. Her body would become less taut, more inclined to lie dormant. She breathed the fabric in that moment, until she was satisfied with her imaginary adventure and returned to the present, when it seemed as if she had been reborn. Velvet embodied the scent of life: the beginning of life and the return to it.

Sitt Qamar loved many other fabrics, although to a lesser degree. She loved guipure lace, specifically black, with its heavy, taut material and broad motifs, resembling the ornaments of openwork crochet; and she loved pliant, delicate, lightly ridged lace, in colors of icy pink, cold lilac, and milky and sky blue. Comparing chiffon with organza she inclined to the former, because of its airy feel. She especially liked chiffon in dark, saturated shades, like royal blue, burgundy, and an evening shade of violet, as the diaphanous fabric would not prevent the appearance of precious parts of the body beneath. Sitt Qamar also loved deceptive silk, as she loved crêpe georgette, with its enticing simplicity and endless possibilities. She took a neutral stance with respect to linen and cotton, and one that changed according to her moods for wool, although she generally favored mohair and cashmere. Sitt Qamar hated many fabrics, and especially despised polyester and nylon. She showed great disdain for very elastic Lycra, and, in general, for all fabrics that stretched.

With Sitt Qamar, Hawwa discovered the wide world of fabrics. Her favorite time was when she went with her to the market for fabrics and trimmings in downtown Amman. Usually, Sitt Qamar was buying the extras called for in designs for her clients—linings, lace trimmings, ruffles, strips of rhinestones or studs, buttons, and belt buckles. Some of her "important" clients would entrust her with buying specific fabrics, such as imported velvet or guipure, not convinced by the cheaper Jordanian or Syrian substitutes, or even the Chinese. And there were select clients who trusted her with freedom of choice in the color, bowing to her excellent taste in design.

Sitt Qamar set trends and embraced fashion strongly. In the seventies she was credited with introducing long sleeves, split entirely down the middle and gathered at the ends by broad cuffs closed with a half dozen buttons. In the eighties she was credited with being the first one seen wearing dresses and shirts ornamented at the breast by brooches of feathers, or shaped like large, blooming flowers, made from silk, with little petals of openwork or embroidery or layers placed one atop the other. She designed them herself and chose their colors with great care, so as to add a color contrast, sometimes stark, to her appearance—putting a red rose on a coal-black dress, or a white, rose-tipped carnation on an indigo shirt, or a lilac orchid on an ivory jacket, or a yellow narcissus on a beige suit. Most importantly, Sitt Qamar was credited with resisting the dominant fashion of the eighties, as she hated those huge shoulder pads that widened the shoulders or that gave jackets, specifically, a rectangular shape or, in exaggerated designs, a triangular one. She refused to include them in her designs, insisting on using small, thin supports, just to "seat" the garment's shoulders. She did not much approve of sequined fabrics, nor was she tolerant of snakeskin prints, leopard-skin prints, or zebra prints. She found them oppressive, coarse, and annoying.

No sooner did Sitt Qamar set foot in a fabric store or in a shop for laces and trimmings than the store owner dropped what he was doing and came to welcome her, placing "the store and the store's owner," as he said, at her disposal. Sitt Qamar was one of those women who dominated a place. She possessed the quality of willingly occupying a picture, standing out clearly in the frame, while all the details around her faded, or at most turned into elements reinforcing her presence. In fact, she didn't settle for being singularly prominent in the picture, any picture; rather, she took possession of it, and she herself became the picture. In her thirties and even her early forties, Sitt Qamar was a woman as a woman should be: sculpted, erect, mature, whole, and perfect. Her great effervescence, even though it had, inevitably, diminished with age, was still like a hidden insurgence. When she would go into a place or walk in the street, everything in her ambit faded except for her, within a relatively wide circle. Everything in the air was quiet; she alone was a shout, simply because she was present. Sitt Qamar was a very beautiful woman. Hawwa in particular considered her the most beautiful person on earth.

Hawwa now stops before the dazzling window of a shop selling traditional gold jewelry. She clutches the green bag to reassure herself; it's now crowded by the new bag she holds, from which the aroma of velvet arises, rich and penetrating, giving a feeling of opulence. Many necklaces and chains, long and short, hang from two metal racks that stretch from the front of the shop window to the back. On the wooden base of the window are displayed sumptuous ensembles of bright-yellow metal, as yellow as twenty-one-karat gold—or so they are meant to seem—arrayed in boxes lined with white satin, like the boxes of real gold jewelry. Each set is composed of a short necklace or pendant with a matching bracelet, earrings, and ring, not incongruent with the original from which it was copied and not differing from it very much, even to the experienced eye. Most of the ensembles are set with glass stones that look like quartz or that are cut like diamonds. On the side of some of the boxes, where the gold gleams blatantly, is written "L'azurde Collections"; near them is a picture of Elissa wearing a necklace from which dangle gold beads that light up a large part of her bare ivory bosom. The singer tilts her head slightly, throwing back her hair, and rests her hand on her shoulder, in a pose intended to display the details of the set in all its components.

Hawwa had learned about "Russian gold" years ago. She was attending the henna party before the wedding of a neighbor's daughter in the camp, and saw the bride lifting her hands as she danced, displaying a dozen twisted gold bangles on one arm and on the other a chain-link bracelet. There was a large string of solid beads, each the size of a marble, hanging from her chest and reaching the top of her abdomen. "Where'd they get all this?" Hawwa leaned over Umm Said, asking her in a whisper, while her eyes followed the mother of the bride, who was returning a bucket to its place near the entrance to catch the water leaking from the ceiling, after the children at the party had kicked it away in their excitement. "Russian gold," answered Umm Said from the side of her mouth. Hawwa didn't understand the difference between Russian gold and the gold she knew. Interest flashed in her eyes as she tried to discover the secret of the radiant golden glitter surrounding the bride.

She asked Umm Said again: "What's that mean?"

Umm Said put her hand on her paunch and blew out the air. She explained to Hawwa that most people had turned away from gold after the price shot up, replacing it with cheap Russian gold, with its designs and patterns that did not differ much from those used in real gold. In fact, sometimes it was hard to distinguish between them, even in the color. "And the brides, sister, they're happy with their gold things—they jingle by day, by night they get laid." She said it with hidden mockery. Then she told her the story of a serious incident that involved their neighbor, Umm Shadi. It was said that she had sold her only two bracelets, her gold snake bracelets, in order to save her son Shadi from a disaster, after he took merchandise worth more than 1,300 dinars from a tile merchant in Amman. The merchant sent two of his boys after Shadi in the middle of the night; they dragged him from his house and took him to a block of garbage containers in the camp. They punched, kicked, and stamped on him without letting up until his face was unrecognizable for the blood that covered it. They gave him two days to get the money. Umm Shadi concealed what had happened from Abu Shadi, and hid Shadi in his grandmother's house. Then she went to the merchant in his big store in Gardens Street and "kissed his feet," begging him to let her son off and promising to return all the money to him, down to the last penny. The merchant gave her a week to come up with the money. The poor thing sold her bracelets, all she had, behind Abu Shadi's back, because Abu Shadi had also had his eye on the snakes, for a down payment on a pickup truck. She bought two bracelets of Russian gold that were almost exactly the same as her snakes, as if they had been cast in the same mold, and they stayed on her wrist for a year. Whenever Abu Shadi pestered her to sell them, she claimed she wanted to use them for Shadi's marriage. When Abu Shadi finally found out what she had done he beat her until her body was swollen all over.

Hawwa couldn't comprehend that there wasn't any gold in Russian "gold." She asked, "Not even a little gold?"

Umm Said raised her head, emphasizing: "Not a bit!"

Hawwa's curiosity was aroused by the flash of the beads reflected on the face of the bride, who was still dancing joyfully, and she asked, "What's it made of?"

Umm Said pulled her mouth to one side, signaling cheapness: "Tin."

When Hawwa asked, lastly, about what someone might get if she thought about selling Russian gold, Umm Said said, decisively, "Shit."

Hawwa now leaves the store, happy and excited, carrying a paper bag with the name of the store in raised gold letters. After long imaginings, comparisons, and aesthetic considerations, she has at last chosen an "Elissa" set. The necklace is short and made of enlaced rings, with a rather large heart hanging from the middle, from which three flowers spring up, inlaid with miniature glass stones, varying in size between grains of fine sand and drops of water that flow like tears on the cheeks of the open flowers. In addition to the necklace, the set includes a bracelet, a ring, and a pair of earrings, all matching the necklace.

On the night of her life, coming soon, Hawwa sees herself in a dress of the violet velvet, in a design she has conceived in minute detail in her head. The dress will be long, flattering the lines of her figure that still retains, despite everything, its firmness and compactness, without much excess fat. It will enclose her waist and her stomach, which have not sagged much during the years of her life that have fallen away so harshly. It will gather her pelvis, with its distinct roundness—large, but not sagging—and then hang down straight to her feet in a single spill, before opening a little at the hem, in a mermaid shape. Hawwa hasn't forgotten to round the boat neck, its edges ending at the top of her arms. From there hang two very short sleeves, half cut away, so her smooth underarms show, and a small part, as if it were pilfered, of the tender skin of her breasts. Then Hawwa smiles, still seeing her image in her mind, and completing it with the Elissa ensemble, which occupies plenty of space on her bare bosom.

Hawwa knows that she will be a beautiful woman. She sees herself as the most beautiful bride a woman could be, at forty-seven years of age.

3

AT THE SWEILEH CIRCLE ROUNDABOUT, Hawwa climbs into the bus. "Safut!" she says to the conductor, as she pays him the fare and takes one of two seats in a row. She sits next to the window and places the three bags on the empty seat next to her. She looks at her watch; the hands are distant from each other, approaching 11:30. A number of weary buses, empty, are lined up in the traffic circle, most of them going to Baqa'a Camp by way of Safut. Soot mixed with thickening exhaust and mud from the days of rain covers the shabby chassis of the little buses. The sooty coating is concentrated on the lower part; it looks like a broad sash of accumulated filth, and gives the buses a dispirited look, as if they're tattered and near collapse. Movement at this suspended, inactive time of day is light—it's neither the beginning of the morning, calling for setting out and undertaking, nor noon or afternoon, urging return.

The bus leaves the roundabout when it's still only half full, hoping to pick up more passengers along the way, cast out on the street at this uncertain time of day. The jolting of the half-empty bus, accelerating in the descending street, shakes the passengers and makes them sway. The seat next to Hawwa remains empty, so the three bags sit slackly in the place of the presumed passenger. But Hawwa isn't at peace. She picks up the bag of fabric and the paper bag with the Elissa ensemble, its shining gold confined in a velvety red box, and takes them in her arms. She steals a glance at the piece of heavy fabric folded in the bag, and from that glance a cascade of violet pours out, in her eyes. Her heart smiles. Serenely, she recalls the precise cut of the dress, and in her vivid imagination she redesigns it. The camera in her mind descends from the boat neck to the narrow waist and moves down the mermaid shape, ending at the fishtail opening. The dress will bring out her tall, resilient stature, and will set off the compact flesh and fat of her body, while the opulent violet color will show off her white complexion with its soft, twilight glow. Then in her imagination she puts on the golden Elissa ensemble. She fastens the necklace securely by the shortest link of the chain so that it frames her neck completely, while a large area of her smooth bosom remains uncovered, and an elusive part of her cleavage appears, a narrow valley between two almost contiguous mountains. For a moment in her fantasy she puts on a narrow, gilded leather belt with an oblong metal buckle, its frame set with a dusting of glass stones. But no; she takes off the belt, since she imagines that it would likely break the melodious, flowing rhythm of the violet velvet. Besides, it might take away, visually, from the dazzling element of the Elissa ensemble. She stands sideways, in the mirror of her imagination, and makes a full circuit, in her mind's eye inspecting the proportions of her body from every angle. In her mental picture, lit by the violet of the velvet and the gold in its artificial splendor, Hawwa sees the glowing possibility of coming happiness. She sees him looking at her, examining her, unable to conceal his dazzled reaction. She turns off the switch of her imagination in her head, which is aflame with yearning and anticipation. She gathers her things in preparation for getting off, as the bus gradually slows down to stop in Safut.

Over the passing years, Hawwa has developed a singular capacity for imagination. It's not just any imagination; her fantasies are multidimensional, with complete details and features, coming with many addenda and particulars that make them possible, very possible. They encompass a full spectrum of colors, sounds, and scents. And the colors might throng and crowd one another, the sounds might clamor, the scents might fill one's nose—many times it's hard for Hawwa to contain them or silence them. She imagines that people are seeing what she sees and hearing what she hears. Her breast fills with the breath of morning, mixed with the scent of dewy jasmine hung in her soul and stored, in her imagination, since ancient times, when she would pick it from bushes whose little branches surged outside the walls of houses in Sweileh, when she was going to Sitt Qamar.

This amazing capacity for imagination that Hawwa possesses was forged from experience—the experience of limited possessions, of life measured in droplets, of many accumulating deprivations, as well as the experience of days of extreme drudgery and of nights drained by sorrows. Perhaps she turned to her very tangible fantasies out of hopefulness and wishing, using them to combat waking nightmares and those in sleep. In fact, Hawwa went still further in sharpening her imaginative faculties, for she was able to bring forth happy fantasies amid the torments of hell. As the torment in her life intensified, so did her capacity to fashion illusions, until it reached a level allowing her to call up all beautiful faces, all places, and all feelings, in bright, glowing, lifelike forms, and she could retain them within her, braided into her being and her senses, for as long as she needed. That was the only way Hawwa able to live.

Hawwa had lived when she was married. She lived as a lesser human being, but her imaginings relieved her somewhat. She was sixteen when she was engaged. Naifa, her father's mother, visited them one Friday and banged on the door heavily, with her foot, in the early morning. Hawwa took up the mattresses, covers, and blankets in haste, to avoid her sharp tongue. Naifa had breakfast with them, and then lunch and supper. Between the meals, Hawwa baked her a pan of hilba semolina sweet cake, which she craved; she cooked rice pudding for her; she boiled her a pot of tea with sage; she peeled two apples for her and cut them into thin wedges, as well as three oranges, which she handed her in sections; she shelled a pound of peanuts for her; and she soaked her false teeth and cleaned them with soap. Naifa didn't budge from her place on the padded pallet all day, except for ablutions and prayers, when Hawwa followed her into the bathroom with a towel and the slippers used in ablutions. When she couldn't lift her feet to the washbasin, Hawwa poured water from the plastic pitcher over her feet, in a wash pan. Then she squatted down, almost suspended over the bathroom floor; she spread a towel over her grandmother's thighs and took her feet, one by one, and dried them well. In the evening, after she had devoured the last section of orange and wiped the sticky juice from her hands and mouth with a towel Hawwa brought her, moistened with soap and water, Naifa got up to leave. Hawwa helped her put on her long toub cloak over her housedress. She looked at Rabia, fastening the belt of her toub over her belly, and said, "Umm Nazmi, the wife of Hajj Hussain Abu Jibril, asked for Hawwa for her son Nazmi." Shaking her kerchief in the air and then tying it around her head, she continued: "The wedding contract is next Friday and the wedding is in a month."

Mousa got up to protest while Rabia stayed seated on the floor, slowly peeling a wedge of apple. "How can you give the girl away without asking me?"

Naifa burned him with the fire in her eyes, folding her hands over her breast. "You got any objections, Ibn Naifa?"

Mousa looked toward Hawwa and then to his wife, to assess her position, but Rabia was avoiding the confrontation by picking up orange seeds from the mat on the floor, deliberately not looking at him. He explained to Naifa that Hawwa was still too young. Immediately she trapped him with her eyes, until she nearly bored through his spirit. She suppressed her fury and spat out, "Too *young? That's* what's botherin' you?"

She reminded him that Hawwa's sisters, Afaf and Sajida, had been about her age when they married. Hawwa broke in, announcing anxiously that she didn't want to get married, not now, and not to Nazmi, who was a con man, in her words. Her grandmother attacked her, pulling her by her thick braid, tied on one side, and throwing her on the floor. She pushed her toward the wall, slapping her face continuously until her nose bled. Then she took one of the bath slippers and fell on her. Mousa tried to intervene, but Naifa shouted, "Stay back!"

Hawwa curled herself into a ball, as she was used to doing during her frequent beatings, so the flaying blows from the bath slipper landed on her back, her legs, and her arms. She was screaming, "Yamma! Mommy! Mommmmmmmmy!" Rabia stayed where she was, paying no attention to her shouts. She was pressing on her stomach as if she had a stomachache, all the while avoiding meeting the eyes of Naifa's son.

When Naifa finished at last, she threw the bath slipper on the floor and shook her arm in the air, before gathering up her henna-dyed hair, disheveled under the kerchief, which had slipped from her head. She replaced the kerchief and tied it carefully, saying, as a matter of information and nothing more, "We agreed on the mahr price. Four hundred dinars." She continued briefing them, watching Hawwa, who was whimpering and wiping her snot on her sleeve: "You'll buy a chain necklace and a few changes of clothes, and you'll send a sewing machine with her in the trousseau."

Then, as if remembering something she had to do before leaving, Naifa went to Mousa, whose face had lost all its color. When their faces were almost touching, she spat on him, saying, "You disgusting piece of filth!"

Then she left.

Nazmi worked in the al-Jurri butcher shop in the camp market. He was eight years older than Hawwa, and he had seen her many times as she passed through the market. But Hawwa was repelled by him, repelled by the mucus and phlegm in

45

his voice when he shouted the prices of meat in the market, repelled by his looks when he fixed the skinned bodies of the sheep and calves on the iron gaffs and hit the bare, bloody flesh with his hands, or when he lined up the severed calves' heads on the large wooden stand set up at the entry to the shop. When the women or girls of the camp passed by, he liked to play with the ears of the severed heads and comment on the beautiful smiles they showed. He might sprinkle water on their unmoving faces, so their glassy, open eyes would continue shining, and give the impression that they were following those who passed by. He had no good sense, and went so far as to frighten the little children who stood in the shop with their mothers. If he saw in a child's face that he was frightened by a calf's head, with its tongue hanging out of one side of its closed mouth and its eyes that seemed to be staring at him, Nazmi would pick up the head and bring it close to the child, who was already terrified and who would scream and jump away, while his mother rained curses on Nazmi: "Go to hell, you rotten idiot! You're nothing but an animal!"

But the tasteless jokes would disappear temporarily when someone shouted that the health inspectors were in the market. The salesmen in the poultry shops would rush to pull some of the chickens out of the crowded cages, the ones whose health or weight were suspicious, amid the shrieks of the terrified creatures, their collective clucking and cackling filling the air. They also rinsed the slaughter sinks, where blood had dried around the edges, with water and cheap soap flakes, gathering up the feathers that clogged the drains with their hands. Meanwhile, Nazmi picked up the calves' heads, which were exposed to all the fumes and filth from the street and the air, two or three at a time, hugging them to his chest with both arms, and ran inside, drawing gloating laughs from people passing in the street.

When Nazmi fell on Hawwa the first time, she nearly choked to death. Aside from his savagery in tearing at her shrinking flesh, an odor of stale, greasy dirt collected in her nose, emanating from his moist, sticky body. It was mixed with the smell of fresh paint on the walls of the house, which were laden with cold, and with another, grimy, smell, stealing around her from no obvious place, in which age, decay, and wear fermented. In that moment, Hawwa summoned the most beautiful pictures her imagination could produce, lively, overflowing with joy, filled to the brim with warmth, intoxicated with beauty, as well as a profusion of scents—of pampered morning jasmine; of closed, fragrant Arabian jasmine buds; of fruits on trees in their earliest ripening, when they're roused by spring breezes that caress their firm cheeks. She also called up an actual desire, wished for, anticipated, resident in her spirit, and summoning a young love, who dissolved her heart's apathy. Hawwa called Murad to her. She sought shelter in his breath, so that it fell on her flesh and burned it painlessly, penetrating her and shaking the joints of her being. In a waking dream, Murad pushed her onto the bed with his well-muscled arms. He lay atop her, spreading out over her body, covering all the regions of her senses, entwining his legs with hers. His smell flooded over her, and his clean flesh, mixed with traces of sweat and recently extinguished cigarettes, covered her fearful flesh. Some of her terror subsided and, for Murad, her limbs lost some of their stiffness. So it was that Nazmi ravaged her and she submitted to him completely.

Murad's breath had often been close to hers, when he came to Sitt Qamar's house to change the gas canister for the stove. Sitt Qamar allowed no one else to come into her house, as he was careful to pick a clean canister for her, untouched by rust. He never cheated on the weight of the canister or the quantity of gas in it, and he was also careful to make sure to connect it safely, and to guarantee that there would be no leaks. Most importantly, he was courteous and well mannered, wiping his shoes well before entering the apartment and following

Hawwa timidly to the kitchen, without allowing his eyes to find their way, stealthily, to the women waiting in the parlor for their turn to have their measurements taken, or to deliver their fabrics, or to receive their finished dresses and two-piece suits. Perhaps Murad was distracted by Hawwa from Sitt Qamar and her women. It was something Sitt Qamar noticed without giving it much thought, though she took a secret pleasure in observing how each of them tried to deceive the other so he would not read what was inside. Murad would walk slowly behind Hawwa, carrying the heavy new canister in one hand, his firm, youthful body slightly inclined; and, without seeing that, Hawwa would be conscious of the distended muscles in his arm that nearly split the sleeve of his shirt.

Murad's breath would come quickly but not brokenly, taking the form of suppressed panting. Another time, Hawwa would feel that his audible breathing might be related to her, and to the fact that she was very close to him and that he nearly bumped into her from behind, more than it was to the weight of the canister swinging in his hand. Many times, when Hawwa slowed her pace as she entered the kitchen, Murad's leg touched her skirt, striking fire from the flint of her body. When Hawwa bent down to open the door of the lower cabinet next to the stove, in the place set aside for the canister, Murad bent down in turn, their breath close, one shoulder near the other, one arm nearly entwined with the other, Murad's face seeming as if it was going to fall onto Hawwa's breast, or what showed of it in the opening of her dress or her shirt. Sometimes Hawwa would tuck a jasmine flower or bud in her hair, which she left loose in back, placing it just behind her ear, so that if their breath met it would be mixed with the sweet aroma of the dewy little flower petals. Or she might intentionally undo an extra button on her blouse or dress, to allow Murad to fall easily, in his imagination, between her pillowy breasts, so she could seize him in her heart and keep him inside her as long as possible. She might pilfer a spray or two from Sitt Qamar's perfume bottle, spreading it on her neck, so the aroma would seep into the fields of his budding desire. When Murad would begin loosening the old canister, handing her the nut and the washer, she would spread out the palm of her hand so the tips of his fingers would touch her soft palm, and a tickle would run through her body that would lift her off the earth where she stood, and that she wished would not stop. She felt she might fall, though she did not fear falling but rather wished for it, as falling would be flying, sweetly, smoothly, lightly.

Murad was eighteen, working with his father, driving a pickup selling and distributing gas canisters to homes and restaurants spread throughout the neighborhoods of Sweileh, Safut, and the surrounding area. Hawwa thought he was very handsome in the jeans that clearly outlined the shape of his backside and the shirts that completely defined the chiseled muscles of his chest and belly. He had a clear complexion the color of wheat, giving off the odor of morning soap, light cigarettes, and a hidden touch of imitation Drakkar Noir scent. When he talked with her, his mouth had the light odor of Marlboro cigarettes and a trace of mint-flavored gum. For a period of over two years they settled for the crosscurrent of their breath, green-stemmed desire, touches that were intentional even if they seemed accidental. During that time, Hawwa's body matured and her breasts like soft buns swelled still more, while Murad went from one set of jeans to another of a similar design, and to a seasonal mustache. Many times he nearly slipped into the curves of Hawwa's body. They hungered for each other when they came together and still more when they were apart.

Hawwa cried for a week after she was engaged. She cried over the inevitable separation from Sitt Qamar, from Sitt Qamar's house, and from Sitt Qamar's life, which had in many ways become a part of Hawwa's life. And she cried more over being separated from Murad. The last day she saw him, she caught up to him after the ceremony of changing the canister.

49

As he was going down the stairs, carrying the empty gas canister, she shouted, "I'm getting married!"

Murad put the canister down on a step and looked at her with frozen eyes.

Hawwa rephrased: "My family's making me get married!" There was a desperate appeal for help in her shaken voice. She was lifting both arms to his ship, which was heedless of her amid a dark sea with surging waves. Death, her death, was the closest thing she could see. Murad stood on two steps, as if he were about to run or flee. He remained silent, staring into space, as if he wanted to call to mind some thought but didn't know what it was. He took out a cigarette and put it in his mouth without lighting it. It trembled at the edge of his mouth, then fell on the floor. At that point he broke out in tears, crying hard, with broken sobs. It reminded her of her brother Ayid's crying, when he was being beaten in the morning after wetting his bed. Hawwa found herself feeling sorry for him, so she went down the steps to be near him. Murad stopped crying without saying a word, his eyes on the floor, watching one of his Top-Sider shoes as his foot played with a wrinkled gum wrapper. One of Sitt Qamar's clients passed them; Murad was afraid she would step on his cigarette with her heavy foot and crush it, so he quickly bent down and picked it up. He shook off the dust clinging to it and put it back in place in the package. "Is Sitt Qamar upstairs?" the woman asked Hawwa, moving her eyes between her and the young man with the canister, not concealing her displeasure at seeing the two of them together. Hawwa nodded while her eyes still clung to Murad, waiting for the next step. He turned to look at her with a face emptied of all thought and feeling, and said, "I'm late. I have to go."

When Nazmi stormed her flesh, Hawwa sought help from her fantasies. She separated her body from her spirit, observing her body being defiled without feeling real defilement, as if at that moment it no longer belonged to her. With time and continuous violations she came to leave her body entirely, standing far away and watching it with compassion. Sometimes she settled for being a neutral witness to the torment of her body.

Rarely did Hawwa's fantasies desert her. She learned to hone them in such a way that they reached the level of genuine reality, a reality that sometimes bordered on magic. Thus, after the odor of the shabby paint in the house dissipated, with its yellow color almost like urine, the house still sagged under the odor of fermenting decay and rot stored in its decrepit joints. But the odor did not enter into Hawwa's system, physically or mentally, for the house remained redolent of the jasmine of her imagination, of carnations on days that might be, of joyful lilies swaying in her dreams, which she alone could smell. Nazmi had rented their conjugal house in the middle of Baqa'a Camp, between his family's house and hers, a site that had no value or meaning. It was nearly a ruin, as many tenants had passed through it, the last a widow who raised baby chicks in it, dyeing them and selling them. It was below the level of the street, entered by going down at least one step. It was made up of two rooms opening onto each other by means of an oval breach that looked as if it had been made in the wall by an exploding shell. For some time after her marriage, the ragged entrance remained without a door; when Hawwa had a child she was forced to trim the sides and install a wooden sliding door that she had a carpenter make to fit the baffling opening. There was also a cave-like hollow that had been turned into a kitchen, in which there was a high sink and a broad, hanging concrete slab, crossing one wall horizontally in the middle. It served as a shelf, with a three-burner gas cooker on it, while the space below the slab turned into storage for junk. Hawwa stretched a rope between the two edges, on which she hung curtains of light linen. As for the bathroom, it was no more than a toilet hole in the ground, a copper faucet on the wall, and a slippery square of concrete, where Hawwa placed a chair to sit on when bathing or doing the wash.

Nazmi bought a small refrigerator, as well as a used bed and wardrobe for the bedroom. His mother made two quilts for him and upholstered some pallets for the other room, as well as side cushions for the elbows of her son, his brothers, and his cousins on both sides—unemployed types, shop boys, hustlers like him, sprawled on the pallets in the evenings, obnoxious guests for Hawwa to serve, never having enough tea (even after two or three cups), or enough baraziq sesame sweets, or melon seeds, or salted snack mixes, or cigarettes, which made a thick smoke in which the men's ashen faces and yellowed teeth disappeared.

Less than two months after her marriage, Hawwa was afflicted by a severe itching that kept her from sleeping and left her tossing and turning in bed. It broke out on her arms and legs, in enormous red splotches. Then little pimples invaded her body, some filled with liquid and pus. When she began to bleed from continuous scratching and scraping, she went with Rabia to the camp medical unit. The doctor did not conceal her disgust, as she examined her from afar with a ruler. She wrote her a prescription for an antiseptic and a salve and hurried her out of her clinic. When Hawwa asked about the reason for the pimples and the itching, the doctor answered her with even greater disgust, as she wiped off the chair where Hawwa had sat with a tissue dipped in alcohol: "Bedbugs."

Hawwa turned the mattress over, and was horrified by the black spots that spread over large parts of it. She inspected the bed, the high headboard that resembled a tombstone, the frame, the sides, and the corners, but she didn't see anything other than the widespread black spots. She brought her nose close to the wood, and was seized by an odor of decay. With her strong arms she pulled the heavy bed to one side and inspected the broad headboard from behind; she was appalled by the numerous hollows in the wooden board, its fiber eaten away. She used a long needle to dig into one of the hollows, which were scattered like smoky black clouds, and the cloud resolved into a swarm of bedbugs, some of which crept out. One crossed Hawwa's hand; she crushed it with the other hand, and the insect disgorged blood. Hawwa rubbed all of the wood in the bed with a rag soaked in kerosene, as Rabia had advised. The bedbugs retreated for two or three days, but they soon recovered their energy and resolve to bite her flesh. She burned the black hollows with matches, after she blocked them with cotton dipped in kerosene, but dozens of nests of bedbug eggs were scattered in other hollows. She asked Nazmi to get rid of the bed and buy another, but he refused. "Are you crazy?" he asked in disbelief. He claimed that the bed was new and clean, and that she was obsessed with a delusion. Then he bared his arms for her, marked with old razor blows, offering her proof that the bedbugs did not exist, because otherwise they would bite him.

One night, when the scratching and bleeding on her body reached an unprecedented level, Hawwa woke up Nazmi in a panic. "I'm going to die!" she shouted. Nazmi lifted his head to her in anger, then tightened his lips and his whole face and kicked her violently, hurling her to the floor. "Out! Get out!" he yelled, then turned and went back to sleep. Hawwa remained crouched in her place until morning appeared in the window. Her mind thought of nothing and saw nothing but Nazmi's face. She made his breakfast in silence and poured his tea without looking into his face. When he left the house for the butcher shop, she went to the kitchen and unsheathed a large carving knife, then headed for the bed. She stripped the mattress of the cover and planted the knife in its heart, and its yellowed foam sputtered. She split the mattress into two halves and threw them on the floor. Going back to the kitchen, she took the sledgehammer from the stored junk. The hammer was heavy and she lifted it with difficulty, carrying it to the bedroom with her back bent. She considered the bed carefully, then she summoned all her strength, raised the hammer in both hands, and brought it down on the headboard. A piece of it broke off and flew into the air. Hawwa felt as if her back was going to break in two from pain, but she pulled herself together and summoned all the injustice her heart held. Then she lifted the sledgehammer high and brought it down strongly on the headboard, and it shattered partially. She followed that with a more violent blow that separated it completely from the bed. The sledgehammer was lighter now and easier to lift, so Hawwa continued smashing the bed—she broke the frame, she broke the wooden slats that supported the mattress, she broke the legs. Sawdust scattered in the air of the room and some of the nails few into the air as well, one of them landing in her hair and another planting itself in the sole of her foot. She pulled it out forcefully, without wiping away the blood that flowed from the wound.

When at last she had given the bed the final blow, she picked up the limbs of the corpse, in a pile on the floor, and carried them in several trips to the camp dump. Then she loaded the two halves of the cloven mattress onto her back and shoulders and threw them on top of the pile of wood. She sprinkled the pile with kerosene and lit it, while dozens of kids from the camp gathered around—they were excited by the fire and intrigued by the rattling sound of the disintegrating wood in their ears, so they tried to enlarge the fire by throwing leaves, wooden sticks, and little branches on the rising flames. When she was sure that the fire had finished off the bed completely, Hawwa walked to a butcher in the first part of the market, all her senses alert, and bought a sheep's liver from him. Then she returned to the house, swept up the sawdust and the nails, and rinsed the floor of the house with water and kerosene. She heated water and took a bath, rubbing her hair and her body with Nabulsi soap. After her bath, she cut the liver into cubes and sautéed them with minced onion in olive oil. She ate it all with two round pieces of pita bread. Then she sat on the floor pallet, waiting for Nazmi.

Hawwa did nothing but wait during the rest of the day, knowing full well what its consequences would be. When Nazmi came home after sunset and asked her about the bed, she planted her eyes in his and answered him without blinking: "I broke it and I burned it."

Her eyes remained fixed on him, even when he pulled his belt from his pants in fury and brought it down on her.

"By God, I'll teach you, you bitch!"

The blows of the belt fell violently on her body, resounding on her skin and rattling her bones. But Hawwa still did not scream or yell, nor did a single moan escape her. She did not try to cover her face with her hands or cower to protect her flesh. The entire time, which seemed very long, Hawwa was looking up at Nazmi's face and neck, his veins swollen; inside herself she took pleasure in his fury, which was coupled with complete powerlessness. As the storm of blows broke on her body, in her heart she let her eyelids droop over the rustling of her skirt as Murad's leg touched it from behind. She allowed the tickling of the fabric to set her spirit whirling, and had no thought of resisting.

Nazmi seemed confused to see Hawwa's eyes fixed on him, unmoving; then terror took the place of confusion. He could not comprehend how she did not feel pain, or at least fear. He threw the belt on the floor, where the metal buckle came off, and went out. Hawwa lay back on the padded pallet and fell asleep. She slept deeply, until she woke after midnight and tried to get up. She could not; it was as if her legs were nailed to the floor, and her back and her arms as well. She tried to lean on one side to get up, but could not. The pain stored inside her, from the sledgehammer and the blows of the belt, had taken over completely, taking full possession of every part of her. Her body was demolished, stiff and hard. She felt as if her flesh were about to fall off her bones.

Nazmi was not in the house, so Hawwa surmised that he had spent the night with his mother to find some fodder.

She tried to go to sleep again, but could not. The October air played with the curtains hanging down over the half-open window, so cold currents hit her body, lying flattened on the floor. She tried to bend her legs and bring them closer to her, to warm them. She felt the cold rising from the floor, piercing the thin pallet and stabbing her back. She shivered, and felt around her for a blanket or a cover to put over her body, but found none. She remained on her back in her housedress, until the morning sun filtered through the thin fabric of the curtains. Between the cold, frowning, unfeeling face of the night and the neutral brow of the morning, Hawwa warmed herself with the promising sound of chestnuts slowly roasting on the little metal tray of the space heater in Sitt Qamar's house. Then she drank a cup of hot chamomile tea that sent lively warmth throughout her body. At the end of the night, as her body swung between hot and cold, covered with a layer of sour sweat, Murad came to her. He stretched out beside her, his clean-shaven face smelling sweetly of lavender and rosemary, as he deliberately, very deliberately, tried to make his jeans touch her dress. Dizziness overcame her and she fell down, easily, pleasantly, without feeling any pain in her flesh or her bones. Then, when the pain increased in her back, which had become still stiffer atop the pallet that was almost one with the cold floor, Hawwa opened her eyes on the lofty blue ceiling—like a cloudless sky—over the enclosed swimming pool to which Sitt Qamar took her. Hawwa lifted her chest, bowed her back, and pushed her legs forward, according to Sitt Qamar's directions, and floated on the surface of the water she imagined in the room. Her body became very light, as if it had been stripped of any remnant of her torture. She no longer felt the pallet below her, nor the cold of the floor that crept into her ribs from beneath it. She actually floated above the ground, on the surface of the water or the air, with light waves around her, massaging her stiff limbs and softening them.

With the advent of the afternoon, Hawwa stood up. When she cast her eyes over the empty space where the bed had been, she felt completely satisfied with herself. She also felt very hungry.

Hawwa has always liked the houses of Safut, and she especially likes walking in the small streets that wind among them, framed by cypress trees. Many of the houses of the town retain their old masonry of uncut stone. There are some where the elements of nature have worked successively on their bare walls, not clad in stone, so the coating of white plaster has turned a pale beige, carnelian has become a dusty pink, light golden brown has become a sandy yellow.

Nonetheless, however harsh the rainy winters, they seem incapable of subduing these houses, since they remain a refuge for wholesome living for Hawwa, a repository for warm lives. Their ample balconies are adorned by pots of green plants, well pruned and trimmed of any excess; the wide, tiled ledges outside always seem washed; their steps are girded with decorative metal railings, painted in shiny black; and their windows, half open, are provided with protective lattices, behind which curtains flit, billowing mildly. The entrance walkways are surrounded by rosebushes, their curving buds closed upon pale possibilities of color and a secret springtime. Concrete walls and rows of stone fence the small gardens of the houses, where there are olive trees, apples, lemons, and apricots, with arching, tangled tops and dense branches. The trees bear the deferred promise of fruit, as December is being kind to them and the leaves haven't all fallen off, but rather kept their green even if it faded or paled or shrank, or if the cold burned some of the smallest leaves. There are trees like the cherries, whose leaves are marked with a reddish orange, as if touched by a wistful sunset; and trees like the jujube, whose shriveled leaves take on a wine-red tint, adding an element of color to the overall scene of December trees, breaking the grimness of winter.

There are trees that stand completely bare of leaves, looking depressed, folded inward on their brittle branches. Some of them look frightening, as if announcing a wasteland, like the fig trees which bend like ghosts over the house walls with their smooth, gray, circular trunks; their enlaced branches, emptied of all leaves, seek the meager sun, but however much they try to rise, they remain bent over.

From the street where the bus lets her off, Hawwa will take a long, winding lane to the house of Durrat al-Ain. It should take her no more than five minutes, but that might extend to a quarter of an hour, with the time she takes to enjoy the houses and their small plots and gardens, which most of their own-ers arrange at random. Hawwa feels that any of these houses could be hers, and that if she were destined to live in one, she would really be able to live.

"Where have you been, Umm Qais?" Durrat al-Ain greets her with a look reproaching her for being late.

Hawwa embraces her fondly and goes into the guest parlor, which she knows well. "I'm sorry. I was in Sweileh," she tells her as she takes off her shoes at the door to the room. "You know the market and how mobbed it is." She takes off her coat, her woolen shawl, and her headscarf, and tosses them on the arm of one of the sofas, then sits down on another broad sofa and puts her bags beside her. Durrat al-Ain excuses herself to make tea and Hawwa extends her legs, feeling great relaxation and warmth, as her feet sink into the Turkish carpet with its eastern designs, mostly in shades of brown interlaced with gold.

Durrat al-Ain has furnished the parlor with a mus-tard-colored set of sofas, having many parts and pieces, which are arranged in a horseshoe. The backs of the sofas are bordered by wide wood frames with arabesque designs. The main table in the middle is square and very large, more nearly a dining table with short legs; when Durrat al-Ain has groups of women as guests, she puts many kinds of refreshments on the table, from fruit and nuts to pastries, sweets, and chilled juices in glass pitchers.

Durrat al-Ain returns to Hawwa bearing a large tray that holds an elegant teapot, two tall, gold-edged tea glasses, a plate of snack seeds, another of date cakes, and a third with two oranges, two apples, and two bananas. Hawwa pulls back her outstretched legs and from the green bag she takes school smocks, smelling of recently cut and sewn cloth. She spreads out the three ironed smocks on the adjacent sofa; two of them are blue and one is a turquoise shade of green. Durrat al-Ain inspects them with pleasure, complaining of how fast her daughters are growing—nothing fits them any more. But Durrat al-Ain doesn't seem bothered by this honorable rite of passage. She's proud of her offspring, and takes even more pride in their growing up and filling out. At thirty-five, she has delivered three boys and three girls, and wants more. She hasn't changed much since Hawwa first met her: the tender, flexible figure is still tender and flexible, and her radiant face still shines with that light that captivates, in any domain in which she finds herself. And then it's as if her skin has never been touched by time, since it retains its baby softness, even if it has assumed a velvety texture, a sign of maturity rather than age.

From the broad parlor window with its curtains drawn back, Hawwa glimpses Durrat al-Ain's neighbor moving around in the small garden of her house, walled by a low row of stones. She has wrapped her hair in a cool green scarf, tied from behind. The scarf has slipped back a little, and a lock of chestnut hair has escaped to cover half her wheat-colored face, as she leans over one of the basins to turn over its muddy soil. A lemon tree bows over her from behind until it's nearly leaning on her shoulder. For a moment the picture is frozen, and Hawwa goes to another time, in the future, her time, which is coming soon. Hawwa sees herself standing in the garden with a spring-green scarf, partially shaded by a lemon tree, its clustered fruit hiding their ripe bellies among the long leaves. Hawwa contemplates her face in the picture of what's coming, and sees the woman she has forgotten, the one she never was: she sees a beautiful woman, a happy woman. The picture clouds over and Hawwa looks up at Durrat al-Ain's outstretched hand offering her a tea glass, steam rising to her nose from the pure red liquid. She takes a small sip, enjoying just the right degree of sweetness.

She will call Munir. She'll tell him joyfully that she's bought the Romeo and Juliet set of dishes; it will be the first thing that goes into "our house." She'll arrange it in the buffet, and she might not put anything else there. She'll put on the dress made from the velvet wave, which she has designed, cut, and sewn in her imagination time and time again. Yes, she will have a home, a home of her own that she will love, a home suited to holding her and her finite desires. As Hawwa's hand strokes the peaceful river of violet in the bag, Durrat al-Ain cuts into the flow of her imagination, asking, "When are you getting married, Hawwa?"

Hawwa loves Durrat al-Ain and loves her house, from which the scent of happiness emanates. She loves her tea, red and pure, flavored with redolent sage in the winter and with intense green mint in the summer.

Durrat al-Ain had spent the first ten years after her marriage in Baqa'a Camp, and then she had moved to Safut, after God had given uncounted gifts to her husband and he had become one of the most prominent vegetable merchants in the camp market. Durrat al-Ain told Hawwa that one day she had dreamed of a little house with its own little garden. The most beautiful features of the house were a canopy extending over the entrance, tiled like a roof, and an upper balcony. When she woke from her dream and told it to her husband, he brought her paper and pencil, and asked her to draw a picture of the house she had dreamed of. Then he took the picture and said, "This will be your house, Pearl of my Eye!"

"And this became my house," Durrat al-Ain had said to Hawwa, laughing, trying to encompass her whole house with her hands, as if she still couldn't believe it.

Durrat al-Ain was no mere client—Hawwa was not accustomed to visiting her clients in their homes, or to delivering completed sewing to them. The truth was that she was infatuated by this fascinating woman, in the loveliest form that infatuation can take. Hawwa had met her for the first time more than fifteen years earlier. The young Durrat al-Ain had come to her with her mother, preceded by happiness. She told her that she was engaged, something she hardly needed to say, since she was proudly playing with the ring on her finger. She was thin, with a tawny complexion that had a watery copper glint. She certainly wasn't beautiful in the sought-after, peasant meaning of the word. Yet her face, with its finely carved features, had something captivating about it, something that seized the eye and the heart; and her entire person had a fine presence, an absolute authority concealed in boundless lightness. Durrat al-Ain was enchanting. At first, Hawwa believed that her magic was related to her very wide, honey-colored eyes; or to her broad forehead, covered by thick, soft, bronze-colored bangs; or perhaps the reason for it was her oval lips, puffed as if they had been injected with water. Or perhaps the matter was related to her even teeth, large without being coarse, and gleaming white—when she smiled or laughed, the white of her teeth joined the avid, pearly white of her eyes and lit up the whole surface of her face. Or perhaps the source of the magic was her fascinating name, Pearl of the Eye, which hinted at tales from ancient books.

But Hawwa realized, with perceptive sensitivity, that the matter was related to love, for Durrat al-Ain loved passionately and was beloved. The love story that joined her to Faris was repeated from onc cnd of Baqa'a Camp to the other. In fact, it was said that it went beyond the borders of the camp, and that journalists came to visit her wanting to record the story, and even that a Palestinian producer who lived in Britain wanted to make a film about Faris and Durrat al-Ain. He was going to sit with her for hours to record the events of the story. But after thinking it over, Durrat al-Ain did not like the idea. She was afraid, as she confided to Hawwa, that the evil eye of envy would disturb her life from the other side of the screen.

Hawwa made the dress that Durrat al-Ain wore to the henna night before she was married, and the dress became the talk of all the women, basically because it contravened the reigning taste. It wasn't made of affected silk or flashy satin; it wasn't adorned with silver, gold, or diamonds; the color wasn't icy or bright. It was, likewise, free of beads, sequins, and glass crystals, stripped of ruffles or any puffed skirt with a bouffant tulle lining. It was above the usual baubles of brides. That's not a dress for a bride, protested the mother of the bride, at first. But when Durrat al-Ain put it on and walked in it, she emerged as a true princess of make-believe—or rather, she emerged as Durrat al-Ain.

The dress was made of velvet. It was a faithful translation of what velvet should be, according to Sitt Qamar, and after her, Hawwa, with no additions except in the strictest limits, and then only in a way that emphasized and did not impose. Durrat al-Ain asked Hawwa to go with her to downtown Amman to buy the fabric, so Hawwa chose for her the most beautiful and expensive piece of velvet, in a wine color, that was luxurious by nature, even though it was also somewhat deceptive. The dress was sleeveless and strapless, enclosing Durrat al-Ain completely at the breast, flowing along the smooth curves of her body, adhering to her firm waist and flat abdomen. When it reached the last line of the abdomen, it opened out into a long, wide skirt, a "double bell," like a broad expanse of sea, with dense layers of waves, some folding over others. One wave would strike another, then more waves would ripple away successively in a movement that saw the color change, as the wine color moved from light to shadow, fluctuating between mellowed wine, jujube red, brick, chestnut, cherry, and crimson. Its silk lining, in the same shade of wine red, gave it greater volume and harmony, so the waves of the fabric seemed boisterous. When Durrat al-Ain stepped proudly in the dress, it seemed as if she were emerging from the sea. Only one addition did Hawwa consider worthy: she framed the line of the breast, which took the form of two domes, in thin black lace, like dark kohl around an eye. From the remnants of the fabric Hawwa fashioned small, wine-red flowers, and in the center of each she embroidered two tear-shaped pearls; Durrat al-Ain planted them in her bronze-colored hair, which she had put up in a wavy chignon. The bride limited her accessories to a strand of pearls around her neck and a pair of earrings from which pearls dangled like large pears, their radiance reflecting on her coppery complexion.

Durrat al-Ain still has the tender velvet relic of that night. The dress no longer fits her body, which has brought forth children, life, and extended love. Nevertheless, she can't bear to part with it, or even to lend it to the many brides who have asked her for it. Hawwa herself hasn't sewn anything like it, for the women of the camp, who reject pure velvet as too expensive, or who undervalue its possibilities and potential, or who replace it with hybrid types of velvet or varieties mixed with polyester—none of them has realized the true value of noble velvet: that it is emotional, that it is eternal. From time to time Durrat al-Ain seeks out the dress, which she keeps hanging in a closet, in a protective bag like a long sheath with a zipper. Her hand slips over its folded velvet waves, and wine-colored billows resound in her spirit. She smells the dense fabric, breathing it in, and is filled with desire.

Durrat al-Ain was fourteen when Faris fell in love with her. He was six years older, and worked in a vegetable store that sold in bulk to other stores and to vegetable carts in the market, overseeing filling the orders and delivering them.

No sooner did he look carelessly into her wide eyes and the overflowing wells of honey in them than he melted instantly within them. Durrat al-Ain was on her way home from school, and her bronze-colored hair, inclined toward a sunny blond, was hanging in two braids over her smooth chest, while her dense bangs floated over her forehead, rifled by the air. She stopped at a shop selling juice and ice cream and bought a vanilla ice-cream cone, licking it as she walked. When she noticed Faris's eyes following her, she tried to hurry her steps, and a spot of ice cream smeared the corner of her mouth, so she put out her small tongue to lick it off. At that moment the sun fell on half her face, so she glowed as a statue of pure gold on one side, while her other half was a coppery shadow of the first. That was when Faris slipped down to the deepest point of the well of her spirit, neither wishing to come out nor hoping that anyone would throw him a rope to save him. He followed her home. As she was opening the door he asked her for her name, but she did not answer. "It doesn't matter!" he told her. Then he added, with a confidence that shook her small being, "Mark my words, you're going to be mine!"

Faris sent his mother on the following day to ask for her in marriage, and she returned with a flat refusal from her family. "She's still young," they told her. Durrat al-Ain was her parents' only daughter among five brothers. Her father owned a store for seeds and spices in the camp, where he sold coffee beans, and za'atar and other spice mixtures. Faris waited a year and then sent his mother again, and again they told her that she was still too young. A year later his mother knocked on the door a third time, and Durrat al-Ain's mother answered her drily that they had no plans to marry her to anyone now. The fourth year, after Durrat al-Ain had finished her secondary studies, Faris importuned his mother to do what she had to do, so the poor woman dragged herself to the home of Durrat al-Ain's unwelcoming family, knowing what awaited her. This time they told her that Durrat al-Ain's cousin had asked for her hand and that her father had agreed. Immediately, Faris climbed onto the roof of a house across from Durrat al-Ain's home and yelled, "I love Durrat al-Ain and I want to marry her! I love Durrat al-Ain, I love Durrat al-Ain, I want to marry her! Listen, people, I love Durrat al-Ain!" People gathered in the lane, looking at him strangely and laughing, thinking he was either an imbecile or a shameless wanton. Durrat al-Ain's family closed the windows of their house, and her father said, "He'll shut up in the end." But Faris kept going up on the roof every afternoon and shouting, "I love Durrat al-Ain and I want to marry her!" He kept on shouting for three successive days, and on the fourth her brothers took him off the roof and gave him a shattering beating in front of everyone. Durrat al-Ain was watching the painful scene from the window of her room and crying silently; every time one of her angry brothers landed a punch or a kick, her helpless heart was crushed under the pain.

For more than a week Faris was unable to walk. Then, when he recovered a little, he went back up on the roof and once again began to cry out his love for Durrat al-Ain. That night, when he was going home, her brothers came out to him in the darkness. They were careful to make him see them, to make him see their eyes seeking vengeance against him. When they had surrounded him, one of them planted a knife in his belly. In the hospital, his mother cursed Durrat al-Ain and her family, and called the plague down upon them. But Faris, who survived because the knife had not torn any of his internal organs, refused to give the police the name of the person who had attacked him or his description—he was masked, he said in his statement. And when his mother tried to dissuade him from protecting them, he said to her, with a wink, "How could I, Mama? How could I even think of complaining about my in-laws?"

The day before the marriage contract with Durrat al-Ain's cousin was to be signed, Faris knocked firmly on her door. Her mother opened the door and saw him standing in a challenge, holding a plastic gallon container in his hand. He poured what was in it on his head, soaking his hair, face, and clothes with kerosene. Then he brought a lighter out of his pocket and told the stunned woman that if they didn't give Durrat al-Ain to him today, he would burn himself up in front of their house. People gathered around Faris, trying to convince him to turn away from this heinous act. Men whose wisdom was acknowledged in the camp tried to take the lighter out of his hand or pull him away from Durrat al-Ain's house. But Faris threatened everyone who came near him that he would set them and himself on fire. When the wise voices besieged the bride's father, he at last yielded to Faris's demand, and promised to engage him formally to Durrat al-Ain within two days. "No, now!" insisted Faris. The wise ones asked him to wash off the kerosene at least, but Faris insisted that the official court maazoun draw up the contract for him and his bride "this minute," while he was soaked with kerosene. The story goes, after the details were filled in and it spread and gained many additions during late evenings in the camp, that the maazoun covered his nose while he was writing the contract for Faris and Durrat al-Ain, and that the groom, who remained standing and was not allowed to sit on a sofa, did not release the lighter from his hand even during the recitation of the Fatiha from the Quran. Some versions of the story maintain that Durrat al-Ain's father demanded from Faris a dower payment of five thousand dinars and a pound of gold, and a delayed dower portion of ten thousand. In other versions, the first payment was ten thousand and two pounds of gold and the delayed portion was twenty thousand. But even if the versions of the event multiplied and differed in their details, the one thing that everyone in the camp agreed on was that the "kerosene groom," as they termed Faris, was the happiest of men that day.

A year after the kerosene engagement, Faris married the Pearl of his Eye in a celebration that lasted three days. Five tents were erected in front of his house and two streets were closed, while the earth shook to the rhythm of hundreds of dabka dances performed by the young men of the camp. They stamped the earth with all the force of passion, and the dust flew into the air, intersecting with the strings of decorative lights, so the motes suspended in the air looked like scattered flecks of gold.

In those days of jubilation, it was hard for a man to ignore that feeling of collective intoxication that came from the triumph of love, if only for one single time in history.

4

HAWWA GETS OFF THE BUS at the entry to the camp market. Despite the bags that weigh heavily on her arms, she feels a great lightness, as if burdens as heavy as towering mountains were falling away, one after the other. In addition to the two bags holding the fabric and the Elissa set, she's carrying a third bag given to her by Durrat al-Ain. It contains six pomegranates, eight apples, two pounds of chestnuts, and five lemons picked for her by that woman of copper and bronze, always fascinating, blessed by legendary love, who plucked them from the lemon tree in her garden. Durrat al-Ain has not forgotten to wrap the fruit, pregnant with juice, in leaves from the tree, choosing the freshest and least liable to break, and Hawwa has been rubbing her hands over them all day. This really is a beautiful day, Hawwa tells herself, as she walks through the increasing commotion of the market.

It's nearly 1:00 in the afternoon. The sun spills its suspended light all at once, sending a pleasant warmth into the joints of the midday. Hawwa feels the heat in her body, so she takes off the wool scarf wrapped around her neck and puts it in the bag with the golden jewelry. The din of the vegetable sellers draws her over, with their tables and carts and competing voices, under dingy white umbrellas of thick fabric stretching between the shops, partially roofing over the space above them. Some have been slit and hang in shreds, while others have been patched with limited success, although most likely they have all lost their waterproofing. The epochal rain has marked the ground with its tracks of rubbish, dirt, and slime. As soon as Hawwa reaches the heart of the market, the vegetables splash their array of colors before her eyes, pyramids of green beans, cucumbers, peppers, mallows, and lettuce, their extreme green broken by fields of potatoes stretching over the tables with their earthen color, dried bits of mud still clinging to their plump haunches, spreading the aroma of damp earth, showing clearly how recently they've been dug up. Boxes of tomatoes are stacked one over the other in the form of benches turned on end, and next to them are boxes of lemons, carrots, zucchini, eggplants, squash, and onions, in a thrusting riot of color. Less pushy, small mounds of parsley are scattered on some of the tables, along with coriander, white onions, and radishes in shades of lilac. Specialty vegetables, in limited quantities, occupy tables all to themselves—scarlet red peppers, orange peppers the color of raw egg yolks, yellow peppers with a tint sometimes like the sun and sometimes like apricots, all displaying their swollen, mirror-like surfaces washed in light. Giant eggplants, coal black, with green stems at their summits, stand on one table, set on three-stepped shelves. The light passing through the openings in the tattered fabric of the umbrellas imprints open eyes and gaping mouths on their polished surfaces, which stare at Hawwa and follow her, casting sheer anxiety into her heart. Hawwa turns her eyes away, deafening her ears to the nasal cry of the vendor: "Black, black as night, black eggplants!"

She goes to a shop with two tables at the entry, almost entirely taken up with a display of mounds of zucchini, cauliflower, and cabbage. Hawwa feels the zucchini. The shop owner, isolated behind a small iron desk inside the shop, takes a last puff of his cigarette before crushing it under his shoe and getting up to welcome her, commenting on her long absence.

"Hello, Umm Qais! It's been a long time since we've seen you. Where have you been hiding?" Then, joking: "Really, all of this on account of a little rain?"

Hawwa answers while still inspecting the zucchini: "Where would I go, Abu Hamza?" She shakes her head as if she's arrived at a philosophical principle: "The rain comes and the rain goes, and we're exactly where we were."

There's a smile on her face, showing her pleasure in the firm texture of the zucchini. She asks him to weigh six pounds for her for stuffing, and four more pounds of the small size for mahshi bil-laban, stuffed zucchini cooked in yogurt. He directs her attention to the heads of local cauliflower, for maqlouba, he tells her. He breaks a floweret from the side of a creamy-white head and gives it to her; she nibbles it, enjoying its hidden sweetness. He shows her the heads of cabbage, with their faint green, and she asks for two. She explains without his asking that her daughter, Umm Abdallah, is coming over "tomorrow, Friday." Then she adds proudly, "And her daughters, Abu Hamza, they adore their grandma's mahshi!" She puts her hand on her chest so Abu Hamza will be certain that she means her own mahshi.

"God willing they'll grow and give you joy! May you live long, Umm Qais, and always feed them well!"

Abu Hamza distributes the zucchini and cabbage in four black plastic bags. Hawwa takes a folded cloth bag out of her purse, shakes it out in the air, and puts the black vegetable bags inside, along with Durrat al-Ain's gift of pomegranates, apples, and lemons. She walks more slowly and heavily through the market. Then she turns off into a quieter side street, stopping at a small supermarket. She calls for Samih, who is counting bottles of shampoo in a carton and recording the numbers on a sheaf of papers he's holding. She asks him for a large sack of diapers and for wet wipes.

She turns the clear sack over in her hands and voices her objection: "These diapers leak." She also complains to him that their adhesive tape doesn't stick.

He agrees with her. "The good kinds don't leak, Auntie Umm Qais . . . but the price is a little high." He stretches his adolescent body to a high shelf, and brings down a package with English writing on it. "This one's foreign. One diaper lasts the whole day, and it doesn't leak or come undone or cause a rash."

Hawwa doesn't understand the writing on the sack and doesn't look at it closely. What attracts her attention is the large picture on the front of the package, of an elderly man and woman with Western features, their faces radiant with signs of healthy firmness and well-being and love, as they are shown in an embrace. It's hard for Hawwa to imagine that either of these two smiling spouses—rosy-cheeked and happy to the point of great joy, beautiful, well dressed, aging elegantly—could need these diapers.

Hawwa feels heat slowly rising in her body, sticky sweat gathering between her breasts and under her arms; her coat has turned into a mobile heater. She slows down more and more, with the heavy load hanging from her arms.

"Umm Qais, Umm Qais!"

Hawwa turns toward the voice. Abu Muhammad the butcher is coming toward her, hunching his shoulders and contracting his naturally dwarf-like stature even more, so she guesses there's some problem. He invites her to come into his shop and she stands at the threshold; the air inside the shop is laden with the smell of carcasses hanging from metal hooks. Abu Muhammad pulls up a chair for her to rest on, wiping it with the end of his sleeve, and calls a boy who's rinsing the blood-spattered floor of the shop to bring her a cup of tea. Hawwa remains standing. She tells him that she can't be late getting home. Abu Muhammad pulls a stained leather register out of the drawer in his table and opens it to a specific page, which he shows her. Hawwa does not read what's there but she understands what it concerns. She heaves a long sigh and surrenders, asking him, "How much, Abu Muhammad?"

He pulls a ballpoint pen without a cap from the pocket of his checked shirt, which gives off the smell of raw meat. He adds the figures recorded on the page, mumbling the calculations, and then announces, "Fifty-six dinars!"

Hawwa puts her things on the chair and takes her wallet out of her purse. She gives him thirty dinars and promises to come back in two days, or three at the most, to pay the rest of the sum. He takes the money gratefully.

"May God make it up to you!"

Abu Muhammad conceals his great embarrassment, as he has no recourse other than to appeal to her, as he says. For her brother Ayid has no compunction about taking meat from him on credit, two or three pounds at a time or even more, on the condition that he will pay him at the end of the month. But two or three months might pass without a whiff of a red cent from him. And what angers Abu Muhammad more than anything else is that Ayid is not satisfied with lamb from Sudan or Australia or Romania; no, he insists on local meat. The boy comes toward her from inside the shop, carrying a cup of cloudy red tea in one hand and a squeegee in the other. His pant legs are folded up to the knee, and he's wading in his thong sandals in the water where the blood is dissolved.

Hawwa places her palm on her chest, in apology. "Forgive me, Abu Muhammad, I must go."

Abu Muhammad drinks down the tepid tea all at once, then asks her, before she leaves, "If Ayid asks me for meat . . . should I give it to him?"

Hawwa turns toward him and answers without thinking, "Give it to him."

"Local meat?"

She continues walking, nodding her head and answering, "Local meat."

The yellow noontide strikes the houses of the camp, accentuating their feeble gloom. The pallor of the walls is not relieved by the map of Palestine stenciled on some of them in blood red, with the word "Resists!" piercing the heart of the map, two of the letters interlaced to form a hand carrying a

Molotov cocktail spouting fire from the top. In fact the map, printed randomly on the walls, seems like a bright stain that only adds to the misery of the houses, some of which are no more than concrete blocks that contain the lowest possible degree of life. The sky crammed between the lanes is choked with an incongruous assortment of colors from the carpets, mats, and quilts hung from the roofs and draped over the walls. The women are opening the doors and windows of their houses to clear the air trapped inside, and they chase their young ones, prisoners of cramped, rotting rooms, onto the ledges outside the houses, so the meager daylight can pour down on their desiccated, extinguished faces, while they nibble on cucumbers or chew dried bread or snack on qarshalla sesame cookies, along with the sticky snot that's collected around their cold noses.

Hawwa opens the door of her house and her mother's voice comes to her, intersecting with the ring of the cell phone in her coat pocket. She puts down the bags at the entrance, looks at her phone, and sees Munir's name on the screen. She starts to answer, but her mother is calling her in a terrified voice: "Hawww! Haaaawww!"

She lets the phone ring, and runs inside. "Yes, Mama! I'm here, Yamma, I'm coming!"

Hawwa had never loved her mother, Rabia. When she addressed her as Yamma, Mama, or called her by that clear, pure name, it was not out of love, or as an initiative on her part, or out of hope. Rather, it was to answer or respond to her, and it came from turning inward, from bowing down, from giving up and from brokenness. During her many painful chastisements, it was an appeal for help or protection, though she found neither. Similarly, Hawwa does not remember that her mother loved her for a single day, or loved any of her daughters, or at least Hawwa did not feel that love, if it did exist. In fact, it was most likely that Rabia did not love life

74

itself, and had not asked for it. She frequently prayed and she frequently cried, but neither prayers nor tears brought her any relief or did her any good.

Rabia kept a volcanic anger enclosed within herself. This anger weighed down her spirit; it swelled in her heart, and it silently undermined her existence. There were times when she translated her anger into biting her tongue until it bled. Then she began to aim her anger at her daughters, yelling at them, hurling ugly insults at them—"whore," "slut," "filth." She might kick them suddenly as they walked near her, or punch them, or pull them by their braids and hit their heads against the wall, without their having done anything to provoke her violence toward them. Her daughters did not try to resist her or attempt to ask her about the reason for her anger. They knew full well that she was broken, weak, and impotent, but that she could at least vent all of that on them. As for them, they also had hearts burdened with festering boils of anger, but they could not express it. Not only that, but with the passing days their anger turned into a deep sense of shame that crushed their very beings, already shattered.

Even if Hawwa did not love her mother, though, at least she did not hate her. She hated her father, Mousa, just as her mother and sisters hated him, and maybe more. The day they heard the news of his death, they were overcome by shock. Many things seethed inside them, many, many things, mixed emotions and contradictory feelings—everything except for a feeling of disaster. All kinds of feelings attacked them, except for a feeling of being orphaned.

Rabia, Afaf, Sajida, and Hawwa received condolence visits for three days in the family home in the camp. Afaf's belly was up to her nose, since she was in the eighth month of her pregnancy with her third child. Sajida was nursing her second child most of the time, and Hawwa came carrying her first and only daughter, Aya. Afaf and Sajida had married at seventeen, having been taken out of school before that. After leaving school, Afaf worked as a saleswoman in a store in the camp that rented out wedding dresses, while Sajida worked in a beauty salon, learning to trim eyebrows and remove mustaches and downy facial hair with string, as well as learning the fundamentals of heavy bridal makeup, and blow-drying and setting hair.

The beauty salon was located in a distant corner of the camp market, far removed from its noise. The door of the salon opened and closed frequently, allowing puffs of air to lift the thin, concealing curtain. That made it possible for the men and boys working in the shops facing the salon to happen upon quick, sharply piercing images of a number of women and girls who had removed the pale hijabs from their heads so their hair flowed in profusion over their shoulders. They had also taken off their concealing jilbab overdresses and strutted around the salon in short skirts that traced the outlines of their bodies, or in tight jeans or tights that encased their firm buttocks. The woman who owned the shop sometimes sent Sajida out to buy things she needed, and that delighted Sajida's heart. She would apply makeup and then simply put on a relatively long shirt over her jeans, without putting on her jilbab. She would put a scarf on her head without tying it well, so that when she walked a few paces in the market it would slip onto her shoulders, and she would not trouble herself to raise it and fasten it firmly.

When she went into the small supermarket she would go to one of the display shelves, seeming to search for something specific. Raif, one of two salesmen in the market, would follow her and stand behind her until he was almost part of her body. She would ask for sugar or packaged cake and the young salesman would lift his arm, spreading the smell of his fevered sweat laden with cigarette smoke and colliding with one of her breasts, which he might pinch. If what she wanted was located on a rear shelf or on the edge of a row, Raif would extend his leg between her legs. She would open them without resistance, and his knee, beneath his pants, would rub the area between her thighs, under her pants. He would stop only if the sound of the friction of fabric on fabric was audible, or if one of them saw someone coming toward them, or if they were startled by the voice of the supermarket owner shouting from where he stood at the cash register: "Raif! Where've you gone and disappeared to?" Then Raif would spring away from her, as if he had been hit with an electric wire, while Sajida folded away her trembling, putting out the small fires in her body by passing her hands over her arms, her panting chest, and her thighs on the point of collapse.

When she came home at the end of the day, Sajida's face smelled of powder and radiated maturity and attraction, with coal-black eyeliner encircling her hazel eyes, with graded shades of fuchsia eye shadow coloring the wide surfaces of her eyelids and pink lipstick lighting up her wheaten complexion. Rabia would give her a long look before attacking her, slamming her head into the wall, then dragging her by her hair to the bathroom. She would make her kneel on the floor and put her head in the water basin. Or, taking the vengeance further, she would spit on a handkerchief and wipe it over half of Sajida's face, from above the eyes to half of the mouth, so the sooty black from the eyes would be mixed with the fuchsia and the pink.

Afaf did not arouse Rabia's ire when she came home. She was very careful not to let the odor of cigarettes, which she bought one by one, linger in her mouth or on her clothes. She bit off fresh mint leaves or chewed a handful of basil leaves, and sprayed the area of her chest and underarms with an antiperspirant that had a soapy smell, which she kept in her purse. Afaf welcomed brides and their mothers in the "Convivial Nights" shop, which rented out dresses for engagement and wedding parties. The shop was in a lane in the camp that was almost roofed over, and near it stood other shops selling women's and children's clothing, displayed on dozens of mannequins of varying sizes that stood at the entrances to the shops. Some of the children's mannequins were without heads or arms, and some had lost a leg, so the empty pant leg would wave in the air. Passersby often bumped into the dismembered children, knocking them down, so they looked like corpses with relatively new clothes. Beside the shops selling accessories and cosmetics, there were a number of shops selling women's underwear, as a part of a bridal trousseau. From the canopies over the entrances to the shops hung plastic models of the upper part of a woman's body, from the neck to the breast, the belly, and the top of the thighs. The owners dressed them in "baby doll" nightgowns of chiffon, silk, tulle, and the cheapest kind of lace, in vivid reds, blues, oranges, and pinks, some decorated with ruffles and feathers, revealing the belly and the smooth, triangular pubic region. However much pious men walking to the mosque at the end of the market lane resolved to avoid looking at them, their eyes would not be able to turn away from the bare plastic flesh. Once the passersby saw half a woman, wearing a pink filigree nightgown, fall on the shoulders of the imam while he was on his way to lead the evening Maghrib prayer.

Afaf's task required her to help the brides pick out a dress for the engagement party, for the henna night, or for the wedding, and to make certain, when the dress was returned, that it had not suffered any rip or tear or been stained by a spot that could not be removed. If she missed anything, Abu Luai, the owner of the shop, would reprimand her. Among her tasks also was tracking the cleaning process for the dresses at the dry cleaners and picking them up at the time set. Abu Luai supervised the shop during the morning and through the midday; his son Luai, who was studying in one of the mid-level university colleges in Amman, took over in the afternoon, until the late Isha prayer. When a bride came with her tribe of women, Abu Luai or his son would usually withdraw from the shop entirely, leaving the women to roam among the dresses at their leisure, stripping down in the fitting room, where Afaf helped them stuff their flesh, usually covered by concealing jilbabs, into tight dresses, low cut or with bare backs.

Traffic was light in the shop during the morning hours, and Abu Luai would often leave to take care of other matters. Afaf would remain alone, sorting the dresses returned by sisters or mothers of the brides, with their remains of powder or deposits of sweat and creams around the neck or chest, or at the underarms. With the shoppers out of the way, she would take a dress worn for an engagement or a wedding, with the traces of the bride still on it, and try it on in the fitting room. She would partially prop open the door of the room so she could keep her ear alert for sounds outside while she inspected herself in the mirror, certain that the fit of the dress and how it looked on her was better than it had been on the bride. More than anything else, she looked forward to trying on the dresses with long side openings, or those that brought out the thickness of the breasts, as those two boisterous waves would be partially crammed into the tight breast cups while the frothy flesh overflowed, and she would consider with pleasure her tall stature, kept firm by design, as the mirror showed it.

On one particular day, when there was little traffic and few people, Abu Luai happened to return a short time after leaving the shop, having remembered something he had forgotten. Afaf's bare arm appeared to him through the cracked-open door to the fitting room. When Afaf sensed his breath coming toward her she tried to shut the door, but he shoved the door with his foot, came in, and closed the door on them both.

Abu Luai did not ask much of Afaf, other than touching, friction, and external rubbing, swearing to her that he would not hurt her. She insisted that they remain clothed and the friction be "from outside to outside." That sometimes annoyed Abu Luai, when his desire hardened under his pants and he could free the zipper only with difficulty. When at last he reached his shudder, he would seem more pained than giddy, more tense than relaxed. But Afaf was less cautious and conservative with the son, who also pledged that he would not hurt her, as she allowed his flesh to come into contact with hers. In fact, she enjoyed his smell, fashioned from his fresh sweat, as opposed to his father's smell of age. When he pulled her to him from behind, pressing strongly on her rear, he would watch the change in her facial features in the dressing room mirror, her skin slackening and clouded with desire, all her senses aroused. Then he would swoon with her in hot panting that burned them both, their tremors intertwined.

Mousa worked as a builder, and it was said that he was skilled. He specialized in pouring foundations, roofs, and columns, and he estimated the proportions of cement, sand, gravel, and water for pourings and for cement mixtures by eye, rarely making a mistake, challenging the most skilled contractors and engineers. He also enjoyed colossal physical strength, which he was said to have inherited from his mother, Naifa, who was five feet eleven and a yard wide. Many of the residents of Bait Mahsir, near Jerusalem, told the story of how at twelve she had helped her one-legged father build their house in the village, since her six brothers had been killed, half of them by the English and the other half in battles with the Jewish gangs. Naifa transported the stones for the house and the rock border around it from the ruins and rocky hills and caves on the outskirts of the village, carrying the rough stones in her hand and piling them up in an iron wheelbarrow, which she pushed before her on the rutted, hilly, winding paths, walking with them upward of two miles at times. When Naifa married Nimr, she left Bait Mahsir to live in the village of Shahma, in the district of Ramla, in her husband's family home. But Naifa could not abide large numbers of people, so she gave Nimr her gold jewelry so he could build a house on a piece of land set aside for him by his father. Nimr did not need to seek the help of construction workers since his brothers helped him, as did Naifa, who was pregnant with her first child; she kneaded the mixed cement herself and did all the plaster work. When she slept the first night in her home, the labor pains came and she delivered Mousa.

With the 1948 Nakba, Naifa and her husband migrated to Far'a Camp near Nablus, and with the 1967 Naksa they migrated again, with their three sons, Mousa, Aisa, and Khalil, and the sons' wives and children (few, at the time), to Baqa'a Camp on the other bank of the river. They continued their uprooted life in their exile, and kept having more children in land that was emotionally sterile. Hajj Nimr, Naifa's husband, had owned an olive press in the old time in the country. When he migrated to Far'a, he put his head in his hands and waited for the return to his house and his land and his press, snatching at any indication of that from the news on the radio. When he migrated to Baqa'a Camp, he still kept his head in his hands, but he no longer listened to the radio. Then, in his last days, he confused the Far'a Camp with the village of Shahma and began to tell tales about other places that Naifa didn't know, and to talk about people she had never heard of. In Far'a, Naifa learned to make Nabulsi cheese, and she took that craft with her to Baqa'a. She would sell the cheese in large tin containers, usually to Palestinian expatriates who took the tins with them on planes headed for the Gulf states. Some of them even took the cheese to America, drained of water and sealed in vacuum bags. She also sold them to shops that made sweets in Baqa'a and Sweileh. Her house in the camp was large compared to most of the other houses, and most of the time it gave off the odor of curdling milk, rennet, and steam fragrant with the saltiness of boiled cheese. She set aside one of the rooms to keep her huge pots for sheep's milk, cheese molds, cutting boards, and fabric for wrapping the cheese. Her daughter-in-law, the wife of her youngest son, Khalil, helped her, and after Naifa's death she took over the house in the camp and the craft.

Nonetheless, even if Naifa was tyrannical and forbidding up to her very last day on earth, she was shattered inside. Her soul had broken in the Far'a Camp, and then it was completely crushed in Baqa'a Camp. She lived what was left of her life as a vengeful woman, angry and vicious.

Far from his mother, Mousa's companions attributed his physical energy to the great amount of food he put down—it was said that during the workers' midday dinner he would consume, all by himself, two pounds of kebab meat rolls with grilled onions and tomatoes, following that with three cups of strong, sweet red tea. Most of his daily wage went to his belly, leaving the people of his household to depend on other, meager financial resources for their living expenses. But along with Mousa's cleverness came stubbornness, irritability, and unexpected changes of temper. He would create problems with the workers for any reason, and might harass them if a period of peace in the workshop lasted longer than his impetuous nature could take. One time he picked up one of the builders and would have thrown him into the cement mixer to be ground to bits, just because he thought he had made fun of him, if the workers on the site had not intervened. He would absent himself from the workshop for days, for no reason, which not only meant less income for the family, but also meant that he stayed with them, a physical and spiritual curse, for longer than the household could bear. He would stretch out on the floor pallet the whole time, while Rabia and her daughters took turns serving him. They put before him a table that was never empty from morning to evening, taking away dishes and putting others in their place, including the tea tray, coming and going throughout the day and night.

Night was the time that Mousa loved the most and that the people in his house hated the most. He would settle in front of the television, his eyes and his desires fixed on the serials of "the Bedouin," even during their irritating reruns. He was infatuated with the lovely Wadha, the white Bedouin who ruined her authentic Syrian dialect with an assumed Bedouin accent, in the drama *Wadha and Ibn Ajlan*. Mousa was especially inflamed by Wadha in the scenes where she disguised herself as a man called Nawwaf to become Ibn Ajlan's companion. He did not conceal his infatuation with "Nawwaf," with his mustache, his beard, his ample Bedouin robe and headdress, the head cord at an angle on his head—he was as taken with Nawwaf as he was with Wadha, and maybe more. When Nawwaf stood sideways next to Ibn Ajlan, Wadha's breasts, concealed only with difficulty under the robe, stuck out clearly. In front of Rabia, who was putting before him a pan of fried tomatoes and a dish of potato and egg scramble, he would say crudely, "Lookit her boobs! How's that asshole Ibn Ajlan not know she's a woman?" And then, still more crudely, with a finger aimed at Wadha's breasts, rising on the screen, "God, if I was in his place I'd give 'em a good squeeze!"

Rabia would not comment, nor did he expect any confirmation from her. He would melt into Nawwaf's very beautiful face, with his narrow, arched eyebrows, his eyes black as kohl, and his polished white complexion, framed by a mustache curved at the tips and a little goatee on his chin. Nawwaf looked very like a young man with a hot body, or an effeminate one, and Mousa often summoned him during his terrifying sexual fantasies.

But Mousa's nights, and so those of his household, would pass also in a way that was darker and more terrifying. He would sneak out of Rabia's bed to the room where the girls lay on the floor on thin mattresses, exhausted in slumber, curled in upon their erupting flesh. Afaf was a year older than Sajida, and they were fifteen and fourteen when their father's flesh fell on theirs, one after the other. Afaf opened her eyes one night as if she were shaking off a nightmare. Her whole being rose up, but Mousa put his heavy leg over her body and pounded her into the floor like a nail. She pulled together her trembling limbs, so Mousa asked her to relax her body and spread her legs, but she remained frozen. Mousa whispered in her ear, pleading, that everything would stay "from the outside to the outside," swearing that he would not hurt her. But Afaf, her tears flowing silently, remained a compressed piece of flesh. When he withdrew from her bed, frustrated, all his pleadings having met with refusal, she realized that the matter had not ended.

The evening of the next day, Mousa met her at the door. He asked her why she was late, and she told him that it was Thursday and that the market was crowded. He slapped her again and again, on her face, neck, and head, calling her a whore and a wanton. All his little women in the house, including Rabia, dissolved where they stood. The day after that he threw the egg platter at her and split her forehead, and the wound required two stitches. The third day he flayed her with the strap. After a week during which her flesh was exposed to every sort of savagery, Afaf at last gave in to Mousa. Sajida gave in to him the first time, sparing her flesh great pain.

Hawwa's flesh rebelled, and she was careful to wind the swaddling cloth tightly around her breasts all day and all night. She would awake to the sound of the floor trembling under her mattress. Her father's panting, when he was stuck to the bodies of her sisters, burned her contracted cells, and her sisters' tears burned her spirit. She closed her eyes, she closed her ears, she closed her senses, and she closed her flesh, concealed from everything painful and everything ugly.

Rabia was left to be consumed by yet more anger, grief, and tears, which dug permanent furrows into her face. When Mousa began spending more time in the girls' bed than he did in hers, Rabia at last complained of Mousa to his mother. Naifa blamed her for her silence and her patience. She remembered Mousa at nineteen, when she caught him numerous times with the little girls of the neighborhood in Far'a Camp, pushing his finger into their underpants. She beat him, whipped him, and kicked him, to no effect. She told him that the girls' families might kill him, but he swore that he was not touching them. One day at sunset Naifa went up to the roof to collect the washing and found Mousa standing with a pale face, while the chickens in the coop were clucking in terror. Naifa opened the mesh door to the coop and the chickens leapt out in her face, screaming. In a corner of the coop was Naila, the three-year-old daughter of the neighbors, curled into a ball and soiled with sand, feathers, and chicken droppings. Naila told her that she was playing hide-and-seek with Mousa. The little girl's dress was up above her small, smooth sex organ with its miniature form. Naifa asked her about her underpants and she said that Mousa had hidden them. The next thing Naifa knew she was lifting up Mousa in her strong arms and throwing him off the roof. His head was split and an arm and a leg were broken. Six months later she married him to Rabia, the daughter of a distant relative.

Naifa married off Afaf and then Sajida. Afaf tried to object at first, but Naifa threw her down too, and kept on pinching her genitals until her face turned blue and she fainted away. Sajida did not try to argue with her grandmother's decision.

With the departure of Afaf and Sajida, Hawwa remained alone. Her surging chest did not subside because of the swaddling; and then the swaddle began to suffocate her when she slept, since it was hard for her to breathe in it. She started to take it off at night and bury it under her pillow, and when she woke up in the morning she was careful to crush her breasts well beneath it. But however hard she tried, it was not possible to contain the two hills or make them sink down. Nor was it ever possible to stop the eruption of her body. When she went to work with Sitt Qamar she did away with the swaddling completely. In fact, she endeavored to wear bras with proper cups, half revealing, most of them from Sitt Qamar, especially since she knew that Murad's eyes would survey her two hills up and down, and that his naughty imagination would wallow in them. In any case, Hawwa became available to Mousa after the marriage of her two sisters.

Hawwa was not like her sisters. She was not apprehensive and she did not bolt, nor did she go rigid or freeze up or collapse into a heap or curl into a ball; she did not shrink or recoil. Her father's deed turned into something mechanical, touching her body on the surface, on the surface of the surface, but never penetrating to her soul. She had learned how to cease to exist when she was violated, how to lose consciousness and comprehension, how to leave her being completely, not returning to it unless she wished. Hawwa died at night, no longer seeing or hearing or feeling. Even her heart stopped completely—until she opened her eyes in the morning and shook off her death, and life returned to her once more.

Mousa died at the site. The news came to them from the contractor, who tried to be kind and proper, as much as possible, while he was telling them of the catastrophe. Mousa was in his late forties, strong and colossal up to his last day. They understood from the contractor that what happened was God's decree and destiny, as half of an incomplete wall had fallen on a number of workers, striking some of them. But it chanced that Mousa received the harshest blow on his head and he bled continuously when they took him to the hospital, where he lasted only a few hours.

Rabia remained dumbfounded, while Afaf, Sajida, and Hawwa were choked with the tears that covered their stunned faces. They were sad, extremely sad, heartbroken—and that aroused the compassion of the women of the camp who encircled them. "How hard it is to lose a father!" exclaimed one. Hawwa cried a lot. She sobbed. God, how she missed Duha! She yearned for her. She tried to recall her sister's face, but she discovered that she had forgotten it completely.

Duha didn't look like any of them. She didn't grow and her body didn't develop; in fact, she began to get smaller as the days went by. Duha would sleep all the time, and when she did move around she was bent over; she would tire quickly and sit on the nearest seat or collapse on the nearest mattress.

When she slept she would pant, as if she were running in her disturbed dreams. At six years of age, her flesh and bones, immobile most of the time, would have suited a child of three. Then one night her temperature rose. The strips of cloth soaked in cold water, which her sisters took turns placing on her forehead, were useless to put out the flame consuming her head. As soon as morning broke, the fire finished her off. She had not yet reached seven years of age on the day she died.

Afaf, Sajida, and Hawwa wept a great deal over the loss of Duha. But they were certain of one thing at least, which was that God loved her. God loved her very much, though He did not love them. In fact God most probably hated them, because they lived.

The lazy, wintery midday sun rests its shoulder on the edges of the closed windows. Some of the dawdling warmth penetrates the sodden walls, nudging a light, hidden humidity into the enclosed air of the house, humidity that diffuses from the cushions, the napped pile of the blankets, and the sponge upholstery of the Morris set. Hawwa vents the window in the main living room of the house and partially opens the curtains, letting a breath of air brush her face, still flushed and panting from her trip home. A beam of light falls on the sewing machine, supplied with a spool of watery blue thread. On the machine table stretches a dress cut from sea-blue silk adorned with satiny spots of a lighter, pearly shade of blue. Under the cascade of light, the spots reflect a faint rainbow traced on the wall opposite. Next to the sewing machine stands a high wooden cutting table, on which are a large pair of scissors, a smaller pair of pinking shears, a measuring tape, a wooden yardstick, a package of pins with a yellow cushion into which several dozen pins have been stuck, soapy tailor's chalk for marking, and three bags standing at the end.

"Haww . . . Haawwwww . . . !"

"I'm here, Mama. I'm coming!"

Hawwa puts down her load at the entry to the room. She takes off her shoes and puts on her house slippers. She removes her scarf, headscarf, and coat, throws them on the nearest sofa, and then hurries to the bedroom, her voice preceding her the whole time: "Coming, Mama . . . coming! I'm coming, Mama . . . coming." Rabia is struggling to lift her body and her head, which have shifted sideways so that she has almost fallen out of bed. Hawwa gathers her in her strong arms and lifts her, supporting her back with her hands and gently pushing up her hips. Rabia seems terrified and clings to her, not wanting to let her go, pulling on the collar of her dress with her left hand. Hawwa gathers the weak, trembling frame of her mother in an embrace, patting her back, which is bowed with fear, massaging her shoulders, and rubbing her upper arms. Slowly warmth creeps into her body, and the grip of her terror loosens. She spreads out a little. Hawwa straightens the pillow under Rabia's head, puts another pillow on top of it, and centers her head in the middle. She lays her on her back, without separating herself from her body, which is nearly stuck to her. "Don't be afraid, Mama, I'm here," she tells her. But to "not be afraid," truly, Rabia needs time. When at last her panic dissipates, she disengages herself from her daughter.

Hawwa lights the gas heater and its three red burners flare, exhaling warmth. She turns the hand crank of the hospital bed, raising the upper half. She sets it at a wide angle and Rabia's face looks at her, half drooping; the twitching of her facial muscles has receded, so she seems less tense. Hawwa puts a fresh pillow under her right arm and rests her right leg on another soft pillow, covering her carefully with a blanket. She opens one of the drawers of a short, heavy dresser, composed of five wide, deep drawers, and takes out three little fabric towels, one large paper towel, waterproof on one side, and a new cake of Nabulsi soap in its paper wrapper. From a second drawer she takes salve for rashes, a bottle of hand sanitizer, and a sterile plastic syringe from a group of syringes in plastic vacuum bags. From a third drawer she takes two small plastic basins and a black plastic bag from a bundle of carefully folded bags. "Thirsty?" she asks her mother, who answers her slowly, "Yeaaah." Then she asks, "Hungry?" as she sucks water into the syringe from a carefully closed carafe, placed next to a large, transparent plastic container overflowing with packages of medicines and salves, on a broad table next to the bed. Rabia answers slowly, "Yeaaah." Hawwa lifts Rabia's head a little, propping it on her tender forearm, then places one of the small towels under her neck and gives her water from the syringe, while the towel catches some of the water that falls from her mouth, slackened on the right side. Rabia seems grateful, emitting sighs as she absorbs the water. Hawwa slips her hand under her mother's cotton nightgown, feeling with her fingers under her diaper. Rabia turns her face away to show her annoyance, but Hawwa tells her that everything is fine. She goes to the bathroom to wash her hands and hears the ring of her cell phone from the pocket of her coat, tossed on the sofa. She can't answer it in time, and reads Munir's name on two missed calls. She starts to call him, but her mother's voice calls urgently: "Haww . . . Haaawwww . . . !" So she leaves the phone and answers, "Coming, Mama . . . coming!"

Hawwa hurries to the kitchen. She lights the fire under the kettle and fills it halfway with water. With her hand she feels the metallic, icy cold of the pan of okra with fresh tomatoes and finely chopped meat, which she had cooked in the morning and left to cool in the kitchen, enfolded in icy air during the winter. Her brother Ayid and her son Qais adore okra, and especially her okra—not only because of the small pieces of okra she uses, no bigger than the joint of a finger, which she sautés lightly in oil before immersing them in tomato juice, as she learned from Sitt Qamar, but also because of the spoonful of coriander and garlic she adds, which Sitt Qamar taught her as well, and the splash of pomegranate syrup that gives the tomato juice a complex flavor in which acidity mixes with a concealed sweetness. Hawwa lights the other gas burner under the pan of okra, so it can heat up slowly. In the evening she'll make rice with vermicelli. Ayid and Qais love her rice with vermicelli, which she makes Sitt Qamar's way, toasting the vermicelli well in clarified butter to brown it and remove any trace of whiteness, before adding the rice, water, and salt. She opens the refrigerator and takes out a small pot of boiled white rice for her mother. She puts the pot on the smallest burner of her four-burner stove, sprinkles the rice with a little water, and lights a low fire under it. Meanwhile, she hears the hoarse sound of the water being heated. "Haaww . . . !" Her mother's truncated cry comes to her. "Yes, Mama . . . coming!" she answers from the kitchen.

At the crack of dawn, Hawwa had washed the towels and bedsheets, her mother's underclothes, her cotton nightshirts, and some of the light linen and woolen blankets she uses to wrap around her mattress. When the light rose fully in the heavens and it was clear that the rain had stopped and the sky had dried out, Hawwa hung out her fragrant wash on the roof. She also changed her mother's diaper, and gave her a breakfast of sweetened white cheese, a boiled egg, and a Marie cookie dissolved in tea. Then she fed her half an apple and half a pear, both mashed, and gave her water. In the morning, when the sun emerged from its overcoat of clouds and shook off the moisture of the long days, Hawwa pulled on a medical glove, put her hand into her mother's throat, scraped out the fungus that collected at the top, and then washed her mouth with mouthwash and rubbed her remaining teeth with the brush and a bit of toothpaste. She also inspected her heels: they were less hardened, the dryness had receded, and many of the cracks had closed. On the last night of the rain, Hawwa had put her mother in her wheelchair, to watch an episode of the Turkish television serial *The Sultan's Harem* with her. She soaked her mother's feet in a basin of warm water in which she dissolved half a packet of coarse salt. When the warmth of an extremely sensual kiss on the screen took them, a kiss in which lips fused in a dark corridor of a palace where every form of intrigue was plotted, Rabia relaxed, while an extraordinary energy came into Hawwa's hands. She abraded her mother's heels, insteps, and the sides of her big toes with a broad file shaped like a spoon, which ended in a rough black oval wafer that felt like black pumice. She kept on rubbing the feet with all her might until she had peeled off the woody clumps and scraped away most of the dead skin. After her mother's feet had soaked in the water and the salt, Hawwa dried them, rubbed them with Vaseline, and encased them in cotton socks, with woolen socks over them so they would not be chilled.

Hawwa now picks up the elegant new bag of diapers and the wet wipes and hurries to her mother. "Coming, Mama . . . coming!" She puts them on the broad table next to the bed and goes back to the kitchen, summoned by the whistle of the kettle where the water has boiled. She picks up the kettle in one hand and in the other a bottle of cold water filled from the kitchen tap, and rushes to respond to her mother's calls, which have become more insistent and nearly continuous. Her quick walk sends sprays of hot water flying to sting the back of her hand, but Hawwa does not slow her pace or take much care. She closes the door of the bedroom behind her, to keep the warmth from the heater enclosed in the small space of the room. She puts the kettle of boiling water on the carpet next to the bed and places beside it the bottle of cold water, then folds her sleeves back to the elbows. She wipes her palms with the gel disinfectant and places them over the steam from the hot water in the kettle, so they will absorb a little warmth. Then she opens her mother's legs and lifts her night-shirt, opening the tapes on either side of the diaper. The urine has penetrated the thin, cottony layers of the lining, which has become heavy from the soaking and crumbled.

A strong tremor bursts from Rabia's thighs, moving upward in a wave until it hits her lips, which turn blue. Hawwa spreads the wool blanket over the upper part of her mother's body, which recoils on the bed from shame and anxiety. Hawwa gathers her shaking thighs in her arms and massages them with her hands until they settle and the tempo of the trembling subsides. She tells her that she's bought a lot of things. "I bought zucchini for Aya and her daughters. Tonight I'll hollow them out and stuff them for tomorrow." Hawwa says this as she pulls the diaper from under her mother's pelvis, and puts in its place the paper towel with the waterproof lining. She adds, "And you like zucchini, don't you, Mama?" Rabia seems to be having fewer spasms, as she follows Hawwa with her confused mind, while Hawwa folds the diaper over its odor of fermenting urine, worse when it's exposed to the air, and puts it in the black plastic bag, which she knots firmly. "Durrat al-Ain says hello, Mama." Then she tells her, to give the name and the greeting greater meaning for Rabia, "Faris's Durrat al-Ain, Mama." Hawwa laughs as she pours hot water from the kettle into one of the basins and adds cold water to lower the temperature. "She sent you some really delicious apples, Mama." Hawwa puts one of the small towels in the basin and rubs the Nabulsi soap with it to make a little foam, then wipes Rabia's bare body with the soapy towel. Rabia gasps at the touch of the fabric and the soapy water on her flesh, but she does not seem bothered. Hawwa cleans the top of her thighs, the area between them, her shrunken genitals, and her bony, shriveled backside two times, all the while soaking the towel in the water and soaping it well. Rabia's flesh glows with the fragrant soap. Hawwa pours water into the second basin and sinks the towel in it, to remove the traces of the soap before using it to wipe her mother's body, now less alarmed. She dries the wet area with the second towel, then applies cream for rashes where the thighs meet the trunk and dresses her in a new diaper from the elegant new sack. "This is a new kind, Mama. . . . They're nice, see?" She shows her the sack of diapers with the ruddy, beautiful, happy old couple on the front. Rabia's twisted face opens in a crooked half smile.

Hawwa takes a wet wipe scented with jasmine from the new package and wipes her mother's face and forehead with it, then her neck and the top of her chest. Her hand slows as she wipes her mother's delicate, wrinkled skin; it seems as if her feelings have strayed to a beautiful place with aromatic breezes, although it's cloudy, filled with joyous images, even if their colors are hazy and their features are blurry. Then her mother's voice returns her to her true place, where everything is clear: "Haww . . . !" She lifts her mother's head to the top of the pillow and tells her, "I've made you okra, Mama." But Hawwa cannot contain her jubilant spirit. She comes close to her mother's face, as if she were telling her a secret, even though they are alone in the house: "I bought a piece of fabric . . . it's violet." She smiles with enthusiasm, but also with some caution, as if she's saying something dangerous: "It's velvet, Mama . . . real velvet!" It seems that Rabia, in her bed, with what remains of her functioning senses, values the grandeur and nobility of velvet, since her body perspires with a heat that Hawwa feels as she rubs her shoulders in a circular motion. She keeps rubbing her mother's shoulders, descending to her relaxed forearms, and then her hands and her fingers. Hawwa is swimming in the folds of the warm velvet, permitting its violet wave to pull her inside, surrendering her yearning spirit to the rich sensation. Rabia lets her face droop. The look of terror has disappeared from it completely, and she gives a long sigh of relaxation.

Hawwa straightens the light wool sheet and pulls it over both sides of the mattress and its air bubbles. She reduces the intensity of the heat in the room, where the warmth has crept into all the crevices, by turning off two of the heater's three red, glaring burners. She spreads the heavy wool blanket over her mother and asks her if she feels cold. Rabia half shakes her head, saying no. Hawwa makes sure the blanket encloses her completely, then pats her belly and assures her: "I'm going to get lunch ready for you, Mama."

Hawwa puts out the slender flames under the pan of okra and the pot of rice. The cooking vapors settle in the kitchen, laden with the aroma of the thick tomato sauce and the starch of the rice. Hawwa opens one half of the little kitchen window, and her senses are assaulted by the smell of sautéed cauliflower, layered with chicken and rice in maqlouba, coming from her neighbor's kitchen. The woman yells at her daughter to turn down the water being wasted in the sink. The sound of a plate shattering on the floor provokes her neighbor's anger: "I wish your hands was paralyzed!"

The midday sun is beginning to withdraw, gathering the far-flung edges of its light to its wintery body. Cold strikes all sides of the main room, so Hawwa closes the window firmly, but leaves the curtains open so as not to deprive herself of the remaining daylight. She hangs her coat, headscarf, and scarf on the hook behind the door of the room. She puts the bag of velvet and the bag with the jewelry set on the cutting table. She sneaks a glance at the red box of the set, inside the bag; then she opens the box and the gold—closely resembling the real thing—splashes its extravagant color in her face. She quickly closes the box, as if she doesn't want the shine of the set to be dissipated or wasted. She's happy. In fact, she's more than happy, she tells herself. And when she stretches her hand lightly to the overflowing yards of violet happiness, folded in the other bag, she cannot suppress the feeling flooding over her, that she possesses some very precious and very beautiful part of the world.

She grasps her cell phone in both her hands, like something very dear that must not be lost. It rings once and gives another half ring before the voice on the other end reaches her, eagerly. "Munir! I'm happy, I'm so happy, Munir! I'm so very happy," she tells the voice waiting for her. She goes on assuring him that she's happy, that her heart won't hold all this joy that lives there. Her heart that "ever so long" has borne what could barely be borne, beats strongly within her. So many feelings are contending inside her—feelings of overwhelming love, to the furthest limit love can reach; feelings of absolute happiness, in a form no logic could describe or explain; feelings of bliss, coming from the fact that the time of entitled suffering might be coming to an end; feelings of safety, as if entire universes were protecting her back; and at the same time, feelings of fear, of anguish, of terror. Munir, in his turn, speaks encouraging words to her. He tells her of the many beautiful days that are coming, that will envelop them both together; he tells her about the good times that they will fill with their story. But Hawwa doesn't hear him well, for her tears are spilling out of her eyes, abundantly, noisily, making a sound like the wind beating down everywhere in anger, or like waves crashing violently on dark rocks. "I'm afraid, Munir . . . really afraid!" she tells him, without even hearing her own voice, which melts into the echo of sobs. She says she's afraid to be so happy. Then her tears subside and Munir's voice begins to reach her troubled spirit. But his voice collides with Rabia's call from the other room: "Hawww . . . Haawwwwwww . . . !"

Hawwa answers, her words rising through her tears: "Yes, Mama . . . I'm coming!"

5

O<small>UTSIDE THE HOUSE, THE BOYS</small>' voices rise in the lane as a soccer ball strikes the windows of the houses and their obstinate metal doors, without damaging them more and without disfiguring further what was already disfigured. They have left school some time before; some of them have not changed clothes, and there are some who have thrown their bags on the ledge of one of the houses, paying no attention to a woman's voice shouting from inside to "get in here, now!" The sound of sandals and athletic shoes striking the dusty earth, along with the sound of their active little bodies bumping into each other, crosscut with their enthusiastic shouts, resounds in the air and traverses the thin glass of the houses' windows. A group of men who have left the mosque after the afternoon prayer are coming down one side of the lane, their elbows held close to their sides like clipped wings, scraping the walls of the gloomy houses. They walk close to each other, almost joined together, bowed over, lowering their angry gazes, stepping carefully, leaving most of the space in the narrow, rutted road to four veiled girls, wearing headscarves of brilliant colors, tight jackets, and jeans that encase their maturely rounded backsides, with embellished fabric purses hanging from their shoulders.

One of the girls continues talking on her cell phone the whole time. The boys suspend their game temporarily and the girls hurry their steps, suppressing laughter. As soon as they've reached the end of the lane, the boys resume their game. One of them passes the ball to his friend and it hits the leg of a man who has lagged behind the group coming from prayers. He's carrying a prayer rug and wearing a long khaki shirt split at the sides, more like a Bedouin dishdasha, over wide pants of the same fabric, closer to traditional, baggy salwar pants. Over this set he's wearing a brown jacket of rubbed leather and a beige Afghani cap, making him look like a jihadi, retired early. A devil suddenly gets into the frowning fighter. He hops crazily in the lane and picks up a large stone, which the enthusiastic soccer players have placed to mark an imaginary goal, and throws it at the boy who kicked the ball at him. With a little luck the boy evades the stone, fleeing with one sandal after the other has slipped off his foot, while his companions continue the game with undiminished enthusiasm. The retired Afghani takes the sandal and follows the boy, his feet striking the dusty earth violently—and the Creator has placed in his legs strength of a sort that makes the defeated run with extraordinary speed. As he runs, he adjusts his cap, which leans to one side of his head, not noticing that the tassels of his prayer rug are sweeping the earth, leaving behind a cloud of gray dust that envelops him. He threatens to teach a good lesson to the "brother of a whore" (as he calls the boy at the top of his voice), who is yards ahead of him.

Hawwa was frightened by the looks of these new men in the camp. It wasn't only a matter of tangled, tinted, untamed beards and frowning faces. There was also the strange dress and the words they mumbled as she passed them in the street or in the market. Some of them, who sold vegetables, were so nervous and easily infuriated that it was impossible to argue with them over their wilted, puckered, or rotten merchandise. If the women took their time in buying or dug into the little mounds of vegetables on the carts or the display tables, or if they turned the piles over more than they should, the men would fly into a rage and sink their cutting tongues into them. But to Hawwa's surprise, people lavished great respect and honor on their returning jihadis, mostly submitting to the conditions they imposed in their daily interactions with them. She remembers well how, twenty years earlier, the camp celebrated the return of the jihadi hero, Abdel-Rahman Shahir, known as Abu Ubada. He was one of the companions of the jihadi Abdallah Azzam, among the many who claimed to be his right arm. It was said that he fought next to him in the battle of Jaji against the Soviets in Afghanistan, showing exceptional heroism and courage, and even that he himself killed no fewer than twelve Russian soldiers. People would describe how Abu Ubada strangled one of those infidels with his bare hands, and how he saw fire coming out of his eyes and judged—and he was most likely correct—that it was the fire of hell that was dragging the man down during his slow death.

Abu Ubada came back to the camp with a lot of money. He said that this was the money of the Muslims for the Muslims, and that he intended to undertake a project from which the believing servants of God would benefit. He asked for advice and counsel from the faithful, so some suggested that he create a soccer field on a large piece of land at the edge of the camp, while others suggested building a vocational center to teach trades such as carpentry, ironwork, and sewing. A lawyer from the Shatarat family, known for his union activity in Baqa'a Camp, suggested building an orphan center for the children of the camp whose families had expelled them and whom state organizations could not accommodate, and maybe another center for training and educating the handicapped, who were refused by government schools and by the UNRWA schools as well. After deep thought, Abu Ubada set up a center to teach the memorization of the Qur'an in the camp, with two branches, one for females and one for males, each bearing a sign that read "The best of you is the one who learns the Qur'an and teaches it." The students would pay a token fee. This charitable project did not prevent Abu Ubada from renting the piece of land suggested for the soccer field and turning it into a lot for buying and selling used cars, as well as spare parts for Japanese and Korean cars, with the help of smart, shrewd agents with sharp tongues, who could sell any sort of scrap, using any sort of deception and swindling.

Six months after his return, Abu Ubada married Umm Barra, the director of the center for females. She was a widow with three children, and it was said that she gave him her box of gold jewelry, contributing it as part of the Muslims' money that Abu Ubada had brought for the Muslims. Then, a year later, Abu Ubada married a female preacher in the center, Umm Hanin, a divorcée with two daughters. So Abu Ubada acquired a good reputation for "comforting" women alone in their distress, those wounded and defeated socially. His reputation was confirmed after less than a year when he was joined by his Egyptian wife, Inaam—Umm Ubada—who had been living in Peshawar in Pakistan, along with their four children. She was the only daughter of one of his companions in jihad, who had met his end in a fierce battle, after bleeding for three days in a mountain hideout in Afghanistan. The wife from Peshawar joined her two co-wives in directing the affairs of the center, and every morning Abu Ubada would drive the three of them, veiled from head to toe, to the center, amid the envy of bearded men over his ability to manage an enormous family, while his wives continued to fill their houses with many pious offspring. Nor did Abu Ubada's reputation suffer much when years later he married Sulaf, a girl of eighteen who was one of the girls who frequented the center. It was said that his wife Umm Barra chose her for him herself, to spite her co-wife from Peshawar, who had tried to monopolize him with her "Egyptian tricks," as she called them.

In her twenties, Hawwa had recoiled from Abu Ubada's appearance, which some of the men of the camp had begun to imitate. She considered him disgusting, extremely ugly, especially because of his pockmarked complexion and long, bulbous nose, which swallowed up half his face. Also his beard, which was sparse, not at all thick, and collected below his chin like thin grass, made him look like an old goat, even though he was not yet forty. "That goat you don't like beds all his women in one night!" Umm Said told her, refuting her incorrect view of Abu Ubada. She assured her that God gives the believing, valiant jihadi, the likes of Abu Ubada, the might of a hundred men. His virility does not flag and his energy does not dwindle and his desire is not satisfied and his appetite is not sated, no matter how many women he goes to. Umm Said, who was her neighbor when she was married, told her also how Abu Ubada's women competed in sating him sexually, raiding "the brides' alley" in the camp market, where the shops specializing in bridal underwear were found. They chose the most risqué, the most shameless, panties and nightgowns. Not only that, but there was Aziza, who went from house to house in the camp carrying a suitcase that contained a hair dryer, hair brushes, a curling iron, for straightening hair and curling it; a complete set of makeup implements and tweezers; string for depilation; rasps and an abrading stone; and creams and bottles of nail polish. Aziza had tiled her house and had added two rooms with all the facilities on the roof, for her son. She had bought him a set of sofas and chairs, a refrigerator, a twin-tub washing machine, and a twenty-inch television set, and she had made him a set of bedroom linens and had arranged his marriage, all from what she had earned from Abu Ubada's women. Aziza hurried to them with her beauty equipment almost on a daily basis. She would remove the hair from their bodies and faces, shape their eyebrows, set their hair, apply their makeup, remove the calluses from their heels, and file their nails and apply polish. Then she began to massage them so their bodies, drained from frequent pregnancies, would remain pliable, firm, and supple. And her visits weren't confined to their apartments in the building where they lived, which Abu Ubada had built for them outside the limits of the camp. At their request, Aziza often went to them in the center for teaching Qur'anic memorization, during the regular hours. They had set aside a room inside the center in which there was a massage table, a chair that could be raised like the chairs in beauty salons, a dressing table with a large mirror over it, and a gas stove with three burners. There, Aziza would prepare her halawa depilatory paste of water, lemon juice, and sugar, and apply it to them one after the other, as they lay half naked on leather couches borrowed from the administrative office.

Now Hawwa looks through the glass of the closed window, with the marks of dirty raindrops on it, seeking the sky over the camp. She sees a cloud with a scowling expression, warning of an early end to the daylight. The light is beginning to gather and fold its edges, withdrawing; she feels a sting of cold. She lights the gas heater in the main room in one of its burners, and cracks the door of the bedroom, so that her ears can closely track Rabia's breathing, which has settled into a steady snoring. She has fed her okra mashed with rice, turned her on her left side, and put her to sleep.

Hawwa is sitting on the sofa near the heater. The heat of the red burner tickles her feet, stuffed into thick cotton socks with wool slippers over them. The heat extends to the limbs of her body. Her heart beats, strong beats that reinforce the heat flowing in her body, settled on the couch. Happiness, overflowing and absolute, envelops every part of her. She's happy because she's spoken to Munir. She loves his voice, she loves it close and she loves it far away, even though his voice at a distance, on the cell phone, affects her being more. It is more beautiful then, rising from the depths, from his depths, and descending to her depths. It clings to her spirit, settling deeply within it; it plunges into her soul until it's submerged. Hawwa is happy. Her soul, bound with happiness, isn't big enough for her when she hears Munir, when he speaks to her, when she talks to him, when she sees him, when the same air surrounds them both, when the narrow space of existence becomes wide enough for them both.

A dark-blue jacket of crêpe georgette is spread over her lap, part of a two-piece suit she has cut and sewn, along with a flared skirt from the same fabric. Sitt Riham, the one for whom she is making the suit, is supposed to come to pick it up tomorrow. All that's left is to place the buttons on the jacket and the zipper in the skirt. Hawwa contemplates the cloud, which is stretching out more in the sky over the camp. The cloud moves heavily, leaning down over some of the houses, spreading touches of gray. Something pains Hawwa's heart, and she feels a twinge in her chest. But she does not allow the twinge in her heart to turn her thoughts away from the happiness rising around her. She begins to set the first of five buttons, whose places she has marked opposite the button-holes. She pulls the thread up through one of the holes in the button. A strong tremor afflicts her hand, and the needle misses her middle finger, protected by the thimble, and plunges into her ring finger. A drop of blood swells out, so she puts her bleeding finger into her mouth, sucking the blood so it won't stain the jacket. She lifts her head toward the window, and her eyes meet enormous smoky eyes staring at her from the heart of the cloud, which is becoming ever thicker.

Nazmi kicked her in the belly with the heel of his boot. Then he rammed her head into the wall and split it open. A thick line of blood flowed from her shining forehead and plunged into the short, dense hairs of her eyebrow. She crumpled on the floor, twisting in pain. She put one hand on her belly, trying to contain the worsening pain, and with the other she wiped the stream of blood, which had changed its direction on her forehead, now flowing parallel to her eyebrow to descend on her temple. She tried to stand but he pushed her down again with his foot, then he stamped on her neck with his boot, the sole edged in nails, and she felt the heat of the sole in the small, hot nailheads burning her flesh. He leaned over her and twisted her single gold chain, which she wore around her neck. He pulled on it violently, so that her eyes nearly popped out of their sockets and her breath was almost entirely cut off. When the chain finally broke she gulped down a lot of air, which she exhaled all at once. He put the chain in his pocket and said he would sell it and use the money to pay for the fabric she had ruined.

Hawwa had been married less than three months when three women, Nazmi's relatives, knocked on her door and put three pieces of fabric on her new sewing machine, which she had brought as part of her trousseau. The family seamstress, as they called her, now took priority over anyone else. They were pleased by the girl who had learned to sew properly from Sitt Qamar, the most skilled and expensive seamstress in Sweileh and the surrounding area. Hawwa listened to them patiently, as they explained to her at length the confused concepts in their heads. They drew their vague designs and erased them many times before settling on their goals, which still floated among many nebulous details and additions. Hawwa did not argue with them about what was proper and what was not, nor did she oppose them—as Sitt Qamar did with her clients—about what would work and what would not. The more she asked them, the more lost she was. She was still lost when she put her hesitant foot on the pedal of the machine and saw the quick, successive stitches follow a path far from what she had hoped for or imagined. While she was cutting the dresses and sewing them, she knew that she had completely lost her way and had gone in a direction the women did not want. So it happened that, angry and threatening, they took the forlorn result to her husband, denouncing to him what had become of their fabric, which they had chosen with great care. They exaggerated the tally of their heavy losses. One of them, his father's maternal cousin, did not scruple to throw her finished piece in his face, suggesting he wipe his ass with it.

For days there was a red mark around Hawwa's neck, resulting from Nazmi's desperate attempt to choke her. She didn't care much about her one gold chain. She knew that Nazmi would not compensate his relatives, and even if he did, the value of the chain was many times more than the cost of the fabric, which meant that in fact he would keep most of the money for himself. But two wonderful things were born of her horrid "thrashing": the first was that her mother suggested to Nazmi that he let her continue training and working with Sitt Qamar, to gain the experience she still needed, and to bring in extra income to help the barren household, from the pay that Sitt Qamar would give her every week. And the second, even more wonderful, was that Nazmi's violent kick caused her to abort, before she had completed the second month of her pregnancy. The whole family was grieved, both her side and his side. Most likely Nazmi felt some passing guilt; if so, his feeling did not last long. But Hawwa's happiness, as she watched the thin stream of blood stain the surface of her thighs, accompanied by severe cramps rising from the very bottom of her spirit and wringing her intestines thoroughly— her happiness was like no other.

Hawwa had worked as a "seamstress in training" with Sitt Qamar for about three years before she was separated from her by her marriage. Without any doubt those were the three best years of her life. She didn't feel that she was working, at least not in the sense of exhausting tasks or bondmen's work. Nor did she feel for a moment that she was spending more than a third of her day in the house of a stranger, for during the time she spent there, a third of every day except Friday, Sitt Qamar's house was her house. It was her refuge. There, the sting of pain was healed; flaring redness faded; swelling went down; her father's boot trampling her neck, with all the filth of the lanes on the sole, disappeared; and fire lit by Mousa's whip on her body cooled somewhat. Better than all of that, Hawwa felt strongly that Sitt Qamar could be her mother. Like a mother, she would be gentle, compassionate, and tender, loving and affectionate. She would check on her daughter, whom Hawwa imagined as resembling her, Hawwa, to the point of being her, at night and during the day. She would miss her during the darkness of sleep and the light of waking; she would be alarmed if she lost her way or were late, on evenings draped with doubt. Her spirit would weep if she were in pain or were sad. Like a mother to her, Sitt Qamar would throw her body over her as a protective blanket or a forbidding wall, so no blow would reach her, no kick or boot, no bruising, no shattering, no squashing, no crushing. The maternal heart of Sitt Qamar would burn with prayers and tears if her daughter were ill—her daughter who looked so much like Hawwa that she could have been Hawwa herself. Sitt Qamar would say to her, "Yamma, it's Mama, my beloved," "Yamma, my soul," "Yamma, my life." She would shower her day and night with hugs and kisses, in scenes like the ones between mothers and daughters in television dramas, scenes Hawwa thought were very real.

Hawwa thought she looked very much like Sitt Qamar. This belief of hers, coming under the heading of wishful thinking, did not lack all foundation in logic, because a number of Sitt Qamar's customers, especially the new ones, would ask her if Hawwa were her daughter. Filled with pleasure, her spirit would flutter like a lighthearted butterfly over lovely green fields, even if Sitt Qamar's answer was negative. But Sitt Qamar did not deny being Hawwa's mother out of rejection or annoyance; rather, she answered with real emotion, and sometimes with a touch of yearning, "She's like my daughter." The truth was that Sitt Qamar, who was on the threshold of forty at the time, approaching it with elegance, dignity, and refinement, could well have been the mother of someone Hawwa's age. In fact her body, with its nobly designed flesh, could make more than one daughter and more than one son.

It didn't seem that Hawwa was in a hurry to learn to sew properly, or at least not in the beginning. She would spend much more time than necessary cleaning and tidying Sitt

Qamar's apartment. Sitt Qamar did not pressure her. Hawwa could do what she wanted in the house, as long as she opened her eyes at nine in the morning to the aroma of coffee penetrating her dry lungs. She would gulp down the aroma without choking on it, and her spirit would be filled with it and refreshed. She had given Hawwa a copy of the key to the house, so Hawwa would arrive between 8:30 and 9:00. She would open the curtains and the window in the living room to air it out, clearing the smell of cigarettes hanging in the enclosed air. The smell would have thickened and fermented during the night, until the tobacco was palpable in the still air. She would pick up the ashtray overflowing with cigarette butts, which had been left on the displaced cushion of the three-seat Morris sofa where Sitt Qamar sat. She would brush the cigarette ashes from the sofa, straighten the cushion, and then put the coffeepot on the stove.

Sometimes Hawwa would bring with her a package of Nabulsi cheese, made by her grandmother, and a little jar of green olives preserved with pepper, made by her mother. She might buy a bunch of mint from one of the vegetable carts near the bus stop, and pass by a bakery near Sitt Qamar's house to buy a package of bread. She might also go a few steps to a restaurant secluded on a side street, to buy hummus and falafel. When the boiling water bubbled on the stove, she lifted the pot from the fire to let the water settle a little. Then she added coffee, in a specified amount, so that the sensual brown liquid would have the proper consistency, heavy and not watery or limp, with a delicate creamy foam floating on the surface.

Hawwa would put the coffeepot on a tray, along with a cup, a matching saucer with a piece of chocolate wrapped in silver paper at its edge, a glass of water, a pack of cigarettes, a lighter, and an ashtray. Then she would take the tray to its place on the three-seat Morris sofa. Sitt Qamar did not put the coffee cup or the ashtray on the table; she wanted her coffee and her cigarettes, which created her day and her mood,

which were her affable and amiable companions, to be close
to her, a natural extension of her hand. When she took her
first sip of coffee, enjoying it leisurely, the foam on top tickling
her taste buds, and followed it with a long pull on her cigarette, she closed her eyes and lifted her head, as if she were
hovering with the eye of memory over a specific place, taking
a picture or some other impression of it. Then she opened her
eyes as if she had suddenly come down to earth, knowing that
her day had begun.

Hawwa took great delight in preparing breakfast. She made
the omelet as Sitt Qamar had taught her. She distributed the
plates of Nabulsi cheese, olives, olive oil, za'atar, hummus (to
which she added a drizzle of olive oil), and falafel on the kitchen
table, surrounded by four chairs. They sat facing each other
over the little table, as a mother and daughter, sharing stories
and the loaf of pita bread. When Sitt Qamar saw that Hawwa
hesitated to reach for a certain plate, she put it before her. Sitt
Qamar did not drink tea with her breakfast—"Only peasants
drink tea with food," she told her, laughing. Hawwa would
drink her cup of tea, a green mint leaf floating on its clear red
surface, with pleasure. Sitt Qamar casually stretched her hand
to a lock of hair that had fallen onto Hawwa's forehead, gently shaking off a bread crumb that clung to it. She gathered
Hawwa's long, chaotic locks and combed them with her fingers,
lifting them behind her ears, then brought her fingers down
over her swollen cheek. She inspected dull red marks, and asked
her about them. Hawwa swallowed a piece of falafel followed
by a bite of hummus and answered in a muffled voice, "I fell on
my face this morning." She looked up at her mentor from the
corner of her eye to see if she had noticed the lie. Sitt Qamar
felt Hawwa's forehead, which still bore the marks of a recently
closed wound, and her cheek. She wiped her cheek gently and
Hawwa's eyes shone, pouring their overflowing morning glow
on her face, the blush of embarrassment and warmth of emotion overcoming the reddening of the swelling.

In addition to the living room and the parlor, Sitt Qamar's apartment had three bedrooms. She made the largest one, next to the bathroom, into a bedroom for herself. In it she put a large closet with six sections and a double bed, of which she occupied the left side. She never changed sides, and she never encroached on the right side, as if she were waiting for her man to return from some absence, to find his place in the bed ready for him. When she woke from sleep, the first thing her eyes would fall on was the empty place in the bed. She would stretch her arm out to some possibility—maybe the one who had come to her in a dream, his features fully formed, had been created next to her, so the plumped pillow and the stretched sheet had wrinkled from the imprint of his body, from his sprawling feelings, from his breath, his pulse, and his sweat.

In the second bedroom Sitt Qamar put a closet with two doors, a single bed, a single armchair, a little dressing table with an oval mirror, and a bedside table. The table held a lamp and the picture of a girl with eyes the color of a blue spring sky and golden blond hair, pulled into a short ponytail on each side, with thick, soft bangs hanging over her forehead. The girl was hugging a white dog and looked as if she were laughing heartily, her milk-white teeth radiating abundant light. But despite the child's laugh, which was almost audible, the room was very cold, and desolate. When Hawwa opened the closet the first time to clean it, she was frightened by the great emptiness inside. On the floor of the cabinet lay only a quilt and a blanket, unused for a long time, and a pillow wrapped in a plastic bag and tossed on the bottom. Wooden hangers empty of clothes clattered when she opened the door, like bony skeletons. Hawwa took fright; she closed the door of the nearly empty closet and fled from the room, shutting the door behind her. She was sure that she had seen a ghost crouching in the closet; she said that to her sisters, Afaf and Sajida, and they believed her. When she became accustomed to the room, which she was obliged to clean, she was careful to stay far away from the closet. One thing only gave her pause: the laughing child. Hawwa looked closely at the picture; the child did not resemble Sitt Qamar. In fact, she did not resemble any girl she thought she had ever seen. The little girl was too beautiful to be real.

Then came times when Sitt Qamar was not the Sitt Qamar to whom Hawwa was accustomed. She would wake from sleep disturbed and smoke a cigarette first thing, and follow it with a second and a third. Then she would cough many times over, her spirit crammed into her dry throat and wrung out. She would gulp down the coffee all at once. She would resist having breakfast and avert her eyes from lunch, and keep to the bedroom with the single bed. She would sit on the edge of the bed, resting her head on the headboard. She would embrace the picture frame, more than the picture itself, hugging the back of the frame to her chest, while the laughing girl with the sky-blue eyes and the clean, milk-white teeth stared into the distance, completely separated from Sitt Qamar.

At first, Hawwa feared for Sitt Qamar. She saw her going away, as if she were traveling to another place. She was afraid she would not come back, as she would stay in that state for hours, and sometimes for the entire day. Hawwa learned not to speak with her or call her or try to bring her back to her known world.

Hawwa would clean the house and cook, and then perform some tailoring tasks left for her, as well as other tasks that Sitt Qamar was supposed to perform, without Sitt Qamar opening her mouth or giving any indication that she noticed what was around her. Her eyes would be fixed, still, looking without seeing a thing. It was as if she had left the world, leaving behind her a bit of body without much value. From time to time, Hawwa would open the door of the room, left slightly ajar, to check on Sitt Qamar. She would see her in the same position, embracing the back of the picture, preoccupied with nothing that could be named. She would come close to her and listen to her calm, regular breathing, reassuring herself that she was all right in that moment, even if she was not completely conscious. She might enter and find her asleep, her body sloughed off from her spirit and slack on the bed. She would gently stretch her out on her side, straightening her legs, and cover her. Hawwa would try to take the picture from her, but Sitt Qamar pulled it to herself, still wandering dazed in another world, her arms folded tightly over the frame as if she feared losing it or having it taken from her forcibly. When she woke at last she would come back to her world as if she hadn't left it for a moment, and the bedroom, with its single bed, would return to its previous desolation, while the face of the child, with her milk-white teeth, was still bursting with happiness. The child still laughed, it seemed, uproariously, a sidesplitting laugh, and her saliva flowed fresh and alive, even when Hawwa closed the room and locked it with a key, according to Sitt Qamar's instructions. She did not permit any being whatsoever to enter it.

Sitt Qamar designated the third bedroom, relatively large, as a workroom for sewing. There were two sewing machines in it, a hand-operated one and a newer one that ran on electricity. There was also a cutting table, made of beech and yellow pine, closer in its design to a long desk. On each side, a set of shelves and drawers had been added, which were filled with boxes containing spools of thread, of all sizes and all degrees and shades of color, as well as buttons, zippers, hooks and eyes, yards of lace and lace edging, measuring tapes, boxes of pins and needles, remnants of interfacing, thin strips of foam, and an assortment of fashion magazines. Near the corner, beside the door, sat a green sofa. All along one wall stood a closet with four sections, two of them set aside for hanging dresses and suits ready to be delivered, and those that were at the stage of the finishing touches. The other two sections were composed of a number of deep, high shelves where dozens of bags of fabric were stacked, their number increasing. Pinned to the openings were pieces of paper with the notes, names, and measurements of their owners. The relatively spacious room had been provided with four long, cylindrical neon lights, giving a bright white light, which meant that the illumination at night was almost like clear daylight. An amber carpet printed with olive green and fire red occupied the center of the room. Every day, Hawwa cleaned the fuzz from the fabric that clung to it with the vacuum cleaner. In one corner of the room stood a wooden screen of bamboo with four panels that could be moved to open or close it. The little space behind it formed a corner for measuring. In it were an oblong oval mirror on a stand and a clothes rack. The women would conceal themselves behind the bamboo panels to be measured for their dresses, and for the first and final fittings. They did not hide their excitement when the pieces, recently cut and sewn, slipped over their bodies, with the mixed aromas of fabrics flowing in the air around them. The crinkle of the fabric flirted with their ears and delighted their imaginations. They repressed their cries when the pins pricked their warm flesh. Many times, Hawwa helped them put on their dresses. Some would stand before the mirror, dazzled by what they saw; for some, it was as if they were meeting themselves for the first time. Their eyes would sweep over their radiant appearance in the mirror, its length and breadth, as if they wanted to seize the moment forever, dizzy with the fragrance of the fabric, recently cho-sen, cut, and sewn, not wanting to let the magic moment go.

Hawwa learned many things from Sitt Qamar. She learned to take measurements and to draw the basic pattern, even if Sitt Qamar did not go by her measurements and her patterns at first, limiting herself to looking them over and checking them. For months, Hawwa was content with simple tasks, such as basting, sewing on buttons and hooks and eyes, inserting zippers, placing interfacing in collars and sleeve cuffs, setting shoulder pads filled with thin foam, and trimming the edges of seam allowances with the pinking shears or binding them by hand. Hawwa especially enjoyed setting pleats with a hidden stitch, showing extreme precision and exceptional skill in setting all kinds of tiny stitches that did not show, from cross-stitches to herringbone stitches to fishbone stitches, all according to Sitt Qamar's instructions. Hawwa tarried before she moved on to drawing patterns on fabric, and then to cutting and assembling the pieces of fabric and sewing them.

Even though over the years Hawwa attained the skill of Sitt Qamar, or a degree that was close to hers, she never acquired the same degree of excessive sensitivity to fabric, and she was absolutely not going to live through the fabric, she who worked most of her years as a seamstress with the cheapest kinds of fabric and the ones most widely sold. Sitt Qamar's sensitivity to fabric reached a degree that fascinated even Hawwa. Some days when the pressure was light, or when their feet pressed less on the sewing machine pedals, Sitt Qamar enjoyed testing Hawwa on fabric, and she enjoyed it more when Hawwa failed the test. Sitt Qamar would bring a piece of fabric to Hawwa's nose, in a test of smell, as if she were interrogating the inner layers of the aroma.

"What does it smell like?"

Hawwa would breathe in the fabric, its creases, its folds, its waves, but she would say innocently to Sitt Qamar that all she smelled was fabric.

"Wrong!" Sitt Qamar would reply, intoxicated as the aroma of freshly lit frankincense came to her nose from velvet. Or it was the aroma of May, moving among the petals of lilies, damask roses, and jasmine, from silk, satin, and chiffon; or the aroma of dried fruit from organza, guipure, and lace; the aroma of aging luxury, sometimes very old, from brocaded, beaded, or embroidered fabric; the aroma of steam rising from roasted chestnuts, from broadcloth and tweed; the aroma of sleeping coals, half lit, from fur and mohair; the aroma of crackling tree leaves from cotton and linen; the aroma of grass washed with water from jersey; or the aroma of newly made plastic from nylon and polyester.

Once, however, Sitt Qamar gave Hawwa a grade of ten out of ten, laughing with all her heart, when she asked her about the aroma of a piece of fabric that looked as if it had been stored for years in the bag its owner had brought. Hawwa put her head halfway into the bag and sniffed the odor for a moment, and when she took out her head, she summoned all her store of aromas, until she produced the evaluation that Sitt Qamar declared was astounding: the aroma was like that of sewers overflowing for more than a week in the lane leading to their house in Baqa'a Camp, especially during the flaming midday, when the sun beat down on the course of the stagnant black stream.

Aside from her skill, which surpassed that of many of the seamstresses of her time and place, Sitt Qamar was also known for her unique taste and her singular aesthetic sense, especially in the final touches that make all the difference. Her reputation extended beyond Sweileh, and women came to her from all over Amman. They would respond to her observations and concepts, very clear in her head, concerning the choice of a design suitable to the type of the fabric and to the form of their bodies. Most of the time, her opinion had dictatorial force and was not subject to discussion. Rarely did women argue with her about the design she thought was appropriate or the fitting material, because "Sitt Qamar knows best." If she did encounter uncalled-for stubbornness in one of them, or a stupid insistence that she labeled "mulishness," then she simply made up the piece "with the back of her hand." The final form of the design would lack her heart and her aesthetic view, not bearing the exclusive Qamar touch. And if her recklessness exceeded all bounds, Sitt Qamar put aside the piece of fabric without touching it for several days, until the client came to her for the fitting; then she would make any lying excuse for not having been able to sew it. Sometimes the discussion between Sitt Qamar and the client would become so inflamed that she would throw the fabric in the woman's face, and the woman would leave, all but thrown out of Sitt Qamar's house.

Hawwa did not wish for the end of the day in Sitt Qamar's house and did not hurry it. But her consolation was that she went back to her family's house at day's end with a small treasure, since Sitt Qamar allowed her to take the leftover fabric that nothing could be done with. Hawwa yearned for the moment when she would sort the leftovers at home, and she often came across valuable finds. She would spend part of her Friday sewing doll dresses for the daughters of the neighbors, selling them for five or ten piasters each. The price of the dress might reach twenty piasters, depending on the type of fabric, the design, and the handwork. Once she made an entire eight-piece trousseau for a doll, including a wedding dress in chiffon and white lace with a veil and a little crown of wire, which she studded with glass beads. It was for a girl who wore short dresses and colored sandals, who had come with her family from Saudi Arabia for the summer vacation, the family staying as honored, celebrated guests with their relatives in the camp. The girl's mother, who wore a black silk abaya from which rose the penetrating smell of eastern perfume, and who showed her hands, with dark, luxurious designs in henna, and with many gold rings adorning her fingers, gave Hawwa a new, red bill, never folded, in the denomination of five dinars. Hawwa couldn't believe her eyes. The red bill stayed new and uncreased for that day and a few nights, until her father took it from her, folding it three times and placing it in his shirt pocket. Hawwa did not have a sewing machine at home, so she stitched the little dresses by hand, using a backstitch, which resembled machine stitching. It was a stitch that wore her out, making her fingers bleed and her neck stiff, since she remained bent over the tiny pieces for hours at a time. Nonetheless, she was able to make ten dresses or more in a day, and so her mother would excuse her from some housework in exchange for the extra income, which was always urgently needed.

Hawwa remembers the day she came across a quarter of a yard of valuable velvet in indigo blue. She was fascinated by it. She showed it to Duha, who enjoyed watching her sister sew the little dresses from shining, sparkling fabric. "How do you like that?" she asked Duha, whose wasted form stretched on the floor pallet. The child's face lit up. The moonlight poured down through the window onto the fabric, its silvery shadows strutting over the peaceful, nocturnal wave of the cloth, bringing out a richer blue. Hawwa set her fresh imagination to the expensive fabric, and from her hands and her needle, quick, tireless, patient, and loving, there emerged a miniature long dress, with a tight bodice and waist and wide skirt, which she gathered just below the waist, giving it volume. She set in puffed sleeves with wide cuffs, which she embroidered with pearl drops, also embroidering the edge of the round collar with two rows of pearl drops. Duha overflowed with joy when the dress hugged the form of her thin doll. The veiled shine of the magnificent velvet blue reflected on the pale plastic complexion of the doll and she looked like a princess—a haughty, conceited princess, beautiful and happy, as if the whole world belonged to her. Duha slept, woke, and lived through her day, for all that remained of her days, in the company of the velvet princess. She would hug her tightly, as if she were afraid the doll would be taken from her. For many nights, Duha sought extended life from the silken pile of the fabric. Afaf and Sajida told her that the velvet would disintegrate or its color fade from her clutching it all the time with her sweaty hands, but Duha would not part with her princess. She went on sleeping and waking with her. Even when the fever was lit in her body and fire devoured her head, her princess did not slip from her embrace. When morning came and at last Duha's temperature cooled and she stopped living, it was difficult for Afaf to take the velvet princess from her sister's twig-like arms, which were folded over her. Some of the pearl drops had escaped from the collar of the dress and rolled on the floor, and with them rolled hot tear drops from Hawwa's eyes.

At first, Hawwa earned five dinars a week from Sitt Qamar. She would give all the money to Rabia, and Mousa took as much as he could from her. After four months of work, Sitt Qamar increased her weekly pay to eight dinars; Rabia rejoiced at the increase and hid it from Mousa, who settled for pestering her for the five dinars, or most of that. Then Sitt Qamar began to pay Hawwa ten dinars, and she hid the two new dinars from Rabia. Even when she began to earn fifteen dinars a week, she would give her mother ten and hide five dinars, as well as the other money she got from some of Sitt Qamar's generous clients, in return for the delicious coffee she prepared for them, pouring it into a gilt-edged white cup and offering it to them with a cookie or date-filled cake and a glass of water, on a tray decorated with a piece of creamy lace— depending on the status of the client. Or it might be for taking charge of the final fitting, for tightening or loosening, shortening or lengthening, after Sitt Qamar had begun to depend on her for many tailoring tasks.

Hawwa also remembers the treasure that fell on her from a completely unexpected place. She was sitting on the floor as usual, straightening the hem of a dress for a client named Sitt Feriyal, who carried some weight. Hawwa remembered the name because it had meant a great deal in its time. Sitt Feriyal would come to Sitt Qamar's house in a black car driven by a private driver, and while the car stood at the entrance to the building, open doors and windows would shut, one after the other, and barely anyone entered the building or left it. As she stood there, Sitt Feriyal seemed like a giant, branching tree, while Hawwa, seated on the floor, seemed like a dwarf plant. Sitt Feriyal was in her late forties, blond, with purely golden hair and small, round, blue eyes with no trace of any other color, almost like two beads. She spoke in a heavy Jordanian dialect, close to Bedouin speech; Hawwa learned later that she was Circassian, and that her husband, Ali Bey, occupied a high position in the regime. Hawwa was leaning forward at the feet of Sitt Feriyal, placing the pins in the hem of a long dress of silk and chiffon that she was having made to wear to her daughter's wedding. Sitt Feriyal was describing to Sitt Qamar and to Hawwa the arrangements for the wedding. Sitt Qamar didn't seem as interested in learning about the details as Hawwa was. She was listening intently to the woman, whose bearing reflected power and rank, as she described her daughter's wedding dress, which they had ordered from Paris. When Hawwa finished straightening the hem, Sitt Feriyal contemplated her extravagant appearance in the mirror. Then she opened her purse and took out a ten-dinar bill. Straightening it with both hands, she tossed it into Hawwa's lap. Hawwa, still seated on the floor, could not believe her eyes. The most she might get from Sitt Qamar's clients was half a dinar, or rarely one dinar—but ten dinars, just like that! She looked at Sitt Qamar, as if asking permission, and the latter closed her eyes, in a sign of agreement. When Sitt Feriyal came, Sitt Qamar greeted her herself at the door, and she saw her out personally, listening to the sound of her heels fading gradually on the steps and then disappearing completely. Then she spat on the door.

Hawwa used the money she saved to buy bras of cotton and stiffened lace, with deep cups, in addition to tops and tight pants that she wore under her jilbab. She told her mother that Sitt Qamar gave her the clothes that became small for her. She also bought shoes, imitation perfumes, lipsticks, creams with a velvety touch, boxes of powder, and eyeliner pencils. When she would go home with a black purse smelling of imitation leather dangling from her shoulder, or milky sandals with a gold buckle on the side, she would say that Sitt Qamar had given them to her. When Rabia expressed amazement that Sitt Qamar would get rid of brand-new shoes or sandals,

Hawwa began to rub the soles of the shoes or sandals she bought in rough earth, so they would be scuffed and look used.

Hawwa hid the bottle of perfume and her makeup kit in one of the kitchen cabinets in Sitt Qamar's house. In the morning, when she had finished preparing Sitt Qamar's coffee and straightening the house, she would wash her face. Then she would spread out her reddish hair, half lifting it on the sides and holding it with colored pins, while letting it hang down behind her in a waterfall reaching halfway down her back. Then she would put cream on her face, apply eyeliner, put on lipstick, powder her cheeks, and spray perfume on the sides of her neck and at the top of her chest. The cream might be denser, the eyeliner thicker, the powder more glowing, the color of the lipstick richer, and the perfume more assertive on the days when Murad was coming to change the gas cylinder. But whatever the case, Hawwa did not forget to take off her beautiful face, the face she loved, at the end of the day and to leave it in Sitt Qamar's house, to reclaim it the next day.

From Sitt Qamar, Hawwa learned to value two things: water and Fairuz. Once every two or three weeks, Sitt Qamar would take her to an indoor pool, and it would be possible for Hawwa to live in peace with her flesh, or what showed of it, amid the flood of bare flesh belonging to women and girls of every size. The most beautiful moments in the water were when she floated on her back, for then she was light, relieved of all the miseries and burdens in her life. She became delicate, and with some induced imagination and hidden desire, she nearly flew. Hawwa felt the light slapping of the water on her body as if it were smooth hands with tender skin massaging her gently. Then all the pain would pass away, or at the least withdraw. In the beginning she was embarrassed to put on the bathing suit that Sitt Qamar brought her. It was a one-piece suit of red and black, which Sitt Qamar forced her to put on. Hawwa could not comprehend how Sitt Qamar could ask her to take off her bra and underpants and put on the bathing suit directly next to her skin—she believed that this in itself was disgraceful in the extreme. She stood in the narrow measuring space, behind the screen in the sewing room, inspecting the bathing suit, which seemed small and tight in her hand, before it stretched over the entire girth of her torso, tracing the shape of her figure. Its firm fabric of nylon and Lycra seemed like another layer of flesh on top of her own. In the mirror she saw the features of her body for the first time, having been taught not only to hide her body but also to oppose and subjugate it. Something made her inspect the effusion of fully formed flesh now visible outside the narrow confines of the bathing suit, as her arms and legs, the top of her chest, and at least half of her back were uncovered. As she examined her flesh, it was as if she were contemplating her essence. Sitt Qamar called to her to show her the bathing suit, and she answered that she didn't want to. Sitt Qamar shouted at her, commanding her, and Hawwa told her in a strangled voice that she couldn't. Sitt Qamar took away the wooden screen and saw Hawwa curled up on the floor, wrapped over herself. She drew her up by her arm and her nearly bare flesh spread out, her eyes fighting off tears. Sitt Qamar inspected Hawwa's body in disbelief. Dark violet spots, bluish in places and yellow in others, with blotches of red, spilled over most of the surface of her body, like spreading clouds, though they were concentrated on her thighs and the tops of her arms, and broad lines crisscrossed the length of her bare back, like the lines caused by blows from a bamboo cane or a whip.

"What's this?" Sitt Qamar asked her in disbelief.

Hawwa summed up the matter in two words: "My father."

As to Fairuz, she was playing all day in Sitt Qamar's house, to the point that her voice was no longer a passing guest or a stranger. Sitt Qamar kept a leather case containing dozens of tapes of Fairuz's songs, every tape in a box, each box bearing the picture of Fairuz and the names of the songs.

Fairuz never stopped singing for a single day in Sitt Qamar's house; and when at times Sitt Qamar had to stop the tape recorder, to deal with her clients and all their overlapping talk, then Fairuz remained suspended in her head. Once the tape recorder stopped working for several days, and Hawwa felt as if her head were falling into a great void. She said that to Sitt Qamar, who agreed with her. But Sitt Qamar didn't seem completely debilitated by the temporary absence of the voice, for Fairuz, as she told Hawwa, was in her flesh. Sitt Qamar did not sing along with Fairuz or hum after her. She listened with her spirit, with every bit of her spirit; and sometimes, with the songs enfolded by a veil of grief, it seemed as if she were mounting towering torments, or rolling roughly over low slopes of renewed pains.

There was one song more than any other that brought Sitt Qamar to leave everything as soon as she heard it, to live in the music and the words. It seemed to be purified completely of all joy, gathering all the sadness that could be conceived. "My home is yours, I have no one. I've called you so much that space has grown large, grown large, grown large. . . . I waited for you at the door, at all the doors, I wrote my torment on the sun of absence, of absence, of absence." Sitt Qamar would close her eyes and call up a distant image or hunt for an impossible moment. When the melody and the rhythm fell gradually on "grown large" and on "sun of absence," before the voice rose again on a long, distilled note, from which filtered a ringing echo that wrapped around the melody at the ends, then she would see Sitt Qamar pull in the ends of her body as if she were afraid it would go to pieces, gathering them in, pressing her shoulders together, raising them, and inclining her head. When the winds of the song roamed in the well of her being and assailed the depths of her spirit, she would tremble, and support herself on anything within reach. With "Don't neglect me, don't forget me, I have you only, don't forget me," Sitt Qamar would shed floods of tears.

Then Hawwa reached a stage with Fairuz's songs, in Sitt Qamar's house, where she was no longer aware of whether Fairuz was singing or perhaps had taken a rest, for her voice had entered Hawwa's head and settled inside her body, also. When she married Nazmi, Hawwa felt that in his dry house, empty of songs and of nearly everything else related to life, her essence might fall into a dark emptiness at any time; that a painful silence, gathered from the ends of the universe, encircled her and was digging into her soul. Two months had gone by without her hearing Fairuz, and the lingering echo of that voice in her body had begun to grow faint. She asked Nazmi to buy her a tape recorder. He refused, and called her a name he thought suited her: tramp. Hawwa contented herself with Fairuz's visits to her, at unexpected times, on the morning radio. It seemed to Hawwa that Fairuz had begun to time her visits to her for the moments when her soul was becoming a desert, or when floods of depression washed over her. She would intervene to save her at the last minute.

No one knew any substantiated story about Sitt Qamar. As much as she was a woman with an appetite open to a pleasant life, to cardamom-flavored coffee, to the touch of valuable fabrics, to spending generously on food with many additions, to the morning air in April that played with her hair—in that same measure she was closed in on her own life, and on her past in particular. Hawwa did not recall Sitt Qamar ever speaking with her, or with anyone, about her origins or her family, or the country she was thought to have come from. Nor did it happen that she referred to an event or to anything that had happened in the past, nor did she ever mention the name of a person whose life had intersected with hers in any way. Sitt Qamar seemed to be a branch cut from a tree, but a firm branch, leafy in its own way, solid, lofty, reaching to the sky, rebelling against breaking or bowing down. At least that's how Hawwa saw her—Hawwa, who imagined that she could grow up one day and bind up her branches, shattered repeatedly, to become like Sitt Qamar. Hawwa wished mightily that she could be Qamar, that the daughter would resemble her mother.

At long intervals, the past would knock on her door, and Sitt Qamar would be compelled to greet it against her will. But the encounter would remain short, tense, and decidedly not susceptible to being extended any longer than necessary. Strange women would stand at the door, covered in dark jilbabs, navy for the most part, or brown or lead gray, reaching to the ankle, with black nylon socks showing below them, and with plain white or beige headscarves. They seemed lost, or as if they had just completed a long journey. Hawwa knew they were not clients, as they would be hesitant, hunching their shoulders over purses they had put under their arms. She would lead them to the guest parlor and they would sit on the edges of the seats, careful not to allow their heavy, tired bodies to sink into the firm foam. Hawwa would bring them cold water, which they would drink down all at once, thanking her and praising God. When at last Sitt Qamar came to them, they would stand up anxiously, as if apologizing for sitting down without permission. Sitt Qamar would not speak with them, turning her spirit far away and wearing a different face, a face borrowed from distant pain that had not yet been effaced. The strangers might try to bring up distant people, but Sitt Qamar would close her heart in the face of their news. She would give them money folded in envelopes, and they would take it in embarrassment, lowering their eyes and stammering, although they did not show much reluctance, consigning the envelopes to their purses quickly and somewhat anxiously. Then Sitt Qamar would turn her back to them and they would know that the visit had ended. When they left, Sitt Qamar would once again close the door firmly on her past.

From the many stories, with differing details, which Sitt Qamar's clients exchanged among themselves in malicious whispers, Hawwa learned that the orphan Qamar came as a girl from Syria to live with her aged maternal aunt in Irbid. The enchanting Damascene beauty who walked so elegantly captivated every boy and his father in her neighborhood. Then her reputation as a skilled seamstress traveled all over Irbid and the surrounding area, and women came one after the other to the aunt's house, to see Qamar's small, quick, graceful fingers turn fabric with vague potential into pieces of art. And while the women knocked on the aunt's door in the morning, bringing with them sacks summarizing their dreams in silk, satin, lace, chiffon, and expensive velvet, crowding the seats in the living room to claim the exclusive services of Qamar ahead of any others, the men would knock insistently on the aunt's door in the evening, asking for Qamar's hand. From among the many men who fought desperately for her affection, who included eminent men from the clans, those with the honorific of "bey," men addressed as "your grace," holders of scientific diplomas, and handsome, ambitious young men, some of whom announced their devotion publicly as if the heart had never loved another—among them all, Qamar's choice was Hajj Faisal, Abu Zaid, one of the most prominent grain merchants in the city. Everyone was greatly surprised. They weren't surprised because Qamar took Abu Zaid, but rather because she turned away from many suitors who were in no way inferior to him in money, position, distinction, and passion. In fact, most of them were younger than he and much better looking, and might be expected to make a greater impression on a girl of Qamar's beauty.

Abu Zaid was an imposing man. When he walked it seemed as if he were an enormous wall in motion. He had been widowed twice, and his wives had left him sixteen boys and seven girls, who had produced thirty-two grandchildren for him. He was more than forty-five years older than Qamar. The old man's sons, daughters, grandchildren, sisters, and brothers held a grudge against the young enchantress who had carried him off. Their hostility was redoubled because the old man had an aversion to his life before Qamar, and to everything that wasn't related to her. Abu Zaid lived with his young enchantress for three years, and then he died. Qamar had not yet reached her mid-twenties; she was a widow whose charms had doubled, who had become a woman more fully developed and more feminine. His sons and daughters gathered up her few belongings, they gave her both her gold jewelry and her share in the estate, as they claimed, and they threw her out. Qamar had buried her aunt a year before her beloved, as she called Abu Zaid, passed away. Thus there was no longer any room for her in a place where the women felt even more threatened by her presence now that she had lost the protection of her man, and where coals of desire were kindled in the breasts of the men; coals that had never once cooled down.

The original story, however, with its factual details, remained tucked away in Qamar's heart. Its specter would visit her later, as she would close her eyes on a delicate love. Abu Zaid had called her Qamar al-Sham, "Syria's Moon." Then he established his passionate possession of her by starting to call her "My Moon." He was in love with her every day and every hour. He loved her in the morning, when he woke to the scent of her moist complexion, to her hair redolent of Syrian jasmine, to her sleepy eyes with their thick lashes clinging to his eyes on the pillow. The coffee color of her eyes, fading into an expanse of cottony white, would drip into his eyes, which never had enough of looking at her. And he would love her in the evening, when she would cast herself upon him, her compact figure less than half of his, and enfold herself in him completely. He would swallow her, and she would be reassured as long as she was wrapped in his spirit, hidden inside him. He was her colossal whale, and the scent of mastic arising from her body filled his nose. Together they would disappear into a single entity.

In Syria, Qamar had worked for Artin, the most famous Armenian designer and couturier in Damascus. His services were limited to women who lived in great houses and villas, behind walls that even flies were afraid to approach. When the number of his hard-to-please customers multiplied, he began to rely for many things on the most skilled girl in his atelier, Qamar. She had been sixteen when her stepmother sent her to work with Artin. He made no secret of his admiration for the girl's beauty and intelligence; and he didn't need long to discover that the stepmother wanted to get rid of the girl, who fascinated everyone with her beauty, on the excuse that her father's income was no longer enough for the family. After Qamar's pay began to help support the family, whose numbers her stepmother doubled with new offspring, her work became necessary. At that point, the stepmother closed the door in the face of grooms, who she thought might well shut off the spigot of money that was pouring into her house. When Artin happened upon Qamar's talent in drawing original fashion designs, he began taking the designs to his clients. When he noticed her ability to learn fast, he did not feel that it was any threat to him; rather, he made ample space for her to create, in sketching, cutting, and sewing. Even the finishing touches, which required precision, experience, and sound judgment, in no way reflected her age. When Qamar found in him sympathy for her, which seemed to her genuine, as well as affection, generosity, and money that exceeded her needs (part of which she hid from her stepmother), she came to work in Artin's atelier as if it were her own. This was especially so since Artin hinted to her, even if it was sometimes out of encouragement or as a joke, that he would leave it to her.

At first, Qamar went with Artin to the houses of his clients. Elegant servants and trim maids would meet them at the door and lead them to large parlors, where Qamar found it hard to take in the contents of the rooms and all the luxury surrounding her. Qamar would even say to Artin that if she were left by herself in one of these houses it would take her months to find her way to the entrances and exits, and that was if she didn't get lost entirely. Artin would agree with her, with a laugh. After she had worked with him for two years, he came to rely on her to the point that he began to send her alone to many of his clients. She would show them suggested designs or draw their conceptions, which she would trim and revise in accord with her ordered imagination. She demonstrated enormous patience in absorbing the frivolity of these women, most likely related to wealth, to emptiness, to their betrayal by their men, and to moods and opinions that changed from one moment to the next. Qamar was determined to take their measurements precisely, and that was not an easy operation, in view of the many directions, orders, and prohibitions that she received from them all at once, as well as having to suspend her task if they suddenly went off to take care of something that was not urgent, or to answer the telephone, or for no reason other than that they felt bored. Nonetheless, Qamar usually achieved her goal directly, complying with the women's aspirations at the first fitting, delighted when she read satisfaction and pleasure on their faces, even if they did not acknowledge it. In this brief period in her history, Qamar learned much about the manners of servility, such as sitting on the edge of the seat, keeping her legs together, placing her hands with clipped nails in her lap, and not drinking more than one or two sips of what was offered to her, even if her throat was cracked from thirst. She also learned not to look around her as she entered or left, not to let her eyes intrude on the place, never to lift her eyes to the face of the client, to keep her eyes lowered constantly, looking at the floor or a few inches above it, as the task required. Perhaps Qamar al-Sham was not lying the day she confided to Abu Zaid that she did not remember the faces of the women whose measurements she took or whose fittings she presided over, because the scope of her view had narrowed to seeing what was necessary.

But the absence of her eyes from those around her in no way meant the absence of others' eyes from her. Artin received a call from the home of Lady Nariman Khanum, asking for Qamar to come quickly. Artin's mind was not at ease with the request; in his heart he felt that some danger lurked behind that house. Among all the houses of his clients, he did not allow Qamar to go alone to Nariman Khanum's house, and the one time he had taken her with him there, he blamed himself greatly. But Artin knew that he could not refuse any request from that house in particular, for Qasim Bey, the lady's husband, was usually behind requests of this sort. Artin realized that completely. But at the same time, he also realized that he could not prevent Qamar from going there. Qasim Bey's influence was decisive in the secret organizations of the regime or, more precisely, in their crypts. It was said that he directed the political division of state security, and his reputation had gone beyond the walls of secret cells and underground rooms to reach the ears of those who walked the earth above, something that spread terror into hearts already anxious. Among the many stories that circulated among people about Qasim Bey, which were classified as great secrets, was the story that he had personally overseen the interrogation of his sister's son, a university student who had been distributing publications from a communist cell. He had extended the fingers of the young man, who strongly resembled his uncle, on the table in front of him, and had crushed them himself with a heavy hammer, in front of young security officers and inspectors. The young man had let out a cry that rent his spirit, and then lost consciousness. When he came to, the uncle gave him another blow that crushed all the bones of his hand. Qasim Bey was among those names that have no face; he saw others, but others did not see him. And he had seen Qamar; he had seen her well, and he wanted her.

When the servant opened the outside door for her, he led her through the main room of the villa to another living room, and from there to a long hall from which branched a smaller hall. Then he took her into a room that looked like a small reception room and stood in front of another room closed with a wide wooden sliding door. He opened the door and asked her to wait inside. Qamar sat on the edge of a wide sofa, in a room with scanty furnishings compared to the furniture in the salons and the other rooms in the house, and even in the corridors. The room was an office, as it seemed. There was a wooden desk, though its surface was completely empty of papers, pens, or office supplies. Only a black telephone with a huge body crouched on a corner of it. In addition to the broad sofa there were two matching leather chairs, one behind the desk and the other in front of it. Near the sofa was a broad table with an empty ashtray on it, where Qamar put the bag in which she carried her sewing tools. The walls were all empty except for a single picture hung on one, of some map, which looked old. There were no windows or drapes; all the walls were covered in wood panels, making the room rather like a closed box. Qamar felt cold and afraid. She felt more afraid when it seemed to her that one of the walls split open to reveal what she later discovered was a door, almost hidden, from which a man with somewhat indistinct features entered the room. He sat on the sofa next to her. Qamar did not see his face clearly, since the room was rather dark. Most likely it had been designed to be that way, and most likely the single lamp, which emitted a thin yellow beam of light, had been placed to make shadows rather than light, for shadows entirely swallowed the room. Then Qamar felt she was plunging into utter darkness, as the man pushed her onto the sofa and landed on top of her. She tried to yell, but he gagged her mouth with his hand. He came close to her, his eyes shining threateningly in the yellow light, half his face draped in shadow. She stretched her arm from under his wall-like body, trying to reach her purse, so he pressed down on her with his whole being. She disappeared beneath him. Her moan, stifled under his hand, met the crash of her purse, and the sound of the box of pins rolling off the table. It was as if the sound of the pins stabbing the floor were rising from her body and her spirit, from every point in her body and her spirit.

On the nights when Qamar woke up terrified, screaming because of two protruding eyes pursuing her from a dark face, Abu Zaid would take her in his hands. He would wipe away her sweat and rain kisses on her forehead and her eyes. And he would swear to her that no harm would befall her ever again.

When Qamar decided to leave Irbid, she asked Zaid, her late husband's son, for one thing only: the set of Romeo and Juliet china that Hajj Abu Zaid had bought for her. She had picked it out piece by piece, and it was the one thing in her trousseau that she wanted to keep. Zaid did not seem to care about keeping the set, but he did want to know one thing. "Why did you marry my father?" Zaid was sure that Qamar had not married his father for his money. Besides, she could have taken any other man with no less wealth or status; in fact, she could have married a much younger man. She could have taken him, Zaid, for example, for he asked for her hand before his father did. He was prepared to divorce his wife for her sake.

Qamar arranged her few belongings, in two small suitcases, in the taxi that would take her to Amman, next to the wooden box containing her china set. When the growl of the motor broke open the space of the question suspended between them, she looked at Zaid and answered, simply, "I loved him!"

Hawwa hangs Sitt Riham's jacket in the closet. Riham is an Arabic language teacher, at the end of her twenties, but she looks younger because of her facial features, inclined to a childlike flatness. It's as if her features have not yet reached the natural size they would have in adolescence and later years, so her round eyes are still wide with recklessness and extravagant surprise, as if they are constantly eager, or experiencing things for the first time. Her nose seems like a small hook planted in the middle of her face, while her cheeks give the impression of two flat plains, not resting on round cheekbones that should have grown, as one aspect of aging or of mature beauty. With her soft brown hair left loose over her shoulders, which she sometimes lifts behind her ears to show delicate earrings in the shape of stars or small flowers or simply shiny beads, she seems hard to place. Hawwa is delighted when Riham comes to her, preceded by her musky perfume and bringing her magazines and stories that are easy to read.

Hawwa had believed that she could be something, not necessarily something splendid or very unusual, but still something important, something of value, or of some value. Never once did Hawwa entertain grand thoughts about how a man can make a difference in the world, but she wanted to make some difference, to matter for herself. She wished she had finished school. For months after she was taken out of school and her small space in the class, she continued to wake up in time for school, to inspect her faded school smock in the closet, and to feel sad as she saw the neighborhood girls carrying their bags on their small backs, hurrying so as not to miss the morning lineup, in their ironed smocks with pockets holding folded tissues and paltry amounts of money for expenses, counted out carefully, and with their braids tied in ribbons and still gleaming with moisture from broad combs dipped in water. It would have been very possible for Hawwa to earn her high school diploma, and if destiny had chosen another path for her, or another time, she would have gone on to the university. Maybe she would have worked as a teacher, like Sitt Riham. For a long time Hawwa had loved the titles of "Abla" and "Miss." Before she took off her school smock for the last time, she believed that these titles were the height of what a girl could achieve.

Riham, who slams the door of her heart in the face of many grooms, has memorized beautiful poetry about love and all that comes with it—ardor, fever, flaming desire, and welcome afflictions. It's something that raises her in Hawwa's estimation, and she considers her one of her favorite clients. When Riham sees in Hawwa's eyes a desire for talk of love, she recites to her poems of ardor and desire with boundless enthusiasm. She doesn't conceal how amazed she is at Hawwa's capacity to memorize the lines, even if she doesn't completely understand the words. What Riham doesn't know is that Hawwa sews the lines into her heart, with firm, adept stitches, and repeats them to herself, as she repeats the songs of Fairuz, which play clearly in her head. She feels that the words lift her from her own dark depths, that they take away her grief, and that they might save her at times. Hawwa doesn't know how that happens, but it doesn't seem important to her to know how. It's enough that she feels it.

Hawwa might have forgotten her small store of letters and words were it not for Sitt Qamar, who had her read the headlines of the newspaper to her every day. Sitt Qamar did not show irritation or impatience with Hawwa when her eyes moved slowly over the words, when she mouthed some of them with difficulty, when she had trouble deciphering some of the letters. She gave her time to understand, to digest the meaning, to read and reread. Sometimes she would supply letters that were missing or enigmatic, and then Hawwa would follow the path of the speech with fewer missteps, with Sitt Qamar's help. As the burden of the letters and their entanglements lessened with the passing days, the words became easier to form in her mouth, and the sentences flowed more quickly and fluently. Hawwa confided to Riham that she liked stories that described people she could see, who resembled people she knew, and who had names like those of real people; and Riham assured her that she also liked stories of people who seemed like real people.

Hawwa keeps the stories for her night, or what's left of it. And when she makes slow progress with the lines, or when she chokes on words and expressions that find no image in her head, or that touch no specific meaning or concept, then she marks them with a pencil to ask Riham about them later on.

Hawwa nibbles on one of Durrat al-Ain's apples. From the other room, her mother's intermittent snoring reaches her. She bites into the smooth, dry, fragile fruit, and its sugary sweetness mixed with acidity tickles her tongue. Fervently in love as she is, she can't keep herself from surveying the warm stream of violet, still in its bag, for the hundredth or the thousandth time. With a sideways glance, she peeks at the waves of velvet lying in temporary calm, as if she's stealing a look at something forbidden, or as if she's yearning to discover some hidden beauty in the color, open to all the possibilities of violet, with its ever-changing mix of light and shadow. She reaches into the bag with renewed excitement, trying to awaken the hidden layers of silk at the deep levels of the cloth. The rustling of the fabric together with the crackling of the bag weave a music that delights her ears. She passes her fingers over the folds of the yielding fabric, handling it with redoubled care, so as not to scratch the extravagant velvety softness. Suddenly, a strong chill runs through her body, followed by a severe trembling. Then it's as if night has fallen on the room; everything is plunged into deep black, except for the gas heater that observes her with its red burner. She looks out of the window and sees a leaden cloud with black spots, as if they are the traces of a fire inside it. The cloud seals the entire sky.

Hawwa wraps her arms around her breast and shoulders. She feels as if her heart is descending to the bottom of a cloud that's even darker.

6

THE CLOCK SHOWS 4:20. A sense that the day is evaporating hovers in the world as it seeps into the room from the window. Nonetheless, the end of the day seems far away—or perhaps it's desirable that it remain far off.

The leaden gray cloud, with its many spreading burn marks, breaks up in the sky. But the sky is still gloomy. To the same extent that Hawwa's anticipated happiness is urgent in her spirit, fear just as urgently grabs her heart by the lapels, spreading inside it a confining cloud, withholding its water and its hope. The cloud is formed from the surprises of time. It spreads out gigantically, building up, until at last it scatters. Even so, it leaves behind a feeling of imprisonment and siege, of dark night even at midday, lurking heavily, deep inside, making the soul tumble down, deep down.

The ring of her cell phone shatters the quiet settled in the room. The picture of her grandson Abdallah at three months fills the screen, and the voice of her daughter Aya comes on the other end of the line.

Aya had waited seven years before a boy came at last. Three girls preceded him, Hanin, Dalia, and Jana. They surround Hawwa with love, tenderness, and gentle kisses, filling her world with stickiness that doesn't bother her, flavored with mulberries and strawberries, from packets of ice cream, kisses planted on her face by small, moist lips. They have soft hair hanging over their shoulders, and colored ribbons; sandals of pink, lilac, and red, with gold and silver buckles; little purses, over-ornamented, that she buys for them; dresses with wide, ruffled skirts; and dolls they put in their grandmother's lap so that she will clothe them in the most splendid dresses. Hawwa is at the height of her happiness when they gather around her at the sewing machine, watching her foot press on the pedal with exciting speed as her hands guide the piece of cloth under the needle that runs atop it. When she lifts her foot from the pedal and cuts the thread at the last stitch, their eyes shine as they watch her putting the final, magical touches on the dress with her hand needle—like lace around the collar or sleeve cuffs, or a few beads on the breast, or a soft ruffle at the hem, or a belt around the waist. They express their astonishment with cries of "Allaaah!" over the obvious difference that a few beads could make, or a strip of damask lace, or a belt from a leftover tape of rhinestones. Their mouths gape and their eyes open wide as they inspect their dolls, whose new dresses give off a special scent, a mixture of warmth, yearning, orange wedges, chestnuts crackling in the oven roaster, the dominant aroma of rosewater on platters of rice pudding, ready at any time—a scent they smell only in their grandmother's house. They assert time after time that their grandmother is something really great. When they come with their mother to visit her, Hawwa senses their feet running in the street as they get close to her door. When she opens it for them, they fling themselves into her open arms, big enough for them all, and no one is left out.

During the time when Aya was yearning for a boy, intensely, the girls were oblivious to their mother's desire for a male, paying no attention to the fact that she nursed them meagerly, from heartbreak. They were happy with the treasures they found with their grandmother, who made them feel beloved, with the greatest love there could be. Throughout the passing years, Hawwa took the position of an observer with respect to Aya's longing for a boy. She did not console her or comfort her. In any case, the advent of a boy didn't mean much to her, even though she did not let her daughter see that; her daughter whose spirit was consumed with worry when she became pregnant and when she gave birth. While Aya feared that a boy would never come, Hawwa feared only that Aya's girls would be lost.

"How's Grandma?" Aya is asking about Rabia.

"Sleeping," answers Hawwa, before adding the obligatory, "Thanks be to God for all things." Aya isn't very concerned about her grandmother; her question is one of those things that roll unconsciously off the tongue. When she visits her mother, she looks at Rabia, crumpled on the bed, as if she were a stranger to her, ugly and pitiable. She doesn't embrace her or kiss her; nor does she address her directly with any words, as a form of interaction with a living person. When Hawwa asks Aya to help her carry Rabia to the bathroom so she can bathe her, she refuses. She's disgusted, she tells her; so Hawwa has to carry her in her arms, obviously weighed down, her back and shoulders collapsing, while Rabia clings to her in terror. Aya does not object to watching Hawwa feed Rabia, or to handing her a wet wipe—at arm's length, and showing great disgust— to wipe her genitals or her buttocks. But she was never able to stand being close to Naifa, her great-grandmother.

Aya called Naifa "the ghoul." One day Aya saw the ghoul— who was riddled with Alzheimer's, all spark of understanding extinguished and her brain completely eaten away—kneeling on Hawwa's chest, choking her with her two strong hands and growling in terror, in a voice quarried from the depths of her age, until life nearly left Hawwa's eyes completely. Her eyes were protruding as if they were watching her spirit leave her and bid her farewell. Aya did not try to save her mother from the ghoul; she simply left the house and began running in the lanes of the camp. She kept on running aimlessly from lane to lane, not wanting to stop—hoping she would reach the end of life at a run, or hoping all of life would come to an end. It was something that wouldn't console her.

Hawwa reminds her of lunch: "Don't forget about tomorrow, Yamma! I'm making stuffed squash for the girls!"

Aya contents herself with an "Mmmmm!" to confirm.

Hawwa tries to seem more cheerful as she asks Aya, "How's little Abboud?"

When Hawwa calls Aya or when Aya calls her, the mother longs for her daughter, she's eager for her. But when Aya's voice comes to her, extinguished at all levels of feeling, Hawwa senses that her daughter is at the end of the universe, that she's not walking toward her except to distance herself from her. Aya doesn't talk on the telephone much. If she does, she doesn't say anything important, or anything of value, or even anything ordinary, the kind of thing that's said between married daughters who live outside the camp, in the modest suburbs of Amman, and their mothers languishing forever in the camp, even if their ambition transcends the miserable neighborhoods and the lanes bordered by sewer water.

Hawwa doesn't know what Aya wants, but she does know what Aya does not want. When her daughter wanted a boy, it was only because she did not want a girl. Aya would say to Hawwa that she hated herself and that she did not want to be the way she was. Hawwa didn't know if her daughter loved her, her own mother, with the great love that should exist between mothers and daughters, and she was afraid to ask. For her part, Hawwa loved Aya with all the power she had, and protected her as much as she could, with all the tools— and they were meager—that she possessed. But that, as it seemed, wasn't enough. Hawwa had not known if her Aya fell in love, or if she wished for a man, or if her delinquent imaginings were filled with the neighbors' son, of if she yearned for a smell compounded of tobacco and fresh shaving cream and cold cologne, or if she surrendered to some secret feeling, sweet and tickling, or if she was carried away by an emotion that dangled from a high branch of a forbiddingly tall tree. When she walked beside Aya in the street, Hawwa saw the eyes of men and boys following her daughter. But Aya's eyes remained preoccupied, like her feelings. When Aya looked at others it was as if she saw faces that were empty, their features wiped away; nothing was ever reflected in her eyes, as if they were dark glass or a clouded mirror. Aya was a beautiful girl. Even after four pregnancies her beauty was still apparent, and her body was firm and compact. She did not resemble her mother except for her light complexion; from her father she took his tall stature, although her form was more harmonious than his. Her eyes were changeable in color, between a mellow green and a cloudy green and gray, with a stroke of sharpness. They were like Naifa's eyes.

Aya was hard. Her spirit was parched, and had been ever since she was girl. All of Hawwa's efforts to bring tenderness to it and soften it had been useless. Hawwa took the lashes from Nazmi's belt, in his seasons of masculine display and viciousness, in her daughter's place. She covered her with her entire body. And when her daughter's body grew and her mother's body became too small to be a blanket spread above her, Hawwa spread her spirit around her daughter, enveloping her completely. What frightened Hawwa was that her daughter did not have any compassion for her, her mother; for when Nazmi's blows rained down on them, splitting Hawwa's flesh and shaking her bones, little Aya would gather her limbs and shrink under her mother, almost completely sheltered from the flood of lashes pouring over them.

Aya would stare levelly into Nazmi's eyes, through a small opening left by Hawwa's arm over her face. He would yell at her to lower her eyes, but her gaze would remain fixed on him, challenging, so all the rancor in the world descended into his arm and was translated into greater violence, turning the blows from the belt into hot skewers that pierced the layers of Hawwa's flesh and bones and spirit. Nazmi kept yelling, "Lower your eyes, girl!" His hoarse voice mixed with the stings of the belt, which tore the air before lighting raging fires in her mother's body. Hawwa would ask her to take her eyes off Nazmi, at least out of mercy for her, but Aya's eyes would remain fixed on him, not closing or blinking or moving away from him, for a moment that was almost eternal. When Nazmi would go crazy and use both of his feet to push the blanket of flesh far from Aya, his daughter's eyes would still be pegged on him, stubbornly. And when Hawwa would try to spread herself over her daughter's form, to cover her again, Aya herself pushed her away, to confront Nazmi alone. Her eyes were sharp and dry, drained of water and light, pouring into his trembling eyes. She took pleasure in enflaming him, raising the degree of his ferocity until it reached its limit, while Hawwa moaned at a distance, begging her in vain to lower her eyes: "I kiss your hands, Yamma, lower your eyes! For God's sake, Mama's begging, look away! I kiss your feet, Yamma, look down!"

When Nazmi was finished with her and collapsed on the floor, exhausted, Aya would get up as if she had not been shattered. But Hawwa saw with painful clarity that a slice was being cut from her daughter's spirit, day after day. Nonetheless, Hawwa continued to be a blanket for Aya, even when Aya threw her off.

When Yusuf came to ask for Aya's hand, she agreed with no hesitation. A client of Hawwa's had suggested Aya to his mother. Aya did not know him and had not seen him before, and she hadn't even spoken with him until after the Fatiha was read from the Qur'an to formalize the engagement. Hawwa asked her to think it over, since she was still only twenty and had just earned a teaching diploma from one of the mid-level university colleges. Hawwa suggested that she find work first. But Aya said that she didn't want to work, and that if it had been left to her, she wouldn't have studied at all, maybe. The truth was that Hawwa had been frightened when Nazmi referred to school as a waste of years for a girl, and said that the best thing for Aya would be to learn sewing like her mother, when he saw his eight-year-old daughter sewing a fabric remnant with ease and skill. Hawwa immediately snatched the needle from her daughter's hand and stuck it into her own palm, making the blood spurt. Aya understood then that she would not leave school early.

For Aya to accept her fiancé, it was enough that he had a neutral disposition and personality, neither making others like him nor driving them away completely; that he enjoyed a physique that was not flabby; and that most of his teeth were free of decay. Yusuf was a schoolteacher, an occupation that guaranteed that he would maintain the minimum of daily cleanliness, at the beginning of the day and the end of it, so he did not come to her with the remains of grease sticking to his mustache or with his face oily and sweaty. He had no beard or mustache, and he wore glasses with thin frames and small lenses. He contented himself with antiperspirant as a scent; he wore white, blue, and beige shirts, usually striped, with pants of polyester-blend broadcloth. He wore formal shoes, black and dark brown, with thin laces, and insisted on polishing them with Kiwi Wax polish. He taught mathematics in a school run by UNRWA in Hussain Camp; he lived in a reasonable apartment with reasonable rent in al-Nuzha, and he was planning to build a detached house on a piece of land he owned jointly with his three brothers on the airport road.

With her marriage, Aya would enter a house empty of the smell of fabric, piled up and proclaiming the odors of camp people, speaking of their rationed dreams. In her house, she would not be forced to get up in the middle of the night or at the end of the night, and all the long nights, at the screams of Naifa, and her pounding, kicking, and beating of everything that fell into her hand. Naifa's screams pierced Aya's essence, full of fury and hatred, even after Hawwa bought her and Qais earmuffs, in the shape of earphones that covered the ear with a thick layer of fur, which they wore when they slept to stop the noise. Nor would Aya wait at the end of the day, at the end of every day, in the hope that Nazmi would not return to the house, preceded by his obscene tongue, which distributed filthy insults to the neighborhood boys playing soccer in the street, before coming in, throwing his greasy, filthy body down on the couch, and asking Hawwa, who was compelled to lift her foot from the pedal of the sewing machine, to get his food ready.

Aya had long wished for Nazmi's death, often seeking his killing in the bloodiest way. She would borrow an imagined scene from a film, of a car going very fast down a street and hitting him, so that he flew several yards into the air before falling on the windshield, smeared with blood. His face with its wandering glances would be flattened on the shattered glass. Then she would sketch a more expressionist scene, of a truck loaded with broad, jagged, heavy rocks rattling down the street coming down to Baqa'a from Sweileh, like a train picking up speed, then rolling over him and squashing him utterly, until it would be hard to distinguish the features of his face, which would have buckled completely. But the most beautiful scene her imagination could fashion involved her, without the least feeling of guilt or hesitation: she saw herself carrying an electric saw and slicing his face into two halves with it, his terrified eyes remaining open even when the halves of his face fell down on either side.

When she married, Aya believed that she would not seek Nazmi's annihilation or wish for it after that day. But his annihilation continued to take every disgusting form of death in her head. Then, when Nazmi divorced Hawwa, Aya's desire to eradicate him became pernicious.

Aya believed that marriage would make her happy, or at least less vengeful and full of hate. But her misery worsened. Her new house did not relieve her, though it differed completely from the house in the camp. Nor did her husband, the UNRWA schoolteacher intent on his personal cleanliness. Nor did her three daughters, who threw themselves at her, seeking her embrace, without finding her warm arms around them. Nor did her little boy, even, who came to her much desired.

"When are they coming?" Aya is asking her mother about her uncle Ayid and her brother Qais. Hawwa's heart contracts. She glues her ear to the cell phone, seeking some reassurance from her daughter. She feels her feet beginning to freeze, and she moves closer to the gas heater. She answers in a voice that's nearly a whisper, "They're going to come at night . . . after the Isha prayer."

Hawwa presses the button to end the call without feeling reassured. Aya's voice leaves her as it had come: listless, thin, as if on the point of death, emotionally.

From the window, Hawwa stares at the calm sky with scattered clouds, the icy winds having died down. She tumbles into another cloud that's gathering within her, a mixture of fear and frost and anxieties, which grows heavier and ever larger.

For long months after she was married, Hawwa had continued to go back to her family's house almost every day, even during the worst of the cold, the rain, the snowflakes, the icy morning air, and the sparse light at the beginning of the day. She would heat the water on the kerosene heater for the bath, and bathe Ayid. At thirteen years of age, he had a thin frame, still weak, cowering by nature, with bowed shoulders and a triangular, mouse-like head. When he grew up he became much taller but his back did not straighten completely, and his shoulders stayed close to his chest. He also continued to gnaw at people and places with his eyes, which would rise cautiously from bottom to top, before sinking to the bottom again. It was something that made him sly and malicious, even though he was still a coward.

Hawwa made a large bag out of oilcloth that she put around Ayid's mattress, so it was not much trouble for her to clean the mattress. She just used a soapy towel or a loofah moistened with soap and detergent, which she passed over the plastic surface to wipe up traces of dampness from the urine, before wiping away the soap and water with a dry rag. When the oilcloth wore out, from time to time, and the mattress would be sodden as its foam held the piss, she was forced to sew a new oilcloth bag. But the real tragedy was washing the covers, especially on winter mornings, when the sun was impounded or imprisoned behind clouds, or on days of rainstorms. Then the water would stagnate in the quilts and blankets for days, storing up mustiness and leaking rot. Hawwa suggested to her mother that she take Ayid to the doctor, to stop up his "faucet of piss," as she described the situation. But Ayid refused to go, although that did not mean that he felt any embarrassment or shame over the nearly daily flood of urine. Even when Hawwa warned him to drink less juice during the day, and to avoid drinking anything after 8:00 in the evening, he continued gulping down liters of artificially sweetened juice during the day and three bottles of Pepsi—at least—in the evening. He bought them secretly, and would bury the empty bottles in one of the pots of dead plants on the roof.

Hawwa didn't know when Ayid stopped wetting his bed, or when her father stopped rending his body with the strap. She no longer covered her brother with her body after her marriage, as she reached her family's house in the morning after Mousa had left. In any case, it was certain that the strap, its leather grown soft and worn, did not retire until after her father died, when it lay on a shelf in the closet like a sluggish snake, whose skin could no longer be heard to slither. Neither could Hawwa determine how she had been selected to be the blanket for her brother, to cover him with her soft, girlish flesh and fat. All she knew was that, from the beginning, Afaf and Sajida did not intervene to rescue her. When they married, it was as if they had rescued themselves from Mousa, Rabia,

Naifa, and Ayid, and even from Lutfi, who faced the walls and floor of the house more than he faced the people in it, living in the house as if he did not live there. Afaf and Sajida cut themselves off from the camp after marriage, as if they had not lived there, or as if the place that had ravished their bodies and spirits basically did not exist. Naturally, it was not to be expected that they would make peace with it, or would try to do so. If it so happened that they visited their mother because they had to, sometimes because they were compelled to, especially on obligatory occasions or in calamities, then they sat at the edges of the place and talked around the edge of subjects, eating very little of what was offered to them. They kept their many children close to them, not allowing them to explore the house in the camp or the camp itself. Thus they prevented (or so they imagined, unconsciously) any continuation of their feelings in the place, or any accumulation of emotions.

Afaf's husband worked as the driver of a passenger bus for a public-transportation company in Irbid, so she lived on the edge of the city. Sajida lived in the town of Dulail, in al-Zarqa, where her husband worked as a supervisor on a cattle farm belonging to a dairy company. The distance between each of their places and the family home was one reason for their marital happiness, if not the only reason. But Sajida and Afaf did not cut themselves off completely from Baqa'a Camp, or from one neighborhood in it, which they considered bearable; they still came to Hawwa's house in the camp every so often, carrying bags of cheap fabric for her to sew for them. Hawwa would ask them if they had stopped at the family house, and they would shake their heads to say no, without being afflicted by any pang of conscience for shirking the traditional family duty.

Hawwa stopped bathing Ayid when he turned fourteen. It happened suddenly, the day she lifted the blanket in the morning and saw before her a tall young man with thick hair on his legs and arms, the shadow of a mustache, and a light beard scattered on a face full of pimples. She told her mother that Ayid had become a man. Rabia answered her, chewing on a piece of dry bread and not looking at this man he had become: "And a pisser." But Hawwa did continue cleaning his mattress and washing his blankets and carrying them to the roof to hang them out even when she was pregnant with Aya, and after she gave birth to her. Then she stopped a few months before giving birth to her son, Qais. Her morning was growing short and her tasks were doubling. She had to get Nazmi's breakfast, set the house in order quickly, and then set the food for the evening on the fire, to half cook. She had to clean Aya, then go to her family's house, carrying Aya and her swollen belly, to clean Ayid's mattress and wash his blankets, before setting off on the bus with Aya and Aya's diaper bag and her belly that cut off her breath, heading for Sitt Qamar's house in Sweileh.

Ayid was fifteen when he left school. Rabia didn't want him to leave, as she was certain that he would not succeed at anything, and that even in the worst case school would pull him off the street. But Ayid, who was never enthusiastic about classes or lessons, wanted to work as a bus conductor. He dreamed about the dozens of green dinars he would hold in his hand, lined up lengthwise, the way conductors held money; and he dreamed about a red package of Marlboros, the top visible from the pocket of his shirt. He would show off his cigarettes in front of the government employees and university students, squeezed into the uncomfortable seats, who made do with smoking Gold Star or Philadelphia cigarettes, which crackled audibly when the tobacco shavings in them burned. He also dreamed of female university and college students, the overpowering scents of their cheap perfume and face powder floating around them as they got on the bus or stepped off it, when he would collide with the protrusions of their bodies, intending to make it appear unintentional. Ayid did work as a conductor for more than two years, on the route between Sweileh and the University of Jordan. He did carry many dinars, folding and unfolding them lengthwise in his hand, moving one or two from the daily take to his own pocket. The girls complained about him and some spat in his face when he rubbed against them or felt their breasts with his hand, blaming a lurch that knocked him off balance when the bus stopped suddenly. And when the complaints multiplied, a university student picked him up by the collar, like a mouse, and dragged him from the back of the bus to the front. Then he opened the door while the bus was moving and threw him out. Ayid rolled out onto the dusty sidewalk and from there fell down into a rocky streambed, without any interference from the driver, who did not slow down the bus. It appeared that the driver had decided to get rid of Ayid after the receipts began to come up short by more than one or two dinars a day.

His broken leg took three months to heal, and during that time his dream of green dinars was lost—dinars he would extend lengthwise, never tiring of flattening and smoothing them with his fingers, riffling them with the nail of his little finger, which he had let grow long and had filed for this purpose. For two years after that, Ayid moved among a number of vegetable stores in the camp market, sweeping up the peelings and rotten fruit, and sorting the crates and cartons. He would arrange the mounds of vegetables and fruit on the inclined stand, and shoo away the flies. Then he worked with an itinerant vegetable seller who roamed through the neighborhoods of Sweileh with his pickup truck, calling out his fruits and vegetables and their prices from a loudspeaker. When a woman would stop him from a window or at the door of the house, Ayid would go ahead of Abu Isam, the driver and owner of the pickup, so he would have the first chance to examine the woman, who might ask for several pounds of tomatoes or cucumbers while she was still fixing her hijab or the flowing prayer veil she wore over her housedress. Often his spirit would be filled when the morning breezes lifted the prayer veil like an umbrella, revealing two well-fleshed arms perspiring from housework and cooking, and a breast full from much childbearing, while in front of her he fondled the eggplants she wanted to inspect, for pickling or for stuffing, in a way that was openly and crudely suggestive. It made one of the women throw an eggplant in his face, once.

When Abu Isam set Ayid down on the road after less than a year, after his excesses with women in houses empty of their men, in the mornings, had exceeded all bounds, he shuffled among a number of jobs. He worked in a watermelon stand, and then in the warehouse of a mill that distributed coffee, za'atar, and spices wholesale to supermarkets, and then as a guard for housing under construction. When he had been kicked out everywhere, Lutfi took him to work with him in the garage. Ayid didn't show any desire to work, finding it hard to perform even the simplest mechanical tasks. The boss at the garage complained to Lutfi about his brother: he was lazy and stupid, and he complained a lot and ate a lot. So Lutfi interceded at last with Abu Ubada, asking that Ayid work with him, to oversee the lot he had set up for selling used cars. Abu Ubada owed Lutfi a favor because, through the garage where he worked, Lutfi did all the maintenance and repair work for the cars on the lot.

The car lot had become twice as large after Abu Ubada added another piece of land to it on the edge of the camp, and Ayid thought that it was his promised paradise. Aside from the basic job of running the lot and organizing the reception and distribution of the cars, Abu Ubada allowed him to set up a little stand on it to sell coffee, tea, and cigarettes to the sellers and agents, and he took "gratuities" from everyone. At night, before the watchman came, he would inspect the cars whose owners had left the keys with him, as well as those whose doors he developed a talent for opening with a metal wire. He searched them for shillings, ten-piaster coins, stuffed dolls, cassette tapes, combs, hairbrushes, buckles, and medicine packages, on the seats and under them and in the inside pockets and in the trunks. He took everything that came to hand, putting it all in a bag and sorting it at home. One time he came across a bottle of arak that the owner had forgotten in the trunk of his car; he gulped it all down the same night, and when the watchman came he found him stretched out on the ground near the stand, a thin strip of human flesh, disturbing the peace of the night with his snoring.

Ayid's greatest find, however, was a videotape he came across stuffed beneath a carpet under the seat of a Mercedes. The VHS tape had no writing or description of its contents, so he was surprised when he watched it at a friend's house. It was a home videotape, copied from the original. The taping had been made, as it seemed, from a single fixed angle, in a room that had nothing in it but a wide sofa and a tall side mirror fixed to the wall, as if the room had been arranged for the purpose of filming. A man and a woman undressed in front of the camera, completely aware of the angle from which they were being filmed. Then they enlaced their bodies, standing, shaking with exaggerated enthusiasm on the part of the man, and with some affected shyness on the part of the woman, whose eyes moved between the camera and the mirror, watching their bodies as they embraced. The man was in his thirties, and his slim, firm figure and the clothes he took off piece by piece indicated that he was a man of means. He was giving instructions to his woman, whose body also showed that she was from a home of ease and affluence. He was telling her how to stand, so that their desire would be completely in the lens of the camera, as they rubbed together, intentionally refraining from complete union, delaying extinguishing their fire in their own burning water. Then the man gently pushed his girl onto the bed, descending over her, so the camera would record the surging of their bodies and their hissing sound (although the clarity of the picture and the sound was undercut by darkness and distortion in some parts of the tape), until they dissolved into an enormous tremor, repressing their final cry.

Ayid refused his friend's suggestion that he make copies of the tape to sell. He wanted to keep it for himself for some time, until he decided what to do about it. Two days later, Abu Ubada's white Audi stopped at the entrance to the lot, and Ayid ran to meet him. Abu Ubada praised his good administration of the lot, which he had heard about from many people. Then he leaned over him, whispering through the steam of the cup of tea Ayid had brought him that perhaps Ayid had something he would like to give him. Ayid understood what Abu Ubada was alluding to, so he gave him the videotape, which he was keeping in a locked drawer in the little supply cabinet inside his stand. He swore on his father's soul that he had come across it by chance in a car left open by its owner, and that he had thought about destroying it, so it wouldn't fall into the hands of the wrong person. Abu Ubada laughed, praising what he described as "his trustworthiness." Then he gave him ten dinars as a reward, and asked him to forget the matter of the tape completely. As he got up to leave, Abu Ubada turned to Ayid and said, "So, a person who cares about his honor doesn't make a scandal of himself. . . . Isn't that so, Ayid, or am I wrong?"

"You're far from any shame, boss!" responded Ayid.

Then Abu Ubada said frankly and directly to Ayid that the cars that entered the lot belonged to him, to Abu Ubada. "But the shillings, the ten-piaster coins, the half liters of arak are licit for you." He patted Ayid's shoulder meaningfully, and went off with the tape folded under the brown abaya he was wearing over his formal suit. (Abu Ubada had taken off his Afghani clothes a few years after he arrived in Jordan. In the beginning he changed to a robe like those from the Gulf; then he adopted a Western suit with an abaya over it, with a checkered headcloth and a headband, which added a touch of the sheikh to his appearance.) Within two weeks, copies of the videotape were being sold on carpets on the sides of the streets. The man on the indecent tape was a well-known television announcer, and the woman was a young singer who turned out to be his wife.

Ayid married his cousin Asma. Rabia thought that marriage would "make him grow up." Then she discovered that "a wife and all those kids" would not in fact fix his situation. His money was meager; if he had any he wasted it outside the house, and if he did bring any of it home Asma wasted it by her poor management. Ayid and his wife lived with Rabia in the family house in the camp, now empty of Mousa and the girls; it was a temporary arrangement that quickly became permanent, after the arrival of two sons and two daughters that Asma spilled out, one after the other. And even though Rabia was the one who pushed for his marriage, and even though she had chosen Asma for him herself—she wouldn't find anyone better than her sister's daughter—still, she was always complaining about her. She was lazy and dumb, just like her husband, she said to Hawwa. Besides, she had "a wicked tongue." But Rabia did not condemn Asma's very sharp tongue. She first showed it when she was a bride, and from that day on her insolence to Ayid did not abate. Ayid's silence, in response, also seemed understandable and expected. When Ayid would pounce on her, in his frequent rages, lifting his hand to bring it down on her face, Asma would stand in front of him, challenging, all her features bulging: "Hit me! Hit me, if you're a man!" And Ayid's hand would stay suspended in the air, before falling to his side in submission. Then, when the door of the house slammed behind him, Asma would open her hands and lament to Rabia: "That's all we needed!" It had been only a few days after their marriage when Asma burst out of their bedroom, about to wail loudly. Ayid attacked her from behind and threw her on the ground, covering her mouth and nose with his hand. When she calmed down, he lifted his hand and implored her, "Be quiet!" Then he put a ten-dinar bill in her hand and went out, without lifting his eyes to his bride or to Rabia. Asma put the ten dinars in her breast pocket and reproached Rabia: "God forgive you, Auntie! Why didn't you tell me your son pisses in bed!"

What Hawwa had feared did happen: Ayid drew her son, Qais, to him, despite her desperate, heroic efforts to attract him to her, or to Lutfi. With a great deal of strain and pressure, Qais finished high school and emerged with a certificate showing he had taken, and failed, the cumulative Tawjihi exam. Abu Ubada had at last thrown Ayid out, after less than eight years at the car lot. Once again Ayid had betrayed his trust, and this time Abu Ubada had not pardoned his "crime," as he termed it.

Two of Abu Ubada's men had stopped in front of Ayid's stand one dark winter night, asking him about the four bags of powder he had found in the spare tire of the silver Hyundai. Ayid swore on his father's soul that he didn't know a thing about the bags they were talking about. One of the men plunged a short, stout, serrated knife into Ayid's right thigh, then he pulled him close and hissed in his face, "Hajj Abu Ubada sends you his greetings, and informs you that the next time the knife'll go somewhere else." Ayid collapsed on the ground and the other man stuffed his mouth full of dirt, until at last he used his sand-encrusted tongue to tell them where the bags were hidden.

Ayid stayed in the house for several long months, living off of the allowance that Lutfi gave his mother. Rabia herself went to Lutfi to beg him to find a job for his brother; but it didn't seem that Ayid wanted to work in the workshop where his brother had become the one and only boss, with the blessing of his father-in-law and the man's two sons. Nonetheless, Ayid did not refuse the money his brother put in his hand from time to time, money that eventually became an established right. He drifted among dozens of taxis, which he rented "at a premium" from their owners, using them to practice his hobbies—harassing women and girls, whom he stopped for selectively and spied on from his mirror when they were secluded in the back seat, and harassing other taxi drivers on the streets. He squandered most of what he made in a day in paying for fines and violations, as well as the expenses of many breakdowns he caused in the cars.

When Qais went to him, Ayid opened the door wide for him in welcome. Qais had already become attached to Ayid's daughter Hind, and it was an attachment that suited Ayid very well; he engaged her to Qais, over the objections of Asma and Hawwa. Qais was not yet twenty, and Hawwa knew that Ayid wouldn't take him for his daughter "for nothing." She discovered that the engagement was going to cost her half a taxi. He approached Qais with a plan to buy a cab, which they would use by turns. He suggested that his nephew make the down payment, and that they share the installment payments from the income. Nazmi washed his hands of the matter, telling his son frankly that since his uncle had given him his daughter, he should be the one to pay him. Hawwa braced herself and went to Lutfi, begging him not to leave Qais to Ayid. But Lutfi did as he always did: he said, "It's no use," and gave her three thousand dinars, the down payment asked for the car, so she could give the money to Qais.

Hawwa loved Lutfi; he was a good man. As a boy he had been almost self-sufficient, "minding his own business"; as an ambitious young man he had almost supported himself, "minding his own business"; and as a capable man he did support himself, also "minding his own business." He gave without great liberality, and he loved without flinging himself on the one he loved. His presence in the house wasn't repellent or tyrannical. He had a low voice and light, almost imperceptible movements—traits that might have seemed strange in view of his huge physique, which far surpassed the build of his father or his brother Ayid. But perhaps the greatest surprise was that he did not spread out in any space he occupied. Never once did he intervene to rescue Ayid, or to take his father's lashes in his place, or some of them. When his father would take the strap to Hawwa on most mornings, and to Afaf and Sajida on most evenings, Lutfi seemed truly pained, and a tear might almost be seen trickling from his eye. Nonetheless, he would remain standing at a relatively safe distance, one that allowed him to watch and feel pain without separating his father and his sisters, and without taking any of the blows in their place, or any of the kicks or any trace of them. Then he began to go to work early in the morning, before everyone, so as not to find himself forced, as a kind and powerless young man, to watch and feel pain at a distance. He also began to come home at the end of the evening, careful not to let his eyes meet the eyes of his sisters, still whimpering after their bodies had taken their full measure of pounding. He went to work energetically and came back exhausted and hungry. He would concentrate on eating, with an appetite, and at the end of the night he would remain piled up in front of the television until he fell asleep, half dead. He didn't talk to anyone and no one talked to him, except when necessary. "Give me five dinars!" Mousa would demand without looking at him, and Lutfi would give him the five dinars, also looking away. In the beginning Lutfi tried not to seem quick to respond, resisting Mousa's domineering requests, arguing and delaying, with some evasion at times. But in the end he found some rest in submitting. "We need ten dinars," Rabia would tell him, and he would hand her the money, without caring to listen to the reasons that made her ask—"because of the electric bill," or "we need to buy kerosene for the heater," or any other reason. It didn't matter much to him to know what it was. He was in charge of buying their monthly supply of meat and chicken, and he didn't complain. Then the responsibility of paying the electricity and water bills was left up to him and he also didn't object, as long as he could keep his distance from the suffering within the house.

Lutfi worked as a mechanic's boy in Abu Karam's garage, and he showed remarkable skill and speed in learning the trade. Then, as a young man, he became a mechanic in the shop, someone sought out by name by owners bringing in their cars for repair, as he could put his hand on the source of the problem at the initial diagnosis. Then he became a supervisor in the shop, and Abu Karam himself asked him to marry his daughter Sahar, who was divorced from her cousin after less than a year of marriage. Abu Karam had two sons, who were less than enthusiastic about working in their father's shop. Karam, the older, was the more fastidious, disliking the dark atmosphere in the shop, the acid sweat and greasy faces of the boys working there, the clatter of metal, the noise of air pumps, the hammering, the rattle of the motors, the exhaust fumes, and the oil and water spewed out by the internal parts of the cars, although he acknowledged that the shop had funded his expensive education in America. For his part, the younger one, Ashraf, toyed with foolish commercial projects, and his father, Abu Karam, was often forced to intervene, to rein him in or to rescue him.

In marrying his only daughter to Lutfi, Abu Karam guaranteed that the garage would continue to yield enough to fund his family, his two sons, their foolhardy ambitions, their families, and their expensive life in Amman. Abu Karam installed his son-in-law in an apartment he built above his house in Kamaliya. His sons showed no enthusiasm for their sister's husband, but Lutfi simply knew how to neutralize them from the start, bringing them over to his side by caring personally for each of their cars and for their wives' cars, assuming all of the maintenance and repair work himself and installing all kinds of accessories. He also became known for his lavish banquets, to which he invited Abu Karam and his sons and their cousins. He even built a large room on the roof, almost a banquet hall, with a kitchen and a guest bathroom, which he furnished with two sets of sofas and chairs and tables, and a huge television screen that he hung on one wall. The men of Abu Karam's family would gather there to watch the

European league matches and the World Cup championship games, during which they never ceased drinking tea and coffee and smoking water pipes, which Lutfi himself prepared for them, inspecting the coals between the shouts over one possible goal and another, and making himself indispensable among people who did not resemble him at all.

When Lutfi stopped his car in front of his family's house in the camp, with his wife and their three children, he brought a bundle of new ten-piaster coins of brightly shining white metal, carefully packed in a paper wrapper, almost like a piece of chocolate. He would break it open and distribute the coins among the neighborhood kids who gathered around him, guaranteeing at least that none of them would run a nail along the sides of his dark-green Mercedes, out of rancor or spite, or intentionally hit one of its two side mirrors with his elbow and knock it off.

Lutfi believed that money solved the hardest problems, and it was a belief that proved correct in most situations. After the death of his father, he began to give his mother a monthly allowance. Later, when Rabia came to him because she wanted to marry Ayid, to pull him out of the arms of a gypsy dancer he was running after, he gave her a thousand dinars for the dower payment for Asma, he bought the couple a bedroom set, and he put five hundred dinars in Ayid's pocket for the wedding expenses. Then, when Fawziya, the wife of his uncle Khalil, sought him out to find an "arrangement" for his grandmother Naifa, he stepped in with the force of money.

Fawziya lived with Naifa in her family home in the camp, and she inherited from her the craft of making Nabulsi cheese. When Naifa was fully rational and at the height of her power, none of the women of comparable age and experience in the camp and its environs could rival her in her trade. For her part, skillful Fawziya remained true to Naifa's original tools and to the flavor of her delicious cheese, which betrayed the luxury of the ingredients and gave an overpowering sense of the village, of the home. When Alzheimer's took up residence in Naifa's mind, so that her reason atrophied and her sense failed her, it took people some time before they discovered that Umm Mousa's cheese, which was unlike any other cheese, was not really made by Umm Mousa. Even when in the end the reputation did pass on to Fawziya, it was still known as "Umm Mousa's cheese," and that brought fortune knocking on Fawziya's door the way it had in Naifa's days, and even more. Fawziya now complained to Lutfi about his grandmother's "crazy stunts." One time she attacked her with the knife used to cut the molded cheese and would have plunged it into her neck, if it weren't for the mercy of God and His protection at the last minute, as she put it, placing her hand on her breast, asking our Lord's forgiveness and thanking him and praising him. Another time Naifa spat into the pot of milk heating on the fire. But the real catastrophe happened the day Naifa peed on one of the cheese molds. "And that's what we live on, Lutfi. . . . Can you accept your grandma pissing on what supports us?" Fawziya struck one hand on the other, warning, in a whisper, that in the end it would mean the loss of her kids' income. She spoke as if she were afraid that her voice would creep through the flimsy walls of the house to the people in the street, and then they would shun her cheese because of the mere thought that it had been contaminated by anything impure.

Lutfi proposed to his brother Ayid that he take in his grandmother, saying that he would assume the expenses of her care and tending. But Asma refused. She flew in Ayid's face and threatened him in front of Rabia, who chose to remain silent, though she seemed to support the position of her angry daughter-in-law. Asma said that the moment that Naifa stepped on the threshold she would leave the house to him and take the children. "By God, even if Lutfi gave us her weight in gold!" she declared firmly. Nor did she neglect to add a gesture, aiming the middle finger of each hand at Ayid's face: "I don't need one more person pissing all over the place!" As expected, Naifa was Hawwa's fate. Lutfi didn't make any effort to convince her, as Hawwa couldn't help feeling compassion for her grandmother, to the point of crying hot tears. That amazed Lutfi, and dug up an old shame buried deep in his memory, of the day he had remained in the bathroom, putting off coming out, when his ears were pierced with the sound of Naifa's shoe burning Hawwa's tender flesh, and when his sister's screams from the depths of her pain pierced his heart. Nazmi did not object to bringing Naifa into his house, personally coming to an agreement with Lutfi about the financial compensation attendant on accommodating her. Nazmi said that Naifa needed a separate space for her care that his little house could not provide her, so they moved to a larger house in the camp. Hawwa thought that the new house might be her grandmother's one gift to her, not only because it was larger, but also because it was at the end of a lane. That meant that the windows on two sides, at least, opened onto the street, so that it wasn't besieged to the point of choking by houses surrounding it on all four sides. Likewise, this house was raised farther off the ground than the old, sunken house, so the winter rains and the neighbors' drains overflowing into the streets no longer invaded them.

Hawwa gave one room to Naifa, in which she put a hospital bed which Lutfi had bought and a clothes closet. She was careful to keep the closet doors and drawers locked with a key, and she kept a lot of keys on a chain she hung on a nail in the wall, out of reach of Naifa. Hawwa took out the two window panes, after Naifa broke them with a strong blow from her big hand, and stuck her arm out through the openings in the protective iron screen, pulling the hijabs off women passing in the street and yanking the men's hair. She replaced the panes with a sliding window made of reinforced, unbreakable glass, which opened and closed with a security latch. She also replaced the protective grille with one that had smaller openings, so Naifa could no longer stick her hand through the screen to prey on passersby, even though she continued hitting the reinforced glass with both of her angry hands. With her confinement to her room and its limited contents, Naifa's belligerence increased. She would hide on the floor behind the door, and when Hawwa came in carrying her food she attacked her and knocked her down. Then she would throw her heavy body on top of her, and Hawwa would shout for someone to save her. Qais would try to lift his grandmother off of his mother, but Naifa would push him far away with her powerful hand. He would fall on his back, swearing and cursing her ancestors, until he got up and went after her, punching and kicking, while Hawwa would yell at him to stop. Later on, Hawwa learned not to call for anyone; when Naifa knelt on top of her she surrendered without shouting or resisting. Many times, Hawwa felt that she would certainly die, and that she remained alive only because Naifa's strength weakened, slackening her arms wrapped around Hawwa's neck, or because she had suddenly fallen fast asleep as she knelt atop her, and started snoring. Then Hawwa would slip out from under her with great care.

Naifa was constantly banging, beating, and yelling. She banged on the closet doors; she beat on the heavy, firmly closed door of the room; she shrieked during the daylight hours until her throat was nearly in shreds, and at night she went on banging violently on the doors and screaming, enraged, until Hawwa thought her nerves might finally give way. Hawwa's clients would be startled by the terrifying screaming of the old woman, and with Naifa's usurpation of most of her time and energy, Hawwa's work receded. Nazmi, meanwhile, applied himself to extorting money from Lutfi, claiming that the three hundred dinars he gave them monthly were no longer enough, asserting that not even God in his heaven could contain Naifa and Naifa's viciousness. "Take me back to my house . . . take me home!" she yelled. Hawwa thought it was strange that her grandmother yearned for her house in the camp, smelling of milk, rennet, and curds. But then one evening at sunset Hawwa went in to her grandmother and found her fingers bloody. She had planted them in one of the walls and was digging with her fingernails, so some of the worn paint had been scraped off and pieces of the plaster had crumbled, baring the rough concrete blocks. Naifa's fingers were bleeding and her face was bathed in tears as she stared at the bare wall. "This's not my house! It's not the house I built!" She kept on crying, and shouting, "Where's my house? Take me home, for God's sake! Take me to my house!"

Then, when her deteriorated brain had lost all power over the movement of her nerves or the direction of her limbs, Naifa fell down. It happened unexpectedly one day. Hawwa went in to her grandmother carrying her breakfast, and found her standing in the middle of the room, as if she were looking for something to lean on. Naifa tried to rein in her own body, for fear it would get away from her. She raised her frame as high as her great height could reach, bracing herself against a convulsive tremor that ran through her, and then she fell: the huge, towering figure, tyrannical in body and bone, fell to the floor. She sank down lengthwise, like a stone tower sucked down from below, or like a skyscraper mined at the base that collapsed all at once. Her fall was accompanied by a roar that welled up from the depths of her soul, and that shook the space around her and every space around it. It was Naifa's very last roar.

For two years or a little less, Naifa stayed in bed, opening her mouth only to mumble or to moan. Her legs were raised to her belly, her arms clasped to her breast. Her flesh diminished, her fat fell away, and she was transformed into a bony shape. Her face was ghostly, as her eyes were sunk deep into their sockets, while her broad, swollen forehead stood out and her jaw protruded, framed by her hollow cheeks. Her sharp jaw lengthened and her lips turned into two downy lines, after she abandoned her set of teeth. When she was sleeping, with her eyes closed, her jaw slack, and her mouth open like a hole, her head looked like a skull from the remains of a human creature who had witnessed horrors before its death. She would cower and shrink into herself, frightened, whenever anyone tried to come near her, but she seemed more at ease and reassured when Hawwa was close to her. Hawwa fed her and gave her water, she diapered her and changed her, she bathed her and affixed the tube for urine in her bladder, she cleaned the bag of urine, and with her hand she removed the feces from her anus, accumulated from her sluggish bowels. She treated the ulcers that formed on her back and around her tailbone, even the decaying ones; she cleaned out the infection and pus gathering in them, disinfected them, and covered them with thin, layered bandages, which she changed constantly.

On Naifa's last morning, after days of moaning, Hawwa was giving her water from a syringe when Naifa gave a great gasp and her eyes bulged. She stretched out her trembling hand to Hawwa's face. "May God bless your path, Grandmother!" Hawwa wiped away quick tears that sprang from her eyes.

At last, Naifa's hand fell away.

Rapid knocking on the door pulls Hawwa out of her cloud. Her whole being shudders violently. It can't be Ayid and Qais—they wouldn't come before the evening prayer. The knocks follow in quick succession, as if two hands and two feet were kicking the metal door. Hawwa rushes to open it before the metallic noise wakes her mother. Six-year-old Lujain is standing there, the daughter of her neighbor Umm Ziyad, carrying a large bag and panting. Her mouth gapes open, the width emphasized by the loss of several of her front teeth. Hawwa takes the heavy bag from her, wondering how the little girl had brought it all the way from her house in the camp to Hawwa's house, through no less than three streets. Lujain follows Hawwa into the main room, taking off her shoes. Her thin frame seems to have shrunk still more with the weight of the bag and the intensifying cold of the afternoon air, and she hurries to the heater, bringing her hands close to the red burner so they can absorb some of the warmth. The heat brings some color to her face, where her features are still shaking off the pallor of the cold air. Inside her holey socks she rubs her toes together, and seems elated with the warmth creeping inside her.

Hawwa sorts the contents of the sack: two jilbabs that need shortening at the hem and the sleeves, the new lengths marked with pins; a skirt that requires a lining; a ready-made school smock with a piece of the same kind of fabric, which Umm Ziyad, as she'd explained previously, wanted made into another smock of the same size. Also in the bag are five pairs of boys' pants, some needing new zippers to replace old ones that have been torn or are broken or stuck, and others that need patches for the tears that cannot be darned or mended, especially at the thighs and the knees. While Hawwa is inspecting the tears in the pants, her eyes are drawn to Lujain, who is looking at the fruit bowl out of the corner of her eye. "Take some!" Hawwa tells her, pointing to the plate where red-cheeked apples and pomegranates beam. The little girl does not hold back; she pulls out the largest and reddest apple, and bites into it. "Do you like pomegranates?" Hawwa asks her, so Lujain takes a pomegranate with a bloodred color oozing over the surface, turns it in her hands, and then stuffs it into her pants pocket, creating a huge bulge at the top of her thigh.

In recent years, Hawwa's work has increased, and her hand-operated machine—which she replaced a few years after her marriage with one that ran on electricity, which broke down many times and which she repaired time after time, before replacing it with a newer one—has never stopped running. But sewing in the sense of sophisticated, complex couture, with aesthetic touches and technical skill and even the taste that Hawwa acquired from Sitt Qamar, has receded in favor of other sewing: patching and repairing, or tailoring the same patterns repeatedly, almost as if she were remaking the same piece over and over, or rudimentary sewing that's so excessively simple that it's nothing of value, in fact nothing at all. Ready-to-wear has put an end to tailoring. She's heard that from her clients, who come to her with ready-made clothes that need shortening or lengthening or taking in or letting out or some other adjustment—maybe the addition of lace trimming here or the removal of a ruffle there, or adding linings to dresses, skirts, jackets, and jilbabs. Then Hawwa began to refashion old clothes that had become too small for the bodies of their owners, or too tight for their spreading, lengthening, and thickening, to accommodate the expensive demands of continued existence. She breathes new life into dresses of styles that have ceased to exist, or extends the life of girls' and boys' pants, passed down among siblings.

Naturally, there is the school season, and the piles of fabric it brings her, blue and turquoise green, which she sews to ready-made patterns for school smocks. She even knows the measurements of the girls of her neighborhood and the surrounding ones by sight, and sometimes by their level in school. She knows them even when they reach puberty suddenly, stretching out and expanding, their breasts maturing and their faces breaking out in pimples, when fat, resulting from heat and overcrowding in the cramped, narrow houses and from poor nutrition, begins to pile up on their hips and thighs.

Then Hawwa happened on a new source of income, which her neighbor Umm Said showed her. She began to buy "stock" fabrics of cotton and linen by the pound, plain and striped and in prints. She cut and sewed them into sheets for single and double beds, with or without elastic around the edges, also making pillow cases, which she sold by the piece or in sets. But the product that was most in demand, from clients within the camp and outside, was the sheets she sewed of durable linen, which could be scrubbed. She lined them with thick nylon that resisted tearing and would not become worn even after repeated washings. With the increased demand for her waterproof sheets (which she sewed in various sizes, the large ones selling better than the small ones), Hawwa began to buy the fabrics and the nylon in rolls. She lined them up lengthwise on a wooden bench near the closet in the bedroom.

The new source of income compensated somewhat for a source that had been closed off, harshly, with the passing of Lutfi about three years earlier. That April night had been loaded with excitement, tea, pastries, freshly roasted nuts, and the burbling of the water pipe, with the smoke from tobacco in flavors of honeyed red and green apples, rose, and strawberry gathering thickly in front of the giant television screen in the large guest lounge in his house. Lutfi was fired up with excitement and jumped out of his chair in great joy after the match between Real Madrid and Barcelona, in the championship game for the Cup of Spain, ended with a victory for Real by a score of one to nothing. Out of this great joy he started coughing, and then the coughing grew worse. He turned red, then blue, and heavy sweat poured from his face and neck and chest. He yelled that a knife was splitting his chest, and then he spoke no more, while his eyes, resisting closing, tried in vain to cling to the hem of life that was pulling away from him. Lutfi was in his mid-fifties the day he died.

The new source of income, however, barely covered many gaping holes, among them the two bottomless pits of Ayid and Qais, who were always hanging around at her house, sitting with their heads bowed, as if they were broken, or shattered psychologically, even though that took nothing away from their appetites. They began by asking her about food, any food in the house; and whatever she put before them they ate ravenously, as if they had been hungry for a hundred years. They hunted out the largest pieces of meat first and then finished off the small ones, and then they moved on to the gravy and the rice and all the other accompaniments, even down to the pickles, which they crunched voraciously. When they were completely full, and had washed their bellies with oranges and sipped well-sugared tea, they once again dressed their helpless faces in expressions of misery and stupidity, spreading out their empty hands before her, complaining of breakdowns in the taxi and the unbelievable cost of repairs, and their car payments that were past due.

Hawwa was alarmed as she saw Qais resembling his father more, day after day. He even looked like him, to the point of being almost identical, as if he had sprung from the same thin, hollow branch, without the least modification or straightening or adjustment in form. But the painful resemblance went beyond the external, for Qais equaled his father in baseness of spirit. It grieved her to discover that the days of her life that she had devoted to keeping Qais from slipping into his father's low, vile ambit had simply been lost. Asma, Ayid's wife, came to her once to complain of him. Bitterly, she described to her how Qais had attacked her daughter Hind, less than two months after their marriage, and twisted the gold chain around her neck until he nearly choked the life out of her, before he snatched it off and sold it. Hawwa felt her neck with the palm of her hand, swallowing with difficulty the saliva that was stuck in her throat. Then she closed her eyes on an image still present in detail in her mind, long after it had made her spirit barren, only to open them on a living horror. She tried to expel the image, but she did not much succeed. Even after Asma left the house, the pain continued to cut into her neck for some time.

When Hawwa was divorced from Nazmi, Qais did not seem to be much affected. Not even Ayid played the role of the jealous brother. If the divorce was for her an emancipation of her spirit, even though she had neither worked toward it nor asked for it, then for Qais, as for Ayid, it was an emancipation of her money, which she gathered with great effort only to have Nazmi wheedle it out of her. With her divorce, they found a larger door before them, which they had a better claim to knock on, unsheathing the authority of the brother and the authority of the son, the established authority of need and the authority of destitution (since destitution turns into violence), and the authority of utter, collective defeat.

Hawwa is now finishing her enumeration of the contents of the heavy bag. Lujain tells her proudly that she got to the bag ahead of her brothers and sisters. Hawwa smiles and opens her purse to hand her two ten-piaster coins. The little girl wipes the stickiness of the apple from her hand on her fuzzy wool shirt, eyeing the shining coins, and then puts them in her other pocket.

At the bottom of the bag Hawwa comes across a small piece of fabric, a scrap of not more than a quarter of a yard, of creamy white satin embroidered with tiny, watery beads. Hawwa turns the scrap in her hands. Lujain lowers her eyes, in a sign of hope, as she asks Hawwa to sew a wedding dress for her doll. As the image glows in her head and elation lights her eyes, the excited little girl, warm now, puts her hands on her waist as she describes the design of the dress. She wants it to have a smooth, narrow waist and a bouffant skirt, with layers and layers and layers of "puffing" tulle under it, "Soooooooooo much!" The little girl sketches with both hands an overflowing circle, while her eyes look as if they're fixed on a pure-white cloud. After all these years, Hawwa still experiences a special kind of pleasure in sewing doll dresses. Often she finds that the supple and capricious imaginations of the girls, who use their hands to sketch in the air images of their desires for the dresses, compensate her for the aridity of the women's imaginations and the retreat of their desires.

Hawwa brings Lujain down from her high cloud to the floor of the room, asking her with contrived seriousness, "Fine, but where's the tulle?" The ideal in the girl's head is dispelled, and she says, resigning herself, "Okay . . . we don't have to have tulle." But Hawwa reassures her, laughing: "We can't have a wedding dress without tulle. I have some!" A smile, unmarred by the absence of a few teeth, frames Lujain's face. "And I'm going to make her a veil, too." Lujain gathers in her excited body, wanting to jump for joy, but seeming to fear that she's not telling the truth.

Hoping to get a confirming, absolute yes, she asks Hawwa, "Really?"

"Really."

"A *veil* veil?"

"A *veil* veil!"

"And long?"

"And long."

"How long?"

"As long as you want."

"Soooooooooo long!"

Lujain's eyes go to the fruit bowl, and she asks Hawwa: "C'n I maybe have another apple?"

Hawwa runs her warm hand over the cream satin remnant, the miniature beads teasing her fingers. Lujain bites into the cheek of another apple, and the aroma of the sweet pulp under the taut skin fills the air.

From the window creeps the gloom of day's end, lowering its trembling gray veil over the satin remnant, and extinguishing the shimmering rainbow of the watery beads.

7

HAWWA IS FEEDING HER MOTHER a mashed apple. Rabia is
delaying the process of chewing, so that the crushed pulp will
stay in her mouth longer. "Does that taste good, Yamma?"
Hawwa asks, as she watches her mother's face begin to relax.
Rabia turns her head toward her and mumbles, as her eyes
light up in a fleeting sparkle. Hawwa gives her some water and
wipes the overflow from her chin and neck. She straightens
her position, nearly flat on the bed, raising her head on two
pillows. "Should I turn on the TV for you, Mama?" Hawwa
flips through a limited range of channels which includes those
that show Arab and Turkish soap operas. When she comes
to a scene in the drama *The Sultan's Harem* in which the Sultana Huyam reclines on a huge bed in the midst of a show of
gaudy colors, Rabia mutters. Hawwa stops at the scene and
says, "This is a repeat, Mama! We saw it yesterday." Rabia
continues her muttering, so Hawwa answers, "Fine, whatever
you want." Huyam's green eyes seem to hiss with desire, and
her bright, flaming hair frames a face of imperial grandeur
and majestic beauty, as she occupies the wide television screen.
The sultana speaks directly to Rabia, and Rabia submits without argument.

Rabia was confined to her bed about a year after Lutfi's
death, a year during which she cried all the time. She cried at
daybreak and with the progression of the day and the lengthening of the night. Asma even assured Hawwa that Rabia's

tears flowed when she was sleeping. Was all this sadness over Lutfi? Asma wondered if it could be, and so did Hawwa. She did not remember that her mother was attached to any of her children; it was as if they had been imposed on her, as life itself had been imposed on her. What was certain was that love—love of a man or love of a son or daughter or love of life or love of a thing, anything in and of itself—was an emotion Rabia did not comprehend.

Certainly Lutfi had not been an exception to this state of unlove. Although he gave Rabia money, in his childhood and in his youth and then in his old age, which did not last long, giving to her from his small prosperity and then from his greater ease, it's certain that the money he put in her hand or in Ayid's hand or even in Nazmi's, when Hawwa began to care for Naifa, was not a sign of love, or even of emotion; nor was it to seek approval. Lutfi used his money to buy his distance from them. When Ayid and Qais went to him bowed down, not standing on any dignity, lowering themselves and their eyes, claiming humility, Lutfi did not argue with them or try to understand any details from them, nor did he take a long time speaking to them. In fact, he hurried them to ask for what they had come for and leave. Anyone could take anything from him, on condition that they leave. That way Lutfi lived free, having loosened all his ties; or so he imagined.

"Why didn't he die before?" wondered Rabia, to Hawwa's amazement, when she visited her mother during the long months of weeping.

Hawwa asked her, in disbelief, "Lutfi? Really, Yamma?"

But Rabia turned away her eyes, overflowing with tears, and said, "Mousa!"

Naifa had taken Rabia for her son because Rabia's father was the only one in the Far'a Camp near Nablus who accepted Mousa. Rabia was the middle daughter among seven girls, none of whom had married. Naifa would have liked to see the other sisters, but Rabia's father told her, "This is what I have for your son." At fifteen, Rabia was not beautiful, but she was coming along, or so it seemed from her breasts compressed under her dress, ready to nurse, and from the flesh accumulated at the top of her white arms. They were bared for her, along with other indicative parts of her body, specifically so that Naifa could inspect them. Rabia exuded the perspiration of a woman, but in her eyes there still lingered the preoccupied, playful, and distracted glances of a child. At least Rabia was something Mousa could "fiddle with," thought Naifa, without causing any harm. And then, the marriage would be enough to pull him out of the problematic lanes and bring him down from the rooftops.

When Naifa checked on her a month after their wedding, she asked her if she had anything "saved up" in her belly. Rabia said to her with no sorrow that Mousa had not come near her, and that when he was home he spent most of his time on the roof. Mousa was sleeping when Naifa sat on him and sank her teeth into his broad cheek. He tried to get away from her, his screams submerged inside, but he was pinned under her heavy body. She got off of him only when the blood spurted from his face, smearing her teeth. Mousa came down off the roof at last, and three months later Rabia became pregnant with Lutfi.

Rabia did not love her progeny. When they arrived in this life, with bodies like jelly and souls still unsullied, she watched them grow from afar. She did not pause much over their needs. She didn't ask them about the reason for their meager laughter, just as she didn't think much about their tears that poured down copiously, bitterly. She did not date the growth of their bodies, which shot up and then filled out, in the corners of the cramped house; she did not anticipate the first words that rolled off their tongues. She did not jump up to take their hands when they walked for the first time, and when they fell as they began to walk; she did not extend her hand to them so they would get up and walk again. She did not extinguish the fevers lit in their little bodies on bitingly cold nights in winter, and in fact she didn't notice them to begin with. She wasn't worried about their thirst, and she didn't rush to satisfy their hunger. She did not sorrow much over their atrophied spirits, nor was she very sad about their decline. She did not live for herself, but at the same time she did not live for them.

When the women of the camp poured into her house to offer their condolences for the loss of Duha, they asked her about what happened. Rabia looked to Afaf, Sajida, and Hawwa, whose eyes were dissolved in tears, so they would explain to the women how their little sister died. Then, when the women asked her how old her little girl was, Rabia looked to Hawwa, who told her and told them that Duha was aged six years, ten months, and nineteen days; Rabia shook her head as if she were hearing about some poor girl she didn't know who had died young, very young.

But Rabia did like pregnancy, and wished that her belly would remain swollen, carrying a child who was never born, or carrying some swelling, as long as she lived. Mousa was disgusted with her during pregnancy, and did not come near her. She was disgusted with herself during the intervals when her belly was empty. During those periods, Mousa would throw himself on her like a concrete block, sticky and cold. She would close her eyes and shut down the areas of sensitivity in her body. When he got up, leaving an accumulation of his sour breath on her flesh, she would vomit.

Rabia did not weep when Mousa died. She did not burst out in tears that had been shut away in her spirit. The women of the camp thought that the dryness of her eyes had some connection to the painful shock. They all said that she would cry in time, when there were no longer people around her. But it took Rabia a very long time before her eyes, folded tightly over reverberating heartbreak, loosened and shed streaming tears over the death that had been so long in coming.

With Mousa, Rabia's life had been afflicted with a great drought, so great that not even in her imagination did she sketch other possibilities for herself, for some possible life. When he was gone, a flood of feelings hit her—sad, gloomy, hateful feelings that swept away her spirit, or what was left of it. For years after his death she walked sideways in the house, bent over, dizzy, her sight and hearing clouded, on the verge of falling and unable to find anything to lean on. Then, during the last five years, she had come to experience brief tremors, or shivers. Some were light, like an electric spark, causing numbness in her arm or tingling in her leg. Others were strong and would stop her in her tracks, and when she would try to lift her foot it would turn into a heavy tree trunk that could not be budged. Then one ordinary morning, when the sound of the twin-tub washing machine mixed with the sound of water pouring from the faucet over a basin of tomatoes in the sink, Rabia was standing in the kitchen holding a glass of water. Asma was washing the tomatoes, complaining to her, as usual, about Ayid. "Every day there's some problem with the car, every day there's a ticket, every day he guzzles a bottle of arak. He barely gets by on two pounds of meat a day, just for him. There's always a lit cigarette in his hand, and when I ask him for money for the house, he says, 'Where am I supposed to get it for you?'" She added, "And as if Ayid wasn't enough he went and brought us Qais, too!" Asma was rubbing off the remains of mud clinging to the tough skins of the tomatoes. "What a mess of a marriage!" Asma's furious words mixed with the sound of the water from the faucet and the sound of the washing machine. Then her voice faded while the noise of the motor became louder and turned into a crazy roar in Rabia's ear. Asma's face turned into a large blob of jelly, moving in the air like slime. Rabia tried to stretch out her hand to grab onto something, anything. The glass fell, shattering, and she collapsed on top of the shards.

As Hawwa expected, Asma came to her complaining of her inability to cope with the new situation. And in the end,

"She's your mother!" she said to her. It was a violent, crushing stroke, which paralyzed Rabia and shut down half her senses. Three years after Naifa's death, Hawwa still had her hospital bed; and when she saw Rabia stretched out on it, she began to await another death that might come soon.

Hawwa raises the volume of the television, and the emotions and dubbed words fill the cold air of the room. She rubs her upper arms. "Are you cold, Mama?" she asks Rabia; but Rabia's senses, or those that function, are still glued to the screen that overflows with color. Hawwa leans over the heater to light another burner, and her body, tall even when she bends, blocks part of the screen. Rabia inclines her head, trying to see the part of the picture hidden behind Hawwa; her mumbling blends with Hawwa's repeated efforts to spark the second burner. "Yes, Mama, right away." Hawwa moves away from her line of sight after the flame has caught in the second burner. Rabia seems content, comfortable, fed, snuggled down, nestled in cleanliness and in Johnson's baby powder, with which Hawwa dusts the wrinkled, folded flesh of her neck. Her eyes are intent on the emotion pouring from the television. Hawwa withdraws from the room, leaving Rabia to the passion in the closed rooms of the castle and to the fire of the heater. The Syrian voices superimposed over the original reach her through the opening in the door she's left ajar.

Sunset falls from the window, shedding darkness on the living-room walls. Hawwa inspects the sky, completely dry and with no trace of impending water, then she lowers the curtain over the window, uneasily, with some hidden anxiety. She turns on the neon light in the room and looks around her. Three open bags await her on the cutting table. She looks at the writing, in her untrained hand, attached to the fabrics folded inside them. She picks up the bags and then puts them back. There are many things she must do. She opens one of the drawers in the table and then closes it. She tries to fashion a single, clear thought in her head, but she's incapable of producing anything resembling a thought. She can't do anything. Night is falling in her heart before it falls on the streets. Obscure feet follow her, treading on the shadows of her heart, and she feels a sense of foreboding.

Hawwa picks up her bag of velvet and hugs it to her chest. She breathes in the richness of its dark, deep violet as its rustling tickles her hearing, like soft murmurs laden with longing. She's reassured, for a time. She can't resist the desire the Elissa set creates, in the other bag. She holds back a little before opening the jewel box, as if she doesn't want to satisfy her desire quickly. When at last she does open it, the lively yellow radiance pours into her eyes. The glow of the gold, which does not look cheap, embraces her heart. Then she closes the box quickly, so as not to squander the luster. She opens her sewing closet, pulls a small key from beneath her dress, and uses it to open one of three inner drawers. Inside lies a small wooden box containing a thin bundle of money and a short golden chain ending in a small, incised heart, given to her by Munir. Hawwa looks around her, as if she wants to make sure that no hidden eyes or specters of any kind lie in wait in the room, and then she plants a fleeting, timid kiss on the heart before consigning it once again to its box. In addition to the box, papers and bills are scattered in the drawer, and Hawwa moves them aside to create enough room for the box containing the Elissa set. She caresses the top of the box and starts to close the drawer when her hand leads her, as it always does when she opens the drawer, to the hidden face.

From under the fabric lining the bottom of the drawer, Hawwa cautiously pulls out the picture. It's of a young man in his late twenties or early thirties. Two dark eyes stare at her from a face ripe with desires, whose features throb with life in the rich black and white of the photograph. As always, the eyes are not neutral; sometimes they blame her, sometimes they try to share a distant secret with her, and sometimes they deceive her. But when Hawwa plunges deeply into the eyes, she can glimpse a glimmer stored in them. The flattened lips open in a half-smile, half disclosed, half full, half joyful, half of a possible life. He looks more like a child moving toward manhood, or a man caught in his childhood. On the one hand, he could be a boy fascinated by having fun forever and ever; on the other hand, he very well could be a crazed lover. Amid many mixed feelings, indistinct in the picture, the face rests at an angle on a closed hand and yearns for the horizon. It seems completely unconcerned about the days to come.

Absolutely, in no way, shape, or form, does this picture of a person who seems somehow secure give any indication of loss, of a loss that's very great.

After getting married, Hawwa worked for about four years with Sitt Qamar, daily taking the same path from her house in the camp to Sitt Qamar's house. The ritualized route required walking through two dusty neighborhoods before arriving at her family's house, on the frequent mornings of urine, then three other neighborhoods, before she came to the bus stop at the entrance to the camp market. All that time she was burdened by the presence of Nazmi clinging to her, even when she washed herself in the morning, in great disgust, to cast off all trace of him, and all trace of household decay, settled in her intestines, which she shook off as she walked. She carried her belly with her, weighed down twice, once when she was pregnant with Aya and once when she was pregnant with Qais. Between the two pregnancies she carried the infant Aya, carrying her as she traversed the lanes covered in dirt during the summer and in mud during the winter.

During the first two years, Hawwa recovered the beautiful life in Sitt Qamar's house that she feared she had lost with her marriage. She did not try to tinker with the order of life. First she aired out the house to remove the odor of stale cigarettes, just as she had always done. Then she prepared Sitt Qamar's coffee and brought it to her on the same tray and in the same cup, with a piece of chocolate, before preparing breakfast. They would sit at the little kitchen table facing each other, two hungry women with an appetite aroused by the aroma of the bread, the white cheese in brine, the omelet, and the hot falafel. Then Hawwa would clean the house according to a weekly schedule, alternating among the rooms, as well as tidying and sweeping the sewing room daily. She would also clean the sewing machine, arrange the work to be done according to priority, organize receiving the clients, and set the dates for delivery, for taking measurements, and for fittings. She also did the basic sewing tasks—basting, hemming, pinking the edges of sewn pieces or binding the seams and borders, adding interfacing to the collars and cuffs, opening the buttonholes, sewing on buttons, setting in zippers, and ironing the dresses and suits before delivery.

Hawwa's energy did not flag when she was pregnant, even when her belly nearly reached her nose. After Aya was born, she got up from childbed after two weeks. She knew she could not stay away from Sitt Qamar, nor did she want to. "Sitt Qamar can't get along without me!" she said to Nazmi. Taking her infant with her, she gave her body (which had become softer and more pliable after marriage and childbirth) to cleaning the house, to sewing tasks, and to taking care of Aya. When Aya began to walk, Hawwa was careful to keep her curious hands away from the many valuable glass objects in the house, closing the doors of the rooms she was not permitted to enter. Sitt Qamar allowed her to put Aya to sleep in the single room, and often Hawwa would glimpse her sitting on the edge of the bed, looking at Aya's face with its obscure, neutral expressions. Hawwa would imagine that Aya could very well have come from Sitt Qamar's belly, just as she, Hawwa, could have, in some dream, in some desire.

Sitt Qamar did not seem annoyed with the chaos Aya created in the house, not even when she escaped her mother's notice one morning and followed her into the parlor, bumping into a vase that stood on a table and causing it to fall, the crash making a sound like an explosion. Hawwa cried and asked Sitt Qamar to take the cost of the vase from her pay. But Sitt Qamar, who was smoking her third morning cigarette before eating anything, shook her head apathetically. Without taking her eyes off the nothingness she had been following from the window for more than an hour, she said, "It's okay . . . this isn't the first thing to be broken."

Hawwa discovered after a few months that she didn't need to learn anything new, but she hid that fact from Nazmi. She wanted her beautiful life with Sitt Qamar to continue forever, even if an anxiety had started to grow in her heart, one that she could not identify at the time. For his part, Nazmi didn't care about following the development of Hawwa's tailoring skills, as long as she came home before sunset and cooked for him after he came back from the butcher shop, and prepared tea for him and snacks for his nightly gathering of "thugs" like him, as she thought of them. He didn't care as long as she handed him fifteen dinars of her weekly pay from Sitt Qamar at the end of the week (hiding from him the other ten dinars), and as long as her machine kept running, as much as possible during the rest of the day, with simple sewing tasks for the women of the camp. The sound of the machine in her bedroom blended with the sounds of the men gathered in the living room, whose jaws never stopped clacking, scraping, and grinding.

Sitt Qamar began to go to sleep late and to wake late. When Hawwa opened the door to the house in the morning, she was greeted by clouds of stale cigarette smoke, ready to pounce on her, and her spirit would shrink from the blackness that tinted the suffocating air of the living room. Even when Hawwa raised the curtains and opened the windows so the room would be washed with outside air, still the blackness did not dissipate quickly. The odor of smoke stagnated in the house, settling into the walls, lurking on the chairs and sofas, even burrowing into the wood. The area of the gray ashes extended seriously, and Hawwa gathered them from the Morris chairs and from the table, along with the cigarette butts from the overflowing ashtray. Aside from the cigarettes of the long night, Sitt Qamar began to smoke half a pack of cigarettes before eating, and to drink three cups of coffee. At breakfast she began to settle for smoking, watching Hawwa as she ate with an appetite. Then Sitt Qamar no longer sat at the kitchen table, so Hawwa stopped preparing breakfast.

"Can I make you a sandwich?" Hawwa would ask, concerned. But Sitt Qamar would take a long pull from her cigarette, without answering; her eyes were following a shadow that had appeared on the street outside the window. She stretched her neck in longing, before letting her eyes fall back, disappointed. Some days Fairuz would accompany Sitt Qamar's preoccupied brooding, in "Yellow September Leaves," while the tape recorder kept bringing back the dreary yellow leaves time after time. When Fairuz's voice would rise in a sorrowful melody reaching the height of grief, in "September has come and you're far away, in a sad cloud under a lonely moon; the rains of September make me weep and wake to you, my love," the cloud of tears in Sitt Qamar's eyes would break open all at once. Hawwa would stand dazed, not knowing how to gather the scattered tears.

Hawwa stopped setting aside enough time to clean Sitt Qamar's house after the tailoring tasks began to pile up, and she found herself obliged to spend most of the time sitting at the machine, her foot taking the place of Sitt Qamar's. Under normal circumstances, Hawwa would sort the fabrics according to the pattern and the delivery date; then Sitt Qamar would design and cut, before seaming together the pieces of the pattern, in preparation for the first fitting. Usually the fitting was a formality, as Sitt Qamar would have measured and conceived the garment correctly the first time, however difficult or complex the cut, and she would complete the final fitting, with all of the finishing touches that followed it, smoothly. Between the first and last fittings Hawwa would undertake most of the small details, which were equally important, under Sitt Qamar's eye and her precise directions.

Then the long time during the day contracted, the time that was packed with creating, designing, and inventing, which Sitt Qamar spent in the sewing room. She began to huddle on the sofa in the living room, glued to the window, for two or three hours, her grave face plunged into a cloud of leaden smoke. Her eyes wandered over the passing seasons in the streets, staring at the faces of people running and at feelings folded away. When her clients came to her, carrying pictures of their designs or their conceptions of them in their heads, she no longer tried to penetrate their imaginations, to adjust them, or to discuss with them what was and was not possible, what would and would not work. She began to content herself with their vague descriptions and many explanations, long and well worn, greeting their ideas with eyes closed, as if by thick glass, with wandering thoughts and a roaming heart. Then, when the time came for the fitting, the women were shocked at the result their imagination had produced.

Hawwa began to be more involved in the major tasks, taking over the precision cutting from Sitt Qamar. For Qamar's hands, skilled, judicious, artistic, demanding, dexterous, were no longer the valuable hands that had brought her favor with the women of Sweileh, Amman, and points beyond. Many times, also, Sitt Qamar would suddenly let slip what she had in her hand. She would go to her room, throw herself on the bed, and plunge into weeping, until at last she fell asleep, an exhausted wreck. Sometimes she would stretch out on the single bed in the other room, next to Aya, looking into her small, curtained eyes, enclosing them in her hot breath. Often Hawwa's worried eyes fell on her as she embraced the frame that held the picture of the laughing golden girl, holding it to her even as she slept. The obscure expression on her face held a touch of terror, as if she were afraid someone would take the picture away from her.

Hawwa was pregnant with Qais when she realized that her beautiful life with Sitt Qamar was coming to an end. It wasn't only because most of her clients had withdrawn from her when they discovered that "her girl," Hawwa, was doing most of what she should be doing herself, but also because Sitt Qamar herself had withdrawn from herself. She would sit brooding deeply for a while, swallow a lot of pills, stay up a long time, and then sleep for a long, long time. In her hours of alertness, her vision would carve its way with great difficulty from inside her hollow, dark eyes to a place outside of her being, where it would roam the streets from the window, looking for something, some face, some shade or human shadow that she knew, while Hawwa read her the obituary page from the paper every day. She read the names one by one, patiently. Often Sitt Qamar would ask her to read the name of the deceased again, raising her eyes to the sky in the living room, weighed down by a fog of smoke, as she contemplated some connection or indication enclosed in the name. Then she would say, without seeming to be much affected, "Go on!"

One time Hawwa read her a name that didn't differ much from all the other names on the page where the dead appeared next to each other, more or less crowded together from one day to another, and Sitt Qamar stopped at it for a long time, longer than ever before. She asked Hawwa to read the name to her once, and again, and again, and yet again. Each time, Hawwa took pains with the three-part name, which resembled many names written in large, black letters, announcing their separation from life, on the pages where "O soul at peace, return unto thy Lord, well-pleased, well-pleasing! Enter thou among My servants! Enter thou My Paradise!" was next to "He that believeth in me, though he were dead, yet shall he live." The first time, Hawwa read the name and the surname quickly; the second time, she read the name less quickly and with some caution, fearing that some letter or part of a word might have eluded her tongue by mistake. Then during the many times that followed, she read the name slowly, shaping the letters with great precision, in a way dominated by doubt: Hajj Zaid Faisal al-Azzam; Zaid . . . Faisal . . . al-Azzam; Zaid . . . Faisal . . . al-Azzam; Zaid . . . Faisal . . . al-Azzam. When it seemed that the name was the name, and when it became absolutely clear that it could not be any other name, Sitt Qamar's face was bathed in tears before she told Hawwa, "Go on!"

Then came days and nights when Sitt Qamar did not stop weeping, her eyes pouring out streams of silent water without interruption, so her face, always wet, seemed on the verge of dissolving completely. The last winter she had in Sitt Qamar's house, Hawwa came into her bedroom one afternoon when the day had been very bleak, bringing her a cup of tea and a cheese sandwich, and found her sitting in front of the dressing table, barefoot, wearing a black dress that was pulled back a little above her knees. It was velvet. Under the meager lighting of the room it disintegrated into shadows that alternated between smoky black, deep black, and still deeper black. This was the first time Hawwa had seen Sitt Qamar in the dress. The zipper sagged open, revealing the lavish white of her back, cut across in the middle by a black bra. The short dress with its simple design seemed to belong to an ancient time, yet it did not look ancient. It was sleeveless, with a scooped neck wide enough to reveal a tender area of her breast, the flesh dappled in some parts with tones of reddish pink. Her belly, which had spread and bulged in recent years in the shape of a flabby apple, was crumpled between the folds of the dress. Sitt Qamar spread her hand over her breast, contemplating herself in the mirror, which was not neutral: her eyes garlanded in black, her receding forehead, her cheeks marked with dark age spots, and her hair, afflicted with severe thinning and fading. She spoke to Hawwa without looking at her: "I've gotten old, Hawwa, I've gotten old." She turned her uncovered back toward the mirror, and through the tears that overflowed onto her face she pointed to her tragedy: "Even the dress doesn't fit me." Then she sobbed in the middle of the phrase "I've gotten old," which she went on repeating: "I've gotten old . . . old . . . old." Hawwa put down the tea and the sandwich on the bedside table and ran toward her, taking her into her arms. In that moment in which Hawwa was overcome by many different feelings, she feared she would lose Qamar, her Qamar. She kissed her head time and time again, she kissed her eyelashes, then she poured kisses over her cheeks and face, her tears mixing with the tears of Sitt Qamar.

"You're still beautiful as the moon, Sitt Qamar!" Hawwa assured her, as she surrounded her face with her hands.

Qamar continued: "The dress has gotten too small for me, or maybe I'm the one that got too big for it." Then she brought her face close to Hawwa's, whispering, with a bit of fear: "I've gotten old, Hawwa, and he's taken a long time . . . he's kept me waiting so long."

Hawwa knelt in front of her. She took the trembling hands between her own and rubbed them, saying, "I'll make you a dress just like it, and prettier!"

"Velvet?"

"The most expensive velvet."

"Black?"

"Black like kohl."

"Soft?"

"Soft, soft, soft . . . for the most beautiful moon, for Sitt Qamar!"

Hawwa promised her that she would visit the fabric shops in Amman one by one, and that she would buy her the most beautiful piece of fabric in the whole world. Hawwa sketched the design of the new dress for her, like the old one, but with simple additions that renewed the dress without stripping it of history. Sitt Qamar stopped crying for a little while, even though the tears remained in her eyes, standing at the door. She imagined her distant figure, which she remembered well and which she had cared for well for a long time, in the new dress that Hawwa would have made for her. And when at last Hawwa closed the zipper, recently set, so that the dress embraced her firmly shaped body and compressed its internal eruptions, bridling its flaming desire, she felt extreme happiness. In that moment, plucked from the spreading tree of imagination, Sitt Qamar was the happiest lover in any universe—until the moment evaporated and the new dress disappeared, leaving her in an old dress, its velvet faded, its zipper refusing to close, much too small for her, redolent of deferred desire, faded flowers, and deprivation. Then, her spirit shuddered as if from thunder, and her tears rained down unbound.

Hawwa did not know why Sitt Qamar's tears flowed in such abundance, as abundantly as tears could possibly flow, nor did she know who it was that Sitt Qamar was waiting for and who did not appear. Why had he not appeared, when she was expecting him? Hawwa did not remember any person who had come and who no longer came, or any face that came into Sitt Qamar's life and then did not come for any reason, at least during her presence in Sitt Qamar's life. Hawwa could not imagine anyone who should have come but who did not. He would definitely come, even if he took a long time. "Who's the one who's kept you waiting, Sitt Qamar?" she asked her. Sitt Qamar closed her eyes in the mirror, sighing. Hawwa wouldn't know. She wouldn't know many things, especially not in that moment. For how could she know that love, all of love, could be created in a single night?

On one distant September night, black as coal and alarmingly calm, pierced between one moment of silence and the next by a single shot, which would be followed by a long, disturbing silence before repeated bullets rang out, Qamar thought she heard a commotion outside the door of her house. She looked out the window but saw no one, no being moving. Even the trees resisted September's fall breezes, deadening the rustling of their leaves, gathering their tangled branches to their cowering trunks. Her work had stopped almost completely with the outbreak of the "events" of September, and then when elements of the Jordanian army chased the Palestinian fedayeen through the streets and the camps, and hunted them inside hiding holes in the towns, no one knocked on her door anymore. The urgent ringing of her telephone became intermittent, the intervals between calls distant. If a worried voice did call her from the deep well of the telephone, she assured its owner that she was "fine, thank God," and then she hung up to the silence suspended outside. From time to time her neighbor Shahla, who lived in the apartment facing hers, would visit her. She would drink coffee with Qamar, and would tell her terrifying stories of extensive killing in the streets. Qamar put her hand on her heart when her neighbor, who was informed, told her the secret of the great barking they heard at the end of the night. Dozens of disintegrating bodies of fedayeen were left in the streets for the dogs to rend. Qamar let the cigarette burn in her hand more than she inhaled the smoke into her breathless chest, as she listened to her neighbor's repugnant description. No sooner had the image of the blood and the torn flesh filled her eyes than she closed them, trying to chase the disturbing images from her head.

Qamar looked through the peephole in the door and did not see anything. She brought her ear to the door, almost certain that she heard breathing. She opened the door and the darkness stormed over her face. The light bulb over the outer door had burned out days earlier and she had not replaced it. During those stressful times no one any longer visited her during the day, or only rarely, and the night was absolutely closed off to her, so replacing the bulb had not seemed like a pressing matter. The scant light that poured from the entry to her house, covering the threshold and its surroundings, was enough to scatter some of the darkness. Qamar looked at the closed door of her neighbor's apartment, but there was no trace of life hiding behind the door. Shahla had gone to spend several days with her husband's family in Karak. Qamar stood at the top of the stairs, penetrated by the night and a deceptive silence. She lowered her eyes, dispelling the darkness, to the bottom of the stairs on the first floor, but she caught no glimpse of any creature or of any creature's ghost. She directed her eyes upward, to the stairs leading to the third and last floor of the building, and the darkness lurking there seemed more absolute. She went back to her apartment and shut the door, turning the key twice in the lock, as a violent shudder enveloped her. She clung to the wooden door as if she were hugging it, or as if she did not want it to open again. When she turned around, she was surprised by a person who appeared before her out of nowhere. She was about to scream but he clasped her in his arms and put his hand over her mouth, whispering in her ear, "I beg you!" They remained in this position for what seemed like an eternity. Qamar opened her hands and put them involuntarily on his chest, as if she wanted to block him or push him far away from her, but she did not block or push him. The truth was that she did not wish to block or push him, she did not wish to resist or attempt to escape his grasp, and her lack of resistance was at once a conscious and an unconscious realization. He was tall enough to crush her, just as he was tall enough to engulf her. He towered above her, high enough to give her shade, to the point of effacing her, just as he towered high enough to bend down over her and collect her entirely inside him, gathering in her very self along with her breath and enfolding her within him. He was tremendous enough to be frightening, and he was tremendous enough to be reassuring. His breath fell trembling and warm into her ear, while his rapid heartbeats touched her frightened, fleeing senses. When Qamar's panting subsided and her trembling lightened, she submitted to him. His hand gagging her mouth relaxed a little, and it seemed as if he was embracing her.

Another thing Qamar felt—or rather, something she did not feel—she did not feel that he was threatening her, nor did she feel that she wanted him to let her go. During some moments, in which the tension of the mutual fear lessened, together with the ambiguity and confused thoughts that tainted it, the enlacing of their two bodies as they stood behind the closed door in the dimly lit hall seemed unforced, not imposed or coerced. For Qamar especially, in some distant point in the murky depths of her thinking, the smell of his flesh pierced the blank surface of her senses in a welcome fashion. It was a violent smell, compelling, overwhelming, wretched; but it was also living and enlivening. He whispered in her ear that he was going to let her go, but that she must first promise him that she would not scream. He assured her that he would do nothing to harm her, and that he would explain everything to her. She nodded, agreeing. When he took his hand off her mouth and stepped back a pace, Qamar felt a current of cold air catch her. In the furthest point of the murkiest depths of her thinking, she wished that he would once again cling to her, his hand over her mouth, his body shading her, his strong, violent smell surrounding her.

Qamar reached to turn on the light in the living room, but he asked her to make do with the pale light of the hall. His voice held a plea. He also asked her to close the curtain of the window in the parlor, so she hurried away from him and let down the curtain, the color of cumin, over the length of the broad window. When she looked at him from enough distance, in the faint light of the hall that fell like a light mist over his head and shoulders, she saw him at last, perfect and complete. In one way he was real, but in another, with the crosscutting of light and shadow on his figure, he was too beautiful to be real. He was tall, lean without being thin, with thick, wavy black hair intermingled with a few white strands. The dim light gave his appearance a combination of mystery and mischief, instead of endowing it with the expected dignity. His complexion was dark and his face was inclined to length, without exaggeration. His features were carved sternly, especially his nose, which stood out in the middle of his face, though without protruding or being overlarge. His sharp brown eyes tended to be narrowed, as if they were constantly probing the depths of things. Neither a moderately thick mustache nor the traces of a beard growing in neglect succeeded in hiding a touch of innocence, which completely contradicted his tattered, half-military appearance.

Qamar was still drinking in his features in the shadow of the available light when he interrupted her inspection, saying, "I'm sorry that I . . . imposed myself on you."

Qamar could not keep herself from smiling, repeating the word *imposed*, which he seemed to have chosen after some thought, with an ironic tone. He returned her smile, showing his understanding of her unspoken interpretation of the word. Perhaps "invaded" would have been more precise, he said to her.

"And why me? Why *my* house?" she asked him.

He assured her that it could have been any other house, justifying himself with a mockery that did not lack bitterness or intended artificiality: "The right quiet, the right darkness, in the right place!"

He told her that he would not impose himself on her for long. He needed to be in a safe place tonight. Tomorrow was another day, another flight. Then, as if he were adding important information: "My name is Ghassan, by the way."

Qamar inspected his appearance: ragged khaki pants, left over from a military uniform, without a belt; a beige cotton shirt with no relation to the pants; and desert-colored military boots. She estimated that he was in his late twenties or perhaps a little older. He read her inquiring scrutiny and explained what he thought must be clear, thinking that she must certainly have figured it out. He spread his hands at his sides and said, "I'm one of the fedayeen."

"And before you were a fedayee?"

He answered as if he were recalling distant information, of no interest: "An engineer . . . an electrical engineer."

"Do you have a weapon?"

"I got rid of it!" Then he added, reassuring her, "I buried it far away, don't worry!"

The truth was that Qamar was not very worried, in fact not even a little worried, about his invasion of her peace, her night, and her house. Even his appearance, prepared for the act of dying or of living despite death, did not embarrass her or make her tense. She was not about to examine the reasons for her unwarranted lack of anxiety or fear, or to wonder about it.

She asked him with genuine concern: "Hungry?"

He answered with true longing: "Dying of hunger!"

She motioned for him to follow her to the kitchen.

Then a more important question occurred to him: "You didn't tell me your name."

Qamar had turned on the light in the kitchen, and it surrounded them both. She looked at him and said, " 'Amar."

In the light, his features appeared sharper than they had in the shadow, and his gaze tended to be more encompassing and wary, in keeping with his habits as a fighter. He sat at the table, watching Qamar light two burners on the stove, one under the teapot and the other under a frying pan. In the pan she melted a spoonful of clarified butter, before breaking two eggs over the hot fat; their aroma filled the kitchen as they cooked. Qamar felt his eyes enclosing her as she put plates of cheese, labneh spread, olives, stuffed pickled eggplants, and pickled cucumber on the table. When she put the bread before him, he realized suddenly that his eyes had not left her, so he lowered them immediately. At first he ate slowly, lifting his eyes between bites to Qamar, who was putting tea in the pot. Inwardly, he was surprised at her complete calm in accepting his presence. Were it not that he was completely sure of the true nature of the situation, he would have thought that they had been introduced or had met before. True, he had not threatened her, but in the end he had "invaded" her house—yes, he must call things by their names—and he had nearly "gagged" her. "Are you afraid of me?" he asked her, as he took his first bites. Qamar put a bottle of cold water and a glass on the table and raised her eyes to the ceiling for a few seconds, as if she were searching for an answer suspended there, before she answered decisively, "No."

He finished off everything on the plates avidly. When he had eaten and drunk his fill, he carried the empty plates to the sink, looking embarrassed at overstepping a boundary. Qamar asked him to leave everything and to go and rest. He told her that he would sleep in the living room, on the floor, and that he would leave at dawn. She led him to the bedroom with the single bed, explaining that it wasn't wise for him to sleep in the living room, which was open to the outside door. He didn't argue. He sat on the edge of the bed, alarmed at the cleanness of the sheet and its newness. The whole room was new, with a strong odor of wood and unused sheets. He inferred that the house was large, larger than what a woman alone would have. Then he was terrified by the likelihood that there might be others with her who were away from the house tonight for some reason, and who might return later, possibly at the end of the night. He asked her if anyone lived with her in the house and she reassured him by saying, "I'm alone." Then she showed him the bathroom and went to the kitchen to bring him the tea. When she returned, she saw half his body stretched out on the bed, while his feet, still in their boots, dangled to the floor. He had dozed off, his head on the pillow and his eyes, narrow in waking, relaxed when they were closed. A smile filtered from his half-open mouth, as if it were a sigh of ultimate salvation. Qamar put the tea on the bedside table next to him and cautiously lifted his feet onto the bed. He did not move. He went into a deep sleep, his body plunged almost into a stupor. She thought about taking off his shoes, but she had heard that the fedayeen slept with their shoes on. She spread a light blanket over him, turned out the light, and closed the door on him.

In her bed, Qamar was visited by many ideas, perhaps all the ideas that existed in the world, even those that seemed unnatural. Some of them tarried, lingering; others shot swiftly through her mind. The bullets that intermittently pierced the night sky frightened her thoughts, making them fly out of her head anxiously, and she needed time to gather them or call them back. She tossed and turned, bumping into many different faces. She saw a little girl with thick black hair and long bangs covering her forehead and her eyes. The girl had sunk to her knees on the ground. The sound of penetrating sobs came from her, and she was shaken by enormous, successive shudders that ran through her curled body. Qamar leaned down over the girl and patted her shoulder with compassion; then she raised the long, thick locks of hair from her eyes, and was terrified. The girl looked a lot like her, to the point of being identical. The girl cried profusely, violently, while the whites of her eyes were stained with a blood red. Qamar reached out to wipe away the girl's tears, which had become so mingled with her own tears that she no longer knew whose tears were whose, and she wiped the whole face of the girl from the screen of her vision. In the place of the weeping face was a blank, and in the blank a heavy body fell on her, with a huge head and no face. When Qamar tried to push away the heavy body, with all the determination and despair she possessed, she was crushed. Her ears rang with the sound of pins streaming onto the floor in a noisy, metallic waterfall, the ringing puncturing her spirit, which had contracted severely. She opened her eyes anxiously and shook the traces of the ringing out of her ears. She looked at the other side of the bed, tinted with dark-blue shadows that penetrated the translucent curtains from the outside heavens, lit with a timid half-moon. She saw Hajj Faisal stretched on his back, his pale face bearing the signs of the impending unhappy end. His hands were folded on his chest and his eyes were directed toward the ceiling, open wide, as if he could not believe what he was seeing.

Barely had she closed her eyes again when she heard a knocking on the door. She got out of bed and ran barefoot, covering the distance from her bedroom to the hall that divided the bedrooms from the living room and the entryway leading to the outside door, in a time that seemed endless to her. On the long, exhausting way from her bedroom to the outside door, she was surprised to find the curtains in the living room torn away; even the windows had been torn out of their frames, so an enormous cavity appeared in the wall, through which rushed violent blue winds. The knocking on the door became faster and she tried to hurry, but the blue wind pushed her back until she almost fell. She was panting, as if she were running in a wasteland. And when she opened the door she was attacked by dozens of dogs, who barked loudly and threw her down, tearing her clothes and planting their teeth in her flesh, eagerly mangling her. The dogs were frightening, like mad wolves, deeply black, with broad, prominent snouts and tongues as red as fire. From her place on the floor she glimpsed Zaid standing at the door, his eyes fixed on her, while the dogs continued tearing her flesh from her bones.

Qamar woke to crimson dawn light entering her room from the window, covering the upper part of her body where she lay. Her senses were gripped by the intermittent barking of dogs outside. It was far away. She hugged her arms to herself, and was somewhat relieved to find that her flesh had not fallen away. She looked at the empty side of the bed. Neither the sheet stretched on it nor the puffed pillow bore any trace or wrinkle to indicate that any human life had occupied it, or even any human death. She got out of bed heavily; she was thirsty, and she went to the kitchen. The bare tiles swallowed the sound of her bare feet. Quiet covered the house, except for the buzz of the refrigerator. She drank water from the bottle and recovered her breath from the emptiness she had traversed in her dream. She stood in the living room, which was still clothed in the remnants of the night. She lifted the edge of the curtain and tried to survey the sleeping street. Suddenly the barking of the dogs rose to her, the sound very near this time, as if it were under the window. She let down the curtain anxiously, moving away.

On her way back to her room, she stopped at his room. She opened the door slowly and peeked at him. She saw one side of his reclining body. She opened the door wider and went up to his bed. His frame looked smaller in sleep than in waking. He lay like a child who has spent his day playing, and then thrown himself on the bed in his clothes, worn out. The slumbering face looked serene, unexpectedly. She brought her face close to his and her lungs filled with the odor of his tanned skin, combining the smells of the sun, the air, and wilderness. The odor was not very apparent, nor was it repellent; it was amassed, hinting of dry roads and sweat and his body shunning water for days. She reached toward his shoulder, then pulled back. Closing the door on him, she calmly retreated to her room.

It was nearly 10:00 in the morning when Ghassan came into the kitchen. His accumulated smell preceded him. She turned at his voice, which was tinged by guilt. "I should have left!"

Qamar told him that she had tried to wake him but had felt sorry for him, as he seemed to be in a deep sleep. He admitted to her that he felt as if he had awakened from a coma. He didn't remember when he had gone to sleep, or how. For the first time in a long time he'd felt as if he were falling into sleep, just like that, and that he was sinking down, far down, in fact going to the farthest possible point, without dreaming. That did not mean that his dreams on ordinary days were pleasant. In sleep his mind was black, and for him that was something restful, in a sort of strange way. Then, as if he remembered something that had slipped his mind, he looked at her and said apologetically, "Good morning!"

Qamar smiled as she put the firm omelet on a shallow plate on the table, amid a collection of small plates containing cheese, labneh, olives, apricot jam, and a cucumber pickle.

In the daylight, his complexion was less tanned and less worn. His face was more relaxed and joyful. His eyes were wider, taking in more of her and her movements; she even felt as if she were about to slip inside him, and that she would keep on slipping until she reached the inside of his soul, and—to her absolute amazement—that was something that would cause her no anxiety. His speech was also less reserved and more fluent. He dug into the food with an appetite. Then, as if he realized that the mistress of the house, on whom and on whose house he had imposed himself, was not eating, he invited her to share the food. "I already ate," she told him, as she put the coffeepot on the fire. As she was placing two cups on a small wooden tray, she asked, "How do you take your coffee?"

He answered through a large bite crammed into his mouth, "Without sugar."

He suggested that she open the curtains of the window in the living room. She should not change the routine of her day. He told her that he would stay in the small bedroom until night fell, when he would leave. He asked her if she was expecting anyone to visit her, and she lifted her eyes and turned down her lips in a sign of uncertainty. During normal times her living room was full of clients, but since the beginning of "the events" the women came only rarely, and sometimes only to chat. She said "the events" with some misgiving, so he felt that maybe he should explain to her that he was forced to become part of these "events," one of those engaged in them. No one wanted these events to occur, he told her; we were pushed into this by force. But on the radio they say that *you* are the ones who pushed them into it by force, she answered him. He lit the last cigarette from a wrinkled pack in his pocket and took the last sip of the coffee, then told her that everyone believes what he wants to believe.

"*I* don't want to believe anything!" she told him as she extinguished the end of her cigarette in her coffee cup, clearly indicating her determination to end the discussion. He offered to help her, with anything at all. He could wash the dishes, for example; he used to help his mother with the housework. She laughed, acknowledging that she could not imagine him bearing arms and washing dishes. He too couldn't keep from smiling. That was before the arms, he told her. His five sisters, all older than he, had gotten married when he was still a child, so he had quickly earned the epithet "Mama's boy."

"And your father?" she asked, mildly curious.

He was drying the plates that she was washing, and placing them in the two-tiered metal dish rack. In a rather troubled voice, he said, "My father . . . he's just my father." His eyes followed her, making a fence around her, as she stood, as she sat, as she worked behind the sewing machine. She seemed to be trying to distract herself from him by anything at all, rather than actually cutting or sewing. He declared to himself that she was too beautiful to be a seamstress. And she was certainly too beautiful to be a woman living alone. She was folding some silky lining fabrics and arranging them in the closet when he knocked on the door of the sewing room and said, "I'm thinking of washing up, if you don't mind."

She agreed. She asked him about his clothes. He smelled his shirt and lifted his eyebrows as if he were shocked, admitting mockingly that the smell was unbearable, but that he would be forced to put them on again after his bath. She went into her room, opened a drawer in her clothes closet, and handed him a set of men's pajamas. He looked at her questioningly.

"These belonged to my late husband," she told him, as she placed a towel and a washcloth in his other hand. The navy pajamas, striped with a lighter blue, looked as if they had not been worn, or as if they had been folded in their place for years. He felt ashamed that he had not asked her before about anything in her life. Once again, he declared to himself that she was too young and too beautiful to be a widow; she was too young and too beautiful to be as she was, alone, young, beautiful—no, more than just "beautiful"—and living in a large, unfriendly, desolate house, even if it was less so during the day, with nothing in it that resembled her.

The smell of soap and water surged from the hinges of the closed bathroom door. The sigh of water falling on exuberant human flesh, vigorous with life, flowed over her. She pressed her foot on the pedal of the machine, and the sound of the successive, jittery stitches overcame the tremolo of the water. The fabric collected under the rushing needle and wrinkled amid a pile of tangled thread. She lifted her foot from the pedal, cut the thread, and pulled the piece of cloth from under the needle, throwing it aside. She tried to stifle the tremor that flared in her body, but she could not. The hot water came down over her and her senses overflowed with soapy steam and the remnants of an aroma stored in a body that had left the obedience of the world, and now here it was besieging her world.

He stood before her in the large pajamas, barefoot, with his aromatic skin, his dewy eyes, and his loose, wet hair framing his face, and she was reassured that he resembled no one she had ever known before. In fact, even though he had borrowed the house, the bread, the bed, the unconsciousness of sleep, the pajamas, the little time between them, and the restricted space that brought them together, he resembled no one but himself, in some way that she was at a loss to understand.

She asked him to give her his clothes so she could wash them for him, and he assured her that he had washed his underwear and his socks and hung them on the shower curtain rod. It wasn't a good idea, he explained, to wash the khaki pants and the shirt, since very little sun and air came in through the small bathroom window and they would not dry before evening. And of course the kitchen balcony was not an option to hang out his laundry. She agreed.

Based on his suggestion, she opened the living-room curtains partway. From afar, at the head of the main street, she glimpsed an open army vehicle in which sat four individuals in military uniform.

He read the concern on her face and tried to relieve her by saying, "Don't worry, I'm going to leave at night! I'm not going to cause you any problems."

"I don't think the road will be safe at night . . . at least, not tonight."

Qamar might have read a desire on his part to stay, but the absolute truth was that she wanted him to stay. She shut the curtain completely, ignoring his suggestion. Their two spirits shone in the daylight, as just enough of the light filtered through the thick curtain.

"Do you like okra?" she asked enthusiastically.

His eyes gleamed in anticipation. His movements were now freer, between the kitchen, the living room, and his room. He answered, "I adore it!"

For the first time since he had invaded her existence, she did not see him as forced upon her life, in any conceivable way. Maybe it was because he was in pajamas, and because he was barefoot, and because the effect of the water and soap had not completely overcome the odor of his own body. In some way that she could not understand or explain, he made the house more complete, or made it more rational. The air of emptiness and silence, the odor of bare wood, the sense of scarce life, all receded from the plentiful, voluminous, empty furniture. That was true even though, in his night and half day, there he had occupied only the single bed, in his long unconsciousness, and a kitchen chair, in his ravenous waking.

By the time night was beginning to fall, he had told her many things. He recounted to her pages from the chapter of his unexceptional childhood. He told her about the first cigarette he smoked, which brought him a painful beating from his father. He told her about the neighbors' daughter, the first and last one he loved, and about how her brother broke his head. He was crazy about her, but she preferred her cousin, who worked in Saudi Arabia, to him. He laughed when he told her how the last time he had seen her, three years earlier, she had been carrying one child and pulling another with her and had seemed happy, very happy— something that terrified him. He laughed more when he told her that his consolation was that her brother became one of his dearest friends and companions. He told her about the schoolmate who had later become a brother in arms, and how they fought side by side in the Battle of Karameh against the Israeli army. He wept as he told her how his companion had sacrificed himself for him, throwing his body over him as they ran fleeing from the bullets that rained down on them. His body, which was being riddled without letup, was trembling on top of him. When the bullets stopped, he was washed in his companion's blood.

Then, in the middle of his tears, he remembered his mother. His mother loved the songs of Shadia in the movies. She sang all the time, singing when she was alone, singing to herself, though he was often able to listen in, behind her back, as she sang while cooking or while hanging out the wash.

"Do you like Shadia?" he asked her.

Qamar smiled, and he didn't wait for her to acknowledge her love. He laughed happily as he called to mind the evenings with his companions in the open air, singing and chanting the rousing songs of the revolution in their gruff voices. He had pretended to join in, but in his heart he was reciting a certain song that his mother loved more than any other. He wasn't going to admit that to them. On the nights when the song crossed his mind, he would repeat stanzas from it. He was afraid that if the strong, rough fighters heard him, he'd become a laughingstock for them. He said "strong, rough fighters" theatrically, roughening his voice and puffing out his chest. Qamar gave him a curious look, inquiring and even insistent. He inclined his head toward her, supporting his chin on his hand, and began to hum in a faint voice, the melody wavering. Then his voice gradually rose and the tune found its groove, without any stopping or deviating or obvious discord: "If from my eye he went away, still in my heart he'll stay. It's a heart that loves but once and never more will stray." Then he sketched on his face a look of menace or threat, while changing his voice to be more feminine: "By all that's happened to him and me, that no one could foresee, I'll take his sleep away, and keep him from leaving me. . . ." Then, when he reached "Let him not harden his heart and forget all we had from the start," his voice intertwined with his mother's voice, and a lone tear appeared on his cheek.

"My father doesn't like Shadia," he told her, having stripped the feminine quality from his voice. When his father entered the house, his mother would stop singing; in fact, it seemed as if she was abandoning life. He looked at Qamar suddenly, his expression full of curiosity: "And you? You haven't told me anything about yourself!"

She told him that her life wasn't as exciting as his. And then she added, as if answering an earlier question: "I like Shadia, but I like Fairuz more."

He laughed, and said, "Me too—I like Shadia like my mother, but I like Fairuz like my girlfriend."

She would have liked him to hold her in his arms. Then she wouldn't slip away, her head would go on resting on his chest, sheltered by his breath, cradled sometimes by his voice and sometimes by his mother's, by Shadia's voice when he would be tender, and by Fairuz's voice, her Fairuz, when he would be passionate. He would be proud sometimes, elevated, unattainable, and at other times easy, down-to-earth, and approachable. She wanted to tell him that his mother's voice was beautiful and that she liked it, but his voice was more beautiful, and she liked it more. She wished very much that she could tell him that.

During the night, Qamar wept. She shut herself in her room and wept a great deal, for a long time. Her eyes hemorrhaged water. Her hoarse weeping mixed with the barking of the dogs outside. Then successive bullets pierced her heart, and she fell on her bed, a corpse.

Qamar was coming up the stairs of the building, carrying bags, when she saw her neighbor Shahla standing at the top of the stairs on the second floor. Qamar's breath suddenly stopped; then she exhaled and put an expression of surprise on her face. Shahla told her that she had knocked on her door several times, since she did not expect her to be out of the house. She added, "It seemed like I smelled coffee inside."

Qamar concealed her agitation and asked her, "When did you get back from Karak?"

"This morning."

Abdallah, Shahla's husband, judged that leaving their house in these times might not be the right decision. Qamar was trying to balance the weight of the bags in her hands when Shahla noticed that her load was heavier than usual. Her eyes fell on one bulky bag in particular, through which she could see many loaves of bread pressed together. "All this bread?" she asked in amazement. Qamar explained to her effusively that this was the first time she had left the house in days, and that she had to stock up from the shop and the baker's oven nearby.

One of the bags fell to the floor while Qamar was trying to open the door with the key, and four packs of Kamal cigarettes fell out. Shahla helped her gather up what had fallen, without stifling her question: "What's this—did you change brands?"

"That's what's in the shop!"

Qamar smiled, as if that wasn't unusual or didn't matter much to her. She didn't escape completely from Shahla's siege, however, since she offered to help carry her things inside. Qamar gathered in the bags so they would look smaller and lighter than they were, and shook her head.

"There's no call for you to go to any trouble!"

Shahla suggested that she have coffee with her, but Qamar excused herself. She told her she had been suffering from a bad headache since the night before, when she didn't sleep a wink—the bullets weren't sleeping, she told her, and neither were the dogs! Shahla showed her understanding, and then she brought her face close to Qamar's, and warned her: "Close the door behind you really well! Those 'dogs' have started coming into houses!"

Qamar's heart was pounding violently when she closed the door. The clock on the wall of the entryway showed that it was almost noon. Ghassan was sitting on his bed reading an old newspaper, and he saw the distress on her face. She handed him the bag of cigarettes and turned to leave, but he caught her hand. That was only the second time he had touched her, even though his gesture was unconscious. He sat her down beside him on the edge of the bed. He had now been present in her house and in her life for seven days, and during that time Qamar had washed his shirt and pants for him, they had eaten, drunk coffee, and smoked together, and they had talked together about everything that had no bearing on anything important. They had plunged into laughter several times, and had sung together some tender songs from Fairuz. She liked "They taught me to love you, they opened my eyes; then we met and they talked, to blame me and chastise." But he liked "Qamara, O Qamara, don't climb the tree; it's so tall and you're still so small, O Qamara." She confessed to him that she had loved Hajj Faisal deeply, even though that seemed to go against all logic and life, and that when he held her in his hands she felt as if she had found her father and her mother, whom she had lost. That did not turn her away from him as a husband or distance her from him; in fact, it was the opposite. She confessed to him that in spite of everything, the man without a face continued to appear to her on many nights. She also confessed to him, with some embarrassment, that she didn't like Shadia, which she admitted was against all logic and life, but she liked her in his mother's voice, brought to her by his voice. Also during their days together they wept, to the point of sobbing out their souls, each alone, at night, in a room. Likewise during that time there had been passing knocks on her door, and brief visits from restless clients, visits that were confined to the threshold. Whenever the sound of footsteps coming toward her door was heard, the blood would rush in his veins and he would isolate himself in his room, repressing his pulse and his breath to the lowest possible point, so that the scattered aroma of his existence nearly disappeared.

He drew near to her, almost panting, and said, "I have to leave!"

They were very close together, in a way that might have been accidental and passing, or that might have been willed and desired. It was very possible that his lips might touch her face or brush against locks of her hair falling over her cheek. His breath scorched her. The accumulated odor of his body pervaded her, like a jolt of electricity that seemed outwardly light and quick but that left a far-reaching stinging and numbing, and penetrated her deeply. He told her that her door would not remain closed in the face of people forever, that he could not stay hidden forever. Also, he was sure that her neighbor would not leave her alone very long. She refused the possibility that he would not be with her tomorrow, and the day after, and the day after that.

She tried to deter him: "But the road isn't safe!"

The road was never going to be safe, he told her, with a resignation that grew out of wisdom acquired early on. It was true that he didn't know where it would lead him when he chose to walk it, but he absolutely knew where it would not lead him. He could not remain in her life, she knew that. The painful thing was that she did know that, very well. In the path of his life he had shunned routine, for he had not kept to the same place or to the same time or to the same land or wood or cave—and routine, as he had discovered to his great alarm, was love.

"I'll leave before dawn."

All her arguments to convince him to stay were useless. She asked him to give her some time to get rid of his clothes, to buy him clothing that would not arouse suspicion. She would buy him new shoes, too, instead of his military boots. He told her that new clothes would not help him much. She brought him Hajj Faisal's brown abaya and red checkered keffiyeh, and told him irritably, "At least wear these!"

She added that it made no sense to go around in the streets with military pants, almost openly. She threw the abaya and the keffiyeh on the bed and angrily closed the door of her room behind her.

The barking of the dogs died down that night, and the nightly bullets dissolved into a continuous silence, so it seemed as if everything frightening, sad, or conducive to unhappy endings was over. Qamar opened her closet and reached into a distant corner of it. She brought out a short dress of black velvet and spread it on the bed. Her hand rolled down over its breast and waist, slipping down to its hem. Her eyes lit up as she drank in its deep black. The neon light of the room fell on it, and it shone with evasive moonbeams. She put her hand on her mouth, smothering a smile tinged with hidden excitement.

It had happened months earlier. Her hands and eyes had been roving among a number of satiny fabrics in a fabric shop when her eye wandered, settling on a single bolt of black velvet on one of the shelves. When the salesman broke open the folds of the bolt before her, the cloth, with its silken substance, had taken possession of her senses. The salesman plunged his hand into the heart of the black billows before her, assuring her that it was of natural silk, and that there was nothing to equal it anywhere in the market. He added, as he passed his fingers over the haughty, arrogant, imperious fabric, that it was free of any trace of nylon or polyester or even synthetic velvet. Then he said, snobbishly, "Not just anybody can buy velvet . . . real *velvet*!"

She herself didn't understand why she had bought this precious broad black sea, but all the way from the market to her house she was overflowing with joy. If her life weren't the life she well knew, Qamar would have thought that the form she had sketched in her imagination wasn't a gift to herself alone, but rather that it was for some potential man, one man in particular, a man who was *the* man. She sketched herself in a dress that outlined the terrain of her body, terrain that she knew well, that she examined secretly when she was alone and desired love. When she unfolded the fabric on the cutting table at home, she was awed by the abundant, billowing black. The black was like luxurious kohl used to outline beautiful wide eyes, like hers. As her hand rolled over the cloth, it revealed an inky black, and then a black like coal, and then the black of a night in which the moon and the stars glistened. When her fingers swam through it, she was intoxicated by its fineness. It was everything she could dream of, everything she could ask.

Qamar did not sleep that night. She worked on it at the beginning of the night and in the middle and at the end. She designed it and cut it and sewed it and lined it and steamed it, until morning came and she put it on, giddy with delight. Its deep black swallowed the light of day, and so even in the light it remained as black as black can possibly be—like ink, like coal, like the night, enthralling. Qamar inspected her appearance in the mirror; she saw herself as beautiful, satisfied, and full. It would have been enough to feel that internal fullness for her to be a truly happy woman.

Here she was returning to it months later. She slipped easily into her velvet, fluidly lifting the zipper of the dress, creating a sound that was the sound of yearning, of deferred opportunities. She let her soft, black hair hang behind her back, where it became a natural extension of the quiet night that enveloped her. She outlined her cocoa-colored eyes with liquid black kohl, and her face shone. When she surrounded her neck with a light cloud of Shalimar perfume, with the scent of vanilla and an overpowering powdery basis beneath it, a light knocking crept from the door of her room to her heart.

He sat beside her on the edge of the bed. His knee touched her knee. He came closer, and his thigh under the khaki cloth moved against her thigh, beneath the velvet. His hot breath mixed with the winged particles of vanilla. He put his hand on the shoulder of the dress and then let it descend slowly down her side, until it settled on her waist and his fingers roamed the forest of velvet clothed in the delicacy of silk. They crept to her flat midriff in its velvet, then rose to her breast, partially uncovered, under the night of velvet lit by longing. In a silence that enveloped the universe, the space that had contracted almost to nothing between him and her velvet was what separated him from rugged night paths, from bullets that were not stray, from barking like that of wolves. The night was completely quiet. Its mist veiled their secrets, and the stars concealed their tidings.

He buried his head in her midriff, gulping the nectar of the velvet, filled with the scents of memories carried forward, memories of jasmine in languid paths, of dewy lilies at dawn, of unhurried morning coffee crowned with foam, of damask roses on lazy afternoons, of riotous grape arbors in late summer evenings, of mint on fresh, nighttime breezes, of sage on cold, austere nights. He traveled her velvet country, the east and the west, the north and the south; he roamed its plains and thickets, plunging into its rivers and valleys and scaling its heights, before settling on her breast, dizzy and dizzying, hoping never to wake. He was smelling her, breathing her, inhaling her, as her breath rose and fell. He floated over her being, which was light and lightened of its reserve, hovering over his being and its wistful aroma. His trembling lips kissed her rising breast, then her pulsing neck, then rose to her temples, then her forehead, descending to the tip of her nose before fusing with her lips that bit his, after long privation. The sound of the sliding zipper broke the silence of the universe and the night of velvet streamed to the floor, its ink flowing amid the clamor of their bodies and the fusion of their breath, rising together on a cloud of commanding rapture and tyrannical desire. He swam in her flesh that was like the full moon, drinking its water, ladling its fragrance, storing from it his provisions for many coming days. She was thirsty but did not want the thirst slaked all at once, hungry without wanting to be sated in a way that would weigh down her body, which had been swallowed by the desert of her days. She wanted to be filled by him, to take him into her and not discharge him. Even when his body left her at last, his pulse had been planted in her heart.

"Don't go!" She knelt at his feet as he was tying the laces of his boots.

He lifted her from the floor and embraced her, whispering, "I'll come back to you."

He stood at the outer door, burying his face in the wood, before he turned to her in farewell. Qamar thought he was afraid; he hesitated. She wished he would run to her and throw himself into her arms, saying, "Hide me!"

"Don't be long!"

He adjusted the folds of the red keffiyeh on his head and gathered in the edges of the dark brown abaya, and then he opened the door. He had disappeared into the dark of the night when she said to him, through overflowing tears, "I love you."

"Do you know that you're too beautiful and too young to be a seamstress?" The bald man with the long head didn't take his eyes off her. "They say you're a skilled seamstress!" He affected surprise as he sat behind his desk, turning over a pile of papers. He was short, his figure inclined to thickening. His extremely blue eyes were the most prominent feature of his spongy, inconsistently white face, with splotches of red almost like traces of smallpox. The blue of the eyes was excessive, artificial, so a person might think they were borrowed from a plastic doll. Qamar sat on a chair facing him. Someone entered, carrying a file in his hand.

"Ali Bey! They're all waiting for you."

Ali Bey aimed a resolute look at his face and said, "Let them wait!"

The man with the file withdrew, closing the door behind him. From the other side of the desk, Ali Bey leaned close to Qamar's face. Qamar recoiled, escaping from his breath, where licorice toothpaste had not succeeded in hiding the traces of tobacco and offensive morning breath.

He tried to make the matter seem normal, saying, "We just wanted to be sure that none of those dogs meddled with you or intruded on you in your house." Then he added, supplementing his words with a suggestive wink, "Your neighbor Sitt Shahla was worried about you."

He took a pack of Kamal cigarettes out of his pocket and offered her one, then lit the lighter before her face. He asked her in a tone that pretended to be a simple inquiry, just for information: "Oh, right, what brand do you smoke?"

Hawwa imagines that she's hearing noise in the sky. Maybe it's thunder, she tells herself, hopefully. She pulls back the curtain and her eyes wander over the roof of the sky, cloaked in the veil of night. But the sky is restrained, showing no indication of any contractions. She's anxious. She wishes it would rain, that it would rain tonight and tomorrow night and the one after, all the coming nights, that it would keep on raining and raining until all the water in history were shed.

A few drops of rain had hit the window earlier, like rapid shots that gave Hawwa's heart a fright before they stopped. That had been the night before the era of extended rain. Ayid and Qais didn't pay any attention to the bullets of water, because the voice of their appetite, which was never satisfied, was louder than anything else. Hawwa had been determined that they would eat supper with her that evening, and she prepared the occasion with care. She made them a platter of grilled chicken and cooked Dawoud Pasha for them, overflowing with round kofta meatballs and swimming in a sauce of fresh tomatoes and thinly sliced onions, as well as rice with vermicelli. She laid out the meal, which included side dishes of pickled cucumbers and peppers and salad, on the long table in the small guest room, where she received her higher-class clients. She had bathed Rabia, dressed her, and put her in her wheelchair in that room, which she had dusted and put in order that afternoon. Hawwa was watching Ayid fill a second plate with rice, pouring over it half a dozen meatballs, while Qais finished off an entire chicken, when she told them that someone had asked for her hand in marriage. Ayid's chewing slowed, and the skeleton of the remaining chicken lay scattered on Qais's plate. They lifted their eyes toward her. Without looking at them, Hawwa went on crumbling a meatball, mashing it into rice and tomato sauce, and feeding it to Rabia, whose eyes trembled more as she looked at her son and grandson.

Munir was his name, Hawwa told them, and then corrected herself: "Abu Laila." He was fifty-four years old, and a widower. She wiped traces of tomato sauce from Rabia's mouth and brushed away a few grains of rice that clung to her chin. She seemed more courageous when she looked at Ayid and told him that Abu Laila was building a house on a piece of land in Ain al-Basha, and that he would take her to live there, with Rabia, and "he's going to take good care of Rabia," as he had assured her. For a little while Ayid's eyes, nearly frozen and unreadable, did not leave her, while Qais's eyes had left her and were fixed on the large, round dish of Dawoud Pasha, where the meatballs were diminished and the sauce had nearly run out. He took advantage of his uncle's inattention and ladled what remained of the meatballs over a hill of rice with vermicelli on his plate. Ayid went back to the table. He swallowed the one remaining meatball in the dish and began gnawing at a half chicken, without saying a word. Hawwa poured them two glasses of Pepsi from a large bottle, and then two more. Then she brought them a fruit platter containing oranges, apples, and bananas. For each of them she peeled two bananas and an orange, which she divided into wedges, and an apple, which she cut into crescents. Then she brought them dessert—cheese kunafa with syrup—and followed that with a pot of sage tea, and then two cups of coffee. They did not speak or try to meet her eyes again. When they stood to leave, Hawwa did not conceal her bewilderment. They had not asked about Munir. They had not inquired about many things that they should have inquired about. It did not seem that they were refusing the matter, but at the same time they did not show any agreement or receptiveness to discussing the subject. In fact, it was as if the subject had not been presented to them at all.

Hawwa stopped Ayid as he was starting to leave. "What about Munir?" she asked. Her face had a questioning expression and showed that she did not understand.

Ayid fixed his eyes on her and said, "We'll talk about it later."

Hawwa appeared insistent. "He wants to set a time to ask for my hand from you and Qais."

Qais exchanged an enigmatic look with his uncle without speaking, and Ayid seemed more insistent than she was when he answered, "I said, we'll talk about it later."

Then he added that he had heard that a severe rainstorm was going to hit the country and God's people the next morning, and that it was expected to last for days. "God willing, things will be better after that." Then he looked at her and asked, "Do you have twenty dinars till the end of the month?" Usually when he asked her for money, Hawwa discussed it with him and asked him to account for the money he wasted, hers and others'. This time she did not discuss his request. She took a twenty-dinar bill out of her purse and gave it to him. She was refolding the rest of the money when he interrupted her: "Or, say . . . what do you say to making it fifty dinars?" She hesitated a little as she counted the money she still had, and then she handed him another twenty-dinar bill and a third bill of ten dinars.

"How are you, Mama?" Ayid looked at Rabia, and she looked at him doubtfully. He bent over her to kiss her head and she drew back in her chair. He left the house, followed by Qais, who continued to avoid his mother's eyes.

Hawwa returns now to the dark eyes with the well-kept shine, in the picture hidden in the darkness of the drawer and the neglect of time. She wipes her fingers over the secret face, which shows compassion, and the eyes flash. She brings the picture up to her eyes, and believes that she sees a tear suspended at the edge of the left eye.

The ringing of her cell phone rises, and Munir's name lights up the screen. But Hawwa, whose eyes are covered with a thick cloud of tears, does not answer. The ringing continues, more insistent than before.

The ringing of the telephone had been incessant in Sitt Qamar's house, as Hawwa was turning the key in the door. It was almost 9:30 in the morning. A passing September rain had washed the houses and the streets, and the smell of the earth rose with the first watering, the first moisture; it was the odor of tyrannical longing, of deprivation, of dried mud debilitated by the thirst of the dirt. The ringing stopped as soon as Hawwa opened the door. Entering her eighth month with Qais, Hawwa had grown very heavy and felt exhausted, so she had started leaving Aya in Rabia's care when she went to Sitt Qamar's house during the day. A heavy silence bore down on the house. Hawwa knew that Sitt Qamar would still be sleeping at this time of the morning; in fact, lately she slept most of the day. But the silence was greater than the silence of sleep. On the floor, Hawwa saw scattered pieces of china. She bent down and picked up a piece, turning it over in her hands, but she could not make out the shape. She swept the tiles with her eyes, and her heart led her to the parlor, whose door opened onto the living room. She was horrified. The floor of the parlor was filled with scattered pieces of china. She looked at the buffet cabinet, its doors open, and put her hand over her mouth to repress a scream. The Romeo and Juliet set had been shattered, and the shell-like china was scattered everywhere. She stepped on an arched piece from a teacup; she lifted her foot cautiously, and saw the wan face of Juliet searching distractedly for Romeo, whose face was lost in the other, shattered, half. Hawwa ran to Sitt Qamar's bedroom; her bed was made, and empty. The silence in the room was dense. Could Sitt Qamar conceivably have gone out? Where could she have gone? The sewing room was just as it had been, with the pieces of a dress on the cutting table, which Hawwa had prepared the day before. The door to the single bedroom was almost closed. Hawwa's heart lurched. She slowly cracked open the door, and Sitt Qamar appeared to her, stretched out on her side on the single bed. Hawwa was surprised to see her lying in the black velvet dress, the open zipper revealing her bare back. On the bedside table lay an empty medicine package. Sitt Qamar was hugging something in her arms, which were crossed over her chest. Hawwa went up to her, and in her hands she saw the frame that held the picture of the golden-haired child. The glass was broken and pieces of it were scattered on the floor. The spring-like face of the child was wrinkled and her laugh was torn. Hawwa pulled the wooden frame from Sitt Qamar's hands and from the open back fell a picture in black and white—a picture of a man with dark eyes that held a hoarded gleam. His head inclined to one side, leaning on his closed hand.

"Sitt Qamar! Sitt Qamar! Wake up, Sitt Qamar! Wake up, Sitt Qamar! God keep you, Sitt Qamar, wake up! For the sake of God, Sitt Qamar, wake up!" Hawwa shook her. The ringing of the telephone in the living room rose urgently. "Wake up, Sitt Qamar! For God's sake, wake up! I kiss your hands, wake up!" She shook her harder. But the silence swallowed her. The ringing of the telephone went on urgently, mixing with Hawwa's screams, "Wake up, Sitt Qamar! Wake up, God keep you, wake up! For my sake, wake up!"

But Qamar's light had gone out, completely.

The cell phone does not stop ringing. On the blurry screen are four calls from Munir that have not been answered. Hawwa looks from the slit of the window curtain to the sky, where the night has come quickly, and weeps. She weeps a great deal. Her eyes drown in the rain flowing from her eyes.

8

THE POT OF OKRA, COOKED this morning and then cooled, is sitting over a tranquil flame, unhurried, to reheat, the aroma rising from the small pieces of okra braised in tomato broth enriched with meat. In another pot Hawwa browns two handfuls of vermicelli in two spoons of fat, then she adds the water, rice, and salt. The starchy steam, scented with the butter, clings to the low ceiling of the kitchen. She closes the pot carefully and leaves the rice to cook at its leisure over a low flame.

Hawwa checks on Rabia. She sees that she is dozing, her head hanging forward, almost plucked entirely from the thin branch of her neck to fall on her chest. The boisterous pictures on the screen and its faint sounds fall on deaf ears and walls. Hawwa moves the crank of the bed and it opens gradually until it's flat. She lifts Rabia's withered body to the top of the bed and adjusts her head on the pillow. Rabia opens her eyes, as if anxious, until she's reassured by Hawwa's face and body, which enclose her; she closes her eyes again and dozes, her face relaxed. Hawwa covers her with a wool blanket, placing a heavy quilt over it. Then she shuts off the television and darkness suddenly flows into the room, except for the two red elements of the gas heater, which stare into the heart of the dark, and some nocturnal light that creeps into the room through the thin fabric of the curtains. Hawwa goes out of the room, leaving the door ajar. She looks at her watch for the hundredth time; it still stands at a few minutes after eight.

The night pouring into the street spreads over her feelings and permeates her. Despite the white neon lights in the entry to the house, in the kitchen, and in the living room, Hawwa feels that she's falling into the night, that she's rolling endlessly at the bottom of the night. She moves to the kitchen and turns off the burners under the rice with vermicelli and the okra, although the tomato broth still bubbles for several seconds before settling. The closed air of the kitchen is moist with the aroma, enriched with meat fat.

The sounds outside diminish gradually, the steps decreasing, and with them the rattles in the throat, the sustained bouts of coughing, and the shoving of small shoulders, in play or quarrels, in the lanes. A dubious calm closes over the street, and the house falls into a deep silence.

Hawwa does not like her house, but she hates it less than the first house with Nazmi, and less than her family's house. In her family's house, Hawwa had not loved herself. In the first house with Nazmi, she hated the house and she hated herself. In the second house with Nazmi, in the last chapter of her life with him, Hawwa no longer thought about loving or hating, especially when Naifa would straddle her and crush her flesh and bones, or put her hands around her neck and squeeze it, watching Hawwa's spirit rising up out of her eyes. In those moments that separated her from a certain death, Hawwa would think that she still wanted to live, and that was something she found strange—how could she love life at the same time that life did not love her? But Hawwa did want to live, in spite of life itself.

Hawwa had been bent over the sewing machine in the daily routine that allowed her to accomplish things without thinking, when Nazmi had come in at the end of the day. He did no more than stand in front of her, staring. Hawwa continued pressing on the pedal of the machine until she finished stitching the side of a dress. When she completed the continuous seam, she lifted her foot and the machine stopped running. She asked Nazmi, without much interest, "What do you want?"

She exchanged looks with him, without reading—as she had done successfully numerous times—what he concealed inside, or picking his locks, which were so easy to break. He didn't want money, the usual explanation. He wasn't angry with her, or feigning anger, for any reason that would or would not justify anger. He didn't seem vengeful or belittling toward her. He didn't seem to be thinking about what he wanted to say, nor did he seem to want to appear intelligent, in an attempt to leave behind the touch of stupidity imprinted on his face as an inborn mark or as a basic feature of it. After a long silence, he said to her, at last, "I'm going to divorce you."

Hawwa placed the second side of the dress under the machine's needle, at the beginning of the seam line. She turned the wheel and brought the needle down at the beginning point, then lowered the presser foot onto the fabric to fix it and her foot pressed on the pedal in a fast motion, continuous and sure. Her hand guided the fabric while a straight seam line formed. A drop of water fell on the lemony, silky fabric and the spot of moisture darkened the delicate cloth. Two drops followed the first. Hawwa's eyes were dripping water.

Hawwa did not weep because Nazmi was divorcing her after twenty years of feeding off her spirit, which had endured miraculously. Hawwa did not weep because at last he was going to leave her, or leave what remained of her. Hawwa wept because lovely things come late. She wept because Nazmi could have assaulted her life for a shorter lifetime; she wept because he could have mounted her flesh for a lesser span, a lesser fate; she wept because all the bitterness that exhausted her heart could have been less, much less.

Hawwa does not remember having lived one sweet day with Nazmi, or one day that was not completely bitter, and when she wrings out all her miserable days with him, she cannot summon one moment of warmth. She doesn't remember that they talked together about anything, however trivial or worthless, that nonetheless yielded something human, in the end. She doesn't remember that they laughed together or rejoiced together or shared a piece of bread out of love or anything like love, such as sympathy, perhaps, or pity.

With him, violent winds raged over her, full of dry dust and ferocious rains. Sewers were constantly brimming, rot stagnated, sweat turned rancid. With him, Hawwa was barren, and when he descended on her she urged her body to numb itself, while she sent her spirit—perforce—into a coma, approaching a state of nearly complete lifelessness. Then, when he had spat out his water into her, she ran to the bathroom to expel it, to excrete it, pressing on her womb till the last drop fell.

Nazmi did not buy another bed after the one Hawwa had destroyed and burned. In the beginning, he replaced the marriage bed with two sagging mattresses, putting them side by side temporarily. When he got off her, Hawwa would take her mattress away from his, in an arrangement that seemed comfortable for them both. Then, when Aya entered her life, and Qais followed her, Hawwa began to sleep between her two little ones, and Nazmi began to sleep on the padded pallet in the other room, in front of the television. But he would descend on Hawwa as she slept, jerking her from her mattress to cram her under him on the narrow pallet on the floor; her spirit would bleed every time, as if it were the first time, and the cruelest. When they moved to the second house with three rooms, Hawwa made one room for Aya and Qais, after dividing it in two with a wooden screen. She began to sleep with her grandmother Naifa, in the room set aside for her. On the nights when Naifa didn't descend on Hawwa and trample her with her heavy foot, Nazmi kicked her with his rough-edged foot, with its hardened toenails, and pushed her roughly into the third room, which opened onto the entryway and served as a living room, a dining room, and a room to receive guests.

He would throw himself on her on the pallet, while Hawwa watched her being as it was spilled.

Hawwa was thunderstruck when she became pregnant a few months after giving birth to Qais. She was still nursing him. For a week she gulped down liters of a drink made of boiled parsley, as Umm Said suggested to her, waiting for cramps and the desired miscarriage, but nothing happened. Then she was told that laxative pills might cause her to miscarry, so she swallowed a dozen of them over the course of two days. During that time she felt as if her internal organs had all melted into her liquid feces and that nothing remained unspilled inside her; even her face became dried and thin, her legs went limp, and her eyes nearly popped out of their sockets. But she did not excrete a single drop of the hoped-for blood. One of her clients suggested a private clinic in Jabal Amman that performed abortions without registering the name of the pregnant woman or any information about her, and without asking "why and wherefore." The client rubbed the tips of two fingers together, so Hawwa imagined that the operation would cost her a lot. Her only choice was Umm Omar, the midwife who had retired long ago from births and who now only received women—most of them strangers to the camp—to perform abortions on them, when they came to her with their heads covered and their faces lowered, preferring concealing nights to dishonoring days. Despite her small frame, which had diminished still further throughout her seventy years, Umm Omar was strong. Her hands with their wrinkled flesh fixed themselves on Hawwa's belly, applying pressure and massaging. She chose strategic points where she thrust her fingers, before applying increasing pressure, beginning with her hips and ending at the base of her pubic region. Between one massage process and another she gave her a cloudy, bitter yellow liquid to drink, which Hawwa felt an urgent need to vomit; but Umm Omar pressed her to brace herself, promising her that her salvation was near. After an hour or more of localized massaging, violent and intermittent, Hawwa went into a near faint. Umm Omar wiped away the sweat streaming from her brow, face, and neck. Then she came close to her with the good news: "Thank God for your safety."

Nazmi slept in the living room. When he wasn't hosting his companions in cigarettes and never-ending cups of tea during lethargic evenings, he would sprawl on the floor cushion in front of the television until he fell dead asleep. Hawwa put her sewing machine in Qais's and Aya's room, specifically in Aya's half, and worked on it there. Qais and Aya never stopped complaining about the rumble of the machine's motor. Naifa never stopped banging on the closed door of her room and yelling for "the whore," meaning Hawwa, to open it for her. And Nazmi never stopped calling "the bitch," meaning Hawwa, to fry him up some eggs and tomatoes, if that crossed his mind at the end of the night.

When Nazmi stood in front of the machine, Hawwa did not ask him, why now? He could have divorced her before this, long before this. She would have cried less; perhaps she would have rejoiced more, and the bitterness, then, would not have turned into a growing, pus-filled abscess in her heart. It's likely that Nazmi explained his motives to her at that moment. Maybe he said a lot, and probably he was direct in explaining the reasons for his decision, but Hawwa heard only a blur of words. A great whistling rang in her head, mixed with the sound of sobbing imprisoned in her breast and intercut with Naifa's shrieks from her room, as she kicked the door with a vengeance and yelled, "Open up, you whore!"

Lutfi tried to intervene in the matter, against Hawwa's wishes. He thought he knew the cure for Nazmi, so he offered to increase the monthly sum he gave Hawwa to care for Naifa. But Nazmi remained firm in his position, and that brought some relief to Hawwa's spirit. If Hawwa hadn't known better, if she hadn't known his vile character and his base soul, she would have thought he was in love. Nazmi married Fariha, a widow five years older than he was who lived in an apartment she owned in Abu Nseir. She had been a beautiful woman in her youth, and she still bore traces of charm even when she had passed through her forties and was knocking on the door of fifty. She had been in her twenties when she was widowed, the second wife of her late husband. He had not given her a son to advocate for her, but he left her a reasonable sum of money that was very useful to her; for she married and divorced three times after that, and in each marriage her husband—who had been after her coin—emerged with only the shirt on his back, and maybe with fewer coins than he had originally. In fact, it was said that she stopped her third husband, who had barely lasted six months with her, at the door of the apartment: she asked him to take off the new shoes she had bought for him, and handed him the old shoes he had come in with.

Fariha stopped at the butcher shop where Nazmi worked one morning and asked him very specifically to cut up half a sheep for her, one raised locally. Nazmi was taken with Fariha's eyes, thick with kohl and blinking from beneath her face veil. Fariha was watching Nazmi's arm admiringly, as it descended on the animal, which gave off an odor of new blood. The admiration did not escape Nazmi's attention. Fariha's breath came fast below her veil, so the black, silken fabric stuck to her mouth and outlined her features. The temperature rose in Nazmi's body, leading him to exaggerate in demonstrating for her his skill in butchering. After a number of visits to the butcher shop, Fariha lifted the veil from her face; it was bursting with abundant life, overcoming time, and it did not disappoint Nazmi. She bit her lower lip, which was very swollen, and her appetite for men awoke Nazmi's imaginings, which his eyes betrayed.

Fariha proposed that he run a butcher shop she had recently purchased in Sweileh. She proposed also that he marry her, in order for him to protect her money, but she stipulated that she not share him with any other woman. Nazmi believed that at last life was giving generously to him, in fact much more generously than he had hoped. He worked in Fariha's butcher shop under her vigilant eye, which was reinforced by the eyes of the boys in the shop, who all spied for her. No slaughter animal came into the shop or went out of it without her knowledge, and when he came to her at the end of the day with the receipts, she questioned him about the pound of meat he had sold on credit to one of his acquaintances, and about the lung meat he had given to his son Qais. She allowed him to use her Kia car, which she had bought new from the dealer; but she checked the fuel gauge daily, and if less remained than what could be expected for the distance between the house and the shop, she called him to account sternly. His relatives began to joke that Fariha was "mounting him and fucking him" for nothing.

With Nazmi's departure the house became more acceptable to live in, for Hawwa. The grimness of the mornings lightened, and the nights likewise became less disturbing and constrained, even with Naifa's mounting violence. Hawwa was happy as she cleaned the house with Aya. They washed the curtains and rubbed the walls clean of the traces of cigarette smoke and the dark sediment of phlegm-filled breath, and they scrubbed the set of Morris chairs. Hawwa moved her sewing machine into the living room, and bought a table for cutting and a wardrobe for her clients' fabrics and for their sewing that she took in. But her heart rejoiced more than at any other moment when she folded Nazmi's heavy floor pallet, with its two pillows and its blanket and quilt, and loaded them all in a huge bundle on her back. She supported it on her shoulder with one hand while in the other she carried a small plastic pitcher. She went out on a morning when the sun was compassionate and the air clear, walking through the lanes with grace and lightness, as if she only had a little bird on her shoulder. Hawwa did not feel the length of the trip or the accustomed weariness, from her house to the garbage dump; and if it were some other time or some other, unconstrained place, she would have danced. "Where're you off to, Umm Qais?" her neighbor Umm Said called to her, as she was hanging out her wash on the roof of her house. But Hawwa continued walking, gaily following a twittering, leaping rhythm playing in her spirit: "So do we pluck the hawthorn, ya yumma, just so, and so does the lovely one walk, ya yumma, just so. From thorns we pluck the hawthorn, ya yumma, just so, and so does the little bird sing, ya yumma, just so." With a little imagination, and there was no harm in it, Hawwa saw herself skipping to the hidden rhythm. A few boys gathered around her and offered to help her carry her things: "Leave it, Auntie!" But she refused, showing strength, skill, and steadiness. Between her house and the garbage dump, Hawwa walked for ten minutes or a little more, and her resolve never flagged. In fact, it was as if she had become taller and greater, lofty and towering; even the boys were awed by her, and cleared the narrow way for her. When at last she reached her goal, she threw the enormous mountain on her shoulder to the ground near one of the metal garbage containers, its walls blackened. The bundle split open and its contents scattered. Hawwa gathered it together and piled it up with her foot, then poured kerosene over it and lit a match. The fire sprang up madly, a flame rising in a column, but soon shrinking and weakening with the contraction of the pile, in which polyester was the dominant fabric. On the evening of that day, Hawwa prepared a platter of grilled kofta and tomatoes, which Aya and Qais shared with her. Even Naifa sat with them for supper, and she was less violent, unusually so. They were hungry, as if food had not entered their bellies for a very long time. They ate with an appetite, and when they were satisfied, a strange peace descended on them, like a kind of revelation. For one moment, they imagined that they had at last found the meaning of joy.

Hawwa tried to like the house, to be happy, to enjoy it, to feel safe, after she had rooted out all trace of Nazmi. She painted the walls and changed the curtains. She reupholstered the Morris set. She rearranged the rooms time and time again, setting up the house for Naifa's needs and then for Rabia. When Aya left, and then Qais, she changed their room into a parlor, placing a set of used chairs and sofas in it and using it to receive the clients who were more comfortable, financially, and who came to her from outside the camp.

One night, Nazmi came to her. It was three years after he had divorced her. He stood before her, humbled, and told her he missed the house. Hawwa put her foot on the threshold of the half-closed door and told him, "This isn't your house any more." But Hawwa knew that it wasn't her house, either, and that no matter what she did or how she arranged it, she could not feel that it was her house. No matter what she did or how hard she worked, she could not erase the long chapters of pain inscribed on its cold tiles or its moist, sticky walls. Throughout all her extended time in it, she never felt it was a home. When she left it in the morning she did not yearn to return to it at the end of the day, just as she did not long to return to her family's house during her defiled childhood, or to her first marital house, where the years of her youth were spilled. This house was better than many in the camp. It was definitely more pleasant, and larger and cleaner, and it had reasonably plentiful bread and water, and windows that opened onto a sky that was less stifling. Oranges entered it, and apples, bananas, and pomegranates, as well as peaches, plums, apricots, and even strawberries, following sudden cravings. Chestnuts crackled in it and sweet potatoes hissed, grilling over an unobtrusive fire; it smelled of mastic, ginger, cinnamon, rosewater, and orange-blossom water; within its confines rustled silk, chiffon, satin, and, yes, even velvet as well. Fairuz awoke early in it, and went to sleep late. Her voice both morning and night was moist and pure, and it made the mornings in the house bearable and its nights less miserable. But in the end it was a house of the camp. In essence, it was a sad house.

Munir promised that he would make her love the new house in Ain al-Basha. She declared to him that she wanted it to be like Durrat al-Ain's house, which Faris erected for her from her dream.

It's going to be her house, and Munir is going to build it for her the way she sketched it, from her imagination. It will have a small garden, with a wall, and in it she'll plant lemon trees, apples, figs, grapes, apricots, and peaches. And of course there will be a grape arbor, stretched like a green sky over basins of roses, carnations, violets, mint, and basil; and when they sit together under the arbor in the summer, they'll be intoxicated by the mood of the playful breeze. She won't take her old furniture with her, from the house in the camp. Fine, she'll take her sewing machine with her, but she won't bend over it for long hours. She will sew less, and she might sew only for herself. She will satisfy her constant appetite for velvet, and then more velvet, followed by velvet, then velvet, and velvet, and velvet.

In the calm of the evening, Hawwa seems less anxious. She wants to believe that life is hiding peaceful nights for her when she would not have to be on her guard, that it will not begrudge her deferred joy. She looks at the screen of her cell phone—five missed calls from Munir. Her eyes encompass the small screen and her face relaxes as she presses on Munir's name, and the name lights up at the heart of the screen. She waits for him to answer. She will tell him, "I love you."

It was two years ago when it happened, suddenly. Hawwa had been standing at the Safut stop when a violent storm sprang up. The bodies of people in the streets were jolted and the treetops were aroused, some of them nearly ripped from their trunks, while it looked as if the earth was being violently pierced. Hawwa thought that the sky was raining down stones of glass and she covered her face with her hands so it would not be wounded. But the pellets multiplied at an insane rate, most of them closer to small pebbles with sharp points and with the frightening force of boulders, and they stoned her from all sides. When she opened her eyes at last, she saw that the sky above was covered with clouds, while the hail—which was still pouring down—collected like mothballs, forming thin, fragile white blankets that covered the earth. A dark-blue car was coming toward her. It slowed, blinked the headlights twice, and then stopped. The driver leaned over the passenger seat and opened the door, saying, "Get in, Umm Qais."

Hawwa was still shaking off the remains of her fright from the attack of hailstones that had surprised her in the middle of the January day, gradually getting her breath, when she noticed that she was inside a private car and riding with a man she did not know. She was sitting in the seat next to his and seemed close to him, very close, so close that she could smell the odor of Nabulsi soap from his face and distinguish clearly a large mole on the side of his neck. She could almost count the faint brown freckles covering the back of his dark hand as it gripped the steering wheel. Nonetheless, she did not feel troubled or upset. She did not recoil within herself, anxious that a suspicious look might find her; she did not tell herself that she had perhaps made a terrible mistake, and she did not think that she would get out of the car to walk as soon as the sky stopped hurling its frigid coals. Not for one moment did Hawwa feel any threat in the company of the stranger, and it took her some time to realize that she had not asked him the most important question, one that she needed to ask him: how did he know her name? His Hyundai car, a model that was over ten years old, was in good condition. It reflected a harmony of understanding between the spirit of the human owner and the metal spirit of the vehicle, steadfastly travers-ing the asphalt and confronting the hailstones, the savage air, and the clattering rain. The seats of the car were clean and the upholstery was intact. Even the floor had no trace of dirt or filth, and that made Hawwa lift her feet, unconsciously, to look at the soles; but the man reassured her that she should not think about the floor, when he noticed her embarrassment in a passing, unintentional glance. A string of wooden prayer beads hung from the mirror, and that gave the warm air in the car a feeling of homey peace, aided by the rose fragrance wafting from a bottle of air freshener on the dashboard.

In a voice as deep as velvet, he said to her, "So, you haven't asked me how I knew you."

He was in the first half of his fifties, tall without being huge, and filled out, not coarsely but sturdily, with some flabbiness related to age. He was wearing coal-black pants and a light pink shirt striped with off-white, with a black jacket over it. Hawwa's eyes fell on his shoes, and she did not fail to notice that the black leather was shiny from polish, and that the narrow laces were tied with care. He was clean and orderly, that much was certain. In addition to the Nabulsi soap, his clothes smelled faintly of washing and ironing, mixed with an aroma of perfume with a faint echo of ambergris. His thin gray hair, combed to the back, added fullness to his face, as did his broad forehead. His trim mustache, the same color as his hair, was neither thick nor thin. "Abu Laila." He gave her his kunya name with a broad smile. Then he seemed to correct himself: "Or Abu Naji." His face showed a sudden seriousness, before regaining its happiness.

Hawwa's spirit was filled with an unexpected serenity. She felt an intimacy in the car, whose closed windows blocked the frenzy of nature outside. Fairuz's voice welled up, singing, "How many were the people, waiting for people at the crossroads? Rain came down and umbrellas came out. But in all my days without rain, no one waited for me." Hawwa felt as if she was in her true place, which she had known for a hundred years, without tiring of it, and without its tiring of her. The car was her "day without rain" and her umbrella, and she no longer needed to wait for anyone. Abu Laila raised the volume of the car's tape recorder a little, and the moving picture on the outside, with the air and water raging over everything, seemed like the perfect contrasting background to Fairuz's calming song. Hawwa nestled into her seat, giving herself to the companionship and the street and their possibilities. She wished she could remain a prisoner of the car's place and time.

When Munir stopped the car at the door of her house, Hawwa wondered at their quick arrival, after three Fairuz songs and a lot of talking. Her face was tinted with a faint red like chiffon, from the heat of the car and from some bashfulness. The air folded away its storm and the sky repressed the rain, at least for the moment. She hesitated a little as she got out of the car, turning to him and saying, "Thank you, Abu Laila." She lifted her face to the sky, which was preparing to pour out more storms of water, then she turned her overflowing eyes on him, adding, "I enjoyed it a lot."

He smiled and said, "And I enjoyed it more."

On the way, Munir, who lived in Baqa'a Camp, had told her that his daughter Laila, who lived in the town of Salt, took sewing to Hawwa. Then he looked at her and said, jokingly, "She swears on her honor that you're a skilled seamstress!" Hawwa covered her mouth with her hand, reining in her laughter. She squeezed her eyes shut, trying to remember a client named Laila, so Munir jogged her memory by supplying his daughter's kunya name: "Umm Rami—have you remembered her?" Hawwa's eyes lit up in a sign that she had remembered. Then her image appeared more clearly in her mind.

"She's lovely, God blessed her! She has a mole on her cheek, like Samira Tawfik."

Munir nodded, his voice weakening and bearing traces of a grief held tightly in his heart. "She looks like her late mother."

Many times when she visited him Laila would stop at Hawwa's house, either to give her a piece of fabric to make up for her, or to have a fitting, or to pick up a dress that was ready, or sheets, or cushion covers, or prayer outfits she had asked her to make. One time Munir had himself taken his daughter Laila to Hawwa's house, and then he happened to glimpse her standing at the door of the house. Hawwa wondered how he had noticed her from a passing glimpse at the door, and she wondered still more that he had recognized her on the street, in the middle of the sudden hailstorm.

Hawwa got out of the car heavily and slowly, and an icy gust of wind struck her as soon as she opened the car door. In spite of the considerable talk that had united them, in an atmosphere of abundant warmth fragrant with rose-scented spray, with whiffs of soap, with the light aroma of ambergris from a man's perfume, Hawwa felt that there were still stories that should be told and words that must be said. She dozed off that night thinking about many things she could have told him, and when she woke up in the morning she recalled the trip in the warm car under the storming hail and then under greater storms of water, and was certain that the trip could have included more talk. In the evening, while she was sewing, she fell into deep thought, and lifted her foot off the pedal in order to be able to hear her thoughts, which were swallowed up by the motor of the machine. She blamed herself for having been silent for most of the trip, perhaps for all of it. Why had she only spoken to him a little? she asked herself. On the third day, she longed for him. On the fourth day, she longed for him a lot. After five days, she went to visit Durrat al-Ain in her house in Safut. Durrat al-Ain was surprised, as she was not used to having Hawwa drop in on her twice in less than a week, but she was still glad to see her. Hawwa claimed that she had been somewhere nearby. She drank tea and ate a date-filled cookie. She was listening to Durrat al-Ain's very enjoyable stories with wide eyes and an open heart, while she observed the hands of her watch move more slowly than usual, and reviewed in her memory—where it was still present—the segments of the trip with its few words; so many essential elements of Durrat al-Ain's stories did not stick in her head. Hawwa's eyes suddenly swerved from the road in her head toward Durrat al-Ain, directing a question to her: "When did you know that you loved Faris?"

Durrat al-Ain stopped speaking, emerging suddenly from the mood of playful storytelling. Her eyes traveled to her past, passing through years and years. She recalled the details of the legend, her legend, and then returned, her sight and feelings dazzled. She was amazed, and as amazed as she could be at herself: "Can you believe it? I don't know!"

Durrat al-Ain was collecting her embarrassment and laughing as she tried to spot the precise moment when she knew she had fallen in love with Faris, and failed to identify it.

But Hawwa insisted: "Fine, how does love come?"

It was nearly 3:00 in the afternoon when Hawwa left Durrat al-Ain's house, covering the distance to the main street with great excitement and an urgent yearning. She was feeling light, in spite of the oranges Durrat al-Ain had loaded her with, and in spite of the wool coat that shackled her body. When she reached the sidewalk of the main street, she stopped to wait. A bus stopped near her and two men got off, and a woman dragging a child. Hawwa turned her face away involuntarily, as if she imagined that one of them might know her. Then another bus approached and slowed down. The conductor leaned halfway out of the open door, looking at her to see if she wanted to get on, but Hawwa did not look at him. She waited about half an hour, then she felt that waiting in her place would attract more buses to her. She walked down the street, her eyes turning back from time to time—every time she heard the noise of car tires turning down from the street above and approaching her. But the cold asphalt swallowed up the noise, and the possibilities of the street were crushed under the tires as they rushed away. After an hour or so, the cold wind, which her coat had not completely succeeded in blocking, had loosened Hawwa's joints. Her sensitivity to the cold was increased by that desolate desert that extended in her soul, exposed to the cruelest and most violent kinds of wind. She was walking clumsily, and seemed worn out and discouraged. She did not even bother to pick up the oranges when some of them burst out of the bottom of the plastic bag and rolled on the ground like defeated suns. "It doesn't matter how love comes; what matters is that it comes." She recalled those words of Durrat al-Ain. But he did not come to pull her out of the blows of the freezing wind and from her own disturbed thoughts. Hawwa finally gave in to a bus that signaled to her; inside she gathered in her lap what remained of the oranges, together with an enormous anger. She was angry with herself, and blamed herself a great deal because she had read into the first trip imaginary things that had not happened, and had freighted it with words that had not been spoken, and with others that should have been said.

Two weeks later, Hawwa was standing at the Sweileh Circle roundabout when rain descended in a tousled mist. She raised her wool shawl over her head in an improvised awning and signaled to a taxi, which ignored her and passed her rapidly. She signaled to another and the driver stopped for two girls, perhaps university students, who were protecting themselves from the water under their bags. Then suddenly, here he was coming up to her in his car, quietly, as if the car tires were moving lightly over the light water, which had turned the asphalt into a shining black skin. It seemed as if his face and his voice had unfolded suddenly before her senses. She heard the words she had longed for more than any others: "Please get in, Umm Qais."

Hawwa gathered in her wet wings and hopped into the car, like a bird seeking warmth and dryness. The car, with its closed windows, was fragrant with the aroma of roses.

The whiffs of Nabulsi soap were concealed, ceding the way to the scent of ambergris that his body disclosed, and that had remained in her nose since their first meeting. She had believed that she had forgotten him in the last two weeks, and that his appearance in her life had been as unexpected as the hailstorm, even though it was less violent. After her anger with herself, because she had expected what she should not expect, and the bitterness that erupted in her deprived soul, marked by drought, Hawwa had realized that in her life, nothing—nothing at all—was to be expected. But as soon as she sat next to him in the car, she was certain that she had been waiting for him, expecting him, that he was the one thing, perhaps, the one being, that she had been waiting for in despair.

The trip was silent, except for the faint whimper of the windshield wipers, and that was submerged by a sound washed in a spray of rain, coming from the tape recorder: "Our date to meet is tomorrow, but it's late, this tomorrow. Do you think it still waits for us, my love? I see you in the clock, in the ticking of the clock, coming from far away, O my love."

Hawwa was not thinking about tomorrow. The world could rain tomorrow and the day after tomorrow, and she would wait on the sidewalk. It could fling hail and stones, it could snow ferociously, it didn't matter—her world, Hawwa's world, would "rain jasmine."

The car did not seem to be in a hurry to get to the end of the road. Hawwa's senses sank into a warm wrapping of rose and ambergris and Munir's warm breath, which fogged the window. All along the way, they did not speak. She did not say to him the many words that should have been said, she who had traveled wearisome roads and borne seasons of burning sun in her life, she who had faced the wind and rain and stones from the sky, and stones from people as well, all for the sake of this. She wondered to herself, does someone who's been defeated lose the power of speech over time? Perhaps Hawwa no longer knew how talk goes, between strangers. Then the strange thing was that she didn't feel that they were strangers. If she had been able to see into the strange man beside her, who was driving his sturdy, clean car under the gossamer rain, perhaps she would have seen that he too felt that they were not complete strangers. The thing that remained a great secret within herself, and that was embarrassing, which she hid in the deep well of wishes, was that as she sat next to him, she felt that her flesh yearned for his. But the silence between them enfolded a great deal of talk, deep talk, talk that climbed the hills of feeling and descended them, that walked in side streets and byways, without losing its way. It also seemed as if their talk, during the eloquent silence, was neither enigmatic nor unclear.

When at last the car arrived, Hawwa got out, less heavily, taking with her the wrapping of rose and ambergris and Munir's breath, covering her spirit in it. Fairuz's pure voice had reached its ultimate yearning, in "O yellow leaves, we're getting old, we're getting old, the streets and the homes are getting old, getting old. The world is ending and you only, O my land, my country, my home, you only are still a little child." She wanted to thank him, but he asked her first: "Will you have coffee with me? One day? Any day?"

That day, Hawwa gathered herself and her jilbab outer dress and sat down on the chair. Her eyes roamed cautiously about the place, examining the tables with metal legs and glass tops, surrounded by bamboo chairs with covered foam cushions on the seats. The cushions were thin with use, without seeming completely worn out. The decor and the sparse, unpretentious furniture were dominated by colors of hazel brown and clay red. A familiar smell seeped into the air, the smell of burned coffee that has boiled over on the gas burner when someone's eye has strayed. Hawwa sat back in the wide space of the oval chair, and the many thoughts colliding in her head subsided for a time. Munir sat on a chair next to her, and he seemed very close, as if he were about to whisper in her ear, and that was something which did not bother her in the least. In fact, Hawwa was amazed at her new self, whom she was meeting for the first time. It was a self she had not known to exist, that perhaps had been sleeping and then awakened, or extinguished and then rekindled, or dead and then resurrected, or—who knew—maybe it had not existed at all and had been created from her ribs, which had been crushed so many times.

Hawwa seemed at ease with how very close he was to her. The only thing was that she was more conscious of the appearance of her exhausted face, even though she had rubbed it with a moisturizing cream of a milky consistency, which Durrat al-Ain had given her before she met Munir in the magical incident of the hailstones. The texture of the cream awoke Hawwa to the possibility of a resemblance she hoped for between her white complexion, which bore the marks of dry days and arid nights, and Durrat al-Ain's complexion, dark, coddled, and pampered, covered with a light layer of golden bronze, and retaining its silken, velvety touch, since it was protected from winter storms, hail, and snow, and was sheltered from sand and the molten sun. It was also continuously watered by Faris's love, and by still more of his love. Hawwa had traced her wide eyes with kohl eyeliner, and placed a touch of pale-pink lipstick, tending to lilac, on her lips. She had bought it especially for her expected outing. Everything on her, in fact, was something she was wearing for the first time, from her brick-red jilbab, which bore no trace of wear, to her cashmere scarf, wine-colored with shades of a smoky black, to her black shoes of shiny leather with wide, medium-height heels, and her black purse with the golden buckle.

When Hawwa wandered in the market downtown, looking for a jilbab appropriate for the coffee date, she felt that the entire universe was dancing to the rhythm of her delight. She didn't understand why her heart was beating hard, and she didn't understand why her spirit was alight with joy. She didn't understand many things related to the complicated mechanism by which her feelings worked, making her feel what she felt, making her long for the one she longed for, and making her like the one she liked, very much, without putting her finger on the reason or reasons.

How, for example, could she have waited for the stranger who headed for her amid the hailstones pounding down from above, without her having spoken to him? How could she want to be with someone she really didn't know, seeking refuge in his being, enclosed within it? What made her yearn for this man who was silent for an entire trip, who smelled of soap, of roses squeezed into a bottle, and of deodorant that did not completely absorb the human smell of his sweat? How could she yearn for a stranger, yearn to the point of her heart burning and her spirit splitting when he did not appear, when the presumption was that he did not even exist? Could a person love someone he didn't know? Was she in love with the stranger?

She didn't give it much thought when she chose this jilbab over the others. It was the least enveloping of many jilbabs, and the least gloomy. What distinguished it was that it had a waist. Besides, the mannequin that was wearing it, showing off her thin figure in it in the display window, called to her to take it. But she took a long time to find the right shoes, which would hold her feet and emphasize her height without exaggerating it. She tried on many pairs before at last she found the ones her feet slipped into easily, as if they had been designed for her alone. The Cinderella inside her rejoiced at the beautiful, splendid discovery. All that was left now was for her prince, the stranger who was not strange, to see her, to make certain for himself that she was the one he was looking for.

The waiter placed the two cups of coffee before them, one without sugar for her and one with a small amount for Munir. There were no more than six or seven people in the coffee shop. Among them was a young man who seemed to be a university student, who sat at a table alone, with a laptop in front of him and earphones in his ears. The other café patrons were distributed between two other tables, turning away from her and Munir.

Hawwa was not worried that anyone would recognize her. She didn't know anyone in the camp, no, not even among her clients from outside the camp, who could possibly come to this café in this clean, distant, and very new quarter of Amman. Neither the place nor the people resembled the camp or its people. And then she herself, with the black kohl emphasizing the width of her eyes, with her pink-toned lips at the height of winter, with her brick-colored jilbab and her Cinderella shoes (the smell of the leather penetrating even if it was cheap, and the soles not yet having picked up lifeless shards from the streets)—she did not resemble the Hawwa of yesterday or of days before. She didn't even resemble the person she had been in decades past.

From behind the glass walls of the café, Hawwa watched the wind outside buffet the heads of the trees planted beside the sidewalk, while the diminished numbers of people in the street were being tossed about by waves of wind, leaning right and left to their violent rhythm. It was not yet 3:30 when the afternoon sky suddenly clouded over; it was as if it had been dyed by the remains of ashes or soot from a huge fire in the universe, which had devoured most of the body of the sun. The heavy darkness of the day fell on the shoulders of the few people in the street, so they hurried their steps, fiercely resisting the force of the wind. The gusts picked up papers and newspapers thrown on the street or piled on the edges of the sidewalks, tossing them and turning them over, before flinging some of them on the heads of the trees with their disheveled hair. Hawwa's eyes followed a woman in her thirties who was running in the street beside the café, and who was wearing a head veil and a long, cream-colored coat with a wide skirt. The blundering winds lifted the skirt high and her legs were revealed, clearly outlined in tight jeans. The woman looked around her as if she was afraid that someone had seen her legs in their jeans. The coat was open like an umbrella in the wind, and she tried to fold it with one hand, while with the other she adjusted the shawl that had almost slipped off her head. A piece of newspaper stuck to the window in front of Hawwa, so it screened her eyes from the face of the woman battling the wind. It was a half page carrying a prominent obituary, headed by the words "We belong to God and to Him do we return," in large, startling letters.

Hawwa turned away her shocked eyes and they fell into Munir's eyes, which had been following her. He met her frightened look gently. Don't worry, he told her. Then he came close to her, so that his jutting chin nearly touched the edge of her scarf, and assured her that no one would recognize her here. "And anyway, what're we doing? We're drinking coffee—where's the crime in that?" He said it in a voice that was more confident and clearer, so she smiled, folding her worry away in distant, unexplored places inside herself. She could be happy on this day, and in this moment specifically; she convinced herself of that. She was happy, and perhaps among the reasons for her personal happiness in that moment was the fact that she was well aware of the undertones of musk and sandalwood in the perfume that spread from beneath her heavy clothes, entwined in the smell of her own body. Sitt Qamar had once praised it, saying, "Your body smells fresh." Hawwa moved as close to him as their presence together over coffee cups would allow, in a café dominated by winter shadows and the colors of chestnuts, hazelnuts, wood, and clay. She surrounded him with her musk and her warmth.

They alternated taking hushed sips of coffee. Their hearts were open and their spirits spread out. They did not say many things that they should have said, but they were happy, completely ignoring the rumbling darkness outside as it sank toward evening.

Munir had three daughters, Laila, Aliya, and Nariman, and five grandchildren. Nariman, his youngest daughter, had finished the last year of high school when his wife, Maryam, at last became pregnant with the son she had been waiting for. He told her that he wasn't waiting for a son. She told him that she wanted a boy, as a support for him. He assured her that he wanted her as a support for him, and a companion, and a shoulder, and a crutch, in the twilight of their lives, not a son. She told him that she wanted a boy so he would love her more. He swore to her that he loved her, Maryam, without her giving him a girl or a boy. He insisted, and she insisted more. The doctor showed some anxiety and told Maryam to end the beginnings of the life, still not completely formed, in her womb. But she refused. He told her that her heart might not bear the pregnancy and the birth, and she reassured him that her heart would bear the stretching of her flesh and blood and the demands of childbirth, even if it ripped apart her soul. The dear boy, the beloved son of the beloved, could be free and easy inside her; he could hit and kick, he could snatch some of her life, enough for his life and more, he could make her sick until the end of time. Maryam preserved the boy as a feeling growing inside her, a feeling that took something from the beating of her heart, which was growing fainter. During the time when the desired being was becoming larger in her weak insides, she was going away, and trying—with some success—to hide the traces of her ebbing existence from the worry Munir felt.

Maryam gave birth. She rejoiced in the boy with the large, radiant face, the shining eyes, the thick hair, as if he had lived and grown inside for a year, and the wide throat that let out a booming cry of life. Maryam rejoiced greatly, and died.

Munir cried for long nights. His spirit was lacerated by sadness. He loathed the world and remained bedridden, his heart failing, wanting to join his Maryam. His daughters begged him to live, for the sake of Naji, the boy, the support.

Maryam had chosen his name for him as soon as his water and blood formed within her, naming him for how she had confided in him the whole time. Laila picked up her brother and stretched him out beside Munir, but Munir closed his eyes and turned away from him.

A month and more went by without Munir going near the boy. Laila and Aliya, both married, took turns taking care of their father and their brother, while Nariman took over the household tasks of cooking, washing, and cleaning. One day, Munir asked his daughters to bring Naji to him. They rejoiced over the sudden change in his feelings. Laila picked up Naji and placed him in his arms; out of the corner of his eye, Munir looked at the face of the infant, who was yawning, meekly. Laila prompted him to hug the boy, so he brought him closer. The baby opened his eyes. Munir brought the fresh face close to his own grieving, unshaven face. He smelled him. The perplexed eyes of the baby widened, startled, and then closed suddenly, avoiding by inborn instinct the tears that were raining down on them. Munir stretched out his arms to Laila so she would take the baby, saying, "Take him. Raise him."

He stopped the car beside the road. All of the anger present in his soul had awakened, and he hit the steering wheel, once, many times. He lifted up his head, wanting to hold back the tears imprisoned in the two heavy clouds in his eyes, and his sight collided with the roof of the car. He lowered his face, his hands gripping the unmoving wheel hard, in an effort to absorb the shudder that flowed through him. The water was too heavy to suppress, so he threw his head on the steering wheel, so the clouds in his eyes split open and loosed their violent rain. His body was swept away with it, and the laments barricaded in his spirit broke free. In the seat beside him, Hawwa's heart was moaning. She wished she could take his weeping head in her arms. She reached out her hand and put it on his shoulder. He sobbed as he told her, in agony, that he had tried to love the boy: "By God, I tried." Many times he would go to Laila's house and wake him, taking him in his arms and raining down kisses on him; but no matter what he did, he was not able to love him, not as love should be.

"The love will come, it's going to come, you'll love him, you'll love him more than anything, you'll make it up to him," Hawwa assured him. Then she patted his shoulder and said, "Look!" and pointed out the car window.

The world had turned white. Snow was falling in cottony flakes, which soon stuck to the ground and made a shining blanket. The moist whiteness swallowed up the noise of the universe, and on the outside peace descended over everyone and everything, and the light of the snow flooded the sky. Munir raised his eyes through the window to the sky that was shedding snow. The tears froze on his cheeks. He turned his eyes toward Hawwa, and was taken by the brilliant white of her eyes, as she contemplated in wonder the falling pearls of the snow. He put his fevered hand over hers, and chestnuts crackled in her heart.

This was the first time she had been touched by the hand of a man, a man who was not rammed upon her or plunging into her, a man who was not stealing her body, so that she was forced to close her eyes and ears to keep from seeing him or hearing him, until he had violated her and finished, and she convinced herself that what had happened was a terrifying nightmare, nothing more. This was not a man leaving his spittle within her and his dirty grease upon her, so that she needed an age, more than an age, to wash away all trace of him. It was a real hand, belonging to a real man, a man who wept, a man who sobbed magnificently, a man who grieved in deep agony. This was the first time Hawwa had seen a man weep, and she thought that the most beautiful men were the sorrowful. This was also the first time she sensed that she might be more than a mere woman; she might be a woman who was loved, who was wanted, who was sought, who was desired, who was adored for who she was, a woman who was wanted simply for the life she pursued vigorously. She might be a woman sought tenderly for the warmth that worked within her, despite the days of cold, of dryness, of emptiness; a woman to be given sympathy for the little love in her past, a woman blessed for her long endurance of her past, a woman to be pardoned for her very few words of love, yearning, or anguish. This was the first time Hawwa felt that she might be in love—who knew? Perhaps this was a love like the love told of in stories, or like the love talked over among people.

That night, Hawwa's thoughts roamed free. She relaxed her hand next to her face, resting on the pillow, and Munir's hand fell over it, like the first rains of spring. A smell arose from it, the smell of the clay of a thirsty body, of a dusty soul. She wished for his hand as a fine mist, a continuous, soaking rain. Then, when her hand had been watered, she sought more water, and abundant rain poured down, welling from all the clouds. When Hawwa closed her eyes at last, her soul, not dried into a desert, had been watered by the perfume of heaven. When she awoke in the morning, the buds of lilies opened dewy and alive in her heart, while delayed lilacs accumulated in her paths.

They had passed their first half winter, and half of the pathways of talking, as Fairuz kept them company and they did not tire of her. Their meadow was smiling, their bashful revelations prolonged. Their laughter and their tears dissolved in their coffee and tea in many corner cafés. They drank from their cups as they drank from each other's eyes, and in their eyes was longing, as in their silence. If their world had confined them in the past, now at last it opened before them, so they believed that the heart thrown into grief was finding tenderness at last.

Their beautiful, shared feeling of the need of each one for the other as part of their existence grew during the winter, under light, drizzling rain, under sweeping downpours. Their yearning endured in the face of raging, cautionary winds and perfidious gusts. Growing in the hidden places of perception was something that might be love, with the sunsets settling on the edges of the cold afternoons, with the early dark creeping over their streets and over their talk, with high-necked jackets and coats, with heavy shawls to cover their faces in furtive encounters. It grew with sandwiches of shawarma and falafel, whose odor clung to the clean car for some time without being annoying, with half pounds of Nabulsi kunafa that they ate on the spot at Habiba Sweets, downtown. It grew with suppers of hummus and broad beans in a forgotten restaurant, with the long roads that were shortened by their talk and that they took every week to the Dead Sea, where they buried their sight in the blue expanse.

"They say love kills time, and they say time kills love. Come, my darling, let us go, before time, before love." At the sea Munir silences Fairuz, but her heartbroken voice remains, despite the great sea and the distant sky and the many winter trips, still singing in Hawwa's head: "The story began under the rain, in the first rain they loved one another, and it ended in the rain, under the second rain they left one another." As Fairuz's voice at the end of the song mixed with the rain drumming violently on the surface of the sea, like daggers falling on its belly and slitting it, Hawwa could not keep herself from crying, while she tried to deafen her heart to the melody clothed in rain when "they loved one another, they left one another, they loved . . . they left . . ." She looked at Munir, asking for compassion and reassurance, and he would spread his broad hand over her hand, turning blue from the cold, rubbing it and saying, "Don't worry. I'm with you, and I'm going to stay with you."

No sooner did they get to the end of winter than the love came. It poured down from the sky of longing in a pulsing rain, burning with love after yearning, pounding the earth after long drought. The love came strong, sweeping, genuine, pure, reaching the end, the ultimate end. Naji returned to the

240

house, a love deferred, a hope, a support, Munir's beautiful son, five years old. He had his father's face, which Maryam had loved so much that she had carved it, an exact copy of the original, in her womb.

During the years of her emotional barrenness, Hawwa had hurried the passing of winter, folding away the heavy blankets in her frozen heart as soon as April knocked on the door. Winter added drought to drought in her soul, and its cold gnawed at the joints of her spirit. Hawwa was terrified of lightning, she shook at thunder, she startled at the torrential frightening rain falling from terrifying skies. She yearned for constant cloudlessness, for the sun, for windows that were never closed before nightfall. The thing she loved most was to walk at the beginning of spring in the streets soaked with the remains of winter's water, inspecting the lone flowers that opened in the rocky earth, stretching their thin necks through the cracks, yearning for the sunny sky, inclining to the rhythm of the gentle breeze and its pleasant melodies. As she walked, Hawwa was careful not to step on the cheeks of the tender flowers or to snap their necks or crush them. During her first winter with Munir, Hawwa did not long for spring. She did not wait for it, hurry it, or summon it; she wished her flowers would remain asleep, and that their hibernation would be longer. Hawwa continued to stare at the dark, swollen clouds, seeking rain, rain, and more rain, sent down in endless torrents. She would not even mind if hail went on pelting the earth.

When the cloak of snow is spread over the days and nights, then her yearning for Munir flames up, for their furtive meetings are possible in the isolated streets, trembling with cold, spread out beneath waterfalls descending from the sky, in the embrace of distant cafés, with white cotton pouring down outside and the fog of thick breath on the windows hiding them from the eyes of curious people. At certain moments, they appear from afar as if they are imaginary, two small embodiments of human beings, sitting alone in a lovely small café in a magical city, as if it were drawn or designed for a holiday card, cut off from all the torments of the real world, a complete scene placed in a crystalline ball where the snow never stops falling.

Spring awoke and so did the sun, in dry skies where stars shone on clear nights. Logically, it would have been possible for everything to be romantic. But spring meant that Hawwa's movements would not be simple and smooth, and that leaving the house whenever she missed Munir would not necessarily be easy. It meant that the cafés and the places they went to regularly would shed their heavy coats and open their doors to outside air; the tables would fill and the air would be crowded with talk and with looks, the talk of others, and their many looks. It meant that the streets they traversed under clouds and wind would open their eyes wide, and it would not be possible for them to melt into the fog or into darkness descending early on the day. It meant that the sun imprisoned in the sky would burst out, and it would not be possible for them to hide from people. It meant that their story, which they had woven in the car during the first winter of love, intertwined with their talk (even if it was scant), with the flavor of falafel and shawarma sandwiches, and with the voice of Fairuz, intoxicated with the clusters of water from the sky, this story would be stolen from them by spring. They would be deprived of the streets of water and wind, and they would not plant their stories in the continuing rain or in the snows. Then no sooner would flaming summer appear than the flowering meetings of the winter would have faded. Hawwa was in a panic.

"Will you marry me?" Munir asked her.

Winter was folding away its water and its wind, squeezing the remaining clouds and sending down the last real rain, when Munir told her that she had become a part of his spirit. Hawwa never once believed that she could be stricken with this thing—she who never truly knew this thing in the life she remembered, nor even in the life she had forgotten, or that which she had buried in the well of the darknesses of the soul. Could this thing come to her now? In the nighttime of her life, or on the edges of it? Could her heart beat, standing on the threshold of the end? Could this be the thing? Hawwa could not reveal it, even to herself; could not give its description, could not say its name: love. Did she love? Could it be that she loved? Was it reasonable for her to love, her? Now?

If love was that her spirit shrank as she waited on the snowy sidewalk, worried that he would come and more worried that he wouldn't, looking at the river of cars rushing past in the street, until she saw his dark-blue car approaching her and slowing down, signaling to her with its eyes wide as saucers, so that her legs went soft and she walked above the earth, her feet splitting billowing space without the winds carrying her off or the rain sweeping her away, then she loved. If love was that her pores clung to his human smell, not exaggeratedly male, with a hidden whiff of silk, a smell that resembled no other that she knew, not even the smell of her precious, dear velvets, so that her blood seethed in her body as soon as the smell filled her nose, then she definitely loved. If love was that she watched the trembling muscle in his neck while he drove, which stretched in his few words and relaxed as he listened unhurriedly, so that she wished she could reach out her fingers and touch the pulse of the muscle or rub it, but she would be too embarrassed to do that, then certainly, very certainly, she loved. If love was that her heart was delighted by his voice every time, as if she were hearing it for the first time, and that it crept into her like the rustling of a new, expensive piece of velvet (if the rustling of his voice didn't have an even greater and more eloquent effect than velvet), then, absolutely, she loved. If love was that her spirit lowered its eyelids every time his eyes embraced her, in the precious meetings in cafés, and that she wished there were no escape from the embrace of his gazes, even if they pressed her so hard that the staves of her heart collapsed, then, necessarily, she loved. If love was that her body suddenly felt an ancient, effaced desire, so that her blood simmered and seethed and in its hidden places secret fluids and burning longing raged, the longing flaring every time he put his hand covered in brown freckles over hers, then, undeniably, she loved. And if love was that in daring nocturnal fantasies she summoned his voice, his speech, his breath, and the feeling of his hand, bringing her body close to his body and stripping them both of their reticence, their caution, their anxiety, the fear of years, and their clothes, as she closed her eyes on longed-for velvet slipping from her thirsty flesh, so that when he was atop her and his cloud poured out and rained within her, then his flood swept away her long history of subjection— if that was love, then she certainly loved, to the utmost degree of certainty that could be reached, she loved, and she loved, and she loved. Inescapably, she loved.

Get married? What would she say to Aya? How would she explain to her daughter, whose heart was hardened, that she, her mother, was in love and wanted to get married? What about Qais? But the biggest problem, Hawwa thought, might be with Ayid. And then, she was still coping with Rabia's new situation. Munir told her that he would take care of her and Rabia, just as he would take care of Naji. Hawwa looked at herself in the mirror of the closet. She was surprised by her face; she had forgotten it. For a long time she had not encountered it or spoken to it; it was a face that was strange to her. Hawwa was used to standing in front of the mirror to adjust her headscarf or settle her shawl over her head without really seeing her face, without her eyes meeting the eyes in the mirror, so like her own and so close to them. "Do you know that you're pretty, Hawwa?" Sitt Qamar had said to her once. "Don't you let anyone tell you any different!"

For the first time, Hawwa sees herself as beautiful, beautiful. For the first time in her life she feels that she's happy, truly happy. She could not believe that she could be happy, at last.

Munir has worked for eight years as a security employee for a private university in Amman. Before that he worked for twenty years in an administrative position in UNRWA, the relief agency for Palestinian refugees. After that he retired, and spent over half of his lump-sum benefit to buy a small piece of land in Ain al-Basha, less than half a donum, an eighth of an acre only. During the time when Maryam was dreaming of a boy, desiring that more than anything else, Munir was planning to build a little house with a small garden around it, designing it in his head down to the plantings, the trees, and the stones of its wall. He told Hawwa that he felt he was aging rapidly, and he did not want to die in the camp as he had lived in it. For him, the camp was a cemetery, its houses were defiled tombs, and it was wrong to count its people among the living. But Maryam's death had made him turn away from leaving the cemetery; he remained buried there, sick at heart. There were even times when he wished that death would hurry.

But now he was going to take his plans out of the drawer in the closet. He would not stay long in the camp: he would build the house, and he would live it in with Hawwa and Naji, and Rabia would live with them. He would love them all until the end of his days, and he would take care of them all. He would carry Rabia, if need be, on his shoulders.

Munir struck the earth with both feet. "This is going to be our home," he said to Hawwa, in what seemed like a celebratory announcement. That was on a Saturday morning that was clear and very cold. He was happy and excited. Hawwa was no less happy, but she felt an agonizing fear, for she had never experienced all this happiness before. She didn't believe that she could even imagine it, just as she couldn't comprehend that a great joy like this could be found in a world that was so stingy with her. They sat on the ground, on a wool carpet Munir had brought from the trunk of the car. Hawwa considered the high piece of land, clothed in pebbles, muddy rocks, and stunted, thorny plants. Hawwa had made sandwiches of labneh and za'atar and of hummus, as well as a thermos of tea. Munir had brought apples, pears, and tangerines. The cold wind was playing with their faces. They wore heavy coats; Hawwa had wound a green woolen shawl around her head and one side of her face, and Munir had secured his white keffiyeh, checked with black, around his head and neck.

Munir pointed to a corner of the land: "Here's the entry to the house," he told Hawwa. He continued sketching the plan: "And here's the parlor, here's the living room, here's Naji's room, this is Rabia's room, that's the kitchen, and here's our room, mine and yours." He carefully pointed out their room in a low voice, as if he were emphasizing that it was private for him and for her, and Hawwa lowered her head, embarrassed, as if the room had suddenly been announced to the world and she had been caught in it with him. Nonetheless, despite her natural embarrassment, Hawwa could not contain her delight. "And the sewing room?" Her eyes went to him hopefully. So Munir pointed to the imagined sewing room, and her eyes rejoiced that the house was complete at last.

The whistling of the wind grew stronger, so Munir put his arm around Hawwa's shoulders, gathering her to him, so the wind would not take her from him. Hawwa welcomed his arm. In that moment, snatched from a beautiful dream, her feeling of being enclosed within him overcame the cold and all her fears. They ate and they drank the tea, so warmth flowed into their bodies, close together. Hawwa imagined that she could measure the heat of his body, nearly joined to hers. When the color of the morning darkened and the sky became foggy, a fine rain patted their hunched bodies, almost joined, and they gave themselves to its light, tickling touch.

Until recently, Munir had worked in the university as part of the shift schedule. His job usually required him to inspect the campus facilities, including the lecture halls, especially after working hours, as well as the courtyards, the squares, and the back garden, where the wall overlooked a wood. He collected the students' possessions, neglected or forgotten—books, notebooks, pens, watches, a little money, cheap jewelry, and, rarely, cell phones—and kept them safely in the lost-and-found area. Aside from the throat clearing and affected coughs that he used to break the embrace of two students behind some elevation, he acknowledged to Hawwa that his work had no value; rarely did he pick up anything important. He remembers only the single time when he picked up a pack of loaded cigarettes—"That's hashish!"—in one of the bathrooms, where it was taped behind the cover of a toilet tank. That was on the night shift. He believed he had discovered something important, so the next morning he gave the pack to his boss. Munir expected that the university administration would take up the matter with the proper authorities. Instead, Munir received strict instructions not to discuss the subject of the loaded cigarettes with anyone, in order not to impede the ongoing investigation, as they claimed. Munir didn't need to think hard to realize later on that they had covered it up. Not only that, but Munir also learned that they had returned the pack of cigarettes to its owner, who, it turned out, was a student at the university, the son of a former Iraqi official who had settled in Amman after the fall of Saddam's Iraq, and who had a bank account worth thirty million American dollars. It was said that an international human rights organization had sent an official request to the government to question the man in the context of accusations that he had committed war crimes in Iraq, and had accompanied the request with testimony affirming that he was involved in acts of torture. But the government had asserted, in a long report that it sent to the organization, that it had conducted a complete and transparent investigation of the subject, and had come to the conclusion that the individual concerned was completely innocent of all of the accusations directed against him, and that everything in the testimony was mere allegations, unsupported by any actual proof.

Munir received a sudden promotion in his work. He no longer worked the night shift, and his position, which bore the title of "security supervisor," was nominally limited to administrative work, drinking tea and coffee, and signing papers and reports that made no difference to anyone.

His voice took a dark turn, as the slow, thin drops of water from the sky were kneaded into their souls. Hawwa leaned toward him while her eyes swept the space where she had built walls and a roof from the bricks of her heart. She opened windows in the walls; their curtains were of ivory lace, and the sun filtered through the pattern, marking their faces and necks with flecks of gold. Munir told her, as he embraced her dewy face with his eyes, that when he built the house, their house, he was going to leave the job. He would look for other work. Hawwa suggested to him, with an enthusiasm kindled by the rain, that he open a shop attached to the house. She pointed to a few houses, most of them still only a framework or bare bricks, which were scattered in the area. A shop would serve their residents—there would be many houses and many people. She assured him of it. Munir's face brightened at the idea. He nodded several times, as if he were studying the possibilities and agreeing. She would sew, also, she said with growing excitement, as before her eyes the house rose up, together with the shop, the surrounding houses, and the voices of women and children shouting in the streets. There would be many people, but they would not be wretched, rash, leaving their houses angry at the beginning of the morning and returning to them defeated and rancorous at the end of the night. The people would be happy, like the two of them, in wide streets and roomy, cheerful houses, with walls that were not peeling, and with small gardens.

When winter locked away its days, gathering its water and its winds, Hawwa's heart paled and her soul clouded over. The eyes of spring were opening, and when summer bloomed, when its suns stretched out and its skies ripened, the eyes stared. It became hard for Hawwa to wait for "the sweet one, her sweet one," who was on her mind, her "sweet basil and wallflowers," in the streets. Even the distant cafés filled with reckless young lovers, who sat on every seat, stealing "their walking and their talk." The last meeting between them was a month earlier, in their excavated spot, where their house was being built, where its walls were rising. Munir took her there to see the poured foundations of the house, their house, and the columns that had been erected and that were still clad in their wooden molds.

From one snatched moment to the next, they met in a mall restaurant, or in a café that was less frequented, in one of the new or renewed suburbs of Amman. Most of the time, Munir was no longer able to pick her up in his car from the summer streets that were not forgotten, with a multitude of human faces in them, many of them liable to recognize them. He could not drop her off near her house in the camp, even at night, for the full moon of summer had eyes, and summer nights did not conceal secrets. Hawwa began to take the bus from the camp to Sweileh Circle, or to the University of Jordan, or to the Sports City Circle. From there she took a taxi to their meeting place. During her trip she felt that all the steps in the world were following her, and she would keep her eyes lowered, looking at her purse, far from the faces on the bus. If a woman recognized her from a nearby seat, the bee of doubt began to buzz in the burning hive of her head, and she feared that her heart would be revealed in her frightened eyes. When she got into the taxi and the young driver would ask her, examining her from beneath his cheap sunglasses, "Where to, Auntie?" her voice would pale and her spirit would plunge into a well of whispered doubts, and she would come close to turning back.

One of their summer meetings nearly ended in a catastrophe. Hawwa had agreed to meet Munir on a June afternoon in a small restaurant and café in the Mecca Mall in Amman, a place that had received them numerous times in easier, winter meetings. Munir had arrived ahead of her, and he sat at a table in the same side corner, facing the entrance to the café, in a spot that allowed both of them to see each other at a distance. Her heart leapt from its place when she was going to him, hurrying her steps, as their eyes met. Then she suddenly stopped stock-still, as if a snake had reared up in front of her with its head in a position of attack. "Umm Qais?" Umm Said stood in the middle of the few yards separating the two of them. "Since when do you go to malls?" Umm Said gaped in surprise. Out of the corner of her eye, Hawwa saw Munir, who was hunching over, shrinking in his place and burying his face in his cup of coffee.

Umm Said was carrying multiple bags, and her daughter-in-law was with her, looking around and inspecting the numerous nearby shops, her eyes yearning to possess everything in them. Umm Said assumed that Hawwa had come to the mall for the same reasons that had brought her, as there were sales in most of the shops. Hawwa confirmed that immediately. "You won't believe it—some of the prices in the shops are cheaper than in the market in the camp!" Umm Said told Hawwa, and her daughter-in-law enthusiastically offered proof of her mother-in-law's words by taking a blouse out of a bag, with its price tag of four dinars, and showing it to Hawwa. Then she laughed as she brought the piece up to Hawwa's nose: "Even the smell is different . . . it's the smell of the mall, not the smell of Baqa'a market." Hawwa was alarmed when Umm Said, who had drawn her away to shop with them, told her that most of the women in the camp came to the mall. Hawwa tried to recall her previous meetings with Munir. In the midst of her tumult, many images passed through her mind, their features confused, but in none of them did she glimpse any of the women of the camp whom she knew. Could they have known her? How could she have seen them in her romantic adventures when she saw no one but him, in adventures that came after long waiting, long desiring, and sometimes after long despair? "Like who?" Hawwa was asking Umm Said about the women of the camp who were regulars at the mall. Umm Said, examining the window of a shop that displayed abayas, galabiyas, and long dresses, casually mentioned dozens of women, who meant nothing to Hawwa beyond being faces and eyes very capable of revealing her secret, which she had enclosed inside with utter care, or so she imagined. "Is this pretty?" asked Umm Said, pointing to a long dress. Hawwa focused her eyes on the store's glass window, and glimpsed a retreating shadow reflected in the surface that was very like Munir.

Hawwa and Munir made do with meeting at night by cell phone. Naji would have gone to sleep in his father's arms, and Rabia would have burped up water, before her head rested on her daughter's hand. When she had dozed off, Hawwa would withdraw her hand and be free for Munir. For Munir's sake, Hawwa came to love the night, all the nights, even Fairuz's "sad northern nights"; she began to want the night to "come back every night," wanting the night, their night, not to go away, "any night," in spite of everything. Munir insisted that they not wait any longer. Life doesn't wait, he told her. She could live in his house in the camp, and they could all move together from there to the new house in Ain al-Basha. He tried to convince her, but Hawwa asked him to give her more time, since she wasn't comfortable with the idea of staying in the camp after they married. She didn't share her true fears with him: she was afraid of Aya, she was afraid of Qais, and she was terrified of Ayid.

How would she tell them she was going to get married? Naturally she would not dare to tell them that she was in love. Even as she thought about love, she exerted superhuman effort not to let her love be seen or heard, even within herself. And then there was Umm Said, and Umm Said's daughter-in-law, and her neighbors, and the women of the camp, and the people, all the people. And there was also Laila, Munir's daughter, who was boycotting her.

Munir did not tell her that Laila had refused his marriage to her seamstress, but Hawwa discovered that for herself. For Laila stopped visiting her. She no longer had her make her two daughters' school smocks, nor did she buy the family's sheets from her, or cushion covers, or prayer outfits. Hawwa called her more than once, but she did not answer. She asked Munir, and he said only that whether or not to marry was his decision alone.

Hawwa endured by means of Fairuz. Whenever she wanted to bring back the winter roads with Munir under the rain, in the company of Fairuz's songs, she turned on the tape recorder, to the same voice and the same songs. She told Munir that she had come to know Fairuz through Sitt Qamar. Before she passed away, Sitt Qamar had given her a leather case with dozens of tapes of Fairuz. Hawwa had listened to them all, time after time. Then she no longer listened. At first her tape recorder broke down, and then her life broke down almost completely. Fairuz unintentionally became an interloper in her many gaunt days. Then, when she won back some life, Hawwa began to open the case and turn over the tapes, wiping her hand across the picture of Fairuz on the cover, and the songs would ring out in her head, according to their order on the tape. In the expanse of her loneliness, she would be intoxicated all alone when the voice would reach its longed-for limits, and the melodies would melt her heart. Aya suggested to her years ago that she buy her CDs of Fairuz, together with a CD player, but Hawwa refused. She was not only afraid that she would lose the Fairuz she knew on the tapes; she was also afraid that she would lose Sitt Qamar, as the tapes were all that she still had from her. That was something that Aya didn't understand, and it didn't matter much to her that she understand it. Munir surprised her when he brought her a tape recorder that looked completely new. He had gone through all of the shops of the

Saqf al-Sail region downtown before he found it: a Panasonic tape recorder, stereo, with a radio. For Hawwa, that was love, the whole of love. And when Fairuz's voice came to fill the air of the house, on sweet mornings or in companionable evenings, intersecting with the sound of her sewing machine, Sitt Qamar's face would appear to her, joyful, as she looked from the window to the streets of the camp, telling her with great delight, "My love has come."

Then her love withdrew. The first night passed, and the second night, and then the third, without Munir calling. Hawwa tried to call him, but his cell phone was turned off. She called him at night, then at the end of the night. Then she called him at the beginning of the day and in the middle of the day and at the end. The same cold voice told her that the number she had dialed was not available. She sent him numerous messages. "Where are you?" "Something good, God willing." "Maybe it's something good." "Tell me you're okay." "Set my mind at rest." "I'm scared, tell me you're okay." "Tell me you're okay, I'm scared." "Why don't you answer?" "Reassure me." "For God's sake, tell me you're okay."

After some thought, Hawwa went to his house. It was located in the fourth neighborhood after hers. She inspected the house from a distance of a hundred yards. The side of the house faced a lane that turned into a street containing several carpentry and used furniture shops, and it was crammed with vehicles for carrying and delivering wood and furniture. Noise from the vehicles and from buyers and sellers filled the place. Munir's dark-blue car was standing at the door of his house. Hawwa imagined that perhaps he was on vacation. She called him, but his cell phone was still turned off. She went to his house in the afternoon; the car was in its place. She watched from a distance and saw that everything was quiet. The activity of the buyers and sellers in the used-furniture shops had receded. A number of boys from the neighborhood were playing soccer in front of his house. A ball collided with the door and Hawwa's heart leapt—she expected that Munir would open the door. But the door shook under the force of the ball at least three times without being opened.

Hawwa returned to his house at night and saw that it was still as it had been, empty of any sign of life. The carpentry and furniture stores had closed, and people's feet had almost disappeared from the street. Under the cover of darkness, Hawwa went up to the car and saw that it was covered in dust, so she was sure that it had not left its place for days. The windows of the house were closed and the curtains drawn, and there was no light coming from inside. Could he have left the house? she wondered. But would he leave the car? Could he be traveling? Where? And why hadn't he told her? She thought about ringing the doorbell. What if it didn't open? What if it did open? Would he tell her that he had left her? She couldn't bear even the thought. While she was vacillating among many terrifying questions and answers, two men passed, one absorbed in talking on his cell phone in a loud voice, while the other slowed down, examining her closely as he walked. He leaned over to the ear of his companion, who ended his call, and whispered something to him that turned his eyes toward Hawwa. She wished that the car were open, so she could hide in it. She opened her purse, pretending to be looking for something inside, then walked away.

Hawwa put her head on her pillow, seeking the sleep that had eluded her for days, and embracing her mute cell phone. The night was quiet, except for Rabia's light snoring. She looked at the sky through a crack in the curtains and glimpsed shining stars. She wished that the stars would be extinguished, that the sky would be choked with swollen clouds, until they split and poured out abundant water. If only July rain could fall, if there were such a thing as July rain in the first place. If her despair could tap the sky then it would send down, now, all the hoped-for water on the dry earth of the camp. Then she would leave the house, move through the streets under the cover of the water, and go to him, to his house. She would knock on the door and keep on knocking, even if that meant that she had to break the door down.

In the morning Laila stood at her door, with copious rain falling from her eyes. "Papa's sick!" she told her. The diabetes had stricken his leg. That was some time ago, but he had ignored all the signs—the faint sensation in his leg, how cold it was, his toes turning blue and then black, and the ulcers on the bottom of his foot. The doctors had told him there was no alternative to amputating his leg, as the gangrene was serious. But he refused. For days he had been bedridden at home, not leaving the bed, not talking to anyone, and not letting anyone in, even his daughters. Laila had had to take Naji back with her. "Forgive me!" Laila said to Hawwa. She asked her to speak to him, to convince him, because she was the only one who had any influence over him.

"But why is he refusing to have his leg amputated?" Hawwa asked Laila, as she was hastily putting on her jilbab overdress and fastening her scarf around her head.

"Because he loves you!" Laila answered her. "And he's afraid that if they amputate his leg you'll leave him." Hawwa cut through the maze of neighborhood lanes, which seemed endless, with Laila, as the beating of her heart went ahead of her to his house.

In his room, enveloped in darkness, Munir lay on his bed. His face was speckled with the beginnings of a white beard, and his eyes wandered, looking old. When Hawwa stood before him he hid his face in the pillow. Laila withdrew from the room, and Hawwa remained alone with him.

She sat on the edge of the bed, summoning her voice, which had fallen to the depths of her spirit, before reproaching Munir: "So that's how it is, Abu Laila! You're not asking how I'm doing?" A few tears formed in her eyes and remained suspended on the edges of her eyelids. "I mean, you didn't ask me even once about Hawwa!"

Munir half turned his face to her, with some curiosity in his eyes.

Hawwa was the name of her great-grandmother, her grandmother Naifa's mother. Naifa had named Hawwa after her. Hawwa was a strong woman, and a loving woman. She was beautiful; in fact, the tales have it that she was the most beautiful girl in Bait Mahsir. When the Ottoman gendarmerie came to take her husband, Ibrahim, for the army, Hawwa ransomed him with her gold jewelry, so they let him go. Then they came again a few months later, so she bargained with them over him, and gave them two gold Osmanli liras. Barely had a year passed when the ill-omened news came to her again, for they were on their way to collect a number of men from the town. Hawwa was pregnant with her first child and she didn't have a single mejdi piaster. Ibrahim was asleep on the floor when she went in to him. She stretched out his leg, and then with a single, well-aimed blow she brought her ax down on his leg, cutting it off at the knee. When the gendarmerie reached the village days later, Ibrahim was still plunged into a fever; Hawwa told them that a wall had fallen on his leg and had caused the amputation. Ibrahim wept over his lost leg, telling her that he was no longer good for anything, but Hawwa convinced him that he was good for her, and for life with her. She told him that it would be harder on her for them to take him from her than for him to stay with her as half a person, and she promised to protect him and shelter him all his life. When Ibrahim lost his sons one after the other, Hawwa stayed by his side and helped him build the house with Naifa. Then, when the Jews took over the village, Hawwa loaded Ibrahim, who in his last days had become skin and bones, on her shoulders, and carried him over the rocky roads all the way to Nablus.

"And you, Abu Laila, are going to stay inside my heart and my eyes, as close and dear as my head!"

Amid the rippling of his overflowing river of tears, Munir pointed to his leg, which he would soon lose.

"It's not important!" she told him. "What does it mean? It's your ransom, it will save your life!"

What was important was that he stay with her. What was important was that he live, for her sake. What was important was that his heart remain intertwined with her heart. Let them take both legs, even both hands! She wanted him as her man, even if he was half a man. She wanted him as a partner for the rest of her life, even if only a day remained in his life. She wanted him, with his white-haired head, his eyes bathed in tears of emotion, his good and loving heart, next to her on the pillow, so he was the last thing she saw when she closed her eyes. She loved him. She would love him even if all that remained of him was a handful of skin and bone. She loved him with a love she had never known in her life; she loved him with a love that folded away the ugliness of her days; she loved him with a love that made her love herself, if only a little. She loved him, him, her Ibrahim; she would put him in her heart, her spirit, and her eyes, and she would protect him from all the evils of time. She loved him with a love she had never once imagined that she could feel for any man, and dare to say it to him.

"I love you, by God, I love you!"

When summer moved on, gathering up its clusters of grapes, and as the longing still burned, Munir returned to work. He attached a new leg and adjusted his car to it. The brick of their house acquired a plaster coating. Hawwa stood at the entrance to the house, which exhaled the odor of cement not completely dry, as currents of October air came through openings for windows not yet installed and played with her headscarf, and as she held the edges of her dress in her hands. "In two months the house will be ready, and after that we'll get married," Munir told her, as he stroked the rough plaster with his hand. He was proud of the house, which was nearing completion. For her part, Hawwa was busy laying out her dreams in the rooms of the house, and she looked up and assured him:

"Definitely, this coming winter!" Then she suddenly thought of the question that had puzzled her for so long: "When did you know that you loved me?"

Munir stopped for moment at the question, turning it over several times in his heart. He told her that he didn't know exactly how he felt what he felt, or when. He had never asked himself that question, and he didn't think to date his feelings. Still, he could remember the moment when he felt that something in his life was different.

He had taken Laila to Hawwa's house one afternoon, in his car. The sun was intense that day. Hawwa stood at the door of her house, and the short awning over the door stretched over her head, like an upper threshold. The sun half fell on her, and half of her flared with light, half her face and half her tall figure, while the other half was sheathed in shadow. In that moment Hawwa looked like an ethereal being, a diaphanous creation, fascinating and captivating. It was a moment he could not describe, that he himself did not understand. But what he did know was that nothing after that would be the way it was before.

For Munir, from that day on, as Fairuz said, the almonds laughed.

It's as if all of night had fallen at once, leaving no opportunity or possibility for the night to become any darker.

The aroma of the rice with sautéed vermicelli is thickening the air of the kitchen. Hawwa lifts the fruit plate from the low oblong table in the living room and spreads two newspaper pages over it. As usual, she makes sure not to use the obituary pages from the paper, nor those containing God's word. She pours all the okra into a large ridged tureen. Sitt Qamar taught her not to put the cooking pots on the table, "like peasants." Why is she remembering Sitt Qamar now, she wonders, making an effort to chase the image of Sitt Qamar from her head. She covers the tureen so the food will stay hot. She puts three plates on the table, and three spoons.

Her eyes long for the bag of velvet. She wipes the traces of steam from the okra off her hands, on her sides. She opens the bag, placed on the cutting table, slipping her senses into it, but a slow knock on the door pulls her away from her velvet.

Ayid enters first, followed by Qais, both wearing stiff expressions. Hawwa greets them cheerfully, or tries to make it seem that way. She inspects Qais's face, which is tinged with yellow. Hawwa does not seem confident that any movement she makes can possibly seem natural. Nonetheless, she takes Qais in her arms, trying to draw him to her. She tries to seem eager. Qais's trunk leans toward her without coming very close, while his arms remain limp at his sides. Hawwa's heart sinks into the void between their bodies.

Ayid takes off his padded jacket with the rain hood and puts it on the arm of the Morris chair, while Qais keeps on his leather jacket, only taking off the checkered wool scarf wound around his neck. Ayid chooses to sit on the sofa, in a place that will make it easy for him to reach everything on the table. He asks her about his mother. "She's sleeping," Hawwa answers him. Then she suggests that she wake her and put her in her chair, and bring her to sit and eat with them. But Ayid says that it's better for her to continue resting, glancing at his sister's son for support, while Qais's face remains completely blank, without any expression. She tells them that she has fed her and changed her. She explains to them that Rabia's face has gotten better, thanks to the massage she gives her. "Her appetite, it's excellent, God willed it!" Hawwa's voice trembles as she makes an effort to add life to it, an element of ordinary life. Ayid is fooling with the buttons of his cell phone, while Qais's eyes settle on her, without appearing to be engaged with her or concerned with following the state of his grandmother's health. "Grandma likes apples, yamma, she eats two apples a day." She's directing her words to her son, entirely aware that the word "yamma" belongs to him, a special distinction she gives him. "Are you hungry?" she asks them, when the silence lengthens painfully.

On her way to the kitchen, Hawwa thinks that she ought to have doubled the quantity of the meat in the okra. It might have been better if she had cooked a platter of chicken with the okra, or kofta meatballs. She should have fried some gizzards—Ayid likes them. Qais also asks her for them. She should have made a platter of harissa semolina sweet, too.

She pours a mound of rice with vermicelli on a large dish, flat and round. The ladle slips from her hand so some of the rice falls on the marble of the sink. She leaves it where it is, without trying to pick it up, and carefully carries the heavy platter to the table. She ladles rice and okra onto a plate for each of them. She chooses the meat for them with extra care. "It's cold out," she tells them, as she sits on a chair far from the table. She watches them and tries to read their separate, silent features, which nonetheless don't prevent them from being interested in the food. Hawwa believes that their inordinate gluttony is a good thing, especially tonight.

Ayid lifts his face to her and asks, "Is there any Pepsi?" She runs to the kitchen, optimistic about how things might end, as long as they are talking to her and making requests. She brings a large bottle of Pepsi from the refrigerator, together with two glasses. She tries to open the bottle and can't. Ayid takes the bottle from her and twists the cap off easily, as the plastic bottle burps out some gas.

"How are you, sis?" Ayid asks her, looking closely at her hands.

Hawwa tries to suppress her trembling as she wipes her neck, and then as she tucks back her hair, some of which has strayed onto her face. "I'm fine, thank God," she answers him.

"So, you didn't eat with us?" he asks her as he guzzles a second glass of Pepsi and jumps up. He puts on his jacket. Qais hasn't yet finished his first glass. Ayid puts his hand on his nephew's shoulder and squeezes it hard, saying, "Settle things with your mother!"

Hawwa tries to follow her brother, but he assures her that he's going out to smoke a cigarette and that he'll be back. Qais contents himself with one glass of Pepsi. Hawwa looks at his plate, and she's happy that he's finished it all. She suggests to him that she serve him another plate. She doesn't wait for the answer, but gives him two ladles of rice with okra on top. She gathers all the remaining pieces of meat and puts them on his plate. Qais sits back, leaning on the back of the sofa. Hawwa offers to pour him another glass of Pepsi, but he shakes his head. With the edge of her dress she polishes the surface of her plate, which she has not used. She covers the tureen of okra, where a little sauce remains with a few squashed pieces of okra. As she gets up, she says to Qais that she's going to go and check on his grandmother, but Qais tells her with a gesture to stay where she is.

"How long have you known Abu Laila?" he asks.

She doesn't miss the reference. She feels she ought to defend herself. "Not a long time."

"How long?"

She tries to draw on the wisdom of lying. "Two or three months."

"How did you meet?"

"By chance."

"How, by chance?"

"In the street."

"What street?"

The December air creeps in to her from the hall leading to the outside door, which Ayid has left open a crack. She opens all the burners of the heater, seeking fire to sear her.

Qais once again corners her with the same question: "What street?"

She lifts her eyes to the ceiling of the room, and notices black mold in some of the corners. She returns to the interrogation: "I don't know. In the camp."

"Did you sit with him?"

"Once or twice."

"Where?"

Cold erupts from under the tiles and the rug, gnawing at her legs. She looks around for a shawl or anything to wrap around herself.

Qais sears her with the question: "Did you ride in a car with him?"

Hawwa cannot feel her feet; it's as if she's wading barefoot in snow. Her eyes sweep the room aimlessly.

"Did you go into his house?"

Then she no longer hears any question. She looks at Qais and sees his mouth opening and closing, along with his eyes, which narrow and widen, narrow and widen.

"Did you go there? Did you sit in his house? Did anyone see you with him? Answer me! Answer me! Speak! Why so silent?"

Her body is cold, tired. Life and the people in life have exhausted it. She pulls the piece of velvet from the bag and wraps it around her shoulders, so it hangs like a receding wave over her chest and in her embrace. But the bombardment of the wind is too wild and vicious to be blocked by the lilac velvet, with its virgin rustling and its aroma of secret delights.

Rabia's shout pierces the night: "Haaawwww!"

Hawwa stands up, and the nestling lilac wave rolls to the floor, breaking at her feet. She tries to move but her legs won't take a step. She tries to drag them, to lift them from the floor, but she can't. She smells a strange odor, as if something were burning.

Rabia continues shouting, piercing the walls of the house: "Haaww! Haaawww! Haaaaaaawwww!"

"I'm coming, Mama, I'm coming!" she answers. But her voice seems shallow, as if she were talking to herself.

"Haaww! Haawwww!"

"Coming. . . ." Hawwa tries to get the words out of her mouth, but the letters stick in her throat. She looks at Qais.

She sees him standing, his face looking as if it's oozing water, his hand gripping a small black pistol.

Her hand slips over her belly and plunges into a thick liquid. She opens her hand and sees blood, much more blood than what spurts out of her fingers when she pricks them with a needle or a pin. Rushing water fills her ears, mixing with Rabia's shouts, which gradually recede.

Her ears are completely blocked, and her eyes stare, dazed, into a deep, dark white.

In the last flare of her spirit, Hawwa draws up her lofty stature, higher and then higher. She reaches the clouds and the sky. Her heart flashes. She gasps. Then she collapses, and her light goes out.

Do you remember how much you told me,
This life does not last,
And that there's no one like me,
My love is the last?
What has happened since that day,
Over several days?
Nothing much has happened . . . nothing, really.

Winter was tiring, and the fire slept in the braziers.

The burners of the gas heaters lowered their eyelids, and the wicks of the kerosene heaters dried and shrank. The sky folded away the quilt of clouds and kept the water behind its closed doors.

April came.

Munir sat on the old wooden settee with the sunken foam cushions. One of his hands rested on his left thigh, while the other leaned on the edge of the window overlooking two intersecting lanes in the camp. On the floor lay his artificial leg, its metal support ending in a black shoe, the laces untied.

"What's wrong with you, Papa! How long are you going to go on like this?" Laila wondered aloud, in despair, as she put the tray of food on the small table in front of him. His face was fixed on the window, his features stiff. She sat on the settee next to him. "Nariman had a boy, Papa—don't you want to go and congratulate her?" His eyes did not leave the street. "Aliya called from Jeddah yesterday. She says hello. They renewed her husband's contract for his work, for another year." She picked up the plate of food and put it in front of him. "I made you okra, the kind that's dear to your heart!" His eyes continued wandering, at a distance. Laila returned the plate to the tray, her tongue tied by her impotence.

Suddenly, he stretched his head out of the half-open window, through the iron grille, opening his eyes wide. They flashed in an attempt to compass the corner of the street, as if they had seen something there, or had seen *the* thing. Laila could not contain herself: "For God's sake, Papa, for God's sake!" Months had gone by since the accident, she told him, and what happened was something he had no control over, and neither did anyone else.

"Look at me, Papa!" She took his face in her hand and pulled it toward her, then planted a kiss wet with her tears on his forehead. The words moved slowly from her tongue, shackled by her sobs. She gave them a sharp tone and a high pitch, as if she were explaining the matter to someone stunned or in a partial coma, or at best deaf: "Hawwa's gone, Papa, she died." He had to forget, she begged him, he must forget. And then he had to leave "this dump," as she described the house, and move into his new house.

Naji came in carrying the controller for the PlayStation Aliya had sent him from Saudi Arabia, complaining to her that it didn't work. She moved her eyes between the father and the son. "And Naji, Papa? Haven't you thought about him?" It seemed as if hope had drained from her voice. She stood up, examining the poorly ventilated and badly lit room, with its odor of depression, decay, and an old man who had not washed for some time.

His cell phone on the table rang with the music to "I, I, you and I, we've become a strange story." The musical ring-tone sounded four times before stopping; Munir did not look at it to see who had called. Laila announced that she was giving up. She said that she couldn't leave her house and her children and come to him every day, and that it might be better if she took Naji with her to her house. When Naji heard his name, he hurried to his father and threw his head on his half leg. Munir spread his hand over the child's head, without taking his eyes from the road, as his unkempt white beard was tinged with tears that flowed freely.

It was late afternoon when the sky suddenly reddened, so that the horizon seemed to bleed. Winds whistled everywhere, laden with sand and small stones, quickly turning into a storm that grew to cover the sky of the camp, stretching, lengthening, widening. It became bad, and worse, thickened by the dust of the lanes and aggravated by shreds of paper and bags.

Laila fastened the windows tightly shut, as the swishing of the sand rose and the savage winds flailed their reckless arms in every direction.

People ran in the streets, trying to cover their faces from the sand slapping them. Their eyes rose to the bloodred sky, hoping, in their sandy state, for a howling, sweeping, sudden rain, a great flood to drown the universe.

SELECTED HOOPOE TITLES

All That I Want to Forget
by Bothayna Al-Essa, translated by Michele Henjum

Sarab
by Raja Alem, translated by Leri Price

Gaza Weddings
by Ibrahim Nasrallah, translated by Nancy Roberts

∗

hoopoe is an imprint for engaged, open-minded readers hungry for outstanding fiction that challenges headlines, re-imagines histories, and celebrates original storytelling. Through elegant paperback and digital editions, **hoopoe** champions bold, contemporary writers from across the Middle East alongside some of the finest, groundbreaking authors of earlier generations.

At hoopoefiction.com, curious and adventurous readers from around the world will find new writing, interviews, and criticism from our authors, translators, and editors.